Nicole Helm grew up with her nose in a book and the dream of one day becoming a writer. Luckily, after a few failed career choices, she gets to follow that dream—writing down-to-earth contemporary romance and romantic suspense. From farmers to cowboys, Midwest to the West, Nicole writes stories about people finding themselves and finding love in the process. She lives in Missouri with her husband and two sons and dreams of someday owning a barn.

Juno Rushdan is the award-winning author of steamy, action-packed romantic thrillers that keep readers on the edge of their seats. She writes about kick-ass heroes and strong heroines fighting for their lives as well as their happily-ever-afters. As a veteran air force intelligence officer, she uses her background supporting Special Forces to craft realistic stories that make readers sweat and swoon. Juno currently lives in the DC area with her patient husband, two rambunctious kids and a spoiled rescue dog. To receive a free book from Juno, sign up for her newsletter at junorushdan.com/mailing-list. Also be sure to follow Juno on BookBub for the latest on sales at bit.ly/BookBubJuno

Also by Nicole Helm

Also by Juno Rushdan

Discover more at millsandboon.co.uk

COWBOY IN THE CROSSHAIRS

NICOLE HELM

DISAVOWED IN WYOMING

JUNO RUSHDAN

MILLS & BOON

First Published in Great Britain 2021
by Mills & Boon, an imprint of HarperCollins*Publishers* Ltd
1 London Bridge Street, London, SE1 9GF

www.harpercollins.co.uk

HarperCollins*Publishers*
1st Floor, Watermarque Building,
Ringsend Road, Dublin 4, Ireland

Cowboy in the Crosshairs © 2021 Nicole Helm
Disavowed in Wyoming © 2021 Juno Rushdan

ISBN: 978-0-263-28365-5

1221

MIX
Paper from
responsible sources
FSC™ C007454

This book is produced from independently certified FSC™ paper to ensure responsible forest management.

For more information visit: www.harpercollins.co.uk/green

Printed and Bound in Spain using 100% Renewable electricity at CPI Black Print, Barcelona

COWBOY IN THE CROSSHAIRS

NICOLE HELM

For everyone who loved Blue Valley
and followed me here.

Chapter One

Elsie Rogers only wanted to get back to her computer. She'd spent the past two days in a bunker on a farm, on someone else's computer. She hadn't minded that so much, until she'd been drugged. That had *not* been fine with her.

She'd been released from the hospital, shuffled back to North Star headquarters by Mallory, one of North Star's field operatives, but when Shay had walked into Elsie's office with that bad-news look on her face, Elsie knew she wouldn't be finding the peace of hacking anytime soon.

She'd only been sitting at her computer for about thirty seconds. It hadn't even booted up yet.

"How are you feeling?" Shay asked. Elsie loved having Shay as a boss. When she'd first started in the tech sector of the secretive North Star group, things had been a lot different. Granger MacMillan had been in charge and North Star's sole mission was to bring down the Sons of the Badlands, a dangerous biker gang.

Elsie knew all about dangerous men. So she'd been more than happy to aid the group, via her expertise with computers, to finally end the Sons. She'd moved her way up to head of tech in no time at all. But working with Granger McMillan had always made her nervous. He'd always been big, gruff and *very* serious. Like most of the men at North Star. She'd grown up not trusting any of those characteristics.

Elsie'd had to get used to the size and serious nature of the men in North Star, and thought she'd done a pretty good job. She'd even made some breakthroughs in her fears and anxieties when it came to men.

But she still preferred Shay as her boss. Even if Shay was just as lethal as any of the men there. More so, maybe, because Shay was the rare entity in North Star who didn't have a specialty.

She was good at *everything*.

"I feel great," Elsie said brightly, looking wistfully at her computer screen.

"We've got the name of the second target."

Oh, good. An assignment. Two of North Star's lead field operatives had been tracking two hitmen. North Star hadn't known anything about the gunmen or whom they'd been sent to kill. They'd only been tracking two shipments of illegal ammunition for guns they knew the mysterious hitmen used. The hope had been that they'd track it in time to stop the assassins from taking out their unknown targets.

Holden Parker, lead agent number one, hadn't found either target, but he'd helped save a woman whose parents were spies and were, in fact, connected to the hitmen.

Elsie wasn't a field agent in any way, shape or form, but there'd been a computer on-site and she'd been sent to the bunker to see what she could find in the computer. Unfortunately, that meant being caught in the crossfire. Being tied up in that bunker by one of the spies who'd lost his grip with sanity had been a little too close to the terror she'd felt as a child trying to avoid her father's fists.

Now there was a second target. Work to do. Elsie could forget her terror and get lost in computer work once again. "What's his name? I'll give you everything there is to know."

Shay smiled, but it was not a real smile. Or comforting. At all.

"We don't quite know what we're dealing with yet," Shay said, and the fact they were so in the dark with this mission clearly bothered her. "Sabrina has some inside information on the second target, but we still have to be very careful."

Sabrina Killian, one of the other North Star lead operatives, was in the Tetons, tracing the ammunition and hopefully the hitman. She'd found the first target and was protecting him, and apparently had now figured out who the second target was.

Go Sabrina.

"Great," Elsie said, feeling a ripple of excitement. She'd been a little afraid Shay would keep her off duty for a few days to recuperate. "I'm ready to jump right into work. I swear. I feel fine. One hundred percent. Give me the name."

"That's excellent to hear." Shay took a deep breath, which wasn't a good sign. And she did not give Elsie the name. Then, even worse, she moved from her standing position to pull a chair up next to Elsie herself.

"Els, I'm going to need you to handle this one."

"Of course. Just give me the name." She had her fingers poised on the keyboard, but Shay shook her head.

Shay studied her very carefully. Elsie wanted to look away, *run* away, because this felt like bad, bad news. But she didn't move. She only stared back at Shay. She had learned a thing or two in her years at North Star.

"No, Els. I mean, you're going into the field."

"I can't go into the field." Elsie laughed because it was *crazy*. "I'm… I'm tech support."

"You're more than that."

"Okay, maybe, but I'm not a field operative. I don't know anything about going into the field! I went to try to hack that computer for you guys and got myself drugged and unconscious."

"That wasn't your fault, or because of anything you did. Look, this first part of the assignment doesn't require skills with a gun or hand-to-hand combat. It requires stealth."

"When have I ever been good at that if I'm not at the keys to the computer?"

Shay's expression went from sympathy and almost *apology* to stoic and cool in the snap of a finger. "You're the only one who can do this," she said, her voice hard. "Nathan Averly, our second hitman's target, is located in Blue Valley, Montana. His hometown, though he's currently at the Revival Ranch in their injured military recuperation center. Do any of those names or places sound at all familiar?"

Elsie heard a strange buzzing in her ears. It had been a long time since she'd had that particular shock reaction to something. But then again, it had been a long time since someone had mentioned her hometown to her. Here in North Star, her past didn't exist. No one knew, or acted as though they knew, where anyone else came from. The only time she heard her hometown's name was when she took time off around Christmas to visit.

She swallowed and, for the first time in her tenure at North Star, she wished she'd never joined. Wished she could lie with any capability. "I can't..."

Shay leaned forward. "I need you to, Els. You're the only one I can send without tipping anyone off. Born and bred in Blue Valley, and your sister is married to one of these guys running Revival Ranch. Small town like that? I bet you even know Nathan."

Elsie felt weak. "I...know of him." She knew more about his brother, Garrett. Because Garrett was a police officer, and had been a sheriff's deputy for Valley County when she'd lived in Blue Valley. That meant he'd arrested her father a few times before Dad had died, before she'd escaped.

Her father. Blue Valley.

It wasn't as bad as all that these days. Her two oldest sisters had built lives in Blue Valley. Dad was dead. Mom had moved. Elsie visited for Christmas because she loved her sisters and her nieces and nephews.

But this was work. A work her family didn't know she did. "Shay, I'm a terrible liar. You know this about me."

"I know. And I know it's a lot, asking you to lie to your family, but I have faith in you. You know I wouldn't ask you if I had any other options. I don't want you in the middle of this, but you're the only one who can go into a small town in Montana on a moment's notice and not create any suspicion. *Anywhere*."

"But Nate… He'll know."

"Yes, he knows someone from North Star is coming. No, he doesn't know it's you. We've had to be careful about our contact with Nate, since we don't know who's after him or why. We don't know what could be tapped or overheard. But you would know. And you'll be able to help him research his theories without anyone knowing that's what you're doing."

"Shay, I don't think I can do this. I'm not…like you or Sabrina."

Shay put her hand on Elsie's shoulder. "I need you to do your best."

Elsie knew she was sunk. She couldn't disappoint Shay. Couldn't disappoint North Star. She managed a weak smile. "I guess I'm headed home."

NATE AVERLY PUSHED the cowboy hat off his forehead and wiped his face with the back of his arm. Hot one for a summer day in Montana. Reminded him of the Middle East, which almost never happened this far north.

A year ago, that might have set him off, but these days he focused all his confusion, anger and frustration into something else. He had a mission of his own. Not rehabilitation.

Retribution.

Something had ended his Navy SEAL career more than the explosion that had left him out of commission. He'd made a mistake, he understood that now. Trusted the wrong civilian. Followed the wrong lead. But being dishonorably discharged after his injury because of those mistakes had never made sense. Especially since his SEAL brother, Connor Lindstrom, had also gotten the dishonorable release when he had never done anything but join Nate on some security checks and questionings.

So Nate had never let it go. He'd dug. He'd collected evidence, and had almost a clear picture of what had happened. He just hadn't been able to prove it to anyone. Because when you were labeled *paranoid*, people didn't spend a lot of time looking into your theories, no matter how much truth they might hold.

Something more was going on. He'd received a very strange email from his former girlfriend. It had been in code—Nate was pretty sure—and had held enough of a hint to let him know she was involved in something.

Then he'd gotten her call, which he was still trying to understand.

It had also been in code. Nate's best guess: Sabrina had been trying to tell him she had somehow hooked up with Connor and that they knew Nate had sent a package, but it had been destroyed.

Nate had backups of what he'd forwarded Connor—he wouldn't have sent all that proof without having backups. But it worried him that Connor seemed to be the target of whatever was going on. Likely *because* of that package.

That meant, if something happened to Connor, it was all Nate's fault.

If the man who'd also talked to him on that call had been Connor. *If* that's what Brina had meant.

There were just too many question marks, which made Nate edgy. About as edgy as the cryptic message that had followed: someone would be joining Revival Ranch to help him with his "quest."

He didn't know how to trust Brina's messages, but he did what he always did. He kept it to himself. He watched. He waited. And he did his ranch chores.

When he'd been a kid, scraping by on his family's small ranch at the southern edge of Blue Valley, Montana, he'd promised himself he'd never spend his adult life breaking his back at a failing spread.

Well, here he was doing just that. Though, in fairness, this ranch wasn't failing and was all about helping military men find their usefulness and emotional and mental health after injury.

His recuperation at Revival Ranch had been just that. A recuperation. His injuries healed, he felt sound in body and mind. The only thing that kept him here was what his therapist termed his *obsession*.

Nate scowled a little at that. He wasn't obsessed. He was determined. He was…focused. He had one singular goal— bring down those who'd wrongfully ousted him from the military—and he wouldn't rest until he'd achieved it.

Hardly an obsession. It was *justice*. Though the more time he spent at Revival, the more ways he understood there was no way to make his therapist or his brother fully grasp what had happened to him. They thought he was exaggerating. Twisting events and memories to suit this obsession.

He wasn't too far away from convincing them all he wasn't fixated anymore. It wasn't true, but he was closing in on making everyone—therapist, friends, brother and parents—believe he was letting things go.

The very opposite of what he was actually doing.

He heard the sound of a car far down the lane and immediately went on alert. The strange message he'd received had said someone would arrive to help him. Could this be his contact person? Was it real help? A trap?

Nate knew better than to abandon his work. That would give away his suspicions and, if this *was* someone after him, he wouldn't give them a clear read on things.

The dusty sedan pulled up in front of the main house. Though one of the men who'd founded Revival lived there, the Maguire house was the headquarters for Revival Ranch.

A small brunette stepped out of the car. He thought he recognized her, and even if he hadn't, she looked enough like her sisters that he knew she was a Rogers girl. Not a girl any longer, but in a town like Blue Valley, once a person had a moniker, it stuck.

Since the two older sisters lived here in Blue Valley, and she didn't look quite young enough to be fresh out of college, he pegged her as one of the middle ones. Billie or Elsie. His money was on Elsie. She'd been closer in age to him than Billie. Maybe three years younger?

Kyle Olsen came over and let out a low whistle, resting his body weight on the shovel he'd been using to clean out the stables. "Well, well, well. What do we have here?" he said, watching Elsie pull a purse out of the back of her car.

"Better watch yourself," Nate warned.

"Why?"

"Aside from the fact you're married?" Nate nodded his head toward the yard where the woman stood, oozing nerves. "Pretty sure if Jack hears you drooling over his sister-in-law, he'll take you apart limb by limb."

Kyle swore good-naturedly. "How many sisters-in-law he got? I've never seen this one before."

"Five Rogers girls." Nate couldn't remember the last time he'd seen Elsie Rogers, but that was definitely her. The Rogers sisters all had dark hair, dark eyes and slender frames. The older girls had always had an edge to them. The younger girls…the hollow-eyed skittishness of children who'd grown up in abuse.

She didn't head for the porch that would lead her to Revival headquarters. He tended to keep track of everyone's comings and goings, and knew that her sister Rose was in there with her kids. Instead of heading for her sister, though, she headed for him.

She walked across the yard, right up to where he stood next to Kyle. Kyle preened. Nate frowned.

"Hello, Nate," she greeted.

"Uh, hi. Elsie."

She released a breath. He couldn't tell if it was relief or something else. "You remember me."

It wasn't a question or an indictment or anything he could sort through. So he shrugged. "Sure. Hard to forget the Rogers girls."

Something on her face changed, but she forced a smile. "Sure. Well, I just came over because…" She cleared her throat, looked around at the men who were watching them carefully. Not just Kyle but two other soldiers who'd returned on horses.

Elsie focused on Nate and smiled, something like panic fluttering at the edges of her lips. "We have a mutual friend out there in the big, wide world."

"Huh?"

"Sabrina Killian? You know her, right?"

Nate blinked. After the strange email he'd gotten from Brina, he didn't think this was a coincidence. Any of it. "Yeah, I…did."

"I work with her."

It wasn't possible. This could not be the person he'd been waiting for. The help he was counting on.

Maybe he *wasn't* of sound body and mind, because if little Elsie Rogers was his contact to some secretive group that was going to help him because Brina had stumbled into this mess…

Well, Nate figured they were both screwed.

Chapter Two

Elsie wished she hadn't come over to Nate, but she'd needed to make some kind of contact. Now he was looking at her less like she was "one of those Rogers girls" and more like she was some kind of nightmare.

Definitely not the help he'd expected.

"I've got to go say hi to my sister and tell her I'm staying for a while. See you around." She nodded to the man who hadn't spoken at all, then Nate, and then turned on a heel to hurry to the main house. Rose hadn't been at her house, so Elsie assumed she'd be here helping Becca with something.

Elsie's stomach turned in awful knots. She had to lie to her sister, and everyone Rose and Jack worked with at Revival. She wasn't excited about doing that, but she definitely wanted to get away from Nate as soon as possible. He was tall and broad, with dark, dark eyes and an edge to him she didn't remember about the Averlys.

Maybe it had been his time in the military. Maybe it was this whole…being the target of an assassin. Maybe it was something else. But she didn't like edgy men with angry eyes.

"Wait a second." It was Nate's voice and he jogged up next to her before she could crest the stairs of the main house. "You know Brina?" he demanded suspiciously.

Elsie nodded. Sabrina. Who wasn't afraid of anyone. Who routinely kicked butt. Elsie had to give herself a shake. She might not be a routine butt kicker, but she was a North Star operative, one way or another. Being at home, she tended to forget what she'd built herself into.

She didn't have the luxury this time around. She had to focus on her task—her *mission*. She couldn't be the skittish girl she'd been here growing up. She firmed her shoulders and looked right up at Nate. Authoritatively. If she were pretending to be at a desk with her computer to protect her, no one had to know except her. "Give me a couple hours and I'll be able to get you on a secure line to her and Connor."

"Connor… So, it was Connor on the phone this morning."

"Well, yeah. Sabrina's protecting him. I'm…" It was ludicrous to say she'd been sent here to protect Nate. It would sound even worse to say she was his tech support. "My expertise is electronics. I'll be able to put you in contact with both of them without any chance of being traced or followed. I figure you have information that will be useful to put this mystery together."

"It's hardly a mystery," he said, but it sounded like he was talking more to himself than her. "They know where I am. They have to know where I am. The only reason Connor would be a target is…" He frowned. "What do you know?"

"Elsie?"

Elsie jerked at her sister's voice and couldn't fight the rising tide of embarrassment that would stamp itself in red blotches across her face. She tried to find her smile as she turned to Rose standing in the doorway, a fair-haired baby on her hip. "Hey, sissy."

The sight of her baby nephew she'd only seen outside of a phone screen once had Elsie forgetting all about her embarrassment. She rushed forward, flinging her arms around them both, Nate Averly and his uncomfortable energy forgotten. She looked at her nephew's wary face. "Look at you, peanut."

"Look at you." Rose studied her, a vague frown on her face. "It's not like you to text you're coming to visit and show up within a few hours."

Elsie worked up to looking into her sister's shrewd gaze. "I know. I'll explain everything." Somehow. "It's good to see you."

Rose maintained the frown but slid her free arm around Elsie's shoulders and pulled her inside. If she saw Nate, she didn't acknowledge him at all as she closed the door behind them with her hip. "I'm glad you're here. I'm just worried."

"Don't be. I have this project to work on, and I needed some…quiet."

Rose jiggled Xander in her arms. "You won't get that here, honey. Or at Delia's. Two kids under three in each place means scream city more than half the time."

"I know. I know. But you know, Montana quiet and family distractions in the evening so I don't get obsessed." Elsie had worked through her excuse and explanation on the drive from the airport. She took a deep breath and forced a smile. It was close to the truth. She wasn't lying. "That's why I was hoping to maybe stay in the little cabin on Revival property. I know you usually let the soldiers' visiting families stay there but—"

"I'll have to double-check with Becca to see if we have any families coming to visit, but I think we're clear there. Though it seems wrong for you to come all this way and not stay with me or Delia."

"Well, if it makes you feel better, I can just use the cabin as an office and spend nights with you or Delia. You don't want my computer stuff cluttering up your houses anyway."

"True. Baby debris is enough on the clutter score." Rose's analytical frown was still in place. "Els, are you okay? You look pale. And nervous."

"Yeah, I'm good. Really." Aside from the whole drugged thing, but Elsie wasn't bringing *that* up. "It's a really big project. It's new for me. I want to get it right. So I'm going to be a little…tightly wound. But that's why I wanted to be here. At home. Somewhere I could pull myself out of it when I get too deep in the obsessive part."

Rose led her into the living room, none of the worry leaving her face. "You've never called Blue Valley home before. Not since you left."

Elsie inhaled. She supposed she hadn't, and in that she hadn't been playing a part or lying. "You and Delia changed it for me." Her sisters had built real, good lives in the ashes of their terrible childhood. Hard not to find her affinity for the place knowing and seeing that.

Rose smiled. "All right. Let's go talk to Becca about the cabin. She's got the rest of the kids locked in the office with her. But first, I want you to tell me why you were talking to Nate Averly."

"Oh." Elsie felt the heat creep back into her cheeks. She cleared her throat uncomfortably. "You never told me Nate Averly was one of the Revival men."

"I didn't know you knew Nate."

"Sort of."

"Honey, I know you're a grown woman and it's *none* of my business, but don't let a little flirtation—"

"Oh, no. *No.* No, no." Elsie laughed, knowing she sounded just a shade too close to unhinged. "No flirtation. We just recognized each other." Though that would make things easier, wouldn't it? If they pretended to have some interest in each other, as an explanation of why they would have to speak.

The knots in her stomach tied tighter. Who would believe Nate had any interest in her? How would she get through pretending without blushing like she was at just the thought? "He's...too big."

Rose snorted out a laugh. "In my experience, big men are not the problem." She squeezed Elsie's shoulders. "Just the mean ones."

"No, I know. I just..." She shook her head. This wasn't about their father. It wasn't about *anything*. Except lies. "I don't know what to say. I've got a big job to do. That's my focus." At least that was true.

Rose placed Xander in a playpen and then turned to Elsie, taking her by the shoulders. Elsie tried to keep her expression placid as Rose studied her.

"Promise me you're okay."

Elsie looked her sister straight in the eye, because this wouldn't be a lie, either. "I promise I'm not just okay, I'm good." This mission was a challenge, but at the end of the day, all she had to do was to lend her computer expertise to Nate.

It was important work. Work that might save lives. Including Nate's.

North Star had given her a purpose. A strength and confidence she hadn't had before. Between the therapy she'd gone through and the work she'd found to be her passion, she wasn't the same little abused girl that she knew her sisters sometimes still thought of her as.

Now she had a chance to prove it.

NATE DIDN'T CONCENTRATE very well the rest of the afternoon. He'd scraped his hands repairing a crooked stable door, and then spilled half a bag of feed and spent too long cleaning it up.

He'd listened to the gossip at dinner in the mess hall and heard Vivian, their cook and Jack's sister, mention something to Jack about Elsie staying in the cabin Revival usually used for visiting families now that Vivian had a place of her own.

So, that's where he was headed. He'd slipped out of dinner, hopefully undetected. If anyone questioned him, he'd say he had an upset stomach. It was a pathetic excuse, but he'd use it if he had to.

He could have waited for Elsie to approach him again, could have waited till dark to sneak over, but he didn't have the patience for it. He'd waited hours now. And if he counted the time since Brina had called him through the ranch line this morning...

She hadn't given him any *real* information. It had been all code. If that. Just enough for him to *guess* Brina was with Connor, and that the evidence Nate had sent Connor a few days ago had been destroyed.

He had no idea *why* Brina was involved. No idea what Connor knew or what danger he was in.

This woman—*Elsie Rogers*—had more information than he did, and Nate didn't know how to deal with that. He'd thought he was in charge, the center, all this time and now...

Well, he'd get his information and go from there. Maybe he didn't have a ton of patience, but he'd recovered from the broken bones and torn cartilage and burns involved in being in an explosion. He knew all about slow and steady progress.

He walked across the property to the little cabin. In the distance, the mountains of his youth stood like sentries. He'd gone off to the Navy, not because he hated Blue Valley, but because he'd felt there was so much more out there.

Well, he'd certainly found it. And it had followed him home.

Nate gave one quick glance behind him, just to make sure no one was watching, then moved around to the back, which allowed the cabin to hide him from prying eyes. If he stayed till dark, no one would have to see him sneak back to the bunkhouse and then he could make up any excuse as to where he'd been.

He knocked on the door and waited impatiently. When Elsie appeared, she seemed...different than she had this afternoon. She stood straight, kept her gaze level, and didn't blush at all as she gestured for him to come inside. The nerves he'd sensed radiating from her had been replaced by a cool confidence that felt a bit like whiplash.

"Did anyone see you come over?" Elsie asked.

"No."

"Good. We'll have to work out something about the time we'll need to spend together, but for right now, we can get down to brass tacks."

She closed the door behind him and he stepped into a cozy if sparsely furnished room. He hadn't ever had cause to be inside the cabin. His family was local, so when they came to visit, they didn't need a place to stay.

There were computers and computer equipment seemingly everywhere. Desktops and laptops and monitors. There was even equipment on the lone couch. It was like walking into some kind of command center.

"First things first, we're going to call Sabrina."

"I can't just call her. I don't know who's listening." He tensed against the look he knew was coming. That considering, slightly arrested look people gave a guy who believed in things like aliens. Or was obsessed over a discharge from years ago.

But she simply nodded, as if she agreed. "That's what all this is," she said, spreading her arm out to encompass all the equipment. "I know what I'm doing with tech." She pulled out a phone. "This can't be traced. This can't be tapped. You'll call Sabrina, and you two can exchange the necessary information. From there, I'll get the information we need to move forward."

She was clearly in her element. Confident when she hadn't been before. An interesting change.

"How do I know I can trust you and Brina?"

She pressed her lips together, as if considering. Her dark hair was straight as a pin, but looked glossy. Her brown eyes were deep and rich. She was a shade too skinny, and a few shades too pale, like she'd just gotten over some kind of illness.

He would know about that.

"I'm not sure I can prove to you that we're trustworthy. But the basics of it are that Sabrina and I work for a secret group. From the beginning of this group, our job has been to…take down the bad guys. Sounds cliché and kind of silly, but I don't know how else to put it. We're a network of people with different specialties. Sabrina is a field operative. I'm a tech operative. Sabrina was tailing a hitman when she connected with Connor Lindstrom. As they worked together to avoid the hitman, they put together a few things. Namely that the gunman was after Connor, and the logical connection was that it had something to do with Connor's dishonorable discharge from the military. That meant it had to connect to you, as well."

That certainly matched his current situation. "Brina called me this morning. Through the ranch line. But she didn't say anything worthwhile except hinted that the package I'd sent Connor had been destroyed."

"Yes, it was. Before Connor got his hands on it. What was in the package?"

Nate considered. While he did, she pressed the phone into his hand. "Look, you don't have to tell me. Yet. Call Sabrina."

Elsie had the number programmed in and all Nate had to do was hit Call. What else was there to do?

"Killian," a sharp, husky voice answered.

"Brina." He'd met Sabrina Killian when they'd both

been in the first phases of working to become SEALs. Somewhere between that first step and the last, he and Brina had gotten involved. She'd been a whirlwind of energy, always ready for a fight, and Nate had been in awe of the woman *determined* to be a Navy SEAL.

Instead, she'd been severely injured in the Land Warfare Training phase. Her SEAL dreams dashed, she'd broken up with him in a fiery explosion of her own, then disappeared.

Nate had gone off to war, pride hurt but heart not mortally wounded, and he supposed that had been that. Brina had become another footnote in his life. A fond footnote, but not one he thought much about these days.

"Hello, Nate. How's it going?"

He eyed Elsie as Brina's familiar voice boomed in his ear. She'd always *boomed* or *sashayed* or *raged*. Something about her not changing set him at some ease. "Fine enough. Your friend is here."

"Els? Yeah, she's a gem. Be nice to her. There's no one like her, and she's going to be able to get you whatever information you need. That, I can guarantee."

She certainly had the equipment for it. "Okay."

"You should talk to Connor. You two understand this better than I do. But everything you tell him, he's going to tell me. We're working on this together."

"Brina..." Nate didn't even know where to begin. "This is serious. Dangerous."

"Yeah. Got it. Here he is."

There was the sound of shuffling, Brina's muffled voice, and then a deep, careful voice Nate knew as well as his biological brother's. Because Connor had become something of a brother to him in the SEALs.

"Hello."

They'd been on missions together. Been friends. Brothers. Kicked out of the military together.

Connor himself had told Nate to let the mystery go all

those years ago when Nate had still been recuperating physically. So, Nate had begun to cut Connor off, slowly but surely. Not because he was mad. He understood why people thought he was crazy. But because he just…couldn't let it go. So, he'd kept everyone who'd thought he was nuts at arm's length. At least, until he'd had enough proof. Real proof.

Nate didn't know how to lead with any of that. "Care to explain how you got mixed up with my ex?"

"Care to explain why my friend's in the hospital and my cabin's obliterated? Oh, and why I got shot at?"

Nate winced. "I know you told me to let it go…"

"I told you to build your life. That's different. Sort of."

"Yeah, well…" Nate eyed Elsie again. Her fingers were flying over a keyboard. "You sure this is secure?"

"Positive," she said without looking up.

Nate sighed. "Okay, Brina's friend here says I can be assured I can tell you anything without anyone being able to trace, hear, or whatever. I guess I have to trust her. I wanted to keep you as out of it as much as possible, Con. I tried. But this is bigger than me. Bigger than us. It's huge. We're talking military corruption on a scale…"

Connor didn't have to say anything. Nate felt Elsie's considering gaze. Felt Connor's frustration through the phone line. "I know I sound crazy," Nate said, irritated with…well, everything. "I know it. It's why I can't go to anyone. But I also know what I've found. What I sent you was evidence Rear Admiral Daria was selling off weapons to the highest bidder. It's what my informant back in the Middle East was *this* close to telling me. It explains everything."

Connor didn't respond, so Nate felt the rare need to fill the silence.

"I know it sounds like I'm making it up, but I'm not. After they kicked me out, all trails led to him. So, I dug.

And dug. I finally got what I needed to prove it. I sent what I had to you because I wanted it in a secure place. I didn't want to involve you, but you were there. You were discharged. You were already involved. So, I sent you the evidence I had—"

"It's destroyed."

"Yeah, Brina told me. More or less." Nate paused. Did he really trust these people? Maybe Connor had gotten mixed up with the wrong "group." Brina being involved was confusing. Everything about this was…weird. Yet he'd always trusted Connor. He couldn't stop now. If Connor was the one to bring him down, maybe it was his just desserts. "I might have some backup of most of what I sent you."

"Nate…"

"You don't believe me."

"I've been shot at and my cabin was blown up. I believe you." Another long pause, but Nate didn't know how to fill this one. "I just don't know what the hell we're going to do about it. They want me dead. They're really going to want you dead."

"It's not the first time people have wanted us dead." But it was the first time they were specific targets, not just a uniform. And Nate didn't know why Connor would be more of a target than him. There'd been no shootouts, no explosions or things being burned down here.

Granted, Connor was isolated. Nate lived on a ranch with a bunch of military men. Still, Nate had been the one digging for evidence. Not Connor.

Was Connor meant to be his warning? Nate didn't know. Maybe he should have kept the evidence. Maybe… Hell, he didn't know. "I'm sorry you got dragged into this."

"I'm not." There was something strange in the way Connor said that, but without Nate seeing his friend's face, he didn't know what. "Have you seen any sign of people after you?" Connor asked.

"No. The only thing I can think of is that they want the evidence taken care of first. Before I sent it off to you, I think…someone was maybe out there. Watching. It felt like paranoia more than actual threat, though."

"You'd think they'd have a bigger…" Connor trailed off, then exhaled harshly. "I know what I have to do. You sit tight. Watch your back. And let this…team of Sabrina's help you. They want to help."

Nate didn't trust Connor's voice, but Brina's *team* being little Elsie Rogers was… "They sent me their computer geek," he muttered, hoping she didn't hear him say it.

"Right, the person who could get us a secure line so I actually know what's going on. How dare they?" Connor said dryly.

"All I'm saying is you got the badass almost–Navy SEAL."

"Yeah, it's a real shame your ex-girlfriend couldn't come save your butt. Would have been a real nice reconciliation story."

Nate actually laughed, the idea was so ludicrous. "Brina and I would never reconcile. Whatever we had was all… kid stuff. Doesn't matter now." Why were they even talking about—

"Yeah, well, I slept with her."

Nate blinked. "I…" His mind was utterly blank. "I do not know what to say to that."

"Just felt like clearing the air."

Then he knew exactly what to say. Because this wasn't about Connor sleeping with his ex-girlfriend. It was about "clearing the air," which meant whatever Connor had to do was a little too close to a suicide mission. "Oh, no. No. Don't you go play hero, Con. No need to clear the air. No getting stuff off your chest. Because you're going to come out of this in one piece and tell me to my face you fell for my ex."

"I plan to. Listen to the computer geek. I don't understand this group at all, but I know they're doing the right thing."

"You sure about that?"

"Yeah. Yeah, I am." Connor ended the call, but Nate held on to the phone as if he hadn't.

Just because Connor trusted these people didn't mean Nate had to.

He glanced at Elsie typing away at her computer.

He could pretend. He'd grown very adept at pretending.

Chapter Three

"Well, that was informative," Elsie said brightly. She didn't know why she was pulling out the *bright* voice or pasting a smile on her face. Discomfort mostly, she figured. She'd listened in on his conversation. Obviously, she'd been right there, so he'd known she was listening. It wasn't eavesdropping, per se.

But Elsie had found out way more than she'd planned to find out.

"Was it?" Nate replied, staring at the phone as if it were a bug he wasn't quite sure whether to squash or let free.

"Sabrina didn't mention your...romantic history."

Nate pulled a face. "We were kids. Do I keep this phone?"

"I just meant..." She had no idea what she just meant. "Yes, keep the phone. Sabrina or Connor may communicate with you on it. They might not. But you can use it to make whatever calls you need to without fear of being traced or overheard. At least, through the phone. This Daria character. What do you have on him?"

He didn't say anything at first. She understood his reticence. They might know of each other from growing up in the same small town, but how was he supposed to trust some random woman who'd appeared, sent to help him by a mysterious group?

It was a lot to accept. Especially when the package was her…computer geek.

But the sooner they got started, the quicker she could be done lying to her family. The sooner the danger would be *away* from her family. Speaking of…

"Sabrina and Connor are handling the hitman after him, but there are two hitmen that my group are tracking. We've lost track of the second, though we're working with someone who was in contact with him. I don't see how he's not on his way here. If you can give me everything you've got on Daria, I can see if I can connect him to a hitman and we'll go from there."

Nate looked around the room at all the equipment she'd unloaded. She wasn't sure if it was a distrust of computers or her stamped all over his face, but it was clear as day.

"It's a lot to take in," she said, not without empathy. "I'd give you more time but, you know… Hitman on the loose and all."

"How do you know all this? Not you personally, but your…group. How is Sabrina involved? I don't—"

"Sabrina is part of the team. Has been for years. Longer than me, actually. Our goal has always been to do good in the world, but without always expressly having to follow the red tape law enforcement agencies do. That means our group was approached by another to partner with them to fully get to the bottom of a mystery of sorts."

"What mystery?"

"Well, that in and of itself is a bit of a mystery. Most recently, our group was tasked with stopping two hitmen. We followed one, which led Sabrina to Connor. Connor and Sabrina put together that you'd be the second target. I assume this Daria wants to silence you because of what you know." Elsie frowned at her computer, where she'd been catching up on the findings she'd missed while she'd been in the hospital. "The main thing that doesn't make sense to me is how Connor has been more of a target than you when it seems you're the source."

Nate stood there. He'd stopped looking at the phone, but he hadn't really moved. He was unnaturally still.

"Nate?"

He took a deep breath and blew it out. "I sent Connor the physical evidence I had. A few days ago."

"That means someone knew you did that." Elsie drummed her fingers on the desk. "But why not interfere before that point?"

"I sent it because I'd started to get the feeling I was being...watched. Followed. So I was careful. I sent the package with a friend who was going into town, to give to my brother, with directions to send it for me. If there really was someone following me, they wouldn't have caught it right away."

His brother. It was such a strange thing to be thrust into the middle of this. North Star and Blue Valley colliding. Computers in front of her, the ghost of her father's abuse hanging in the air. She could tell by Nate's careful look that he knew as well as she did that Garrett had arrested her father.

And many times, hadn't.

But that wasn't the point of why she was here. "So, you snuck the evidence out. How would they know to track it to Connor, then?"

"I don't know."

Elsie typed that question into the document she had on her screen full of questions. She wouldn't be able to find the answers to all of them herself, but it was good to keep track of them. "Is it possible they think Connor has the evidence, so now they don't need to mess with you?"

"I guess."

"You'd still be able to tell people. You still *have* the information. It might not be concrete enough for a trial or arrest, but—"

"No one believes me," he muttered. So low and grumbly, she barely made out the words.

"I'm sorry?"

He clenched his hand into a fist and let it go. "In the beginning, I tried to tell people. I tried to report Daria to whatever military and law enforcement entity I could think of. Everyone thinks I'm suffering from some sort of PTSD paranoia."

It was Elsie's turn to blow out a breath. "Everyone?"

"More or less."

Elsie knew he wasn't paranoid. She had too much evidence to the contrary. Maybe it was wrong, but it gave her more confidence she was actually the right person for the job. With her computer expertise, she'd help Nate prove what no one had believed.

"So, they've discredited you. You're harmless. But the evidence isn't, so they go after Connor." Elsie frowned. "All to keep quiet that this one guy was illegally selling military weapons?"

"He was. I *know* he was," Nate said. There was a heat to his gaze and an edge to his voice that made it easy to see why people thought he was paranoid.

She felt a little guilty for seeing it, but that kind of zealotry wasn't often accompanied by the truth. She had the uneasy feeling that maybe... Maybe this had more twists than North Star was banking on.

But she wasn't a field operative. Her job was to obtain evidence. Track movements. She'd do her job, and ideally arm North Star with not just Nate's take on things, but the true facts of everything.

She wasn't totally sold they were one and the same.

"Great, even you don't believe me."

"It isn't—"

"I have evidence."

Elsie looked up from her computer, eyebrows raised. "Have or had?"

He looked at her, those dark eyes edgy, broad shoulders tense. Like a man holding on by a thread.

Elsie's pulse scrambled. A mix of the kind of fear she'd never fully eradicate from her psyche, and something else she didn't fully recognize or understand.

She swallowed and held his gaze, no matter how nervous he made her.

"If someone was following me, if someone knew about that evidence and it going on its way to Connor, then someone could…" He gestured around the house and to her, and she understood he was worried her and North Star's involvement made him a larger target than he already was.

"No one can connect me to my group. As long as you don't go around telling people we're working together, no matter what anyone who's watching you sees, they can't connect it to this."

"Who's to say they're not listening?" He winced a little, like he understood that sounded like a very paranoid question.

"This cabin is a safe place. No one can listen in here. I've set up every precaution. We wouldn't want to be caught talking about evidence outside of it, but here, we can talk. I promise you."

"If someone is watching, won't they wonder why I keep sneaking in here?"

She'd found no other way around this. She'd tried. As she'd set up all her equipment, she'd tried to come up with every plausible story. But there was only one she could think of. "Well, I think we're going to have to make up a story about that."

"A story?"

"I think you're going to have to pretend to have an interest in me, Nate." She felt the heat of embarrassment sweep up her neck. "Sure hope you're a good actor."

NATE FOUND THE words didn't make sense. Not in any order he rearranged them in his head. "You want me to pretend…" He blinked.

"All I want you to pretend is some reason you'd be hanging around this cabin. If you've got a better idea than…"

She was blushing. He couldn't force himself to look away from her face, where cheeks turned a pretty color of pink. It helped the slightly sickly pallor.

"Jack would kill me." That was the only thing he could think of to say. He didn't know what to do with…*this*. He'd given up hope of people believing him. Given up on anyone helping him to prove what he *knew*. He'd been working on this alone, in secret, and now suddenly there was a group, and little Elsie Rogers, and fake…interest.

"Right. Well, I guess you have to decide which hand you'd rather die by." Then she *smiled* as if that made any sense.

Nate had been perfecting his acting skills for years now, but they were failing him. So he had to rely on military stoicism. Mouth shut instead of hanging open. Keeping his spine stiff and ramrod-straight instead of fidgeting about. He had to wrap himself in the stillness of a Navy SEAL.

It might be the only way to survive this.

"You probably need some time to think it over. That's okay," she said gently.

He sighed because the world didn't always afford a man time to think things over, to act. To make the right decisions. Would he be here if he'd had time to think back in that Middle Eastern town where trust hadn't been thick on the ground? Between anyone.

No matter how gentle a person might be, sometimes a man had to make a choice. Best as he could.

"We'll build up to it. Rush in too fast, too many people will wonder, question, speculate. They'll pay too much attention to it."

"I'm afraid we don't have that kind of time," Elsie said. "Not with a hitman on the way."

"We'll have to make it. When I need to talk to you, or need the safety of talking freely, I'll find a way to sneak here. Probably at night. During the day, we'll see what we can do to be in each other's way. Look...interested in each other."

Interested in Elsie Rogers. Not exactly crazy, but his world had narrowed to a point. The point of proving his discharge was a lie. Proving he wasn't paranoid and some-one *was* watching him to make sure he didn't get to the bottom of things. He hadn't thought about a woman ro-mantically in...years.

He thought about Brina. And Connor. His friend had slept with his ex-girlfriend. And, quite honestly, he didn't know how *that* worked. Connor was honorable and, while he was a good-natured guy, he didn't put up with an un-reasonable amount of attitude.

Brina was *all* attitude. Or had been. Maybe she'd changed. Nate himself sure had.

"Nate," Elsie said with a gentleness that made him bris-tle. Reminded him of therapy. "You said you have evidence Daria stole weapons from the military and sold them for profit," she continued, as if he didn't remember what he'd said. As if she was just another person carefully humoring him. "More than the physical evidence you sent to Connor that was destroyed."

Nate looked around the cabin. He'd familiarized him-self with hacking as best he could, but he already knew she had him beat there. To move forward with this, he'd have to trust her, and he wasn't there yet.

Trust, like fake relationships, had to be built. Tested.

So he'd build a test. "We'll talk tomorrow."

She frowned at him as he strode for the back door once more. "Nate. This is… I don't think you understand. There might be a hitman after you. Like *now*."

He'd been living watching over his shoulder for a while now. Felt scrutinized. Hunted. Played with. "They've had two years to kill me, Elsie."

That didn't seem to comfort her any. She stood, looking away from her computers and directly at him as she crossed her arms over her chest and stepped in front of the door he'd planned to exit through. "You don't know why they haven't pulled the trigger, so to speak, which means it could be anytime. The years before don't matter. Your friend was shot at. Not a year ago but *this week*. And from everything *I've* been told, the only reason he isn't dead is because Sabrina has been protecting him. If you're withholding evidence, you're risking…" She held up her hands as if she didn't have words for the magnitude of the situation. "Too much, Nate."

He considered. Rejected. Then moved past her. She moved out of the way rather than stand up to him. Just as he'd figured.

"We'll talk tomorrow, Elsie," he said. Firmer this time. Then he walked right out the door. And didn't look back.

Chapter Four

Elsie didn't plan to wait for *tomorrow*. Nate might hold a lot of the cards, but *she* had the means to get information at her disposal. Now that she had a name, all Elsie needed to do was start digging.

Rear Admiral Ronald Daria was, on the surface, unassuming Navy personnel. Spotless if sparse military record. Nothing particularly interesting about the guy.

But Elsie knew how to dig deeper, and then deeper still. She used all the information Holden had uncovered about Ross Industries—a group supplying weapons to elite hitmen—to cross-check anything potentially interesting about Daria.

She glanced up at the clock a little bleary eyed. She'd thought it had been about fifteen minutes, but it had been two hours. Still, in those two hours, she'd figured out Daria had been instrumental in putting military-grade weapons into the hands of Ross Industries.

It would be interesting to see what kind of concrete evidence Nate had, because most of what Elsie had dug up was circumstantial. Obviously, Daria had been careful. Though Elsie could find hints and lines to tug, it would take her even more hours to really locate anything concrete on Daria.

She was prepared to do just that—even if she had to stay

up all night. Let Nate keep everything to himself. She'd present him with an entire dossier of all the evidence it had probably taken him those two years to collect.

She'd need some sustenance, though. No doubt tomorrow Rose would foist nutritious groceries on her, and Elsie would feel honor-bound to eat them, but for now she could live the way she preferred.

Sour gummy bears and an ice-cold Coke. The doctor who'd released her had said to hydrate. Coke was hydrating enough, wasn't it?

Before she could make her way to her suitcase and the snacks she had packed, a knock sounded on the door. Her first thought was that Nate had come back. Maybe with his evidence.

When she opened the front door, it was her oldest sister. "Delia." The world behind her was dark, causing nerves to skitter up Elsie's spine. Someone could be out there. "You didn't come out here alone, did you?"

Delia raised an eyebrow. "Was I supposed to come with an armed escort?"

"No, of course not. It's just late and dark and…" And Elsie should have gone to see Delia right away. The Shaw ranch where Delia lived with her husband wasn't that far away. She should have been the one to make the effort, but she'd gotten set up, then Nate, now Daria.

"Els, it's Blue Valley. Nothing ever happens in Blue Valley."

"Don't say that," Elsie said. It felt like a jinx.

"I guess that's not altogether true, but I'm safe. Are you?"

"Of course."

Delia peered around Elsie. "This looks…heavy duty."

"It is. It is, but it's not dangerous." Elsie had always looked up to Delia and Rose. They'd been tough in the face of the terrible childhood they'd had to endure. Delia had tried to take care of them, gotten them out of Dad's clutches one by one. She'd sacrificed everything for Elsie.

Now Elsie was standing here lying to her.

Delia surveyed the computer equipment with some suspicion. "I don't even know how to use my laptop."

"Sis…" She couldn't tell Delia what was going on. She *couldn't*. But the words were there on the tip of her tongue, wanting to tumble out.

"You're working. You don't want me to bother you."

"It isn't that." Though she should take that excuse. Let Delia believe that was the problem. Not lying. Not secrets. Not danger.

"It *is* that. And it's fine. More than. I like seeing you in your element, even if it makes no sense to me. But I want you to come over to Shaw for dinner some night this week, no matter how busy you are."

"Absolutely." Elsie swallowed at her tightening throat. "I bet Sunny and Gideon have grown like weeds. I want to see them. All of you. I do. I just…"

"Have important work to do. You don't have to feel guilty about that. We like seeing you be successful computer lady."

"But you worry."

"I'll never get over worrying about any of you. That's just the luck of the draw." Delia pulled her into a hug. "I'm proud of you, and I'm glad you're home. Even if you stay holed up in this cabin for a bit at first." Delia released her and pointed a finger. "At *first*."

Elsie managed a smile. "I promise."

"Okay. I'll leave you to it, then." She surveyed the equipment one more time and shook her head. "Beyond me. Just beyond me." She walked back to her truck and, even though Delia was sure nothing ever happened in Blue Valley, Elsie watched until Delia was safely inside it and driving away.

Nate had to take this more seriously. He lived in the middle of all her family. Of course, an elite hitman *shouldn't* take out the wrong target, but no one could be sure, could they? A cold-blooded killer might kill anyone.

Why hadn't she gotten an update from Betty or Sabrina? It had been hours now, and there hadn't been a peep from any North Star people. Sabrina and her team could still be tracking the men after her and Connor. Elsie knew they had a whole team and they were in the Tetons—meaning a lot of wilderness in which to hide.

But there should have been an update. She closed the front door against the early fall evening chill and found her phone. She dialed headquarters first. When no one answered, it was the first real sign something was *wrong*.

She went down the list of people least actively involved with Sabrina's mission. Shay, Betty, Mallory. No one answered. By the time she got to Holden's cell, she was shaking with worry.

"Parker," he barked.

"Holden."

"Els. Hey. Things are a circus, can you—?"

"I've called everyone and anyone. You're the only one who's answered. What's going on?"

Holden sighed, which was odd. Even if he'd been through a lot this month, he was usually his over-the-top charming self. Not a stress ball.

"Sabrina's been shot."

Elsie dropped into her chair, her knees simply giving out. "What?"

"It's…bad. We're all working on this. Someone will update you when there is one."

"But—"

He'd already ended the phone call.

Shot. Bad.

It couldn't be true. Sabrina was…

Elsie inhaled a shaky breath. She'd been here before. Reece had been shot a few months ago. Granted, as part of the team on that mission, she'd always known what was going on. She hadn't been sitting there in the dark.

She glanced at her computer. She didn't have to be in the dark. Some hacking into the hospital system might give her more answers than anyone else had.

But if Sabrina had been shot, it was probably by the hitman after Connor Lindstrom. And there were *two* of them. One had to be moving on Nate.

This wasn't hypothetical anymore.

NATE LAY IN his bunk, tossing a baseball up and catching it as it fell. One of the coping mechanisms his therapist, Monica, had offered him. Do something familiar with his hands would help keep his mind focused.

His mind wasn't falling for it. His mind was on Elsie Rogers, and Brina, and Connor. His mind was on all the things he'd uncovered in his years since discharge. Things that, for *years*, people had dismissed.

There was a relief in the fact that he was right, or that some people thought he was kind of right. But there was also a strange feeling of…anxiety. Who would he be if someone actually believed him? How would he proceed if Sabrina and Elsie and Connor actually followed all his leads?

A heavy, incessant knock sounded on the bunkhouse door. Since Olsen was closest, he glanced out the window. "Averly, it's that chick from this afternoon."

Nate got up off his bed. "How do you have a wife, Olsen? *Chick?*"

Olsen shrugged as Nate nudged him out of the way so he could answer the door. He was going to have to give Elsie a lecture about the appropriate time to have their conversations. Coming to his bunk that he shared with three other guys? Not it. Ever.

He opened the door, immediately stepped outside and closed it behind him so Olsen and the other two guys couldn't eavesdrop.

"You have to take this more seriously," she said without preamble.

"Take *what* more seriously?"

"This. You. There is a hitman after you, and you dismissed me. I let you dismiss me, but there's a hitman after you, and my entire family is wandering around and—"

"Slow down."

"No. I won't. People are in danger. *You* are in danger."

"Like I said before, Elsie, I just don't know why they'd shoot at me after all this time."

"Well, they shot Sabrina." She spat the words at him.

Nate didn't hear anything at all over the heavy thud of his heartbeat for a good few seconds. "What?" he managed to croak.

"I don't know if she's okay." Elsie held up her phone, like that meant something. "I don't have any clue as to what's going on because, instead of being at headquarters, I'm here babysitting you, and you won't even take the threat against you seriously."

She was panicking. That meant he couldn't. "Whoa, whoa, whoa. Back up." He had to get his facts lined up. This had to make sense.

"Holden said it's bad."

Nate didn't know who Holden was, but clearly someone who would know. "This hitman after Connor shot Sabrina?"

Elsie stopped her pacing and blinked. "I... Well, I don't know for sure *who* shot her. She's shot. It's bad. That's all I know."

"That's not enough information to go on."

"I have enough information to go on! There is a hit-man after you. Unless just about everyone I work with is wrong—and they're not—there is a second hitman out there, and you are the most reasonable option for second target. Why wouldn't you take that seriously?"

He didn't know why that ticked him off. He'd been trying to get people to take him seriously for years. It was enough to drive a man crazy, and he'd been on the edge for a while. Now she was marching up to him, accusing *him* of not taking things seriously.

When Sabrina was shot and Connor was…what? Did anyone in her group care about Connor? Did anyone in her group care about anything? How would he know? Why was she demanding a response out of him in the *hours* after they'd met. When he'd been living with this for *years*?

No, she didn't get to be mad at *him*. She didn't get to lecture *him*.

He marched farther out into the yard, to stand in the glow of the outdoor light. "How's this for serious?" He spread his arms wide. "Come on, hitman. Take your shot."

Elsie's face went mutinous. It was fascinating, really. Maybe it was the shadows of the darkness around them and the lone glow of the outdoor light. Maybe it was the sheer strangeness of seeing Elsie so *angry*.

She stalked right up to him…

And punched him in the stomach. A surprisingly decent punch. If she'd been anyone else, he might have seen it coming and dodged, but since it was little Elsie Rogers, he took the blow in complete and utter shock.

"You're an idiot. And I don't like you," she said, shaking out her hand and vibrating with rage. A rage that had her storming off into the darkened night.

Nate managed to suck in a shallow breath and then another. Well, Elsie could certainly gut punch a guy.

And he kind of hated to admit it, but he'd let his feelings get the better of him. His frustration and his confusion, when clearly the real serious issue was that Brina had been shot. And it was bad.

All because of this thing with Rear Admiral Daria. *His* thing.

Nate scrubbed his hands over his face. For years, he'd been living with this. Alone. No one to share with, and then suddenly, out of nowhere, people believed him. People were involved.

Brina had been shot.

That meant, whether he liked it or not—whether he knew what to do about it or not—he needed to let some people in.

He went back into the bunkhouse. Olsen was at his heels immediately. "How'd you move so fast?"

"I'm not moving. I've basically known Elsie my whole life." He brushed Olsen off and knelt next to his bed.

"Known how?"

"Mind your own business, Olsen," Nate muttered. "Why don't you call your wife?"

Olsen didn't back off, but Nate couldn't care less at this point. Brina was shot and Elsie was mad and... He couldn't play it safe. Wasn't this what he'd been waiting for? Someone to *believe* him? Here she was, not just believing him but wanting him—*him*—to take this more seriously.

Yeah, it was time to stop being bowled over by this flip. He finally had what he'd wanted. He had to act on that. He dug out the folder he kept hidden under his mattress and tucked the flash drive that fell from it into his pocket.

He ignored Olsen's looks, noting that no one else really seemed to care. And then he went back outside. To find Elsie.

To do the thing he'd been waiting for the chance to do for *years*.

It was time.

Chapter Five

Elsie was so *furious*. At the situation, and worse, at herself. She paced the inside of the cabin, having to twist and turn around her tech equipment.

She'd never hit anyone before. She'd promised herself she never would. Oh, she'd done no damage to abs-of-steel Nate Averly, but she'd been a little girl who'd been used as a punching bag. Whether the blows hurt or glanced, they were an expression of anger that wasn't right.

It wasn't *right*. Sabrina had been shot. She'd punched a near stranger and told him she didn't like him.

Why had Shay trusted sending her into the field? She wasn't built for this kind of thing. She was the girl in the corner, nose pressed to the computer screen for a *reason*.

She plopped onto the couch and let her head fall into her hands. She was getting worked up, and she had to find some control. She did one of the breathing exercises she'd learned from her therapist when she'd been having panic attacks.

It was strange. She'd been a mess, drowning at her old job for a tech company. Not because the work had been hard. It had been a breeze. But because the world had felt too big and too scary, and the rote computer work hadn't challenged her in the least.

When Granger Macmillan had approached her—

because of some paper she'd written in college, of all things—she hadn't trusted him at all. He'd given her a challenge: hack into a security-laden server.

She'd done it in ten minutes. He'd given her more tests after that, each one more complicated than the last. Even though she hadn't trusted him, the tests had become her center. When she lost herself in a *complicated* computer problem, she felt in control, confident.

Right.

When he'd finally convinced her to join North Star, she'd found a life she'd never had. She didn't panic in North Star. She rarely had nightmares. The work had given her something to hold on to.

She couldn't let that spiral out of control. She wouldn't let Nate or anyone else take that away from her.

If Nate wouldn't take this seriously, there were things she could do. Revival had its own security systems, but she could stealthily make them more secure. It was a big ranch, and there were too many places to hide, but she could make it harder.

She would. Not for Nate, but for her *family* and all the innocent people milling around this potential powder keg.

She was halfway through a remote diagnostic test on the security feed when someone knocked on her back door. It was late, so Elsie doubted it was one of her sisters again.

She went to the door. She couldn't see anything, but she doubted very much a bad guy was going to *knock*. So she opened the door. Nate stood there in the shadows. He stepped inside without a word. There was a folder under his arm.

"What's that?" she asked by way of greeting.

"My evidence against Daria."

He set the folder on the first free space he could find. "This is what I have."

She blinked. She'd gotten through to him. With a punch?

She shook her head. No, punching him had not been right. "Before we...go into that, there's something I have to say."

His eyebrows rose, but he didn't say anything else. He just stood in the cabin, looking too big and far too edgy for any comfort.

Elsie wasn't *afraid* of him. Heck, she'd punched him and he'd taken it and hadn't even demanded an apology. Though he deserved one. "I'm sorry. I shouldn't have hit you. That was wrong."

"Are you worried you injured me?" he asked somewhat incredulously.

"Not in the least. It probably didn't even hurt, but expressing anger through violence isn't right. Ever."

"I'm going to have to disagree with you," he said somewhat flippantly. Then he winced and looked at her uncertainly.

Because the ghost of who she'd been was always front and center in Blue Valley—even if her sisters had reclaimed something here. She hadn't. "If we need to acknowledge it, we can."

He shoved his hands into his pockets and rocked back onto his heels, looking deeply uncomfortable. "Acknowledge what?"

She wasn't worried about his discomfort, she was worried about moving on so they could accomplish something. "My dad used to beat me and my sisters up. The town was aware. Your brother arrested him a time or two, but sometimes his hands were tied and he couldn't. I don't hold anything against anyone except my parents. My dad was the one who did it. My mom was the one who facilitated it."

"And someone should have done something. That's just the bottom line."

She wasn't sure it was better to hear that, or worse. Because no one had. She'd had to work through that, accept that no one had. "Sometimes there isn't anyone with the means to do something. That's just…the bad luck of the draw."

"Garrett…"

"Your brother tried. But the law doesn't make it easy to do much of anything without evidence or an adult willing to talk. I don't blame Garrett or, through extension, you, if that's what you're worried about."

"I wasn't…" He trailed off, frowning, but still with that aura of discomfort.

"That's the beginning and end of it. I'm just fine. Can we move on now? I'm not an abused little girl anymore. I'm an adult woman with a tough job, and I do some good in the world."

He studied her then nodded. "Then let's do some good. Together."

It felt like relief, but before she could enjoy even that small step forward, her phone rang. "Hello?"

"Hey, Els. It's Betty."

"What's the news?"

"It looks like Sabrina is going to pull through. It's a bad one, and she had to have some major surgery, but she's strong and stubborn."

"What about the others?"

"Still in the field. I'm at the hospital with Sabrina, so someone else will have to update you on that."

"I guess they will when they can." But it worried Elsie that everything was taking so long and she was so far out of the loop.

"Your assignment going okay?" Betty asked, but she sounded beat. Just exhausted.

"Go get some rest, Bet. I'll take care of my assignment just fine."

"Call if you need anything."

"Sure." But she wouldn't. She had to handle things on her own, and she would. For Sabrina in a hospital bed. For the little girl she'd been who'd thought she'd never have a chance to do anything. For her family—her sisters and North Star.

She said goodbye to Betty and hung up. She turned to Nate. "Sabrina is going to be okay. I guess there's still a small chance she won't be, but she's strong. She's... Sabrina."

"She's come back from bad odds before."

Elsie nodded. It helped to hear him reiterate her own hopes. Sabrina would be okay. But that didn't mean the work was done. "Someone is coming for you, Nate. They have to be."

He nodded, his expression grim. "Let's see what we can do to stop them."

NATE COULDN'T EVER remember feeling true panic before he'd been discharged. Even when the building he'd been in had exploded, he hadn't felt *panic*. He'd been trained for that. He'd accepted the odds were he might not make it out of the SEALs alive. He knew what to do when all seemed lost.

What he hadn't been prepared for was the dishonorable discharge. People dismissing all his evidence. Friends and family, and even a licensed therapist, thinking he was unhinged. He'd accepted all that at this point. Even gotten used to it.

So used to it that trusting someone with everything he had... It felt insurmountable. So he kept the flash drive in his pocket and handed Elsie the folder. Even that had his heart racing as though he'd run a sprint out of a burning building.

She didn't say much. She looked through the papers, studying them with the weight they deserved. That was more than he could say about anyone else he'd ever showed them to.

"You hacked into his bank records?" she asked, eyebrows rising.

"Well, I paid someone to when I couldn't manage. I doubt that's all his bank records, either, but it's got some weird payments that coincide with some military operations."

She flipped to another page—presumably the one he'd cross-referenced with Daria's missions and where he'd been stationed. It was clear to Nate. Perhaps not the kind of evidence that could go to trial, but enough to prove Daria was shady.

Elsie was carefully analyzing the information, and he didn't know what to *do*. He felt like jumping out of his skin. Instead, he stayed exactly where he was, close enough to the back door he felt he could make a quick exit. Falling back on his military training and standing with legs apart, hands behind his back.

Like he was waiting for his dressing down.

"This is what you sent Connor?" she asked, flipping to the front and going through the papers again.

"Yes."

"It just doesn't seem like enough to shoot down a helicopter over," she said with a frown. "This is all circumstantial. You'll need something stronger to really pin it to Daria."

Nate thought of the flash drive in his pocket. He hadn't been able to bring himself to give it to her. There were just some things... He didn't have to trust her completely. What if she ignored it? Disproved it?

He could give her the info about Daria and work on the rest alone. Where it was safe. Where no one could tell him he was *reaching*.

"Yeah, but it's a starting point."

"Oh, it's more than that. But why go after Connor and not you? It doesn't make sense."

Nate didn't know what to say. He couldn't seem to come up with a lie that had become second nature to him when talking to his brother, his therapist, any of the guys.

With Elsie, the only thing he could think to tell her was the truth. Luckily that was terrifying enough, he just kept his mouth shut as she studied the papers again.

Her phone rang and he jumped at the sudden jangle, wincing at the weakness he showed by being startled by a *phone*.

If Elsie noticed, she didn't acknowledge it. She pulled her cell out of her pocket. "Rogers." She pulled up something on her computer, the phone tucked between her ear and shoulder as she typed away. Her dark hair had fallen out of its band. As whoever began talking, she sat a little straighter. Nate had to wonder if she was talking to some kind of superior.

She *was* pretty. He wasn't sure the last time he'd paid attention to the way a woman looked. The way he reacted to those looks.

So, you're going to do it now? That's healthy.

"What are my next steps?" she asked, pushing away from the computer. "All right… Sure… Take your time. Thanks, Shay." She ended the phone call then stared at him.

She swallowed and opened her mouth, but it took her a few seconds to actually form words. "They arrested Daria."

It felt a bit like a blow. Nate didn't know why. "What?"

"His whole team is wiped out." Elsie looked at her phone as if she didn't understand it. "Sabrina was the only injury. Daria is in custody, as is anyone who worked with him." She looked up at him. "I'll make sure the evidence against Daria sticks, so I guess…it's over."

Nate's stomach sank. He could let that be it. He could go back to the way things were.

But he knew things weren't over. He knew this didn't end with Daria.

He didn't have to tell her. He didn't have to risk it. But he thought of the way she'd come to his cabin, all worked up that he wasn't taking this seriously enough. That he was in danger. That her family could be caught in the crossfire.

If someone figured out he still had information—and that he might actually get someone to believe him about it—he'd be in danger, yes. But so would the people around him.

Maybe even Elsie herself.

If he couldn't trust *her* with it—or the group who'd taken down Daria when no one else had or would—then there was no hope. He might as well give up.

He closed his eyes and sighed. "No, Elsie. It isn't over." There was no turning back now. If Daria was taken down, great, but to do the rest, he had to accept he was going to need help. And it looked like Elsie was his help. "Daria was just the beginning."

Chapter Six

Elsie didn't know if she had any surprise left in her. Between being home in a North Star capacity, Sabrina of all people being seriously shot, and this Daria already being taken down with no help from her, she was already reeling.

Now Nate was standing there grimly saying…

Elsie shook her head as if that might clarify things. "I don't understand."

"When I was looking into Daria, I found more. Bigger. He was a small cog in a big, messy machine."

"You mentioned military corruption on the phone with Connor. But I thought…"

"That I was crazy?"

She glowered at him. "Why is that the conclusion you keep jumping to? Why can't you give me five seconds to work through anything without assuming everyone thinks…" It dawned on her then.

Everyone *had* thought he was paranoid. No one had given him any credit. No matter what he'd found, he'd spent a while being dismissed and discredited. That kind of thing… Well, she knew what it was like. But even when she'd been living through it, she'd had her sisters. They'd built their own little world of belief.

Nate was alone.

Elsie was not tough like the North Star field operatives.

She had too soft a heart for a sob story—and Nate sure had one. She knew he wouldn't appreciate her feeling sorry for him, but it didn't eradicate the feeling.

"No one has believed me in a very long time," he said, his expression intense but also…defeated. Like he'd given up. "Not my family. Not anyone here. Why would you believe me? Why would *anyone*?"

"I guess sometimes the people who know you, who care about you, have to worry. Naturally. Honestly. And it… colors their perception of…well, what's going on."

"A lot of things have colored their perceptions," he said, an edge of bitterness to his tone.

"But I don't have any of that. I just have the facts, and the facts I have back you up." He looked at her, those dark eyes just a little wide, as if surprised, even standing here surrounded by her computer equipment. But they didn't have time for his reticence or surprise, and she had to remember that. "So if you've got more information, you need to give it to me. You need to stop holding back. I can't help you if you're keeping little pieces of things hidden because you're afraid I won't believe you."

He straightened, his frown turning into a deep scowl. "I'm hardly *afraid*."

"What would you call it?" she retorted, looking at him expectantly.

"I…"

Elsie waited. Maybe she should have said something out of kindness. Changed the subject so he didn't have to flounder. She'd been afraid too many times to count. She knew how that could warp your perception of the world.

But she needed him to understand what he was doing—and why—so he'd stop. So North Star could do what it set out to do—stop the bad guys. If Daria wasn't the only bad guy out there…

She huffed out a breath. They didn't have time for *any*

of this. "We have a lot of work to do, Nate. It doesn't matter if it's fear holding you back, or some amazing courage I couldn't even begin to fathom." Though she knew it was fear. "You have to work with me. Or there's no point in me being here. Sabrina was shot for nothing. Maybe I could figure this out without your help—but it would take time. Time we don't have. There's still a hitman on the loose."

"If they really wanted me dead, they could have done it already."

"Do you want to wait around to figure out if they will? Maybe you'd like me to figure out why they waited—you know, after they kill you."

He shook his head, but she could read some conflict inside him. Even as he told her no, he was letting her words sink in. He was weighing the importance.

"I need time," he said, his voice a rough scrape.

Elsie didn't groan in frustration. Sometimes you had to beat your head against a brick wall a few times to make it through. Hacking and her computer work was often painstaking. Running into blocks over and over again and trying new things until there was a breakthrough. She could beat his stubbornness.

She had to. "You don't have time. Beginning and end of story."

He jammed his hands in his pockets, scowling. "Well, I never thought I'd be bossed around by little Elsie Rogers."

"And I never imagined I'd escape Blue Valley and be someone who *could* boss people around." She took a moment to fully absorb her own words. No, she never thought she'd be here. But here she was. She wouldn't be afraid of it. "Sometimes change is a good thing."

"I hope you're ready to prove it," he muttered. He pulled one of his hands from his pocket and held out a flash drive. "This is two years' worth of work. Everything I have. I only sent Connor the things on Daria, but whoever is above

Daria wouldn't necessarily know what—*if* they know I have anything. They'd only know I sent stuff, and if they knew what I had…" Nate shrugged.

She took the flash drive, relief that he'd hand it over and satisfaction she'd gotten through to him coursing through her. But his words made it clear. "The timing means they know you know. You sending that package to Connor was the tip-off."

She could tell he didn't like that, but with all the information at her disposal, it was the only sensible conclusion.

"Fine. They know. They acted because I sent information. We'll work from that hypothesis…for now. They wouldn't know I didn't send Connor everything."

"Why didn't you?"

"I didn't think he'd believe me if it was too big. A lot of the stuff I have pointing to a bigger organization is circumstantial. I just needed one person to believe me, to work with me. Connor was already involved, so it had to be him. I was going to take it step-by-step. Daria first."

Elsie couldn't blame him there. "You sure this is everything?" she asked, holding up the flash drive. She didn't know if she'd believe him even if he said yes, yet she had to ask.

Nate nodded. And he looked mad enough that she was compelled to take that as the truth.

So she put the drive in the computer and got to work.

"Not bad for an amateur," Elsie said, her nose practically pressed to the screen. She'd spent silent minutes pulling up everything he'd saved to that drive over two years. He'd had to pace the room to keep himself from demanding what she thought.

"Gee, thanks," he muttered irritably. When was the last time he'd been an amateur at something? But that's exactly what he felt like while she sat there fingers flying over the keys of her computer like some kind of fairy princess of tech.

She blinked up at him, almost as if she'd forgotten he was there. She scratched a hand through her hair then stretched, the material of her shirt stretching over her—

Nate looked down at the floor. Yeah, being attracted to her didn't work on *any* level. There was clearly something wrong with him, but he didn't have to succumb to it. He would stare at the floor and escape as soon as he could.

"Since you don't know how to do it stealthily, the biggest problem is that anyone can see what you're doing and immediately delete or change the information you're collecting," she said. "Every time you saved something, they probably knew. Now, they might not have always known it was you, but they didn't need to. They only needed to alter the information so whatever you saved no longer looked real."

The words had him forgetting about her stretching. His gaze jerked up. "Is that why no one believed me?" He'd sent proof—or so he'd thought—to everyone he could think of in the Navy, and gotten nothing in response. Except a call to his therapist here.

If the information had already been changed, that made him look as unstable as people seemed to think. And there was a *reason*. Not just people's distrust in his stability.

Elsie shrugged, nose pressed to the screen again. "Probably. I mean, if someone thought you were even kind of right, they could start digging and see what's been changed, but someone would have to want to do that. My guess is, going against the brass—especially someone like Daria who has nothing bad in his record—isn't something most people are willing to attempt without solid, irrefutable evidence. Unfortunately, someone probably made your evidence look really refutable."

"So…" It worked through him then. That it might not

just be as simple as his friends not trusting him enough. That it might actually be people working against him to discredit whatever he found.

Could it be true? It all seemed far too good to be true.

Except that Sabrina had been shot—no matter that she might survive. Brina had been through enough. She shouldn't be caught in the crosshairs of this...

But if she had been, didn't that lend credit to everything he believed? Finally?

Elsie leaned away from the screen, blinked her eyes a few times and sighed. "This gives me a place to start. I might be able to uncover what they changed, when, how, who. That will be the next step. Who's above Daria?" She yawned as she asked the question.

"It's the middle of the night. Don't you sleep?"

She waved that away. "Don't need much usually. Doctor said I might be more tired than usual, but I can push through. Plenty of supplies." She pointed to the two empty pop cans next to her.

Nate couldn't think about the fact her "supplies" apparently meant sugar. "What do you mean the doctor said?"

"Oh. Right." She shifted in her chair uncomfortably. Her attempts at being casual failed miserably, and she kept her eyes on the screen though he didn't think she was actually looking at anything. "Just a little...incident a few days ago."

He folded his arms across his chest. "Why don't you explain that?"

"It doesn't matter."

"Explain it," he insisted.

She rolled her eyes and huffed, glaring at him. "It's nothing. I wasn't shot, like Sabrina. I don't do field work. Mostly. I happened to be on-site trying to hack a computer and...someone drugged me."

"You were *drugged*." It explained the sickly pallor, but

what the hell was she doing working this hard when she'd been drugged. And apparently not that long ago?

"It's really not that big of a deal. I don't even remember it. I feel bad for Willa. She's the one who had to witness her dad losing it. Willa, she's… It's complicated, but basically her dad was a spy who lost it a little and was ready to…well, kill us all, I guess. So, she had it way worse than me. Her own father was going to kill her."

Nate couldn't help but stare at Elsie. Hadn't her own father been capable of the same? And why did their conversations keep coming to this awkward place where he knew…exactly what she'd been through?

She said she didn't blame anyone, but Nate didn't understand how that could be possible. How she could still think someone else had it worse than her.

Something on her face softened and Nate didn't know why that was so hard to look away from.

"You know, your mom tried to help us once."

"What?"

"She brought a meal over. It was after Garrett had arrested my father, one of the times he did that didn't stick. You know that old sheriff—my father was buddies with him or whatever. He'd find a way to wiggle Dad out of things, and CPS could never find any evidence. But Garrett arrested Dad anyway this time. It must have been his first year with Valley County. I was pretty young. Anyway."

"Garrett is sheriff of Blue Valley now. He actually… got community support to start a Blue Valley PD instead of be patrolled by the county."

"Is he?" Elsie actually smiled. "I'm glad. He'd be a good one. Hard to believe he'd have a whole department."

"Oh, it's only him and Mrs. Linley as dispatcher." But that wasn't what he really wanted to talk about. "My mother…?"

"Oh, right. Garrett must have told your mother about it.

She came over, brought us dinner. A chicken noodle casserole. It smelled amazing."

Nate's stomach felt like lead. Since he'd never known his mother had done such a thing, he had a feeling this didn't have a happy ending.

"You must have been in the Navy by then, and Rose and Delia were gone. It was just the three youngest of us, I think. Your mom told my mother she could take us to Billings right then and there before Dad came back." Elsie smiled, even though, clearly, her mother had not gone. "My mother refused, of course. Threw the casserole in the trash. But your mom tried."

Nate didn't know what to say. It sounded like his mother. She was not a particularly effusive, friendly woman, but she believed in right and wrong.

"My mother never left, even when people offered help. She always told Dad, and then Dad wouldn't drink or knock us around for a few weeks while he waited for someone from CPS to show up—usually if someone came by trying to help, CPS would come out as soon as they could. But my father knew how to work around the system. And when you're as isolated as Blue Valley, he always had warning."

"I don't know what to…say."

"You don't have to say anything. It's not…poison. You know? I'm not going to fall apart if you mention it. If *I* mention it. There were people like your mom who tried to help. Like Garrett. There's just only so much you can do for five girls whose parents don't want the help that's being offered."

"There should be more."

"There should be. And sometimes there is. I've helped kids. Kids stuck in worse situations than even I was in. He didn't win, and you don't have to act like I'm more fragile because of it. That's why I tried to clear the air earlier."

"I don't think you're fragile."

"Good."

"But if you were *drugged* not that long ago, maybe you should rest."

"Maybe I should, but Sabrina was shot today. Betty said she's probably going to make it, but there's still that *probably*. There's a hitman somewhere, and you're the likely target. You live among my family and friends. I'll rest when we figure out how to make sure everyone's safe. How can I rest before that?"

"I was a Navy SEAL. Even we rested sometimes."

"Well, feel free to go rest, Nate."

He scowled. He was hardly going to *go rest* and leave her to do all the work on her own. "What can I do?" he demanded.

Elsie studied him, a frank appraisal that made him want to fidget. Since he *had* been a Navy SEAL, he didn't. But it was uncomfortable, that impulse.

"Notes," she said with a nod.

"Notes?"

"Yes. We're going back to high school, Nate, because I'm going to need you to write down and organize everything I tell you. Do you think we can get a whiteboard?"

"A whiteboard."

She waved it away. "We don't have time. Paper will do."

"I was not a good student."

She flashed a smile at him, one that had some uncomfortable tightening passing through his body. "I'm sure you'll figure it out. I've got faith in you."

No one had for a very long time, and Nate found he didn't know what to do with it. Except do as she said and take…notes.

Chapter Seven

Elsie woke with a pain in her neck, and what felt like a keyboard pressed to her face. As she straightened, she realized that, yes, she'd used her keyboard as something of a pillow.

Not the first time.

She rubbed her face as she yawned and looked around the room. She startled when she noticed Nate on the corner of the couch he'd cleared off so he could sit to take notes. The notebook was in his lap, the pen was in his hand, but he was fast asleep.

His head was tilted just slightly, his eyes were closed and his breathing was slow and even. She got the feeling that if she moved, he'd jump to alertness in the snap of a finger, so she found herself sitting very still.

His dark hair was messy, and a day's growth of stubble gave him an even more dangerous look than he usually had about him. She would never have considered him *her type*, what with the sheer height and breadth of him, but he was objectively handsome.

The flutter of attraction in her chest was so novel, she just stared at him. She'd had boyfriends before…in college. She'd made a point of it. But working at North Star the past three years, and all the problems she'd been having at her previous job before that had taken up all her time, and male companionship had fallen to the wayside.

And why on earth are you thinking about male companionship on a job, with a man from your hometown?

As if he'd read her thoughts or sensed her staring, Nate's eyes blinked open. Elsie knew she should look away. Her mind screamed at her to, but she just couldn't seem to take her gaze from his sleepy dark one.

"Fell asleep, huh?" he said, his voice rumbly.

Her stomach did a strange swooping roll, like she was on a roller coaster. Before she could say anything, a knock sounded at the door. Elsie jumped a foot. Oh, this was not good. "You have to—"

"Disappear," he finished for her. He was already up and heading for the back door.

Elsie swallowed at the nerves battering her. So many different kinds of nerves, she didn't even know what to do about them.

The knock sounded again and Elsie went to answer it. Nate was slipping out the back, but Elsie needed to create a little bit more time. She opened the door a crack.

Elsie's eyes widened. "Rose," she squeaked. "It's early."

"Yeah." Rose studied her skeptically through the crack. "Open the door, Elsie."

Elsie made a big production out of it, going as slowly as she could and hoping any evidence of Nate was long gone.

Rose stepped inside, frowning.

Gabrielle wiggled and held her arms out to Elsie. Elsie took the toddler and smiled winsomely at her older sister.

"What are you hiding?" Rose demanded.

"Nothing. Nothing!" Elsie jiggled Gabs in an attempt to get her niece to laugh.

Rose was clearly not convinced. She walked deeper into the cabin, little Xander peacefully asleep in his chest carrier.

"Doughnuts!" Gabriella shouted, boisterously wiggling in Elsie's arms.

"Yes, we brought doughnuts," Rose agreed. "But this is not a place for children. You could have said that instead of acting all weird about letting us in."

Elsie looked around at all the equipment. "Sorry, I fell asleep at my computer last night and I'm just...out of sorts. Sorry."

Rose reached out and touched her cheek, and there was that *worry* Elsie had needed to stay away from. She loved Rose and Delia with all her heart, but the real reason she avoided Blue Valley these days wasn't the ghost of her father, it was *this*. Being treated like she couldn't handle anything.

"Don't be sorry. What's really going on with you, Els?"

Elsie swallowed. "I told you. This project..."

"If it's making you this jumpy, and has you falling asleep at your computer, maybe..."

"Don't do that." Elsie stepped away from Rose's hand, trying to keep her voice even since she was holding Gabrielle. "Don't underestimate me."

"I'm not," Rose said, sounding hurt.

"I can handle my life. Sometimes it means falling asleep while I work. Sometimes it means..." Well, it was no time to bring up Nate. "I'm capable. And an adult."

"I know."

"Do you?"

"Yes," Rose said, still sounding hurt. "You could do anything, Elsie. I believe that for all of us. If I can be *here*, married to Jack, mother of his children. Mother, period. I think any of us can do anything. But... I don't want you pushing yourself so much you end up... It isn't always healthy to work so hard."

"And sometimes it is. Sometimes you put in the hard work because the outcome is worth it." Elsie nuzzled Gabs. "I know kids and work aren't the same, but it's similar.

I've watched you and Delia enough to know that being a mother—a real mother—is hard, hard work. But you do it."

"Yes. Because they're living, breathing human beings who don't give you much of a choice."

"We know there's a choice. We saw the other side of that choice."

Rose sighed. "I worry about you girls. I can't help that."

Elsie knew she couldn't, but she also thought if she could *show* Rose all she did, maybe Rose would get to that point.

Would Rose ever really believe she could handle Nate Averly, though? Elsie barely believed it herself. But she had a job to do. A *job*. "This job saved me, Rose. I need you to understand that. As much as you and Delia did."

"I didn't—"

"As much as you and Delia did," Elsie repeated. "So, I need you to trust me when I say I know what I'm doing."

Rose nodded. "Okay. Okay. I'll back off." She glanced at the computers once more, then frowned, picking up the notebook on the couch. "This isn't your handwriting."

Elsie did everything she could—channeled every North Star field operative she'd ever worked with—to keep her face impassive while her mind scrambled. "No, it's notes on the project I'm working on from…my boss." She even managed a smile as she lied to her sister.

Rose shrugged and dropped the notebook.

Elsie knew she should beg Rose off so she could work this morning. She wasn't sure where she and Nate had left off. Apparently, they'd both conked out when it really hadn't been an option. She had to focus on Nate and the potential hitman after him.

But a girl had to eat. Especially doughnuts. "Is it warm enough to eat those doughnuts on the table outside?"

Rose smiled. "Yeah, we can do that."

NATE KNEW HE'D made a tactical mistake last night. If he hadn't fallen asleep, he might have been able to sneak into the bunkhouse before the first early morning alarms went off, but even that would have been difficult.

He did live with a bunch of former soldiers.

The real problem was that he shouldn't have stuck around Elsie's and taken notes. He really shouldn't have allowed himself the luxury of falling asleep on her couch—not that he felt like he'd *allowed* it. He wasn't sure how it had happened. One minute he remembered her talking about some group she'd worked a mission on—and she'd said *mission* with all the seriousness of a military general—and the next...

Waking up to her dark eyes staring right at him, and that pretty little blush creeping up her neck and—

Nope.

Nate pushed into the bunkhouse knowing that most of the guys would already be up and at the mess hall eating breakfast. Even if they didn't care, they would have noted his absence last night and this morning.

And they'd be forming their own conclusions—conclusions that would likely get him into trouble with *someone*. Whether it was his therapist, or Elsie's sister, or her brother-in-law.

Nate could have explained it away in any number of ways, *if* Olsen hadn't known Elsie had come to the door last night. And Olsen had a big fat mouth.

Nate ran through the shower and got dressed. He had no choice but to follow his usual routine for the day. Breakfast at the mess hall, his therapy session with Monica, then whatever ranch chores were on the docket.

When he got to the mess hall, he ignored the way it felt like all eyes were on him. He might not be delusional, but the paranoia thing wasn't always so easy to dismiss.

Nate made his way through the food line then took a seat at a table with only two other soldiers.

"You work fast," Drake Worthington said, looking up at Nate with a grin.

"Don't know what you mean."

"Yeah, you do," he said with his booming laugh. "And Olsen's told everyone—not just our bunk."

"Told everyone *what*?"

"That you spent the night in a cabin with Jack's sister-in-law."

Nate scowled. "Olsen's a liar."

"You weren't in *our* bunk."

"I didn't realize that made Olsen a great teller of truths."

Drake shrugged, and Nate knew he hadn't gotten anywhere in convincing him the truth was not the truth. But he didn't dig himself a deeper hole. He did what he did best. Kept his big mouth shut.

He ate his breakfast and headed for the stables, where he did most of his therapy with Monica. Equine therapy was the staple of Revival Ranch, and he knew it was a draw for a lot of the guys.

But since he *wasn't* paranoid or delusional, it didn't do a damn thing for him. He'd come here only because his family had all but begged him to.

"Morning," Monica greeted in her efficient, friendly way. For the whole of the time he'd been here, Nate had tried not to take his frustration out on Monica. Deep down, he knew she was doing her best, but it was hard not to lay all his emotional baggage at the feet of the person always so bound and determined to bring it up.

"Morning," he offered. Their usual job was to saddle up whatever horses would be needed for work that day, then take them out to the various stations while the men who did the morning ranch work and had their therapy sessions in the afternoon were waiting.

Those men would rub down the horses in the afternoon, or exercise the ones that didn't get used. Revival was a well-oiled machine, and between Monica doing the therapy work, and Becca Maguire acting as the organizer and stand-in when necessary, Nate had to step back and admit that what they'd built here was something pretty impressive.

But that didn't mean he enjoyed being a part of it.

"Nate. Where were you last night?"

Jerked into his current reality by that question, he tried to tamp down his annoyance. "What's it to you?"

She didn't answer his belligerent response, just cinched the saddle onto the horse. "You know, if you want to leave the ranch, there are protocols to follow. Letting someone know where you're going is top among them. For your own safety."

"And yet I'm fine," Nate returned.

He *knew* he tested Monica's patience, but she never showed it. Not in any way he could see. He should give her credit for that—a thought he hadn't had this whole time. But there was something about Elsie believing him that made him look at everything in a new, less uptight way.

In fact, he found himself coming up with excuses. They might be lies, but usually he'd just firmly refuse to talk to Monica. Or his lies were specific to getting her to believe he was doing better. But these lies were just a cover-up. To keep the focus off Elsie.

"I was going to take off. Go to Garrett's or my parents'. Somewhere… I just needed some quiet. To work through some stuff. I realized, belatedly, I went about it the wrong way. I just didn't think you'd approve me being alone, so I didn't seek out approval. I should have at least…discussed it. With someone."

Monica nodded and they worked together to secure the next saddle, giving each horse a little treat once they were finished. When Monica finally spoke, it was in a calm delivery that totally belied the words she spoke.

"What about Elsie Rogers?"

"What about her?"

"There's talk. And while I usually ignore gossip—especially of this variety—I was concerned."

Damn you, Olsen. "I don't know what you're talking about."

"There's talk you spent the night in Elsie's cabin."

"Talk from Olsen. We both know you can't trust that guy."

"It's not just Olsen, Nate. But it's the kind of gossip that can make everyone's life a little harder. Elsie isn't part of the ranch."

"I'm well aware. I've known Elsie my whole life. Probably know her better than you do." He had to keep his hands gentle for the horses, but it was a hard-won thing. If anything these therapy sessions had given him, it wasn't healing. It was the ability to control an emotion.

Isn't that part of healing?

"Which means what exactly?" Monica asked, bringing Nate out of his thoughts.

"It matters to you how?"

Monica sighed, and it wasn't frustration on her face. It wasn't any of the things he'd expect, just that infinite well of patience and something that had always made him edgy. Concern.

"I know you don't believe it, Nate, but I am on your side. I want to help."

For a year he'd been here, having these sessions with Monica, and he'd always viewed her as the enemy. But he realized…knowing someone out there was changing any evidence he found, having Elsie offer him some belief… Monica really was just doing her best with the information she had.

Someone was working against him. Maybe not specifically—maybe not with the intent to make everyone in his life think he was off-balance. But by covering their tracks, he constantly looked delusional. And thinking, on occasion, he was being watched didn't help matters.

Because he wasn't always sure he was.

But Connor was targeted after you sent stuff, even though you were sneaky about it.

He wasn't unhinged, and he'd spent a lot of time being angry at the people around him for thinking he was. If he actually took a breath and put himself in Monica's or Garrett's shoes… Why *should* they believe him?

Would he?

And he knew, with a clarity he didn't particularly appreciate, he would have done the same as Garrett and Connor and tried to offer help in a way that did not bring up all the wild stories Nate might *know* were true but couldn't prove.

Elsie could. He had to believe she could prove it.

Nate stopped what he was doing and summoned all his calm, all his renewed faith that everyone *wasn't* right about him. He actually did have a good enough head on his shoulders. He'd need to access that to convince Monica what he needed.

He could leave Revival without her permission, but his life would be way easier with it. "I want to take a break. From Revival. I think it'd be good for me. And, you know, maybe when I get back, Elsie will be gone again and these dumb rumors can die off."

Monica studied him, and he knew she was carefully considering his words. He might not *like* therapy, he might have often taken that dislike out on Monica, but he knew she was a good person. A good therapist. If he dug under all his own issues, he believed she wanted to do the right thing.

She shook her head. "I don't think it's in your best interest to go somewhere alone."

"Fine. I'll drag… Garrett along." It would require lying to his brother, but a plan was beginning to form. One no one in his life would like. Including Elsie.

So, he just wouldn't tell her.

Chapter Eight

Elsie returned to the cabin full of doughnuts and that warm feeling of *home*. Rose had truly built something amazing for herself. She'd found a loving husband. They were both great parents to their adorable kids, and they were involved in this ranch, which did something important for people who needed it.

That brought her mind to Nate. She thought he was finally starting to take everything more seriously, which was a good first step. Would he have needed this place if people believed him, though?

She shook her head. She couldn't concern herself with what might have happened if things had been different. She couldn't concern herself about *Nate* aside from his function in her mission.

The break to eat breakfast with Rose *had* given Elsie an idea. Revival had all sorts of security systems. Alarms and cameras here and there. She could hack into their system and look at the footage over the past few days to see if anything was out of place.

It'd probably be easier to do with Nate, but even if she thought he should be slightly more concerned about having a hitman after him, she realized him doing everything he normally did was both important to keep *her* cover, and not to give the hitman any idea they knew what might be coming.

But what if it's coming right now? And some innocent person is caught in the crossfire?

Elsie blew out a breath. She remembered Reece telling her once that you had to take a mission step-by-step, because the whole would overwhelm you.

She missed Reece Montgomery. He'd once been a lead field operative and, after her initial discomfort at his quiet, intense ways, she'd appreciated that he was always calm. Sabrina was a ball of energy. Holden was always trying to *charm* someone. But Reece was steady.

Now he was getting married, expecting his first kid, and coaching baseball for his stepson. Like some kind of perfect suburban dad. It *delighted* Elsie to no end. In fact, she'd call him tonight. He did still owe her some candy, and she wanted to know how Henry's latest baseball game had gone.

For now, though, she had to get to work.

She hacked into Revival's system with such ease she gave half a thought to telling Becca she needed to upgrade her system. Maybe Elsie would even offer to do it pro bono… After this mission was complete.

Like she often did, she got lost in what she was doing. Forgot to check the time or to eat a meal. She drank the pop or snacked on the sour candies next to her computer. She watched footage, noted odd comings and goings, and cross-referenced people on the video screen with members of Revival Ranch based on the pictures in their files.

Confidential files. She tried not to pry into anyone's business. Just got a name and a picture, and an idea of what bunk each soldier was in so she could make sure they were where they were supposed to be.

There was one face, however, that popped up now and again that seemed off. A quick search showed the woman was the sister to one of the soldiers, but why would she be walking around the ranch by herself? Most of the guests spent all their time with their family member.

Elsie took some screenshots and was about to do a check through whatever police database she could sneak into without detection when her back door eased open.

Nate slid inside, clearly sneaking around. That was good. She didn't need any more close calls like this morning. Rose could have easily just come inside without knocking and seen...

Well, she wouldn't have seen anything incriminating considering Elsie had been at a table and chairs and Nate had been on the couch, but Elsie would still have had some explaining to do. Explaining that couldn't be covered up by saying she and Nate were...

Her face got hot as Nate frowned at her.

"Don't you have any of those blue ray blocking glasses or whatever?"

"Oh, blue light glasses? I think so. Somewhere." She waved at the counter where she thought she'd left them. She always meant to wear them, but then she got caught up and...

Nate held out the glasses. She blinked up at him. And like this morning when he'd woken and met her gaze, her stomach did that long, slow roll.

It was really kind of nice. Nice enough she forgot herself and just stared at him. Until he jiggled the glasses at her.

Right. She took the glasses and slid them on. "I might have found something. I hacked into Revival's security systems. Just seeing if something was off anytime. Do you recognize this woman?" She pointed at the screen where she'd paused it.

Nate stared at the image. Something went across his face, but she couldn't read it. He stepped back and then frowned at her.

"Justin Sherman's sister."

"Yes. She's one of the few family members who routinely shows up on screen alone. And she shows up a lot."

"She lives just outside of Blue Valley. Her and her husband visit a lot," Nate said.

"So where's her husband?" She pulled up another screenshot of the woman standing outside Nate's bunk. "Where's her brother?" Elsie knew she was on to something. A sister of a soldier seemed a little odd, but there had to be *some* reason this woman was lurking. And with everything going on—

"Listen, I'm going to be scarce for a few days."

Elsie blinked at Nate. Had he just spoken a foreign language? Or maybe received a head injury. "We don't have *a few days*. We have a lead."

He shrugged, as if it didn't matter. "Rumors all over the place because of last night. Jack was glaring daggers at me. All the guys are ragging on me. Even my therapist brought it up."

"Maybe don't fall asleep on my couch."

"Look, you do your thing. I'll do mine. We'll reconvene in a few days."

"You aren't the boss of me, Nate." She thought he'd finally got it through his thick skull he was in trouble. Or that he could at least trust her. But she knew…he was lying to her. Something else was going on.

"And you aren't the boss of me, Elsie." He gave her an infuriating shrug then left her cabin as if that was that.

She seethed at the closed door. She knew—she *knew*— he was lying to her. He had something up his sleeve, or some new lead to follow, and he was cutting her out.

Oh, no. No, no, no. Nate Averly was working *with* her, whether he liked it or not. That meant she'd need a little muscle to get that across. She grabbed her phone and punched the number for North Star headquarters.

When Shay answered, Elsie grinned at the door. Perhaps a little menacingly. "Shay? I need backup. As soon as you can get it here."

MONICA HADN'T BEEN keen on his leaving Revival right away. She'd also only okayed two days when he might need more.

And would take more. Therapist approved or not.

The next step was lying to his brother. Something Nate didn't relish, but necessary steps were necessary. He packed the backpack, made sure to mention his absence to a few of the guys—giving Justin Sherman a slightly different story than the rest.

He told Justin the truth.

Because he'd known from the beginning something was off about Justin's sister, and her showing up on Elsie's screen had proved it. He'd let his...discomfort with Courtney's *overtures* keep him far away from the woman.

But Brina had been shot and there were hitmen involved. He had to take the reins and make something happen.

Because no matter how many times he'd told himself for two years he wasn't paranoid, he wasn't suffering delusions from PTSD, there had been a small part of him that had sometimes wondered if he wasn't...just a little crazy.

He shook his head. Didn't matter. In the here and now, he knew what he was doing. And he knew he had to keep Elsie out of it.

She just wasn't...

He paused in his packing, trying to determine what Elsie was or wasn't, but then packed away. Elsie wasn't his problem, and he didn't owe her much of anything. Except maybe thanks she'd showed him that video.

He'd given her the information he had—information she

could likely use to prove whatever needed to be proved. But she wasn't the target of this. And shouldn't be.

Nate caught a ride into town with one of the guys headed to Bozeman to pick up the food delivery for the mess hall.

Blue Valley wasn't much. Mostly just a main street with a diner, a bar, a few specialty shops mostly geared to ranching folk, and then, at the end of the street, in a tiny stone building, Blue Valley PD.

Nate walked into the building, which boasted one main room with a jail cell built into the corner. There were two desks—one for the sheriff and one for the dispatcher—and a little door at the back that led to a narrow hall with bathroom and a cot that Nate knew his brother used a lot more often since his wife had taken off last year.

This afternoon, Garrett was at his desk, his dog Barney at his feet, per usual. Garrett's lone dispatcher had made Barney a little scarf with a badge and insisted Barney wear it if he was going to be within the tiny department walls.

Garrett's eyebrows rose when he saw Nate walk in. Barney, fierce guard dog that he was, continued to sleep. Mrs. Linley was on the phone in her corner desk, but she waved at Nate all the same.

"Coming to confess your crimes?" Garrett asked good-naturedly, but there was the way that Garrett looked at him. Always sizing him up, like he could *see* the PTSD on him.

As oldest brother, as police officer for this tiny town, Garrett would never consider that something might not be under his jurisdiction—and therefore not his fault.

"Hey, listen. Monica gave me a few days' leave and I wanted to borrow your fishing cabin." That, at least, wasn't a lie. Garrett had a very isolated fishing cabin, only accessible by boat. Nate would be able to watch for the inevitable ambush.

The genial smile on Garrett's face immediately melted away. "Nate."

"Therapist approved. I'm going to hike over and grab Mom's car. I'll be at your fishing cabin the whole time. Just a little breather."

God, he hoped the ambush was inevitable so he could end this. Far away from anyone who might be caught in the crosshairs.

Elsie's face popped into his mind, but he pushed it away. She might be part of some group, but she was a tiny slip of a thing better suited for sitting in front of computers rather than running real missions.

He could handle this himself.

"Nate…"

"You can keep saying my name in that condescending big-brother way, but Monica okayed it. She said it'd be good for me to have some time to myself."

Garrett's frown didn't dissipate. "I want to search your pack."

It wasn't a surprise. In fact, Nate knew exactly what Garrett would be looking for. He handed the backpack to his brother.

"I'm not going to kill myself, Garrett."

"That's good to hear." But he still checked Nate's bag like Nate was some kind of common criminal. Barney watched the proceedings without lifting his head from his paws.

When Garrett handed the bag back to Nate, he held Nate's gaze. "I love you. I'm not letting anything happen to you, even if that hurts your feelings."

"I'm not in a bad place. I promise." Nate supposed that was only half a lie. Mentally, he wasn't. But…well, there *could* be someone after him.

That's why he'd left his gun in the flowerpot outside. He knew the way his brother thought.

Garrett opened a drawer and pulled out a keychain. He slid one key off it, but didn't hand it over. "Grab some food before you go. It's not stocked. I haven't been up there in a while, and Dad hasn't, either."

"If I tell Mom I'm headed up there, she'll load me down with food."

"You gonna tell Mom?"

"Yeah. Like I said, it's just a break, Garrett. No need for you guys to worry."

The words Garrett didn't say hung between them. *But we will.*

And that irritated Nate enough to turn the tables on his brother. "Maybe you should be more worried about *you* being in a bad place."

"I'm fine," Garrett said gruffly.

"How many nights you slept on the back cot this week?"

"All of them," Mrs. Linley chimed in from the corner, her hand covering the receiver as she gave Garrett a disapproving look before going back to her conversation.

Barney gave a little growl as he rolled over, like he was agreeing with Mrs. Linley.

"You tell me how much you want to sleep in your own bed after you find out your wife's been sleeping with someone else in it."

"So burn it. Sell the house. Find something new." Nate shrugged. "Start over, Garrett. It's been a year."

Garrett blinked, because while everyone in the family liked to chime in about Nate's PTSD, the subject of Garrett's wife was always so off-limits. How was that fair?

"Where's your fishing gear?" Garrett asked, clearly changing the subject.

That was fine enough for now. Nate had bigger fish to fry for the time being.

"At Mom and Dad's." Nate held out his hand, waiting for Garrett to finally relinquish the key.

Garrett handed it over, but he was frowning. "I could go with you."

"And leave Blue Valley unmanned? Whatever would the good citizens do when roving bands of criminals come sweeping through?"

"Oh, fine, go," Garrett muttered. "If you're making fun of me and Blue Valley, you can't be that messed up."

Nate held up the key and grinned. "Your faith in me is earth-shattering, Garrett. I'll drop this back off in a few days."

"Forty-eight hours, Nate. Check in every night. With me."

Nate rolled his eyes as Garrett kept calling instructions after him, probably long after Nate had escaped the building and closed the door.

He grabbed his gun, stuck it in his pack. He pretended to be fully absorbed with that, but really he was surveying the town around him. Was someone waiting? Watching? He didn't notice anything out of place, didn't feel any eyes on him.

But the time would come.

He set out on the trek to his parents' ranch and made sure to leave a clear trail.

Step one down. A few more to go.

Chapter Nine

Elsie didn't know how she was going to explain this one to her sisters. So, she simply didn't yet. After Nate had left, she'd done some digging and figured out where he would go if he left the ranch.

She didn't believe for a second he was saying they'd reconvene in a few *days* if he wasn't planning on leaving.

He wouldn't go to his parents' house. It was too much like Revival—a working ranch with people who knew him hanging around. A few days meant he wouldn't go too far, she didn't think.

He'd known that woman on the video, and he'd been suspicious enough to clam up. And if Nate had suspicions... Why wouldn't he tell her?

Did he think she'd been born yesterday? Or was he just that used to doing things on his own because everyone thought he was paranoid?

No. She would *not* feel sorry for him. No, no, no. He knew she believed him. So, regardless of everyone else, he should trust her. Confide in her. She was *trying* to help.

But he was running away. To accomplish something. She understood—deep in her gut—that he was up to something.

That meant, after looking through all his and his family's properties, his brother's isolated fishing cabin was the best candidate. If the woman on the ranch premises—who, for all intents and purposes, had a reason for being at Revival—tipped Nate off to *something*, he was likely getting off Revival to lay some kind of trap.

When Elsie caught movement in her cabin out of the corner of her eye, she didn't even startle. Knowing she'd asked for backup meant knowing a North Star operative might show up like that at any moment.

"You got here fast," she said to the woman in the corner wearing all black—down to a black cap to hide a riot of red hair.

"I was already on my way," Mallory Trevino said, peeling off the wall and walking toward Elsie at her computer. She was one of the newer operatives, but Shay knew Elsie liked working with the women on the team the best. "I've been waiting for you to need some help."

"Well, I need it. Our target thinks he's so smart, but he's about to realize he can't shake me that easily. My theory is he's going somewhere isolated, alone, to try to face down whoever's watching him. I've got a line on the woman it might connect to, but I want to show Nate a thing or two." Elsie pressed a few keys on her keyboard and brought up a map. She pointed to the computer screen. "I think he'll be here. Do you know how to pilot a boat?"

Mallory smirked. "Naturally."

"Gotta love a North Star operative. You didn't come by bike, did you?"

Mallory laughed. "No, I leave the motorcycles in this kind of terrain to Sabrina." She sobered, just a little bit.

"Everyone told me she's going to be okay," Elsie said, trying to smother the little blip of panic and worry.

"Yeah, she is. I just hate that I was sitting around here twiddling my thumbs instead of there with her."

"That's the job. You can't be the one to save everyone. That's why we have a team."

Mal smiled, if sadly. "Yeah, I know. I've got a Jeep a few miles out. Be a bit of a hike, but I didn't want to arouse suspicion."

Elsie nodded. "That'll be good. I'm packed and ready to go. Hike, Jeep, this cabin. I've got it plugged into my phone."

"So, just to be clear… Your plan is to get there first, break into this cabin and lie in wait?" Mallory asked as Elsie shoved her laptop into the backpack she was planning to take along.

"Yes, and hopefully scare the tar out of him in the process so he learns his lesson about lying to me." Elsie still hadn't figured out what she was going to tell Delia and Rose about her absence for a day or two. It depended on how Nate reacted when she caught him red-handed, she supposed.

"Who knew Elsie had a bloodthirsty streak."

"I'm not sure I knew it. Or had one, until I met Nate Averly." She wanted to punch the guy. *Again.*

"Uh-oh."

Elsie looked up at Mallory as she shrugged into the backpack. "Uh-oh what?"

"I mean, you see what's been happening here."

"Where?"

"Since this whole thing started. First Reece," Mallory said, holding up one finger then a second. "Then Holden. Sabrina, too. Though word is Connor's joining North Star rather than Sabrina defecting once she's better."

Elsie laughed, Mallory's meaning dawning on her. Because Reece had fallen for his mission, and then so had Holden. Apparently, Sabrina too. "You can't honestly think…"

Mallory shrugged.

"I'm not an operative."

"But you are a woman. And Nate Averly *is* a man."

"An infuriating one."

"Tell me one thing," Mallory continued as she slid out the back door of the cabin, scanning their surroundings before she started striding for the trees. Elsie followed. "And you can only answer this question with a simple yes or no. No equivocations or explanations. Is he hot?"

"I…"

"Yes or no, Els."

Elsie scowled and hunched her shoulders. "Yes," she muttered. "I'm not attracted to traditionally hot guys, though."

Mallory let out a little hoot of laughter. "Stop, Elsie, we're trying to be stealthy. You can't make me laugh like that."

"Why is that funny?"

"You can't think a guy is *hot* and not be attracted to him."

"Of course you can. I'm being objective about his looks."

"Either you think he's hot or not. You're attracted or you're not. Sure, you don't have to *act* on it, but you better watch yourself. If *Sabrina* can get knocked over by the love stick, even if it was by a former Navy SEAL, who is *definitely* hot by the way, and Holden is besotted with a *farm* girl, and Reece can be taken out by a little blonde with a kid, any of us is vulnerable."

Elsie frowned at Mallory's back. That was all pure silliness. Attraction didn't equal love, and the thing about Reece, Holden and Sabrina was that they *were* formidable. It made sense on both sides—that they'd fallen and the person they'd fallen for had fallen right back. Sure, she could see someone thinking *she* might fall for Nate—the nerdy computer girl and the imposing former Navy SEAL who was wounded in more ways than one.

But the other way around? LOL.

They hiked for a good hour before they made it to Mallory's Jeep—and Elsie knew she was the one who'd made it take that long. Her head pounded and she felt awful. Likely the aftereffects of the drugging, but that didn't mean she could ignore how out of shape she actually was. Maybe she'd start working out once she got back to North Star headquarters.

"You haven't been listening to the doctor's orders, have you?" Mallory asked, eyeing her suspiciously as they got in the Jeep. "Let me guess…little sleep, nothing but junk food."

Elsie pouted but she didn't answer. Because, of course, Mal was right on target.

They headed out, Elsie giving instructions. When they reached the lake, Mallory drove around a little bit to determine the best place to park her Jeep where it wouldn't be easily visible. Once they'd parked and gotten out, they walked toward the rickety dock and even ricketier rowboat.

"This really going to get us across?" Elsie asked, eyeing the watercraft wearily. If they capsized, her laptop would be toast.

"Sure thing. I'll row you over and drop you off at the cabin. I'll row back and then hide in the woods with my Jeep until you give the signal."

Elsie nodded. From shore, she could see the cabin on the little island. The sun shone brightly on the small dot of land and the rough-hewn cabin in the middle. But there was a storm brewing in the distance, and Elsie thought it looked a lot more ominous than charming.

She straightened her shoulders. Hopefully, Nate thought it was charming or relaxing, and then *bam*.

Was he in for the surprise of a lifetime.

IT FELT GOOD to row, to be away from the ranch and the men and be *alone*.

The sun was already setting—thanks to the hours he'd

had to endure at his parents' house being loaded down with food and advice. The storm clouds in the distance were tinged with a riot of red and orange.

He understood why Garrett came here. It was isolated, but a person didn't feel *alone*. The craggy mountain peaks, the gently lapping water of the mirror-clear lake, that famous big sky above—it all felt like it was teeming with life. A beautiful one at that.

Something Nate didn't have the luxury of thinking about because he wasn't here to rest his soul. He was here to prove that Courtney Prokop was shady as hell.

Nate had spent a lot of time looking into all of them—her brother, her husband, the woman herself. But he'd never been able to unearth anything.

Well, Elsie would work on that and he would work on *action*. Whether it was Courtney herself or a hitman who met him here, it would be an answer. Because, aside from his family, no one else knew this was where he'd been heading.

Except Justin.

About halfway across the lake, Nate knew someone was in the cabin. From his vantage point, he could see the flicker of a light through the curtain of the window. He could see that the mud around the dock had been recently disturbed.

He didn't stop rowing. This was what he'd been working toward. He rowed right for the dock, but took some time to carefully and stealthily take the gun out of his backpack.

He docked, pretending like he didn't have a care in the world, even as he watched every flutter of that curtain. Once on the dock, he drew his gun and kept low to the ground. He tried to scan the banks of the lake, but it was too dark now. Still, he had a feeling someone was out there. Watching. Waiting.

And someone was inside.

He was surrounded.

Maybe you should have trusted someone for help.

He pushed that thought away as a low rumble of thunder echoed across the sky. He could—and *would*—handle this. He inched toward the cabin, watching the shore for some sign of something. Once he reached the door, he could see enough of a swath of light that he realized it wasn't fully latched.

He frowned. What kind of careless criminal was this? Maybe a trap? They thought he was *that* dumb.

Aren't you going to be?

He ignored the voice in his head as he eased the door open, feeling like he was a SEAL again. All those tactics came back to him—without the gear, without the backup.

But there was no team of people to take him out. No spy—or whatever Courtney Prokop was.

There was only Elsie.

She sat there on the floor, legs crossed in front of her, a laptop balanced there. Her hair rioted around her shoulders, and she was wearing the same clothes she'd had on yesterday...because clearly she hadn't done anything except stare at that computer all day.

She yawned, completely unconcerned by the gun pointed at her. "What took you so long?"

Nate was frozen. He didn't even lower the gun. He just stared at her. How... *How?* "What the hell is going on?"

She raised her dark gaze from the computer—apparently dead set on ruining her eyes—and looked at the gun with an air of boredom. "Do you *mind*?"

He lowered the gun, stepped fully in and closed the door behind him. "What are you doing here, Elsie?"

"That was going to be my question for you."

"This is *my* brother's cabin. *I* have every reason to be

here. You, on the other hand, do not." How had she figured out he would come here?

She kept staring at him, her gaze even and, if he wasn't mistaken, trying to hide a flare of temper.

His gut should *not* tighten at the sign of a little temper on Elsie Rogers.

"I was sent here to work *with* you, Nate," she said calmly, as if talking to a child having a tantrum. Or a man with PTSD. "Something you seem to have a really hard time getting through your thick skull."

"I didn't ask for your help."

"But you need it."

"I do not. I don't need you here. If I did, I would have asked. How…how the hell did you know I'd come here?"

"You're hardly unpredictable. It was obvious the second you looked at that woman on the screen that you had something up your sleeve. Saying we'd reconvene in a few days? Well, it doesn't take a genius to figure out that means you're going somewhere. I know enough hardheaded former military men who think they can save the world one-handed to make the leap to what your plan would be."

"I don't think you're stupid," he muttered.

"No, I don't think you think beyond your own nose. But you're going to have to. We are a team. Whether you asked, whether you like it or not. That's it. And you can keep trying to sneak off and have a manly showdown, but it's not happening. I will be able to figure out your every move before you make it. So stop making things difficult and work *with* me."

Elsie did not get up. She did not move the computer off her lap. She looked more like a waif than even a computer nerd, but the haughty, almost regal look she directed at him gave her the aura of someone very much in charge.

He was about to tell her she needed to get over the idea

she would ever be in charge of *him*, but something outside the door moved. He whirled, gun aimed, ready to shoot the intruder just as Elsie let out a heavy sigh.

"Relax. She's with me."

"Of course she is," Nate muttered, dropping his gun arm as a woman appeared seemingly out of thin air. "Why wouldn't she be?"

The woman grinned at him. But when she turned to Elsie, her expression went serious. "Someone is out there. I can't tell if they're just watching or if they're planning on coming out here. I didn't think I should wait around to find out."

"Good call. Mallory, this is Nate. Nate, this is Mallory."

"Hey," she said with a nod. "Got anything, Els?"

"Not yet. Do you think if I got the camera on the Jeep up and running, we'd be able to get an ID?"

The woman dressed in black—Mallory—seemed to give this some thought.

"There's no reason to get an ID. I know who it is, or who sent them, anyway."

"The woman on the video," Elsie said, her voice was cool. Detached. Like she was *mad* at him.

Why did that make him feel bad? He'd made the right choice. Even if she'd figured him out. It was the *right* choice and her and her friend needed to get the hell out of here.

"I have never been able to figure out what the Prokops have to do with this, but I know they—or at least Courtney—does."

"Ah, so you suspected they had *something* to do with it and didn't think to tell me? Interesting."

The accusation made him defensive even though she was right. "You knew who she was. You decided she was shady all on your own. I figured you'd research that."

"While you went off and played hero?"

"While I went off and ended my yearslong nightmare, Elsie."

"Well," Mallory said, studying him and then Elsie, "I'm going to go watch the actual threat while you guys argue. Cool?"

She wasn't asking him. Elsie nodded and Mallory slipped back out again.

"Are you…in charge?"

She snorted. "Hardly." She frowned a little. "Well, lead operative on this mission, I guess. Anyway. That's not important. You being thoughtless and a liar isn't important, either."

"Hey—"

"What's important is figuring out what this random woman has to do with a military cover-up. I looked up her brother…this Justin Sherman. He was in the Army. So, presumably, had no connection to you and the SEALs."

"As far as I can tell."

"I know families are all different, but Courtney and Don uprooted their whole lives to come live in Blue Valley when her brother got accepted to Revival." Elsie frowned at her screen. "Maybe it's less about the branch of military, the connection to you, and more about the timing. Once you were discharged from the hospital, you came home to your parents' ranch."

She typed some things, and Nate found he didn't particularly care for how much she knew about him. Down to *dates*.

"A year later, you join Revival. A month after that, Justin joins. It's not totally suspect timing, but… I need to get into applications and when those went through. Oh, and maybe Justin's military references. Yeah, and…"

"How do you have all that information?" Nate demanded.

She looked at him over the laptop. Her eyes were a little blurry, but she blinked and they sharpened.

Because she was still mad at him. Clearly.

"I could get all sorts of information on you, Nate," she said with the wave of a hand. "I could read your therapy records if I really wanted to. Luckily, I have a code of ethics I'll only break if someone is in mortal danger. I'll only hack into the information I actually need to do my job."

"I don't have anything to hide."

"Except Courtney Prokop."

She turned the laptop toward him. It was another security video. But instead of Courtney sneaking around outside, it was her following Nate into his bunk.

Nate winced. "That's not…what it looks like."

"Oh, and what does it look like, Nate?" Elsie asked, all faux innocence.

Nate was saved by Mallory, because she stuck her head in the door. "We got one in a boat coming."

Elsie nodded at Mallory, but that did not work for Nate on any level. "You get her out of here," he said to Mallory. "I'll take care of this."

Chapter Ten

Elsie laughed. She should probably be more offended, but Nate trying to boss around a North Star operative *was* hilarious.

Mallory smiled at Elsie. "Is this guy serious?"

"I think so. You'll have to forgive him. He's not used to people helping him out."

"Pro tip—don't order people around. They don't like it. And I don't take orders from you. You two stay here. I'm going to watch his approach. If I can incapacitate him without help, I will. If I need backup, I'll whistle."

"No. Absolutely not. You two will stay here—"

"Is this because I'm a woman?" Mallory returned, crossing her arms over her chest and serving Nate a killing look.

Elsie watched frustration chase confusion on Nate's face. But he shook his head and kept digging the hole deeper.

"I don't care if you're an extraterrestrial—this is *my* deal," he said, jabbing his thumb into his own chest. "My problem. My threat. *I've* been dealing with it—alone, I might point out—for two years. I didn't ask for you two to crash *my* problem."

Elsie sobered, because there it was again. She felt for him. She was sure he meant well, in a strange sort of way.

Maybe he simply didn't know how to let go of all those guards he'd built around himself when no one believed him.

No one. Not even his own brother. She honestly couldn't imagine what that might be like. Because, no matter what, she'd always had her sisters.

Nate didn't know how to be part of a team since his discharge from the military and felt betrayed. He didn't know how to trust. And that gave her an idea.

"We could bring Connor in, if that would make you feel better about help."

Nate's gaze turned from Mallory to her. His eyebrows drew together. "You… What?"

"It'd take probably a day at least to work out, and he'd have to be willing, but we can make it happen. Connor worked with Sabrina. He was integral in taking Daria down. He's capable of handling whatever this is. If it would help for you to have someone you trust here, we can make it happen."

Nate looked at Mallory then back at her. Confusion etched all over his face. "I don't understand."

"We're working with you, Nate. That's the point of us. To work with you, to help you, to figure out who is behind these hitmen…and whatever else is going on. Because, clearly, there's more going on than we know. You're a hitman target, so Mallory's job is to protect you. Sure, I get why that might be a little hard to swallow, and that's fine. We'll find a way to help you swallow it. Now, *my* job is to get to the bottom of this, and while you've been actively working against me, my hope is you'll get to a point where you stop."

Nate rubbed his hand across his jaw. Conflicted. Lost. It took a lot of willpower, and probably Mallory's presence, to keep Elsie seated rather than crossing to him and offering him some physical comfort.

A totally friendly physical comfort. Totally.

"Let's take this one step at a time," Elsie said gently. "The threat currently. You said someone's in a boat, Mal?"

"Yeah. One guy. Heavily armed. Might be the hitman."

Elsie nodded. "Okay. For right now, we'll go with Mallory's plan. She takes care of the guy. If she needs backup from you, Nate, she'll whistle."

Before Nate could argue—and Elsie had no doubt he'd been planning to argue—Mallory slipped back out into the night surrounding the cabin.

Elsie took a deep breath, to center herself and keep the calm. She gripped her laptop maybe a little tightly because the computer was her security blanket. She didn't relish being in charge, but she would have to be until Nate really let himself be part of their team. "Now, we can talk about bringing Connor in."

"I don't want Connor mixed up in this any more than he already is."

Elsie nodded. She should have known his hard head wouldn't just accept the easiest answer. She set the laptop aside and got to her feet. It made her feel exposed, but this really wasn't about her and her feelings.

She stood in front of Nate, met his gaze and tried to find words that would get through all that…hurt. He'd been hurt. For years. By people he'd trusted.

She knew that was the kind of thing you didn't get over just because someone told you to. But she had to try.

"Look. I need you to really absorb this, and I'd love to give you time—but I keep telling you, we don't have it. Dude in a boat with a gun out there. You are part of a *team*, Nate. You have to let people in. Lean on people and let them lean on you. We all want the same result. All of us. And we're here to *help*. The thing about help is, you have to accept it. You have to work with it. Or instead of working against the bad guy, we're all working against each other."

He looked at someplace on the wall beyond her, big arms crossed over his chest. "I don't want anyone in danger."

"We're already here. Mal and I? We've been in plenty of dangerous situations. It's our job. A job we both love. It isn't a duty. No one is forcing us to be here. We chose this job, this group, this work. You didn't. I get that. But *we* did."

His dark eyes met her earnest gaze. "Why?" he asked, baffled.

"I'm sure a wide variety of reasons."

"I don't mean them. I mean you. Why would you put yourself in harm's way after...?"

She shrugged, uncomfortable that everything seemed to keep going back to her bad childhood. Still, she held eye contact, because she knew he needed to believe her. *See* that she meant everything she said. "Everyone has a little harm's way in their life, Nate. You can't avoid it. Especially as a woman in the world. But this way? I'm in charge of it. I'm helping people get out of it. It gives me all those choices I didn't have as a kid. And it lets me give those choices to other people who are stuck. You have *choices*, Nate."

"Choices?" he repeated.

"Yes." She didn't fully think the movement through. It was too instinctual. She reached out and grabbed his forearms crossed over his chest. She squeezed. "And you'll have more when this is over. We can help make this over, faster, and with you safer. But you have to trust me. You can't run off. You can't argue with us. You can't cut us all out. Trust us. Please. If not all of us, at least me."

"It's not that I don't trust you."

"Well, start acting like it, then."

"It's…hard."

"I know." She should pull her hands away. She should focus on the impending danger. She should do anything over this getting all soft and mushy about him. But he seemed so lost and…and… "I know." And she just…stood there. Stupidly. Looking up at him. Words lost in that dark, direct gaze.

He wasn't looking at her any special way. He was thinking. About hitmen and Connor. If it *looked* like his gaze was on her mouth, she was clearly having some kind of delusion. But the delusion came with a kind of longing she didn't know what to do with.

A gunshot rang out, followed by the sound of something breaking.

Nate jerked, stumbled forward and swore as a bloom of red appeared on his shirt.

NATE LET THE stream of curse words fall out of him. The pain in his arm was sharp and hot, but bearable. No other shots followed.

He realized, once he was done swearing, that Elsie was babbling a mile a minute.

"You're bleeding. You're shot. You're… Mal. No. I…"

"It's just my arm, and it's not that bad. Take a breath, Els."

She did so. Immediately. "You've been shot. We have to…" She swallowed, took a long, deep breath and then slowly let it out. "Okay. We're going to bandage you up." She walked stiffly to her pack and pulled out a little first-aid kit.

He doubted a Band-Aid was going to fix this problem, but he had to think. The shot had blasted through the cabin wall. There wasn't a window there, and it was dark, so it was unlikely the bullet had been meant for him.

But that meant Mallory was out there being shot at. Or had already been shot since she hadn't whistled.

Elsie took his arm and studied the wound. In the weak beam of her lantern, she looked pale. Worried. But her hands didn't shake. She'd pulled herself together.

Because she was part of a team on a mission. She'd seen danger and perhaps gunshots before. No matter how slight or pale, little Elsie Rogers wasn't *new* to this.

A team. The last time he'd thought he'd been part of a team, he'd been injured and dishonorably discharged—all for trying to do the right thing.

She put a bandage over the bloody wound, but he knew it wouldn't do much to stop the bleeding. He didn't have time to worry about it. "You stay put." He already had his gun out, so he started for the door.

"You can't go out there!" She grabbed his arm—the one that had been nicked by the bullet—but immediately dropped it when he hissed out a breath of pain.

"That hitman wants you dead, Nate," she said, stepping in front of the door.

"And what do you think Mallory is doing out there? Having a picnic? I have to go help her. Unless you want your friend to die?"

She was wide-eyed and shook her head.

"Let me go. Stay put. Do you have a gun? Do you know how to use a gun?"

She scurried over to where she'd left her computer and picked up a small pistol. Nate didn't have time to frown at the puny weapon. "Keep it loaded and ready to shoot. Anyone who's not me or someone in your group, shoot. No questions asked. Got it?"

She nodded, holding the gun in a death grip. If he wasn't in immediate danger, it might have been funny. Elsie talked a good game about being some operative who knew how to deal with danger, but one gunshot had sure changed her tune.

"Stay put. I mean it," he said and then slid out into the night. Frogs and insects were making their evening noises. The storm hadn't started yet, but flashes of lightning in the distance illuminated the world around him in intervals.

He saw the second boat drifting back toward the center of the lake, unmanned. Whoever had rowed over hadn't secured it. Hadn't had time?

He walked silently around the perimeter of the cabin. He heard a rustle in the trees—sounding a little too loud to be animal. He moved toward it, seeing a light deeper in the trees. His military training had already kicked in, and it was easy to fall back into those old habits. The awareness was still there, the calm that settled over him when he accepted his only goal was to keep himself alive.

He stopped short when he realized what the sight before him was.

Mallory had a penlight in her mouth and was tying a very large man's hands behind his back—and then to another man's hands.

Nate blinked at the two unconscious men tied together. "What—"

"Sorry," she said around the penlight. Once she'd secured the knot, she dropped the light into her hand. "There was someone else here besides Boat Guy. He jumped me before Boat Guy landed. Fought him off, but then Boat Guy came around and we struggled with his gun. Went off in the struggle. Luckily not at me."

"There was someone besides Boat Guy?" Nate's eyes immediately went to the little island's cluster of trees. It hadn't occurred to him someone besides Elsie had beaten him here.

"Yeah. Came from the trees. My guess is he'd been there for a while." Mallory rolled her shoulders and swore.

"Gonna be sore tomorrow." She pointed her penlight at him. "You're bleeding."

"Yeah, bullet nicked me."

"Hell. This is a mess. You go get more than a Band-Aid. I'm calling my boss. I think we need more men on the ground here before we search the island."

Nate hesitated. More men. This secret group. Everything was getting out of control. Out of his hands. He wouldn't know all the moving parts and, in his experience, being in the dark meant you ended up getting the short end of the stick.

"Look, I don't know you and you don't know me," Mal said, stepping over the defeated men and toward Nate. "But I know Elsie. She's the real deal. If you can't trust all of us, you can at least trust her. She trusts you, wants to help you—so I'll do the same. But we need it from you, too."

"Yeah, I..." He didn't know how to do this, but he knew he had to. What's more, he knew Elsie wanted him to. And, for whatever reason, that made him want to and...

Hell. "If Connor doesn't mind, it'd help if he was one of those men."

Mallory nodded. "Let's get back to Elsie and see what we can do."

Chapter Eleven

Elsie hadn't handled that very well, she knew. Even now, her palms were sweaty as she held the gun pointed at the door.

She didn't like guns. Shay had insisted she learn how to shoot one, along with basic self-defense and a few other field operative–type things. Elsie knew she could shoot it, and with good enough accuracy if she was calm enough.

Didn't mean Elsie *liked* it. Or the fact Mallory and Nate were out there with a hitman and she was sitting here, sweating like a...weakling.

She was not meant for the field. Last time she'd been outside headquarters, she'd been drugged and all she'd been doing was sitting in a bunker trying to hack a computer. Now, Nate had been shot and she was just sitting around waiting for everyone else to take care of things.

Because she was *not* a field operative. She was a computer genius. How could Shay have put her in this situation?

How are you going to disappoint Shay in this situation?

Voices were getting closer, and Elsie swallowed and tried to listen over the heavy pounding of her heart. Relief swelled through her when she finally realized it was Mallory's and Nate's voices. They were the ones who opened and came in through the door. *Thank God.*

She immediately turned the safety on, put the gun down and got to her feet. "Are you guys okay?"

"All good. Took down two guys—tied up out there." Mallory nodded toward the door. "I called Shay," Mallory said as she closed the door behind Nate. "She's sending a few more operatives, including Connor, but they won't be here till morning."

"Do we stay?"

"I think so. Not sure if there's more here, but it's a good place to hunker down and watch for any more threats. Nate and I will take turns watching out, so we can each get some sleep. Rain's starting, so hopefully that keeps everyone laying low."

Elsie stepped forward then stopped because she just felt…superfluous. Still, she pointed to his arm. "Nate, you need better…"

"I've got some field dressing in my pack." Mallory was already digging stuff out and taking off the silly bandage Elsie had put on his serious wound. She took care of it and, while she did, she and Nate talked in low tones about everything that had happened outside the cabin.

They did not include her in the conversation. Elsie knew it wasn't fair to feel hurt. They'd done the hard work. *They* knew how to deal with guns and threats.

They were…in charge. Doing things. Leaning into their strengths. She couldn't be a field operative. She didn't know how to be a soldier or a spy. She could let all she didn't know or couldn't do overwhelm her.

Or she could remember there were things she *did* know. That she *did* have a function here and that it was time to stop worrying about guns and bandages and *do it*.

She was here for a reason. Maybe a large portion of that was her family ties—but she wouldn't let that be the *only* reason. She grabbed her phone and marched for the door.

"Elsie." Nate tried to stop her from opening the door,

but she shook him off. She walked into the dark and went to where the men were tied together, starting to come to. Thunder rolled, lightning flashed, and she got progressively wet as she walked. Still, she pulled out her phone.

"Say cheese, boys." She took one picture, the bright light of the flash making them wince, then the next while Nate watched her. Speechless apparently. When she turned back to the cabin, he gaped at her.

"What are you *doing*?" Nate demanded.

"What I'm damn good at," Elsie said, back to feeling in control. "Pull them inside. We're going to figure out who they are." And by *we* she meant *me*.

Nate and Mal worked together to drag the men into the cabin. Only one was fully conscious and fighting his bonds. They were all soggy puddles by the time it was done, but Elsie hardly noticed.

She'd settled in with her computer, ignoring the men, ignoring Nate and Mallory. She uploaded the pictures and began her search.

"You don't have to look this one up," Nate said, scowling at the bald guy who was still unconscious. "That's Don Prokop."

Elsie's eyebrows rose, but she didn't look at Nate. She kept her eyes on her computer. Just because they knew who he was didn't mean there wasn't more to know.

"He was the one waiting in the trees," Mallory said. "Other one's the hitman."

"Funny." Elsie typed a few things in and it took her less than a minute to find what she was looking for on the first guy. "That's not the only name Don goes by, FYI. He has at least two aliases, and rap sheets for both."

"Well, that's new information," Nate said.

"We'll look deeper into these other names soon, and who else they might connect to, but first let's figure out contestant number two." She typed and searched. This man had come to, and while he didn't fight his bonds anymore, his eyes were full of fury, like he was just biding his time.

His picture was proving trickier to connect to an identity, but that only convinced Elsie his identity was important.

"Good luck, little girl," he growled.

Elsie raised an eyebrow at him then pushed a few more keys. Dug past a few fake names with ease. She knew exactly what to look for. And how. "You like a fake name, don't you?" she asked cheerfully. "But Lee Braun is the real one, huh?"

The angry expression on the man's face slackened into shock.

Elsie smiled sweetly at the criminal. "I'll take that as a yes."

NATE COULDN'T SAY he had time to *reel* exactly, but watching Elsie go from shaking mess over a flesh wound to in-charge snark queen was…well, it left a man a little off-kilter.

It certainly left Lee Braun, hitman, off-kilter. The man looked like he'd been dealt a blow by a two-by-four instead of some information unearthed by a computer fairy.

"That was enjoyable to watch," Nate managed to say. Elsie turned her smile up to him.

"It was enjoyable to do, too." She was so *pleased* with herself, he couldn't help but smile back. She had the faintest little dimple in her cheek when she smiled and…

Mallory cleared her throat.

Elsie blinked and turned her attention back to the computer, a blush creeping up her cheeks. But when she spoke, her voice was easy and even.

He was sure his would have sounded perfectly strangled.

"Now. I'll need some time to a do a little deep dive.

What are we going to do with these guys? They need to be detained. We could get local law enforcement to pick up Don on any number of these charges. Based on his record, he's not much of a threat. Definitely not the brains of the operation."

Dread leaped into Nate's gut at the words *local law enforcement*. Luckily that dread was much preferable to the complicated, uncomfortable thing twisting his gut when he'd shared a smile with Elsie. "Let's not…do that," Nate managed to mutter.

"Oh, too late on that," Mallory offered. "Shay already delegated cleanup. That means she'll likely come to the same conclusion Elsie did and send locals."

"You can't send locals. You can't…"

Mallory looked at him like he'd lost it. "They can handle Don. He's a nobody. We'll keep the hitman and—"

"Call this Shay back and tell her no. Or she can call Valley County. You don't want Blue Valley. Small PD. Just one guy."

"You got a history with this one guy?" Mallory asked suspiciously.

"You could say that."

"It's his brother," Elsie supplied, though she seemed like she wasn't paying too close attention to them. She was tapping away. Face far too close to the computer. The woman needed to get outdoors and stop staring at a screen all the time. She was going to be blind by the time she was forty.

And she needed to stop rattling off things he didn't really want to tell Mallory or anyone.

"So, let's keep him out of it," Nate said firmly. "For his own good." And for Nate's. If Garrett saw Nate was hurt…

"It's already been done," Mallory replied with a shrug. "Whoever Shay was going to call to pick him up has already been called. No undoing it."

Nate didn't groan, though he wanted to. What would his

brother be thinking if he got a call for the fishing cabin? He was probably worst-case scenario–ing everything. And Nate *had* been shot.

"You really can't expect a one-man department to handle this guy. They barely have a real jail. They—"

"Nate, relax. Whoever Shay called, she knew what she was doing. A smaller department is actually better, because it allows us to bend some rules. I'm sure Garrett can handle it, if she did indeed call Garrett."

Nate didn't argue more. It was clearly pointless. His arm throbbed, but that was the least of his worries. Garrett. Here. How was he going to explain…any of this?

And how had he gotten to the point where he'd been shot, and had absolutely no control? When this had been his entire world for two years, and no one had come after him or hurt him or…

"You should go wait for whoever is coming on the banks, on the off chance there are more men here. We don't want locals ambushed," Elsie said, looking pointedly at Mallory and nodding toward Nate.

"What about these guys?" Nate asked, eyeing the two large, dangerous men in the cabin.

"They're tied up and incapacitated. Besides, I'm going to enjoy telling Lee all the information I'm finding out about him."

She was just bound and determined to get herself hurt. Bound and determined to complicate this thing. If she'd left him alone, he could have handled Don and the hitman. He could have handled everything. On his own, and…

Well, he might have been able to incapacitate the two men after him. But then what? He didn't have any mysterious group or computer skills to figure out Don's aliases or Lee Braun's identity. He didn't have anyone—except Garrett—to handle the two men. And that would have been only if he'd gotten Garrett to believe him.

So, he had to accept, no mater how hard it was, that he needed Elsie and Mallory and their group. To *really* finish things. Not just to prove he was right, but to stop whoever was after him from hurting more people.

It was the strangest, most out-of-body realization he'd had in his life—and he'd had a *lot* of those in the past few years.

He *needed* these women and their associates.

He shook his head. Need didn't mean he'd allow Elsie to get hurt in the process. Nate picked up the gun she'd put down the minute they'd walked in and placed it next to her on the table. "Use that if you need to."

She wrinkled her nose, but she nodded.

Nate followed Mallory out, looking at the tied-up men as he left. Don was still unconscious. Lee was glaring at Elsie. Nate didn't like it, but he didn't like *any* of this.

They moved to the bank. He could hear the soft sound of a motorboat rather than a rower.

"He moves fast."

Nate grunted. Garrett would take any call seriously, but Nate knew one that potentially involved him would in fact get Garrett to break land and speed records to be there. "You should have let me handle this," Nate muttered.

"Sorry, I wasn't informed your brother was law enforcement."

"It wouldn't have mattered if you had been. You'd still have done it."

Mallory chuckled. "You're right." She had her gun drawn, and her gaze kept sweeping the world around them. The rain had let up, but thunder still boomed like another patch of showers might move through. "You sure that's him?" she asked as the boat got close enough to make out most of his features, aided by the flashlight Garrett had strapped to his chest.

"Yeah, that's my brother."

Garrett motored the boat—God only knew where he'd gotten that motorboat since they weren't legal on this lake—to the dock and then exited with ease. He started right for them. Mallory let out a low whistle. "What's in the water in Montana?" Then she winked at Nate before sauntering back into the cabin.

"You're okay," Garrett said, standing with his arms crossed over his chest. His badge glinted in the flashlight beam like this permanent wall between them. Garrett had been made to be a cop: that strong sense of right and wrong with a core of fairness and an understanding that justice and the law didn't always go hand in hand. That was why he'd managed to work toward his own Blue Valley department.

Nate, on the other hand, had gotten out. He'd joined the military because it sounded like an adventure, not because he had any special desire to help people. But he *had* helped people. He'd done good things.

Until he'd had to come home and then he'd done… He blew out a breath. He'd been right. All this time he'd been occasionally worried that Garrett and his parents and Monica were right about his mental state, but Elsie had proved… Nate was actually right.

Now they had to do something about it. Nate hadn't wanted Garrett as part of this fight, but here he was.

"Nate," Garrett said darkly as they stood in the night, the lake lapping around them. Anyone could be watching, waiting, but Nate felt rooted to this spot where his brother stood before him like some kind of shining beacon of what was *right* while all Nate felt was wrong.

"Yeah, I'm okay. Where's Barney?" It was an inane question. Nate didn't know what else to say. There was no conversation he wanted to have right now. Might as well talk about his brother's dog.

"Nate. What is going on?" Garrett looked at the cabin.

"And who on earth was that woman? Is that why you're... Are you mixed up with this shady character?"

"Not exactly. Not..." Nate trailed off as Elsie came out of the cabin. She had her hands clasped together and Nate could see even in the faint light of the lantern she held there was a tension about her that hadn't been there before.

"Is that...?"

Elsie stopped in front of Garrett, next to Nate. "Hi, Deputy Averly. Sheriff now, Nate said."

"You're one of the Rogers..." Nate watched Garrett very carefully swallow the world *girls*. "Elsie, right?"

"Yes." She smiled. "I'm afraid we're in need of your help. I could make up a very complicated story about how or why, but I think since Nate is deeply involved in this, it might be one of those rare cases where the truth is necessary."

"I have no idea what you're talking about."

"Come inside. We'll get it all hashed out."

Nate wasn't sure any of this would ever be *hashed out*, but he followed Garrett and Elsie into the fishing cabin, which was definitely not built for four people let alone six. Elsie sat with her computer—she'd moved from the floor to the kitchen area with its small table and two chairs. Mallory stood next to the door, watching the world outside the window, and Nate stood in the middle of it all feeling like he was in an alternate universe as Elsie explained everything to Garrett.

Everything. That she was with a secret group. That Nate had uncovered a massive military cover-up. About Brina and Connor and the whole shebang.

Garrett sat there, taking it all in. When Elsie finally stopped giving him details, he shook his head in silence for a good full minute before speaking.

"I'm sorry. I just don't..." Garrett dragged a hand over his face. "This is for real."

"I've been telling you," Nate muttered. His brother's shocked acceptance didn't make him feel any better or vindicated. It made him uncomfortable.

He knew his brother had never *meant* to hurt him with his distrust, so he'd never had any dreams about proving them all wrong. He'd only wanted to…prove it to himself. To end the threat and then move on.

Now Garrett was looking at him like someone had kicked a puppy in front of him.

"Look, we can deal with all that later. Right now, we need you to take care of Don Prokop. Right?" Nate looked at Elsie.

She nodded. "What we need is for you to keep him in a cell for a few days, and make sure no one comes for him. We'll set you up with communications with one of our people at headquarters, so you can contact them if someone does come for him. We can also set you up with some security, so you're more protected."

"And this will help Nate prove…all the things he's been trying to prove?" Garrett asked, eyebrows drawn together, forehead wrinkled.

Elsie nodded. "Yes. And it will help stop this group who's been smuggling guns and sending out hitmen and who knows what all else."

"All right." Garrett raked his hands through his hair and shook his head. "But the unconscious one needs medical attention first. As does my brother."

"I'm fine. All patched up," Nate said, moving his injured arm even though jostling it hurt. Garrett frowned, but at least seemed to believe him. Nate looked over at the two women.

Elsie exchanged a look with Mallory. They seemed to have a whole nonverbal language going on.

"Okay, I'll take Don back to the station with you," Mallory said. "We've got doctors on our staff. We'll do a video conference and one of them will talk us through the medical procedures. One of our tech guys will talk me through figuring out the security situation. Good?"

Garrett looked up at Nate, clearly overwhelmed and lost. But he gave a firm nod. "Good."

Chapter Twelve

Elsie had never shared a small cabin with two fuming men—one of whom was an incapacitated hitman who wanted the other one dead. And the other one was…

Well, a problem. One she didn't have the time to think about.

She had to email directions to one of her tech operatives to set everything up for the Blue Valley PD. She had to field a call from Shay, updating her on their progress, while Shay gave her an ETA for the two operatives she was sending to take care of the hitman. All while she was searching names and delegating certain tasks to her remote tech team.

After Mallory and Garrett had left, Nate had positioned himself by the window, looking out into the night. He held his gun pointed at the man now handcuffed and tied up on the floor.

Nate was angry, certainly. The scowl told Elsie that—no deep analysis necessary. But she knew underneath that anger he was worried. About his brother. About Connor. And, she thought because she was starting to understand him, about what came next.

He acted like his wound was no big deal, and perhaps it wasn't. He'd been a Navy SEAL. Maybe getting shot in the arm was routine for him. And Mallory *had* wrapped him up with something far more effective than a Band-Aid.

That didn't mean he shouldn't take care of himself, though. She got up from her computer and pulled a snack from her pack. She walked over and stood next to him by the window. "You should eat something."

Nate grunted as he took the granola bar she handed him. She stood there while he unwrapped it and took a grudging bite. "This has chocolate chips in it," he said around a mouthful of food.

"Well, of course it does. Who wants to eat plain granola?"

He swallowed. And then handed the bar back to her. "You have a problem, Elsie."

"I have a sweet tooth. It's hardly a problem." She shrugged and ate the bar herself. She looked out at the black outside the window. She should be at her computer, searching. Doing the work she was good at, but she thought Nate needed some conversation.

Or maybe she did. "What do you think happens next?"

"I don't know. I don't understand what's happening now." He glanced at the hitman. "What did you find out on him?"

"As far as I can tell, he doesn't have any ties to the group that wants you dead—if it's a group, which makes sense. If a hitman doesn't have ties, aside from the money he's paid, it can't be traced back to whoever hired him." But she had found someone who *did* have ties and whose husband being mixed up in this made things all the more suspicious.

She found herself really not wanting to broach the topic. But that was weak. And foolish. "What about this Courtney Prokop?"

"What about her?"

He wasn't defensive exactly, but Elsie knew what she'd seen on that security footage and... Well, it was possible

Nate had been taken in by the woman. Maybe he'd told her things he shouldn't have when they'd done...whatever they'd done in that cabin. Elsie supposed it didn't matter what he'd done with Courtney. That was over. But it would help if they all knew what exactly had gone on, and she definitely needed him to know Courtney was shady.

It wasn't *personal* interest. It was necessary. "Courtney has ties."

"To what?" Nate demanded, his gaze whipping to her.

Elsie didn't flinch. While the crackling anger in him might usually make her nervous, she *was* used to people being none too pleased about the information she found in the course of a mission.

"She has ties to the military, which wouldn't be a big deal on its own. Lots of people have enlisted or done work for the military. But, connected to everything else going on and how much it's hidden in her records? I have questions. I have a few of my tech people digging deeper since I was focusing on our hitman, so they're sending me reports as they find things. We'll need to study everything more comprehensively, but—"

"I didn't sleep with her," Nate grumbled, looking back out the window. His expression was tense, all hard lines and angles. She wished she could put her hand on his face, somehow soften all that tension inside of him.

And she really had to stop being so soft-hearted. "It's none of my business."

"Well, I didn't. Not for her lack of trying."

Elsie rolled her eyes. "Don't put too fine a point on it, Nate. I'll believe you didn't sleep with her if you really need me to."

He gaped at her, which Elsie had to admit she enjoyed. That she could surprise him into gaping and sputtering. When he finally got a word out, it was a little bit outraged.

"She *did* try. You don't have to believe me, or can

think I'm being conceited, but I know what went on in that cabin."

"*Not* sleeping together," Elsie replied, trying and failing to keep her voice from sounding sarcastic.

"Among a million other reasons I didn't sleep with her, she's *married*."

"I'm actually not so sure about that."

Nate's expression kept turning more and more incredulous. "What?"

Elsie blew out a breath and nodded at the hitman in the corner. "Maybe we should talk about this later."

Nate reached out and took her arm, pulling her toward the door. It was a simple touch, his fingers curling around her forearm. It should *not* send a buzz through her skin like she was suddenly all jangling nerves and…

And it was *not* the time or place for those sensations, she reminded herself.

"Explain," he ordered once they were outside. The night had cooled considerably since the storm, but Elsie only felt heat where his hand was wrapped around her arm. He'd situated them so he could look through the window to where their prisoner sat. He kept his gaze on the man, but Elsie knew she had his full attention.

She also knew he held her with his injured arm, so she could escape his grasp easily enough if she wanted to. She was sure she should want to.

But she didn't.

"Courtney and Don are definitely connected, but there's no record of any marriage. Nothing legal binding them together."

Nate's grip loosened, though he didn't take his hand off her arm. "I guess it doesn't really matter, does it?"

"Yes and no. The thing is, if you're dealing with people in a secret group, or people working together to do bad things, it's not going to be easy to find actual physical evidence you could use against them in a court of law. But I can find clues, connections and hints that lead us to the people or group, or what have you. Her not being married to Don but using his last name is a clue. A hint."

"To what?"

"Well, I started looking into her maiden name. Unlike him, she doesn't have any aliases—at least that I've found, and I'm very good at finding those. But she has a bank account under that maiden name still. I've got my team following that money right now. Money that seems to have military strings. Maybe she just worked in the military, but we need to know for sure. Obviously, if she were trying to be really sneaky, she'd choose a completely different name, but I'm having my team look into if a Courtney Loren pops up anywhere else. A connection to you or Connor or Daria, or any of the places you guys were stationed, et cetera, et cetera."

"Wait." Nate's grasp on her arm tightened as he seemed to work through everything she'd just said. "Loren? Isn't her maiden name Sherman? Like Justin?"

"No. I checked into that. They have the same mother, but different fathers. Courtney's maiden name is Loren. L-o-r-e-n."

"I…" Nate looked like he'd seen a ghost before he shook his head. He dropped her arm, even took a slight step away from her. "Surely that's a coincidence," he said, more to himself than to her.

"What is?"

"Garrett's ex-wife. Her maiden name was Loren. But…" Nate scraped his free hand through his hair, making it a little wild. "Elsie. Good God."

"First name?"

"Savannah, but it's not poss—"

Elsie hurried into the cabin without waiting for Nate to finish. Could this connect to Garrett? Could Garrett himself be involved? Immersed in discrediting his brother? Wouldn't that make a horrible kind of sense?

She had to find out ASAP. Mallory was *with* Garrett and a man who'd tried to take her out. Elsie hadn't even watched the boat to make sure it had crossed. Mal could take care of herself, of course, but…how would Elsie feel if she'd sent Mallory off with a *dirty* cop?

Elsie's stomach roiled. Rose and Delia might have hated every Valley County sheriff's deputy from their childhood, but Elsie had always tried to keep an open mind. And she'd known Garrett had tried to help. She'd never hated him, or thought he'd done anything wrong.

Was she that off base? Could he be a traitor to his brother and his badge and everything else?

She began to type on her keyboard. She was going to find out. ASAP.

NATE FELT A bit like he'd been gonged. He vibrated with an energy he had no outlet for, and his brain buzzed with thoughts he couldn't seem to follow to completion.

The only reason his brain was tethered to consciousness at all was the hitman inside the cabin. There was no way he was leaving Elise alone with him, so he followed close on her heels.

But that didn't mean he understood anything else. He stood in the doorway and looked at her. She sat at the tiny table, already hunched over her computer, tapping away while her dark hair curtained most of her face. She looked like some kind of feral creature, and he had no idea why that was charming.

But he certainly didn't have time to be *charmed*.

This name thing had to be a strange coincidence. It *had* to be. How could Savannah be wrapped up in this? In military stuff? And neither he nor Garrett had ever known?

It wasn't possible. He hadn't liked the woman who'd

married his brother, but surely she wasn't… Nate rubbed a hand over his face. He couldn't let his brain go bounding forward. They had to deal with this one step at a time.

The first step was Elsie doing her search. They'd go from whatever information she found.

He moved to stand next to her. When he caught sight of what Elsie was typing on the computer, he forgot everything else.

"What are you doing? Search the ex-wife not…" He stopped because as little as the hitman could do sitting there tied up and incapacitated, Nate wasn't going to feed him any information about Garrett.

Elsie didn't stop typing and clicking. "He's the one my field operative is with, so he's the one I'm going to search."

Nate didn't want to get all that close to her, not when the soft warmth of her arm in his grasp was still too much a part of him. But he had to lean down and get in close so the hitman didn't overhear. "Garrett isn't shady," he whispered into her ear.

She glared up at him, dark eyes flashing with fury. "How do you know?"

He had to remain in place, and he had to make sure his concern for his brother overrode any sort of physical reaction to being this close to Elsie. "I know my damn brother. I also know his wife. Who cheated on him and up and left out of the blue a year ago. A year…"

The timing of it all came crashing down. It couldn't be… It couldn't…

"What is it?" Elsie asked, some of her anger turning into concern. "Nate. What is it?"

He didn't have to work to whisper this time. His throat was tight and his voice little more than a strangled rasp. "She left right around the same time I told… After all my military contacts didn't believe me about Daria, I started gathering information beyond Daria, right?"

Elsie nodded, leaning even closer so they could continue to have this conversation in a whisper. If his stomach wasn't full of lead, he might have been distracted by how close her lips were to his, but as it was…

Hell.

"I took it all to Garrett. I thought maybe him being in law enforcement and my brother, he'd believe me. Help me. But he didn't. That's when he insisted I join Revival. I thought I'd eventually convince him, but then Savannah left. A few days after that, he found out she'd been having an affair. She just disappeared. I joined Revival, and I left Garrett out of it because he had bigger issues to deal with. How does she connect? Why would she…?" It didn't make *any* sense, but how could the name *and* timing be coincidental?

"What other information do you know about Savannah? Birth date? Where she was born? Anything?" Elsie was typing away, but Nate didn't know much. He'd never really gotten to know Savannah. She'd been very clear she'd thought he was unhinged and wanted nothing to do with him.

So he'd kept his distance as much as she'd kept hers. He hadn't even really blamed her, because everyone thought that about him. But then she'd left and… "I really don't know anything."

If Elsie thought that was weird, she didn't mention it.

"Garrett would know more, obviously, but…"

Elsie waved it away. "I can find records of *their* marriage, and divorce, and go from there." She typed and tapped and her screen zoomed from one window to the next. He didn't understand how she did any of it, or absorbed the information she was skimming. It all went too fast for him.

"Oh. *Oh*," Elsie said breathlessly after only a few minutes.

"Oh. *Oh* what?" Nate leaned closer to the computer, trying to read what Elsie had brought up. "It's a death certificate."

Elsie looked up at him, something warm and caring in her eyes. "She's dead."

"What?" Nate forgot to whisper that demand, but Elsie continued to keep her voice low as she looked back at the screen and read.

"It's from four months ago," Elsie said, pointing to the date on the screen. She used her finger to show him the necessary information as she whispered. "She was admitted to a hospital in Texas. She…" Again Elsie looked up at him. She swallowed. "When did you say she left Blue Valley?"

"About a year ago. Almost exactly." Because it had been summer and he'd finally agreed to join Revival, so he knew to almost the day.

"Um. I don't know how to tell you this." Elsie inhaled then tapped the section about cause of death. "She died in childbirth. Complications to giving birth to twins."

At this point, Nate's brain was just blank. None of this computed, and he didn't think it ever would. "That doesn't mean…"

"I don't know what it means," Elsie said gently when he didn't finish his sentence. "The twins survived. They were awarded to Savannah's grandparents and… God, there's more, Nate. So much more." She leaned in, and it was like the more she found, the more her nose practically pressed to the screen. "She's related to Courtney."

"How?"

"Cousins. And here's our military connection. Their

grandfather, the one who's currently guardian of these babies, is a vice admiral with the Navy."

Nate thought his knees had simply turned to jelly. He remained upright only by gripping the table in front of him, even if it sent a jolt of pain through his injured arm. "I don't understand."

"Neither do I," Elsie said. "But we've got an awful lot to look into."

Chapter Thirteen

Elsie had no luck convincing Nate to sleep—not even reminding him he'd been shot budged him.

She'd kept digging until her eyes had gone blurry and her head was throbbing. Vice Admiral Ray Loren had a squeaky-clean record. She'd gotten nothing interesting from his bank accounts.

The more she didn't find, the more convinced Elsie was that he was the center of everything. But she was reaching the point she simply couldn't get her eyes to focus.

She closed them for a second. She'd just count to one hundred and when she opened them, her eyes would be fine and she could keep digging.

But she heard the snap of her laptop clicking shut and her eyes flew open. She glared at Nate standing there with his hand on her closed laptop. She scowled up at him. "Don't touch my equipment."

"Then be smart. You're not invincible. You're wilting."

Elsie straightened her shoulders. "I know my limits, Nate."

"No, you don't."

"Are you always so arrogant and condescending and bossy?"

"Are you always so determined to take such poor care

of yourself? Weren't you just in the hospital or something? Take it easy."

"Oh, yes. Let me *take it easy* right now. Sounds smart."

"Even soldiers have to rest."

"I'm not a soldier, Nate. I think that's obvious. What I can do is find information, sitting here at a computer. It's not a Navy SEAL mission or brain surgery. It's just tapping some keys."

"Just tapping keys." Nate laughed bitterly. "Yeah, that's why my life has been upended. Because you're *just tapping keys*."

Elsie felt unaccountably hurt, like he was blaming her for the twists and turns his life had taken. "I'm just the messenger."

He dragged his hand through his hair. "I know that." He blew out a long breath, because much as he clearly didn't want to admit it, he was as at the end of his rope as she was. "Elsie, take a break from the computer. You said you have a team, right? Get some rest. Just a little."

"And if I get some rest, what will you do?"

He scowled but looked at the watch on his wrist. "We've likely got a few before your friends get here. If you take a break for two hours, I'll take a break for one."

Elsie crossed her arms over her chest and gave him a disparaging look.

"Fine," he muttered. "We'll split the three hours in two, but *only* if you go first."

"Only if you promise to wake me up fair and square under threat of…of… Something bad I'll figure out at a later date."

"Fine. Deal."

She stood and held out her hand so they could shake on it.

There was *something* about the way he looked at her outstretched hand—like he just wasn't so sure about touching her—that made her want to *insist* upon it. She jiggled her hand at him until he scowled.

He closed his much bigger, much rougher, hand over hers and shook. When he tried to release her hand, she held on. She didn't let him pull away. It was a strange impulse.

She just...wanted. And it was probably delirium from lack of sleep. Maybe she was already asleep and this was a dream. That would make a lot of sense, actually. And if it was a dream, she could do anything.

So she stepped close to him. Really close. She looked up at him. He stared down at her warily, but the thing was, he was much bigger and stronger than she was. He could remove his hand from her grip if he wanted to. He could step completely away from her instead of look at her with that expression.

"Nate—"

Then there were three people in the doorway, on top of the hitman bound up in the corner. She hadn't been dreaming, but clearly she'd been delirious. Elsie let out a long breath. "Nate, that's Shay and Gabriel, and I'm assuming you know Connor."

Nate looked at the door, a million emotions crossing his expression before he schooled them into a kind of military stoicism that matched the look on Connor Lindstrom's face.

And Elsie was still standing far too close to Nate, her hand in his. She *knew* she should step away, but her brain wasn't functioning at that level. "You guys are a bit early."

"I guess so," Shay replied. Her voice was cool and even, but Elsie knew her boss well enough to know that didn't mean she wasn't already filing away impressions. Ones that might not look so favorably on Elsie. Still, she stood there.

Nate didn't, though. He pulled his hand free and stepped back from Elsie.

"Let's load up our friend here," Shay said, nodding at the hitman whose furious expression hadn't changed the whole time he'd been sitting there. "Gabriel?"

Gabriel moved into the cabin and to the hitman. Lee Braun didn't struggle as Gabe dragged him outside. Elsie figured he knew he didn't have any hope against *four* ex-soldiers and/or highly trained operatives.

"Why don't you and I step outside while Connor and Nate get reacquainted?" Shay said, raising an eyebrow at Elsie. She made it sound like a question, but Elsie knew it was most certainly not an invitation. It was an order.

She didn't look back at Nate or make eye contact with Connor. She just forced herself to smile and follow Shay outside.

There was the faintest hint of dawn in the east, the storm having passed over and leaving the world shiny and new. Gabriel was in a very tactical-looking boat, loading the hitman up and then motoring into the dark.

Shay was quiet and still as the boat slowly disappeared. The sound of the water lapping against the shore mixed with the chill of the early morning should have given Elsie some space to find her bearings, but her exhaustion was making her emotional for absolutely no reason.

Shay said nothing. Elsie had to break the silence or burst into inexplicable tears. "You guys got here fast," she said cheerily. "Aren't bosses supposed to stay behind and delegate?"

Shay laughed. "Yeah, supposed to. But this is getting big, and Holden's back at his farm with his wife. *Wife.* Sabrina's out of commission for a while. I even tried to convince Reece to come back, but that was a no go."

"You have other operatives."

"I know. Gabriel and Mallory work well together, and they're definitely in the running for taking lead roles. But we're talking military higher-ups. I thought we needed all hands on deck."

"You miss the field," Elsie said, feeling for her boss. Shay was an excellent head of North Star, but the leader so often had to sit back and pull strings and coordinate. Not *do*. Shay wasn't the kind of woman who liked to sit around pushing papers.

Shay shrugged. "I've been in the field plenty this year."

"Yeah, because you miss it."

"Maybe I do." Shay looked at Elsie. "And you don't want to be in it, so you can go back to headquarters, Els. We'll take it from here. I don't want you going with Gabe and the hitman, so we'll have you—"

"What?" Her stomach sank like a rock. Go back? *Leave?* "Wait. I can't leave."

"You did what we needed you to do. We made contact with Nate without anyone being suspicious. You've uncovered deeper connections. Mallory can—"

"You can't send me back to headquarters."

Shay's eyebrows rose. "I can't?"

Elsie swallowed. So many emotions battered around inside her, and she *was* exhausted, so she didn't know how to catalog or deal with them all. "My family could be in the crosshairs. I should be here. On the ground. With you guys."

"You don't trust us to keep your family safe?" Shay asked, her voice carefully devoid of any emotion.

Elsie knew her boss well enough to read the surprise. And the hurt. "You know that's not it, Shay," Elsie said.

Shay eyed her. "What's really going on, Els?"

"I just…know these people. Not just my family, but I grew up with them. Garrett Averly tried to help my sisters and me when almost no one in this town ever did. Nate is…"

Shay's eyebrows rose farther and Elsie knew she

couldn't afford to blush, but the heat was creeping into her cheeks anyway.

"I'm no operative, but I need to see this through. Don't send me back, Shay. Please."

NATE DIDN'T KNOW how to talk to Connor. All of a sudden, this friend of his, who Nate was responsible for dragging into this mess—from the very beginning—was here. Standing in the cabin.

"We should probably search the island," Connor said. "Make sure no one else is here. It'd be a good base, I'd think."

"I'd think," Nate echoed. The hitman was gone. Elsie was outside. And he was standing in his brother's fishing cabin in the middle of Montana. But it was like he was back in the Middle East. Sand in his mouth and Connor standing there—tall and honorable—wondering what Nate was dragging him into.

Yet this time, Connor was in some…group. They weren't on the same team, even if they were hoping for the same end result. "You're just a part of this group now?" Nate asked, not knowing how else to break the oppressive silence between them.

"Yeah," Connor said. Effusive as always.

"I thought you liked search and rescue?"

"I love it. But this is similar. Well, except for the fact I had to leave my dog back at headquarters."

"Why would you leave something you love for something 'similar'?"

Connor shrugged. "Sabrina's there."

Nate didn't wince exactly. "I guess that's a weird topic of conversation." Nate's ex. Connor's current. Yeah, that was weird.

"I guess."

Brina in a hospital somewhere. "How's she doing?"

"Okay." A ghost of a smile flitted with Connor's mouth. "Mouthy and irritable, so she's getting better."

Nate shoved his hands in his pockets.

Connor took a deep breath and slowly let it out. It was only when he spoke, Nate finally understood what all this awkwardness was really about.

"You were right. All this time."

"So it appears," Nate agreed. Connor's guilt didn't sit right, though. "I didn't always believe myself, so don't take it so hard."

"But you were right."

"And Elsie's theory is that someone or *someones* were working to discredit every accusation I made. It's hard to trust a guy who's been blown to hell when none of the evidence supports his theories."

"Except the evidence you supplied."

"I wasn't a trustworthy source. I didn't always see that at the time, but I get it now. And I don't have any hard feelings. You shouldn't, either."

Connor studied him in that silence Connor had always done so well. Eventually he smiled. Imperceptibly.

"So, what now?" Nate asked.

Connor shook his head. "I guess we sort through this mess and figure out who tried to ruin our lives."

"And stop them."

Connor nodded. "I'm not sure we could have done that on our own, Nate, but I think we can do it with North Star."

"Then let's get to work." Before Nate could move, Shay and Elsie reentered the cabin. Their expressions were inscrutable. The tall, built blonde and the slim, brilliant brunette.

"Okay, let's get up to speed about what happens next," the blonde said. Shay. The boss. There was no doubt that everyone would do as she said.

"Gabriel is taking the hitman to our military contacts—

good guys, I promise. He'll be interrogated there, and we'll get all the pertinent information. One of Elsie's people found a connection to Ross Industries. It's very slight, but considering the hitman was still after Nate even after North Star took down Daria, we're looking beyond Daria. Elsie said you've got evidence, Nate."

"Some. I gave her everything I had. She's got far more skills than me."

"She's got far more skills than everyone," Shay said proudly. "So, she'll keep gathering information. You can't go back to Revival," she said firmly. "There's no way to hide the fact the hitman came for you, that Don waited for you, and they've been arrested. Anyone after you, or who thinks you're a threat, knows you're involved in something fighting that now. This is a good place that we can easily defend. We'll have men on the ground around the island and you'll stay put here."

"How does this connect to the Lorens?" Nate asked.

"That, we don't know yet," Elsie said, clearly trying to hide a yawn. She opened her laptop and Nate thought briefly of when he'd closed it. When she'd held his hand. When…

Not the time for that. Shay was continuing on, reminding him of many a commanding officer he'd had in the Navy.

"No one knows Elsie's connected. So, I'm going to get her back to her sister's and hopefully no one suspects she was gone tonight. She'll communicate with us from there."

Nate glanced at Elsie, but she was frowning at her laptop. She needed some rest. She needed…probably quiet to focus on her task. Them separating was for the best. For both of them.

So, why did it feel like a loss?

"Mallory should be back from Blue Valley any minute,

and Gabriel will return by afternoon. I'm staying on, so we'll have four operatives on the island."

Nate began to shake his head. It didn't seem like anyone was going to argue with Shay, but she was missing an important piece of all this. "Someone needs to be on Elsie."

"They don't know I'm connected," Elsie said with a frown.

"That we know of. If Courtney Prokop's brother is involved, he knows there's rumors about Elsie and me."

"Rumors?" Shay said, looking at Elsie, eyebrows raised.

Elsie blushed, but Nate couldn't care about that. "If someone's been watching—and someone had to be to know I tried to send Connor evidence—they could have easily been watching me. Who knows who Don communicated with before Mallory went out there and he tried to ambush her? We don't know who's out there, who's watching, or for how long. How can you send her to Revival without someone watching out for her?"

Everyone in the room looked at him like he had grown a third head. He was used to that. God, he was so much more used to that than people believing him and making plans around the things he'd thought for years.

Shay's expression changed, imperceptibly, bit by bit. "He's right," she finally said, clearly a little shocked by the fact. "We don't fully know if Elsie's been compromised." She looked back at Elsie, her expression grim. "I guess you're going to have to stay here."

Chapter Fourteen

Relief coursed through Elsie, even if it shouldn't. How was she going to explain this to her sisters? That she'd stayed with them a few days then up and disappeared—leaving a majority of her equipment behind.

But no matter how guilty she felt over that, she got to *stay*. She got to continue to be part of this. If they'd shipped her back to Revival, she'd always be a step behind, doling out information as she found it, not as it happened in front of her. It was for the best that she stay here.

For the best.

And had absolutely everything to do with wanting to be close to Nate, to continue to work with him on this. Together. She understood that, even as she told herself it was stupid and way beyond the point. She couldn't help it. They'd become…a team in these short few days.

She needed to see this through *with* him.

Mallory entered the small cabin, so that it was now chock-full of people with not a lot of space to breathe. But no one acted like that was weird or uncomfortable as Mallory explained she'd gotten Don situated with Garrett and some new security and North Star communications.

But then Mallory's gaze turned to Elsie with some apology in her expression. "Uh, Els. Your sister was in the police station when I left."

Since those words didn't make sense together, Elsie could only manage one word. "What?"

"Yelling at Garrett. Demanding to know what Nate had done with you."

"Oh. Dear," Elsie managed. She didn't look at Nate. She didn't look at anything except her computer.

"Garrett was handling it okay, but I'm pretty sure anyone in a ten-mile radius is going to know Els and Nate are connected, and if more people are out there looking at Nate…"

"Yeah, we know," Shay said on a sigh. "We've already decided to keep Elsie here. But someone is going to have to shut the sister up."

"I'll call her," Elsie said, dread filling her as she forced herself to sound firm and in control. "I'll get her to stop looking for me and making demands. But if the wrong person *did* hear her… Shay, you have to make sure no one hurts Revival."

"Like we aren't spread thin enough. I'll call in—"

"Shay. I need *you* to make sure no one hurts Revival. Not part-timers or friends you call in for a favor. This is my *family*, who don't even connect to what's happening. I need someone I trust. Someone I know will—"

"What about Granger?"

Elsie stopped on a dime. Granger Macmillan had been the first leader of North Star. When he'd been injured, Shay had taken over. Granger had gone off to some mysterious ranch deep in the mountains and, for a while, only Shay had known where he was. It was just in the past few months that Shay had been getting him to come back and help with missions—though he wouldn't return to the group officially no matter how they tried to convince him.

Still, Elsie trusted Granger just as much as Shay and the rest of the full-time North Star team. He'd hired her. Believed in her. He would protect her family, she was sure of it. "All right."

"I'll give him a call. You call your sister and make damn sure she shuts up about everything. And don't go telling her..."

"I know," Elsie said. She managed a paltry smile.

North Star was, and stayed, a secret for a wide variety of reasons. Elsie might not always have a clear idea of what those were, but she was the one who often wiped a person's history for them. Then put it back when they decided to rejoin civilian life. She could make things disappear and create fictions that everyone in the world would take as fact. She had *no* idea how she was going to convince her sister to stand down. She couldn't even give Shay an I-told-you-so about her not belonging in the field, because she very much wanted to stay in *this* particular field for reasons that were entirely inappropriate.

"Can I go outside to do this in private?"

Shay shook her head. "We'll go out. Plan where we're going to be." She nodded her head at the door and the team, including Nate, followed her outside. Nate did give Elsie one look over his shoulder, but she couldn't really read anything in it.

Right now, she had bigger fish to fry. She closed her eyes and gave a quick prayer for some kind of genius lie to pop into her head, and then dialed Rose's cell.

"So help me God, Elsie Marie Rogers, I am so furious with you, but if you're hurt or need help, tell me when and where and—"

"Sissy, I'm fine. What are you doing up so early?"

"I have two kids and a husband who works on a ranch— and don't think you're going to get around this by wondering why I'm up so early. Where are you? What's happened? If Nate Averly put his hands on you—"

"He hasn't. It isn't like that, Rose." She blew out a breath and rolled her eyes at herself. She should have gone along with it. Said she was in love with him or something ridiculous. Swept off and away by a dashing cowboy.

Besides, she kind of wished Nate Averly had put his hands on her. But that was beside the point.

"Explain. Now," Rose demanded.

"Are you still at the police station?"

"Damn right I'm at the police station. How do you know that? Where are you, Elsie? Why would you scare me like this?"

Me. Well, that was something. "So you haven't told anyone else?"

"I wasn't going to worry Delia until I had to. Jack knows, obviously. But he's home with the kids and… Why am I explaining myself to you? Explain to me what is going on."

Elsie wished she could tell her sister the whole unvarnished truth, but maybe… Maybe she could give her enough. Maybe it would be enough.

"I can't tell you everything. I wish I could, but it's not… This is all part of my job. I promise you, I'm safe and sound. But sometimes I have to move fast. I thought I'd be back by morning and you wouldn't have to worry, but now I have to stay away for a bit."

"Stay away? With Nate Averly. I do not think so."

"My job helps people. *I* help people. Right now, I'm helping Nate. He's in trouble, and my team and I are going to get him out of it."

There was a long pause on Rose's end and Elsie felt like holding her breath. Would her sister buy any of this?

"So, you work for people who use your computer genius to help people?"

"Yes, and that's all I can tell you. For your own safety, okay?"

"Safety. Are you in danger? You didn't look right. Were you hurt? Is this—?"

"Rose. Listen to me. I got this job because I know computers and information. I've helped save people for three years. Innocent people. Good people. In those three years, I've only been in real, serious danger twice, and I always came out the other side, because there are people who know what they're doing protecting me. But I found myself here, and I promise you I am not just good—I need this. Now, I need you not to worry. I need you to…"

"I will damn well worry," Rose said.

"Okay, then I need you to trust me. To believe me. I know what I'm doing. I'm good at what I'm doing. It's why I don't come home much. I wouldn't have come home this time, but the job was Nate. So, it made sense."

"None of this makes any sense. Are you a spy or something?"

"Not…exactly."

Rose laughed, though it was more baffled than amused. "Elsie…"

"I know it's a lot to swallow, but I wouldn't lie to you like this. You know that, right? I wouldn't make up this far-fetched thing. We've been through too much, come too far. Please. Believe me."

Rose was quiet for long enough that Elsie knew she was seriously thinking about what Elsie had said. "I just need to know you're okay."

"I'm okay. I'm better than okay. This job…" Elsie's throat got tight. "It saved me. It showed me who I could be. I can't do my job if you're in Blue Valley yelling at Garrett. I need you to go home and…take care of your babies and your husband. I promise you, once this mission is over… I'll come home and spend some time. For real. No job. You can see just how good I am."

"Mission. Hell, Elsie. I…" She blew out a long breath.

Elsie didn't know what else to say to convince Rose. To make her understand.

When Rose spoke, it was with a fierceness that had always been with her. Because Rose was fierce and strong and, honestly, Elsie wasn't sure how she was the one at home with babies and Elsie was the one fighting roving gangs and military corruption with an elite, secret group.

But here they were.

"If this is all on the up-and-up, and you're really some secret spy or whatever, then I'm proud of you. Amazed by you. But if you get yourself hurt, I'm going to kill you and everyone involved myself."

Elsie managed a laugh as she tried to fight the wave of emotion and tears. "Deal," she croaked. She cleared her throat. "I have to go."

"Please…keep in touch as much as possible."

"I will. And I'll be home soon."

"Good. Take care of yourself, Els."

"I will. Bye." Elsie clicked the end button. She wouldn't cry. There were a bunch of tough operatives and military men out there who'd probably never cried a day in their lives. She had to be strong. Even if Rose's trust and belief and *pride* meant everything to her. Filled up an empty space she hadn't known she still had.

"Oh, screw it," she rasped into the silence of the cabin. She gave in and let herself cry.

WHILE ELSIE TALKED to her sister, Shay laid out the island, and where she wanted pairs stationed. She put Connor and Mallory together on the east side, and said she'd be on the west with Gabriel when he returned. It was a small enough island. That should keep the cabin protected.

"What about me?" Nate asked once she'd made the assignments clear.

Shay eyed him carefully. "You're on Elsie duty. Whatever info you've got that she needs, supply it. You'll also be the contact to your brother." She nodded to his bandaged arm. "That doesn't look too bad, but it's a weakness we can't afford out here."

Nate didn't know what to say to that. He should be annoyed by the assignment. Annoyed by her calling a little gunshot wound a weakness.

But he wasn't.

"While Elsie and her team at headquarters keep digging, we watch and wait for more hitmen or what have you. If we get anything on the original hitman, the info will be sent around. If we need to meet, we'll do it at the cabin. Consider it our epicenter for the time being."

There were nods and murmurs of assent.

"Right now, we're in a waiting phase until we've got information to move forward on. Any threats we run into, we just want to neutralize and ideally use to further our mission."

"What *is* our mission?"

Shay looked at Nate, and he couldn't figure out what she saw, what she thought. But she spoke with a clarity and surety that helped center him.

"To take down the group using the military to arm and fund their unlawful purposes, to bring all perpetrators to justice, and to keep you, your brother and all members of my team safe in the process. Does that work for you?"

"Yeah, it does."

"Good." She nodded to Connor and Mallory. "Let's get situated." They started to move away, but Connor stood where he was, studying Nate.

Per usual, he said nothing for the longest time. When he finally spoke, he held out his hand. "See you on the other side."

Other side. Nate had sort of stopped believing in another side. An end to this. A world where he got to—not just be believed, but vindicated.

He shook Connor's hand and then watched his friend

melt into the trees, feeling a bit like there was quicksand under his feet.

The other side.

What life was he going to have on the other side?

Nate stared at the cabin door. He didn't let his mind go there. One step at a time. Elsie was the current step.

God help him.

He walked into the cabin then stopped short.

Elsie sat on her tiny chair, but she was sniffling. Her cheeks were tearstained, the tip of her nose red. She wiped at her face in an attempt to clean herself up, but she didn't exactly hide the fact she'd been crying.

"Everything okay?" Nate asked warily.

She nodded. "Got my sister to stand down." She stood and started fussing in the kitchenette. "Took some doing." She flitted from one thing to the next—sink, counter, table—without settling anywhere or completing any task. "But she said…she said she was proud of me." Her voice cracked and, though her back was to him, he had the impression she was crying again.

"That's…bad?"

"No. It's wonderful," she squeaked. "And awful."

"I really don't follow."

She kept her back to him, but shook her head. Then her shoulders began to shake, though she made no sound.

Hell.

He had half a thought to leave the cabin. To let her have her inexplicable emotional moment while he went…far away. But that would be cowardly. She'd had a long few days. What she really needed was some rest.

He crossed the small room with the thought he'd tell her that. Maybe pull her along to the couch so she'd rest. Yeah, that's what he'd do. Gently, he placed his hand on her shoulder and turned her to face him.

But instead of moving with his hand, or away from

his grasp, she stepped right into him. Burying her face in his chest.

Nate held himself perfectly still. What…was he supposed to *do*? He was not used to emotional breakdowns. He'd never seen his mother cry. He was pretty sure she'd jump off a cliff first. He'd grown up and worked mostly around men. Never had much of a long-term relationship, aside from Brina—and if his mother was rock-solid, Brina was granite.

But he couldn't remain immobile while Elsie cried into his shirt. He slowly and carefully wrapped his arms around her and held her there. Crying against his chest. She softened into him, like it was exactly the right move.

Like this was exactly right.

"I just hate that they're worried about me," she said, her voice muffled. "That they're somehow dragged into this. And it isn't just them. Poor Garrett. He doesn't even know his full connection yet, and I'm sorry."

"You're sorry?"

"My group."

He held her a little tighter. "My digging. Don't blame yourself for any of this. You said it yourself. You're just the messenger."

"I've never had to be the messenger to people I care about before."

People I care about. She meant her sisters. Surely not him.

Dangerous ground.

"Come on." He led her over to the couch and nudged her into a sitting position, but she just looked up at him like he could…fix this. He hadn't fixed a damn thing in so long, it was like being in a tractor beam. He had to sit next to her, to put his arm around her and let her curl up against him.

They sat on the couch together like it was normal. Like he comforted her all the time and it just felt right to sit here cozied up together. He had never wished for a future that didn't simply involve everyone who thought he was crazy realizing he wasn't. He'd never gone any further than that.

Until now.

"You're going to have to call Garrett," Elsie said after a while. She yawned as she said it and he wondered if he held still enough, if she'd finally doze off. She'd stopped crying, but he knew she was hardly over the emotional upheaval.

"Do we have to tell Garrett about Savannah?" Nate asked. "Couldn't we just… It's bad enough she cheated and left, now he's got to know he was some weird pawn in we don't even know what."

"I need more info on her, and he might have it. I think I'd rather know I was a pawn and cheated on and left than think it was *real* and I was cheated on and left."

"You do not know my brother." But Elsie was right. It wasn't about what Garrett would rather know. It was what he needed to know. "I'll want to tell him in person. Over the phone…it isn't right. It needs to be in person."

"Did he love her?"

Nate didn't shift, but only because Elsie was leaning against him. Love didn't seem like the best topic of conversation. But how could he ignore it? "I assume so. Garrett isn't the kind of guy who'd get married without taking that commitment really seriously." Commitment. Marriage. How were they talking about this?

Elsie lifted her head from his shoulder, which felt like a loss. But then she looked into his eyes and he didn't know what to do but meet that warm gaze. Her hand was on his shoulder and they were still hip to hip.

"Maybe she loved him, too," Elsie said hopefully. "Maybe that's why she ran away?"

"While she was pregnant with twins?"

Elsie wilted a little, but she didn't give up. "Maybe she was trying to save Garrett from something."

"I could maybe believe that if she wasn't related to Courtney. You might not believe me, but that woman is a snake."

"A person can't be judged by their family members."

"Maybe not," Nate agreed, knowing she was thinking about herself and her parents. "But it's a lot of coincidences to believe in love."

That word seemed to echo between them, and Nate really, *really* didn't know what to do with that. He'd never considered himself bad or awkward at interactions with the opposite sex, but the Nate who'd come back from war, injured and dishonorably discharged, and certain he'd been about to uncover something terrible…was not the same Nate Averly who'd left.

Elsie leaned forward, eyes on his. There was no subterfuge, certainly no mistaking that look. It and she should have been easy to resist. There was nothing particularly seductive about the move. She looked a mess from crying and he should…

Her lips touched his. Soft, but not tentative. Just gentle. Like *he* was fragile. Or they were. Together.

That gentleness made the kiss impossible to break. He knew—God, he knew—this was wrong, but no amount of knowing changed what he felt. What he did as he smoothed his hand over her hair, changed the angle of the kiss.

Her hands on his face felt like a new lease on life. Erasing the past few years and building something new and possible right here in this moment.

Which you know isn't possible. Thankfully, that thought managed to penetrate. He eased away from her mouth. He had to clear his throat to talk. "Elsie."

She opened her eyes on a sigh. "I know. You're not… It's okay. You're not into me. I get it."

"Not… What?" He got to his feet and raked his hands

through his hair. What was his life? "I kissed you back, Elsie. It's not a question of being into you."

She blinked then smiled. That was bad. Very bad. He had to put a stop to that self-satisfied smile or he might forget there were three or four other people on this island waiting around for a threat against *him*. *He* was in danger and...

He had to nip this in the bud. Immediately. No matter how that kiss had rearranged things inside him. "It's a stressful situation and I'm just not sure you're seeing things clearly."

She shook her head. "No. Don't ruin it. I kissed you. You kissed me back. It was nice. Let's leave it at that."

Wait. "Nice?"

"Don't get all bent out of shape. It *was* nice." She smiled up at him innocently.

"I see what you're doing. You're not going to goad me into this."

She quirked an eyebrow at him like that's exactly what she was going to do.

Maybe she was.

Chapter Fifteen

Elsie felt like a live wire. And something more. A blooming flower. A cart of dynamite with the fuse lit. She felt all these *amazing* things she'd never felt. Not once.

It was all ridiculous and she didn't care. The voice of reason telling her she was exhausted and delirious had died when his lips had touched hers. She would have backed away after the kiss if Nate had said he wasn't into her. Let it go.

But he *was* interested. Just too...noble or something.

She stood and crossed to him. He didn't retreat, which was probably as much ingrained habit as anything else. Nate wasn't a man who backed down from a challenge.

So, she'd challenge him.

She knew the timing was terrible, but her whole life was full of terrible timing. If there was one thing she'd learned, it was that you had to take whatever came, whenever it came.

She wanted to take Nate.

"Your friends are out there," he said, sounding vaguely strangled as she slid her hands up his chest.

"My coworkers," Elsie agreed, studying him as she linked her fingers behind his neck. There was something adorable at how stiff and uncomfortable he was. Because he was *not* unmoved. That much was clear. "Outside this cabin. With us inside. Alone."

"I should tell Garrett," he said somewhat desperately. "About everything. With his ex-wife."

"Now you want to tell Garrett?"

"Yeah, I should. I'll call him."

"You didn't want to do it over the phone," she reminded him.

"Oh. Right." He swallowed. "Elsie."

She looked up at him, sure she would come up with something pithy and challenging to say, but his gaze was so dark, so...intent. "What?"

He sucked in a breath then seemed to find some iron will. Gently, he pulled her hands from around his neck and nudged her back a step. Before she could do anything to retaliate, he took her face in his hands. His expression was so serious, she actually paused. It wasn't a game, she knew that. But she also knew that for some people sex could be casual. Easy. Something to move on from.

Eventually.

But he didn't look any of those things. He held her face and looked deep into her eyes. "I don't want you to misunderstand me. It's not that I don't *want* to, but it shouldn't be like this."

"Be like what?"

"In the middle of all this. In my brother's tiny fishing cabin. Not some fumbling impulse."

"I'm sorry...you'd rather plan it out?"

His grip on her face tightened and he leaned forward, so serious. So... Nate. "I'd rather it *mean* something."

Her heart fluttered, like a fragile butterfly. Something she'd been very careful to avoid her entire adult life. Anything too fragile, including herself and her own feelings. She'd needed armor and North Star had given it to her and now Nate was...

All her bravado and certainty fled. *This* wasn't what she was looking for. *This* was dangerous ground. Because this was real, and he was talking about…the kinds of things she'd always avoided without fully realizing that's what she was doing.

Now she wanted to lean into all that she'd avoided, even knowing it was dangerous. Even as her mind yelled warnings at her, her heart reminded her that he'd held her when she'd cried, and they understood each other in this strange, complicated way. He knew who she was and he didn't *treat* her differently because of what she'd endured.

She felt completely immobilized by all of this. Want and need and a genuine care she hadn't counted on. She didn't care for it, but it was inside of her. Blooming against her will.

Still, Nate's hands were on her face. Still, he looked at her intently. "It's not the time. And I won't be the same guy on the other side of this."

She reached up and covered his hands with hers. Because she knew that excuse. She knew that belief. It had been a core part of how she'd struggled once she'd gotten away from her father and Blue Valley. "Yes, you will."

"You don't understand." He tried to pull his hands away, and though he got them off her face, she gripped them before he could withdraw completely.

"No, I do. When you go through a trauma, you think eventually you'll move past it, heal from it and be some new, shiny thing. But you won't. You're still you. You can heal, but you don't become a new person."

He pressed her hand against his heart. He didn't say anything. Just looked at her like she'd sliced him in two.

This was the part she couldn't walk away from. How *much* she understood. No matter how scared, how worried, that this little glow was breakable and could ruin everything, it was the understanding that kept her rooted to the spot. Staring at him. Waiting for...

And then it was too late, whatever this was. Mallory was in the doorway. If she'd heard anything, she didn't let it show. "We've got company."

NATE FINALLY MANAGED to get himself out of Elsie's grasp. Not because she'd been stronger than him, but because all that emotion and connection was finally broken by a third party.

And he could remember who he was, not what he wanted to be.

Even if the next few pieces of this proved he was right all along, it didn't...

Elsie had said it herself. It didn't change who he was. A man who'd spent the past two years of his life mired in the past. He didn't have a job. The future was unclear—because in the past he'd only been working toward proving he wasn't insane.

Elsie had this job she loved. She was a *genius* putting her skills to work to help people. Nate had only ever been after helping himself.

"It's Courtney Prokop. Alone. Unarmed," Mallory stated grimly.

"That doesn't make any sense," Elsie said, frowning.

"No, it doesn't," Mallory agreed. She looked at Nate. "But we thought you could be out there to help greet her while we figure out what she thinks she's doing."

Nate nodded. "You'll stay put with Elsie?"

"Yeah."

"I'm not some weakling who needs protecting," Elsie said, frowning at both of them.

"No, but it's hard to point a gun when you're eyeballs-deep in the computer screen like you usually are," Mallory said, giving a much better explanation than Nate would have. She was no weakling, but that didn't mean she had to turn down protection.

Elsie huffed out a breath. "Fine. Babysit me," she muttered. "I'm going to find out what Courtney Prokop is up to."

Mallory nodded at the door, a clear sign Nate was supposed to go. He found he didn't want to. He didn't want to face Courtney. He didn't want to deal with all the inexplicable happenings around him.

He wanted to stay right here with Elsie.

And that wasn't an option. He stepped outside. Morning had dawned, pearly and pretty. Courtney's boat was nearing the dock. A small canoe she was paddling. Odd. This whole thing was bizarre.

Nate stood at the dock and scanned his surroundings without moving a muscle. Though he couldn't see anything except a little glint of reflection, he could tell someone was positioned right behind the cabin, eyes on him and Courtney. Nate believed it was Shay since it seemed there was only one person. He presumed she was purposefully letting him see that she was there.

But Courtney likely wouldn't know, unless she was trained to look for some kind of small hint that something was amiss.

Who knew? Maybe she was.

Still, Nate didn't let his gaze linger on the person behind the cabin. He focused on Courtney as she docked and then tied up her canoe. She stepped onto the dock.

"Oh, Nate. I'm *so* sorry." She came right up to him and flung her arms around him like they were old friends. Or more than.

Nate stood stock-still. He didn't understand anything that was going on, but felt his only course of action was to let it unfold. Much as he'd like to push her off and demand what the hell was going on.

"What are you doing here?"

She looked up at him from underneath her lashes. She looked distraught, but Nate found himself utterly unmoved. He'd seen her emotionally manipulate a few too many people—her brother, her supposed husband, some of the other men at Revival—to believe that she couldn't just put on a mask whenever she wanted.

"I just couldn't live with it any longer."

"Live with what?"

"The truth." She sucked in a breath. "I have a bag in the boat. You're not going to hurt me if I grab it, are you?"

"You're not going to hurt me if I let you, are you?"

She smiled and patted his chest, letting her hand linger. "I promise, Nate. I'm here to help you. We've been pawns in an awful thing, and I just couldn't live with myself if I didn't tell you."

Nate didn't let his distrust or his unease show. She pulled a messenger-type bag out of the canoe and then slung it over her shoulder. "Can we go into the cabin?" she said, pointing at it in the distance.

Nate looked at the cabin. No doubt Mallory was watching, same as Shay. Maybe even Elsie. He looked back at Courtney and the way she was gripping the bag.

"I'm going to have to look through the bag first."

She sighed and held it out to him. "I totally understand. You've been through so much. You have every right to be paranoid."

He took the bag, trying to keep his movements practical and devoid of emotion even though he wanted to jerk it out of her grasp. "Paranoid isn't the word I'd use." He looked through every pocket, but the only thing inside was a laptop and a cord. The computer looked legit. Elsie would know if it hid explosives or could trigger something.

But he was hardly going to take this woman into the cabin with Elsie.

He handed the bag back to her. "Why don't you tell me what you've got to tell me here?"

"I'm afraid it's something I have to *show* you. I need an outlet of some kind. What do you think I'm going to do? Kill you?"

Nate shrugged.

Courtney rolled her eyes. "Nate. Honestly. You were a Navy SEAL. You can take me." She smiled up at him. "I promise."

Nate didn't know what else to do but agree. He walked toward the cabin, keeping his pace slow. Hopefully, he was giving Mallory and Elsie enough time to hide if they needed to.

He didn't trust Courtney for a second, so it was probably best if she didn't know he now had an entire group helping him out.

Unless she already *did* know. It was hard to say what anyone did or didn't know. But it was worth a few minutes, he supposed, to figure out what she was trying to pull over on him.

Nate opened the door and stepped inside, once again standing still as he scanned the area around him. No sign of Elsie or Mallory, or even Elsie's things. Good.

Courtney brushed past him, unnecessarily, on her way in. Nate really couldn't figure out her angle, so he just kept his mouth shut.

"Let's see." She wandered the interior of the cabin and then settled herself at the table Elsie had been situated at not that long ago. It made Nate frown even though he was trying to maintain an unemotional expression.

He'd much rather be staring at Elsie eating her granola bars and ruining her eyes than Courtney plugging in her laptop and then tapping some keys.

Nate forced himself to move over to her. Best to know what she was doing just in case that computer *was* a threat.

She brought up some kind of video player. "I know this is going to upset you, but I knew you deserved the truth."

Garrett appeared on the screen. With his ex-wife. Nate recognized the room as the kitchen in their house, a cozy Craftsman just off Main Street where Garrett could walk to the police station and Savannah could walk to her job as a cashier at the hardware store.

"You have to convince him to enroll at Revival," Savannah was saying.

"For his own safety?" Garrett asked. He was sitting at the kitchen table and Savannah put a mug of coffee in front of him. In the corner of the screen, Nate could see Barney snoring away on the floor.

"Of course," Savannah said but then smiled. "And 'for his own safety' will become for our own gain."

Nate frowned. That didn't make any sense.

"What if he suspects something?" Garrett asked, sounding less worried and more...practical about the whole thing. Very Garrett.

"He suspects everything. Isn't that the point?" Savannah stood behind Garrett and wrapped her arms around his neck. "And if he's at Revival, your parents are going to take him off their will."

Garrett smiled and patted his wife's hand. "That is the plan. Mom and Dad bought the box of fake information hook, line and sinker. They're convinced he's crazy."

"Well, he is. So, we're doing him a favor."

Garrett pulled Savannah onto his lap, nuzzled her neck. "We're doing ourselves a bigger one, and that's what really matters."

Nate didn't move. It was like being turned to ash in a matter of seconds. His brother. Working with his ex-wife. To discredit him. To make him seem so unhinged their parents would make Garrett sole inheritor.

It didn't make sense. Mom and Dad's property was

small, and they were only in their late fifties and in excellent health. Why would Garrett be concerned about their estate? Garrett had never been concerned about money.

But Savannah had, and Garrett had loved Savannah. Would he have done...anything for her?

"I'm sorry, Nate," Courtney said.

Nate barely registered the words. He was still looking at the computer screen, the image now frozen. Garrett and Savannah in what he knew to be their kitchen. Barney was there. It was just...an actual scene out of their life from a year ago.

Courtney rose and put her hand on his shoulder. She stood between him and the screen so that he had to look at her instead of it.

"We're just innocent victims in this, Nate," she said sadly.

He stared at Courtney. He'd been taken in there for a while. Watched his brother say horrible things and believed them. For a few minutes, his world had crashed around him.

But listening to Courtney say *innocent victims* like she was somehow part of this—when what would it matter to her if he'd been discredited? Something was a fraud here.

And he didn't think it was his brother.

"How are you a victim?"

"Someone is blackmailing me. They said I had to show you this, even though I knew it would wreck you."

"Someone?"

"I don't know who. I was just given instructions to show you this. I'm not supposed to tell you it's blackmail, but my heart's just breaking for you, Nate. I'm so sorry and—"

"What are they blackmailing you with?"

Courtney blinked then looked at the floor. She was a damn good actress...if she was acting.

She *had* to be. Garrett didn't care about estates. Savannah had left him. This had to be fraudulent. Somehow. Some way.

"Well... Don and I aren't really married."

That was true. Elsie had found out that was true. Could Courtney actually be...telling the truth? Could this awful thing be real?

"Why don't you come back to Blue Valley with me, Nate? I'd hate for you to be out here alone. Feeling so hopeless, like it might not be worth it to go on," Courtney said, leaning her head against his shoulder.

Much like Elsie had. But Elsie had belonged there. Elsie told the truth.

He didn't know what this woman was doing, but it wasn't anything to do with the truth. It couldn't be. He knew better than anyone that when things didn't add up, no matter how real they looked to other people, you kept digging until the math worked.

"Are you trying to get me to commit suicide, Courtney?"

She pulled back, eyes wide, her hand fluttering to her chest. "Nate. How can you say such a thing? I'm going to insist you come back with me. You have a therapist at Revival, don't you?"

"You should go now, Courtney," he said, not bothering to hide the ice in his tone. "You can leave the laptop."

"I can't do that." She moved to it and packed it away again. "I have to give it to my blackmailers."

"At least give me a copy of the video."

Courtney shook her head. "It would only depress you farther, Nate. The truth was enough. Don't go doing something drastic—"

"You can go now." Maybe Elsie could dig up a copy through her computer hacking or something. Or maybe she'd seen something or... It didn't matter. He needed Courtney out of his orbit.

"Don't be angry," she said, her eyes sad and her voice pleading.

Nate remained unmoved. "Goodbye, Courtney."

She lifted onto her toes and pressed a kiss to his cheek, for far longer than was necessary. Her hands trailed down his chest and pulled away just at his waistband. "You can always call me, Nate. I promise, you can trust me."

He pointed to the door and she left, bag on her shoulder, with just the hint of a frown.

Nate scowled after her.

He'd trust Satan himself first.

Chapter Sixteen

Elsie wondered if Nate had any idea she'd set up a camera and microphone that enabled her and Mallory to watch everything that happened from where they hunched in the woods.

She watched Courtney brush past Nate as she sauntered into the cabin and wanted to do a bunch of violent things she'd promised herself she'd never want to engage in. But having a violent thought in anger and acting on it were two different things, as her therapist had always told her.

Nate seemed unaffected. He played it well—neither acted too suspicious of her nor too comfortable with her as she pulled out a laptop.

"This is weird," Mallory muttered, though her gaze didn't stay on the screen but instead kept scanning their surroundings as if she half expected someone to jump out and surprise them all.

Elsie couldn't look away from the screen. She could make out what Courtney was showing Nate. It was a video. It looked like Garrett and some woman in a kitchen. The voices from the video were quiet but clear enough to make out.

Elsie's heart sank to her toes. She felt *sick* over this. Garrett was saying awful things. Hadn't she considered that it was an option? That he was somehow in on it. The ex-wife was dead, even if the babies weren't and…

Did Garrett know Savannah was dead? Had he been involved? Was he playing them all?

But… Elsie squinted at her screen. Something wasn't right. Some interference, a pixilation around the dog. Whatever footage that was, it had been tampered with.

"This isn't real," Elsie said.

"Sucks, huh? Your brother being a dirtbag. Rough."

"No. No, Mallory. This *footage* isn't real. Or isn't the whole story. It's been altered. I have to tell—" Before she could dart off, Mallory grabbed her arm and held her still.

"Wait, Els. Courtney can't know we're here. *Especially* if that footage is altered."

Elsie knew she was right, but the idea of Nate sitting there thinking Garrett had said all those awful things… It hurt. What's more… Mallory believing her when it was a crazy assertion—that the video they'd seen was altered to make things look a certain way… Nate didn't need any more disbelief in his life.

Mallory didn't question it. She trusted Elsie's expertise. Not only did Nate not have that, all these years he'd been trying to prove himself right, he now also had to believe his brother was actively working against him.

It wasn't fair, and Elsie needed to end that suffering for him as soon as possible. But Mallory didn't let her arm go. As if she knew Elsie couldn't be trusted to follow reason because her feelings were *way* too involved.

Courtney packed up the laptop, gave Nate a kiss on the cheek that had Elsie's hands curling into fists, and then left the cabin.

They didn't have a camera on the dock yet, so she had to sit and wait for Mallory to let her go.

"Mal, I want that laptop. Can you get it without her knowing?" Elsie whispered, just in case Courtney hadn't gone straight for the dock.

Mallory blew out a breath. "Eventually. But Shay wants me here."

Elsie didn't say anything else until Mallory finally let her go. A sign Courtney had to be rowing away by this point.

"Connor says it's clear," Mallory said, tapping her earpiece.

Elsie needed that footage. "Get it cleared with Shay and get after her ASAP. I need that laptop."

Mallory nodded then peeled off in one direction, already talking into the com unit. Elsie moved for the cabin, watching the lake carefully to make sure Courtney was out of sight first.

She was a dot, far off near the other bank. So, Elsie slid into the cabin without hesitation. "It isn't real," she blurted even before she saw where Nate was.

He stood in the same spot he'd been when he'd told Courtney to leave. Elsie thought she'd see anguish on his face. Maybe banked fury in his gaze. But he nodded. Like he'd already figured that out.

Still, Elsie continued on, just in case he was being stoic for the sake of it. "That video isn't real—not fully. If it were real, she'd let you have a copy. Or would have just sent you a copy, not come all this way. I saw some pixilation that…" Her technical explanations would take too long to detail—nor was he interested in them. "It's just proof that it's been modified. It was an altered video. Without the hard copy, I can't tell you what was real and what was changed, but if it was changed at all—"

"I'd believe a lot of things about Garrett, but being after my parents' estate isn't one of them. None of that made sense, so it makes just as much sense it's altered video."

"Well. Good." He believed her and in his brother and… good.

"They showed me that for a reason," Nate said, staring at the table Courtney had put her laptop on. "They want me to think Garrett is against me and Courtney isn't. But it has to be more than that. What do they care what I think?" Then he focused on her fully. "How did you know what was going on?"

Elsie went over to the phone hanging from the wall. She tapped the speaker. "I put a bug here." Then she pointed up at the light fixture, where she'd fastened a tiny camera that was as black as the fixture, making it hard to see if you weren't looking for it. "Video up there."

"You think of everything."

"Not everything," Elsie said, a slow, horrible realization taking hold. What did they care what he thought? That wasn't the important question.

"How did they know to include Savannah in this? And why send Courtney as messenger? It connects them. It connects both of them to whatever is going on."

"Maybe they think I'm too stupid to put that together."

Elsie shook her head. "If they thought you were stupid, they wouldn't work so hard to discredit you. They want you dead, but…they've had time to make that happen." There were too many contradictions. But there was one clear fact Elsie knew, and whatever happened because of it was all her fault.

"The problem is, if they know we made a connection to Courtney and Savannah, they know what I'm researching. They have to know or assume you know about Courtney and Savannah's connection."

"Or they're trying to get me to know. Maybe it supports this fake story about my parents' estate."

"Maybe." Too many twists and turns to see clearly. "I sent Mallory to get the laptop. That could help us answer some questions."

"How many more of these people are in your group?"

"Why?"

"I want someone on Garrett. And someone on my parents. I want…" Finally all that stoicism melted and his shoulders sagged. He sank into the seat at the table and rested his forehead on his palms. "Hell, I want this over."

Elsie swallowed at the tightness in her throat at all she wanted to tell him, to give him. She crossed to him, but she didn't know what to say.

He blew out a breath. "We need to get some rest. I think I heard somewhere that you can't take down military groups who make no sense when you're exhausted." He got up and took her hand. She was so surprised by the move, she let herself be led into the back of the cabin where there was a bedroom. A *bedroom*.

"No funny business, Rogers," he said, walking with her into the tiny room.

She laughed and flipped on the light. The room was barely big enough for the twin bed that took up most of the floor space. She supposed it worked for whatever fishing weekend you might have, but it certainly wasn't going to fit two people.

"What about a little funny business?" she asked, looking up at him and hoping to take his mind off of all of this, if only for a moment.

She did get a half smile out of him. Then he looked at her that way he did that had all those fragile pieces of herself melding together until they almost felt stronger than anything that had come before. He pressed his lips to hers. A brief, gentle kiss.

It felt like a promise for something bigger than kisses or funny business. "Come on, Els. Let's sleep."

THEY DID IN fact sleep. She was dead on her feet before he'd even gotten her horizontal, and he wasn't far behind. He should have left her on the small twin bed and gone to sleep on the couch. But somehow he'd ended up tangled with her in the tiny bed. Sleeping.

Just sleeping.

There wasn't anything complicated about sleeping in the same bed as Elsie—he'd been dead to the world, after all—but, boy, was there something complicated about waking up with the woman. Elsie was all wrapped up around him, strands of her hair tickling his jaw, the steady rise and fall of her breathing making it next to impossible to move. His arm ached where he'd been shot, but he barely felt it when he looked at Elsie's sleeping face.

His life was wholly devoid of this type of thing. He lived on a ranch meant for rehabilitation, which meant he slept in bunks and was surrounded by men for the most part. Added to that, he kept to himself, focused on the mission of proving himself right or sane or *something*.

There wasn't a lot of softness in his life, and there never had been. But Elsie was soft, and lying with her felt like a kind of domestic comfort he'd never had or thought he'd wanted. It was strange to find contentment in it.

He couldn't dwell on that for long. He heard the faint squeak of a door being opened. No doubt Elsie's team already knew they'd crashed, but he doubted they knew he and Elsie had crashed together.

They certainly didn't need to draw any of the wrong conclusions.

Nate eased out of bed, carefully disentangling himself from Elsie. She murmured something then buried her face in the pillow and stilled.

Nate moved silently out of the bedroom.

Mallory was sitting on the couch, scrolling on a phone. She glanced up when he entered the room. "Could have slept longer. Looking a little rough there."

Nate grunted. "I was awake."

Elsie stumbled out of the room with a big, loud yawn. If Mallory thought anything of that, she kept it to herself.

"I've got the laptop," Mallory said to Elsie.

Elsie lurched forward. She said something, but it was mostly a mumbled garble.

"Coffee?" Nate asked, knowing Garrett would keep at least that in the kitchenette even if he hadn't stayed here in a while.

Elsie shook her head. "Does anyone have any pop?" She plopped herself at the little table.

Mallory put the laptop on the table and then went to the mini-fridge and pulled out a can of Coke. "I stocked up while you two got your beauty rest."

Elsie yawned and didn't tell her friend to go jump off the dock, so Nate figured she was a better morning person than he was.

"Do you subsist solely on sugar?" he muttered in Elsie's direction.

"If I can help it," Elsie replied. She was already studying the laptop, though she was looking at the outside, examining all the ports and jacks and whatnot. "You dusted for prints?"

Mallory nodded. "Collected what I could. It hadn't been wiped since her trip out here, but it might have been before that."

Elsie nodded then opened the laptop. She took a big gulp of pop, making Nate wince. But she got straight to work as if she was indeed powered solely by sugar. She frowned, tapped, leaned too close to the monitor. "It looks like it's only got the video on here. Imported from somewhere else."

"So, it's a dead end?"

Elsie made a *pfft* sound. "With computers, nothing is a dead end." She looked up at Nate, eyes soft and full of all those tangled emotions he hadn't quite figured out. "But this is going to take some time. You should probably talk to Garrett about everything."

Nate winced. God, that was the last thing he wanted to

do. He knew he had to, but that didn't make the prospect of actually doing it any easier.

"He's here," Mallory said.

Nate whirled to face her. "What?"

"Shay's orders." Mallory shrugged. "Once he got Don situated with the state, he started asking the kinds of questions we can't really have people asking, so Shay told me to pick him up."

"You kidnapped my brother?"

"I mean, I would have enjoyed that and all," Mallory said with a grin. When Nate did not return it, she sobered. "No. He came willingly." She nodded to the door. "I'll take you to him."

"Who's going to stay with Elsie?"

Elsie rolled her eyes. "I might survive what with the three other operatives patrolling the island."

Nate didn't particularly like that answer, but Garrett was here and deserved some answers. So, Nate followed Mallory outside.

"We figured it's his cabin, so it wouldn't raise too much suspicion for him to be here. And Courtney knew you were here, so it could be a brotherly fishing trip."

"Unless they know you guys are also here."

Mallory shrugged, leading Nate into the wooded area at the far end of the island. "Maybe they do. Maybe they don't. We'll do our jobs either way."

"I still don't understand your 'job,'" Nate muttered, ducking under a low branch.

"To help. It's just that simple." Mallory stopped in a small clearing. Garrett was pacing the area, Shay was sitting next to a small campfire.

Both Shay and Garrett looked up. Garrett stopped pacing but Shay stood. "We'll give you guys some privacy." She nodded to Mallory and they disappeared into the trees.

"Somehow I doubt we're really getting privacy," Garrett said, scowling at the trees.

"Yeah, me too. Mallory said you were asking questions."

"Yeah, I've got questions. I think I've got this all figured out, then a million what-ifs pop up. Someone tried to *kill* you, Nate. Someone was hired to take you out."

"Yeah, turns out corrupt military leaders don't take kindly to the truth."

"This isn't a joke."

"No, I guess not."

"Someone wanted you dead. I want answers. I want to know how we're going to stop that from becoming a reality. I can't sit in my office twiddling my thumbs. Not when a hitman is after my brother."

Nate wished he could feel comforted by that. Wished he could tell his brother this had nothing to do with him and he could take a hike—just so Garrett would be out of harm's way. But…well, aside from the fact Garrett wouldn't take any hikes, no matter how much of a jerk Nate pretended to be, Garrett was involved. At least tangentially.

Nate didn't know how to say that to Garrett, except plain and quick. "I'd love to tell you I can handle it, but unfortunately you're more connected than you think. Savannah is wrapped up in this somehow."

Garrett's expression shuttered. Immediately. It had been like that this entire year since Savannah had left. One mention had him closing everyone off. He didn't rage. He didn't get upset. He shut down.

"Apparently she's Courtney's cousin. They share a grandfather who's a vice admiral in the Navy. Those facts alone wouldn't be that big of a deal but—"

"Connected to military conspiracies, it's not so far-fetched."

"Yeah, and Savannah left when…"

Garrett's expression slackened. "When you told me. You…" He stood there, looking like he'd been shot. He'd gone pale. He turned away from Nate, stalked toward the trees then back into the clearing.

"Garrett—"

"You told me, and I told her I thought it was worth mentioning to a higher-up. Maybe you weren't quite adjusting the way we'd hoped, but maybe there was some seed of the truth in it. You gave me those printouts and…"

"And what?"

"They were gone when she left. I was dealing with other things, so it never occurred to me to connect it. It never occurred to me…"

"You never told me you were going to send those printouts to anyone." That there'd been some small belief mixed in with all the worry over him.

Garrett shrugged. "You were certain."

Nate didn't have time to deal with the emotions battering him. Garrett deserved the whole truth. "There's more."

"How could there possibly be more?" Garrett rasped.

"Savannah…died."

"What?"

"In childbirth." Nate swallowed. "With twins. Who survived."

"You're telling me I have children out there…and I… Where?"

Nate didn't know how to deal with the ragged emotion on his brother's face, or the fact that it wasn't even that simple. "They might not be yours, Garrett. But they're with Savannah's grandparents."

"If they were someone else's, don't you think they would be with that someone else?"

"We don't know. We just don't know."

"She didn't…" Garrett stood there, and Nate knew his world view was crumbling bit by bit. Nate had been in the same situation too many times to count. Everything you thought you knew or understood upended. All the people you thought you could trust turned out to be someone else.

"Look, Garrett, we're still figuring this all out. It's confusing and complex, and yeah, someone wants me dead for it. You're connected, so I want you to stay safe, but you don't have to—"

"Elsie. She's tech. Computers and hacking, right? And this team she's with… They don't have to follow laws, so to speak."

"They're the good guys, Garrett. I'm sure of it." He wasn't sure of much else. But that, he'd come to believe.

"I don't care about that. I need to know if those kids are mine. We need to know…where this started, and why you. We need to stop this, whatever it is. Someone wanted you dead, Nate."

"I think it's more than some*one*."

Garrett clearly did not find his words comforting. "I took that guy to the station, booked him and got him sent off to state. But I'm sitting there, hands tied, while you're with this group. Someone wanted you dead, and I was playing small-town cop. Now—"

"We need you to play small-town cop."

"Not anymore. I'm part of this now. You. Savannah. Whatever it ends up being, I'm part of it."

"I know I joke about the crime in Blue Valley, but you're the only cop. You have to be there."

"Even the only cop has sick days. I'll call Valley County to send out a detachment the next two or three days. Mrs. Linley will dispatch all calls to them."

"You sure?"

"Someone wants my brother dead. My ex-wife is dead and maybe left my children with her crooked family. Yeah, I'm damn sure."

Chapter Seventeen

Elsie's head throbbed and her vision was blurry, but she was used to that. Working at a computer screen day in, day out took a weird physical toll some days. But the part she wasn't used to, the churning, awful part, was realizing she might be a computer genius...but she was hardly the only one.

When the door opened, Elsie looked up from her computer. Nate and Garrett walked in, looking grim and handsome. They didn't make her nervous anymore. She trusted them, knew they were good men. Good men who'd been drawn into this awful thing simply because Nate had once wanted to do the right thing.

Shay came in next. "You got an update, Elsie?"

Elsie tried to smile, though she knew it faltered. "Do you want the bad news or the really bad news?"

"What is it?" Shay insisted.

Elsie took a shaky inhale. She'd made mistakes before. There was no way to be perfect when it came to computers or hacking. But she'd never felt the weight of responsibility sit quite so heavily on her shoulders. She'd never before felt quite so outmaneuvered. No one in this room was going to take any of her news well.

So, she had to be the calm one. The one who knew

what she was doing, even in the face of her own failure. "They've been tracking me."

"What? How?" Shay demanded.

"I haven't figured out the technology of it yet. It's virtually unheard of—in fact, a lot of tech people think it's an urban legend. It's complicated but, bottom line, they have a program that can attach to the hack and follow that computer's movements. As far as I can tell, they can't get a location or an IP, but they can watch your computer moves."

"So, they don't know it's *you*."

"No, but it wouldn't be hard to figure out. Maybe if I'd stayed at headquarters, but my arrival in Blue Valley... Nate's subsequent leaving Revival... Honestly? That hitman could have been after me as much as he could have been after Nate."

Shay swore. Nate looked apoplectic. Elsie felt strangely calm. What else was there to feel? They were all alive and well, and Elsie had caught on before an ambush had happened.

"But wait." Shay held out an arm. "That hitman was after Nate before I sent you here."

"Not exactly. We don't know where that hitman was. He certainly wasn't *here*, even when the hitman after Connor was in Wyoming. Maybe he didn't have a target yet. Maybe he had another one first. But I can't find any evidence Nate was ever the target there."

"This is my fault," Shay muttered.

That made Elsie feel a bit like a useless child. But she smiled at Shay and kept her voice even. "Don't go mourning me yet. I'm still alive."

Shay glared at her. "I shouldn't have sent you."

"You said there was no other choice."

"I should have found one."

"I'm not dead. I'm not even hurt." She pointed at Nate's arm, because he had been. "I wouldn't have found this if

I'd stayed. I wouldn't have figured it out if I didn't have *this* laptop. Besides, this is where we are. There's no room for should-have-beens. We have to deal with what is. Now, we can wait for them to show up—"

"Can someone clarify to me who this 'them' is?" Garrett said. He held himself still, much like Nate did. There were similarities in height and breadth of shoulders, dark hair and eyes. A lot of similarities. But they were two very different men.

Elsie exchanged a glance with Shay. Shay's imperceptible nod was the go-ahead to share what North Star knew.

"Connor took down Daria, right? He was stealing weapons from the military and selling them to a group—which our team took care of. Based on my research, I think we're dealing with either one guy or a small group of what I'd call idea men. Whoever set the whole thing into motion is removed enough, it's almost impossible to make a connection to the actual group doing wrong. That means all they have to do is start a new group—if they haven't already."

"Yet we know, thanks to Courtney and Savannah, one of these idea men has to be their grandfather," Nate said. "We wouldn't have known that if they hadn't showed some of their hand."

"But they've already existed in Blue Valley together, and no one's put it together until now," Garrett pointed out.

"Yes. Now. Before Courtney arrived, I put it together. Via the computer. That they're tracking. They know someone put together Savannah and Courtney *and* Vice Admiral Loren."

"Let's discuss Courtney for a second," Shay said. "Why is she putting herself in the middle of this? Why not take out Nate via explosives in the computer or something? She had sufficient chance."

"Why they haven't killed Nate is an interesting question. Because I have to believe they've had ample opportunity. They're tracking what I'm doing. That hitman? It makes more sense for me because I'm the one making connections. It made sense to go after Connor first because he's receiving evidence."

Nate swore under his breath.

"But listen. Everyone, think about this. For two years they haven't taken out Nate. He's dug into information and told people, but they haven't killed him. They've only worked to discredit him. To destroy his evidence. Presumably, they had someone marry his brother. Presumably, they had Courtney's brother installed at Revival. Why?"

Everyone was silent because there was no good answer to that question. But there was *an* answer.

"They think I have something," Nate murmured, his scowl deepening. "Something they need before they can kill me?"

"It isn't simple enough to just extract the information from you. There's more to it. They think you have something *big*." Elsie paused. She didn't want to believe Nate was still holding back, but he had before. Multiple times. "Do you?"

"Not that I'm aware of."

"Why not kidnap him, then?" Shay said. "Force him to give the information. Or hurt his family. Blackmail. Why not force the information out of him?"

"I'm not sure. But I think it has to do with Nate not being aware. They're waiting for him to do something. But we interfered. And still, the worst they did was send Courtney out here to try to convince Nate that Garrett was against him, setting him up all for their family money."

"The *worst* they did was send a hitman for you," Nate growled.

Elsie knew that everyone was frustrated, confused and irritable because of it. But these were the kinds of puzzles that made sense to her, even when they didn't.

"The important thing is, I didn't think this kind of tech they've got was possible. But it is. That means I can turn it around on them."

"You can?"

Elsie nodded. "With the right plant. We need something to happen. Something they'd want to look into—and then I could turn their trap around on them."

"Like what?"

"Courtney gave me the idea, actually. She acted like she was concerned Nate would hurt himself, even insinuated he might end his life. What if they thought he did?"

NATE FOUND HIMSELF SPEECHLESS. He'd been thrown a lot of curveballs, but faking his own suicide was pretty up there.

"Fake kill him ourselves?" Shay asked.

"They want something from him, and they're afraid to get close enough to get it. So—" Elsie shrugged "—we eliminate the threat. I think suicide makes the most sense, since that's what Courtney was getting at."

Nate didn't know what to say. Garrett rubbed his hands over his face and Shay stood stock-still, presumably absorbing the information and coming up with a plan.

Nate had no idea how he'd ended up here, with multiple people believing him, setting up traps to prove everything he'd believed alone for so long.

"They'd need to be sure," Elsie continued. "They'd have someone hacking into police reports, hospital records, maybe even death records. All I'd need to do is watch for it. From there, I can use their own tactics against them. I bet they've got a lot more to hide than we do."

"Won't they just find out it's a fake?" Shay asked.

"I could make the documents look real, but I think it's better if it's fake," Elsie returned. "They'll think we think we've pulled one over on them, but what we're really doing is setting a trap. We watch them, instead of them watching us. We make sense of it, and once we do, we can really stop them."

"I'm sorry. You can't put my parents through this. Or Revival. It isn't right. It isn't fair."

Elsie's gaze met his. "While I'd argue the ends justify the means, we don't have to. We've got Blue Valley's sheriff right here." She pointed to Garrett. "We've got the tech expert who's going to fake the records." She gestured to herself. "We don't need to bring in anyone else to make it look real. We only need *them* to think it's real, and then do one search on one specific event, and then I've got them."

"You're sure?" Shay asked.

"Thanks to Courtney's computer, I'm positive."

"So, what do we do?" Garrett asked. He sounded tired, and everything about his expression and the bleak look in his eyes reminded Nate of when Savannah had first left. Garrett had been wrecked, and this was the same. If not worse.

Before he could help his brother through his turmoil, they had to end *this* thing.

"Does anyone know you're out here, Garrett?"

"When Mallory so insistently said I had to come with her, I told Mrs. Linley I had a meeting and to route dispatch through Valley County. I didn't say where the meeting was or who it was with."

"So, you'll call in a potential suicide and—"

"No, I can't lie to Mrs. Linley. Not about that. If I tell her where I am, she'll know. Besides, she'd have it spread around Blue Valley and Revival in five seconds flat."

"Okay. Well, what if you called her to say you were going to check on your brother at your cabin? She doesn't have to know the end result we're trying to create, and you'll be able to help me generate a fake report from here."

Garrett clearly didn't like it, but he nodded. "Okay. Then what?"

Elsie and Garrett hashed out the details of medical examiners and records. Of his fake death. Nate didn't have anything to add to all that. It was mostly just an out-of-body experience standing in the middle of his brother's fishing cabin while people *helped*.

But he didn't have time to be completely useless. He had to think over two years of events—even ones like Savannah leaving, which felt unrelated—and try to figure out why this group wanted *him* alive, but weren't going to press him for the information they needed.

He had no possible idea what they could think he had, but he supposed he should be grateful for whatever it was.

Garrett was leaning over Elsie's computer. "All this is how you figured out Savannah died?" Garrett asked Elsie, frowning at the screen.

Elsie looked at Nate briefly and then nodded at Garrett. "I promise you, when I can, I will use whatever is at my disposal to either get some kind of paternity check, or to prove that you have a right to one."

Garrett inhaled, but he shook his head. "First, we do this."

"Yeah. First we do this." She looked up at Nate and offered a smile. A clear attempt to lighten the mood. "Just a couple Blue Valley kids taking down military corruption. Who would have guessed?"

Chapter Eighteen

When Elsie looked up from her computer some time later, she was alone. Well, she doubted she *was* alone. Neither Shay nor Nate would leave her unsupervised, but the cabin was empty save her.

She rolled her shoulders and rubbed her eyes. She'd worked through the night, but that had been fine because she'd slept for half the day yesterday. She'd been totally unaware of people coming and going, so she had no idea if people were asleep, outside or what.

She'd done all the work to make it look like Nate had died. It was going to be a pain to undo, but she'd cross that bridge when she came to it.

For now, for all intents and purposes, Nate looked dead to someone who would look. Since she'd had Garrett call Courtney and ask her to come into his office today to make an official statement about her visit to the fishing cabin, she thought Vice Admiral Loren or someone he employed would start looking into that death soon.

If Courtney didn't spread the word to her grandfather, they'd have to come up with a new way to carefully make sure he got the information.

Elsie got up and stretched. She needed a five-minute break from looking at the monitor, and then she'd get back to it. Waiting for *someone* to start looking into Nate's alleged death.

She looked out the window. Everyone was outside in the dim light of morning—Shay, Mallory, Gabriel, Connor, Nate *and* Garrett. It was the thing she'd always appreciated about being part of North Star. No matter how bad things got, they were a team. They worked together and fought together. All without coming unglued.

For a while there, Elsie had only known how to come unglued. North Star had saved her from that, and now here she was. In Blue Valley. With people who'd known her then and people who knew her now.

She hadn't fallen apart. She wouldn't. She had a job to do. She'd do it because North Star meant the world to her. She'd do it because…well, now so did Nate.

She sighed and watched as it looked like they were putting up targets for doing some sort of practice.

Guns and shooting. No thank you. Elsie would stay inside and keep to her computer work. She got herself a can of Coke and then settled back at the computer.

It didn't take much longer, and she got so absorbed in what she was doing, she didn't even hear the gunshots outside. Someone was poking into things. Now, all she had to do was run her program.

She got lost in it, like she always did. Here, she was all powerful. She got everything she needed to use Courtney's computer to reverse the program that would now stalk their every move. She might even be able to hack into a computer or two—figure out who was behind it.

Her fingers flew over the keys and she ignored the crick in her neck.

"Jackpot," she muttered. Emails. Including one about a chartered plane. She jumped to her feet and hurried outside. They were still shooting, and Elsie tried not to let her distaste show as she crossed to Shay. Gabriel liked to give her a hard time for being squeamish about guns while working for a secretive group that used a *lot* of heavy artillery. She understood why North Star operatives or even police officers needed to practice this kind of thing, but there was nothing about the noise or the machines themselves that Elsie had ever found any comfort with.

Elsie kept her distance until Shay told them all to stand down.

"Come to show us how it's done?" Shay asked.

Nate eyed her skeptically. "*Can* she show us how it's done?" he asked, clearly not believing Elsie'd had any training. It was hard to blame him. She'd been a shaky mess when holding the gun earlier.

"She's a phenomenal shot," Shay said proudly. "When she's not nervous," she added.

"Really?" Nate clearly thought Shay was trying to pull one over on him.

Elsie lifted her chin. She was not going to be drawn into this banter. "I really prefer to *not* handle guns."

Before she could tell them all that they had more important things to concern themselves with, Nate moved to pass her his gun. "Show me."

She didn't take the gun, but there was something in his expression. Not disbelief exactly, but a kind of good-natured humor that was hard to resist. "Fine," she muttered and took the gun.

They'd hung debris from tree branches using fishing line, so that the targets fluttered and moved with the breeze. Elsie chose three pop cans, raised the gun and aimed. She nailed three cans in a row. She could have done more but she *really* didn't like guns.

She looked over at Nate. "Satisfied?"

Garrett let out a low whistle and Shay was chuckling. Nate was smiling, and it made that fragile thing flutter in her chest, which she was very afraid Shay would see right through. For some reason, the thought of tough, indestructible Shay potentially seeing what she felt for Nate embarrassed her.

"Now, can we focus on what's really important?" she said primly, carefully handing Nate his gun.

"What's that?" Shay asked.

"Loren chartered a private plane about an hour after Garrett called Courtney. He'll be landing in Bozeman in about three hours, barring any airplane difficulties."

THE CABIN WAS a hive of activity. Plans were tossed out, rejected, altered, rejected again. Nate stood in the middle of it all and felt a bit like a Navy SEAL again.

There was something comforting about the fact it didn't fit so well. Though he'd been discharged, he had no desire to go back. It eased something inside him he hadn't even known he'd worried about.

He might not know what came next when all this was over, but he knew he didn't want to go back into the military, even if he was cleared.

Cleared. He still didn't know how to wrap his mind around that, so he figured he should focus on the people around him. Who were trying to find a plan to get to the bottom of this. Once and for all.

"We'll want a full team at the airport," Shay was saying. "We can't get around that."

"And one of us has to lead the team," Gabriel pointed out. "Me or Mal or Shay."

"Granger could—"

"My family is in danger here. Especially with Justin at Revival. Keep Granger with my family," Elsie said firmly.

Shay nodded, and Nate was a bit surprised she didn't pull rank and tell Elsie how it was going to be. They weren't like any team he'd ever been part of. Shay was clearly the one who made the final decisions, but she listened. She considered. It didn't have to be her way or the highway.

"You don't need to babysit me," Elsie said, frowning at her computer. "You can all go."

"Nate can't," Garrett pointed out. "He's *dead*."

"So, I'll stay here and watch after Elsie."

"Garrett, too," Shay said, standing.

"I can—"

She shook her head. "You're the distraught brother, and the fact of the matter is, we don't know what's going on. He's coming here, but why? I want pairs."

"Do I not count?" Elsie demanded.

"Not with your nose in a computer, you don't. You do your thing, Garrett and Nate will guard you so you can fully concentrate on *your* mission. I'll take Mallory with me to the airport. Gabriel and Connor will go keep an eye on Courtney. Surely, if Loren comes here, he's going to hook up with his granddaughter at some point."

The activity went full buzz as they hashed out details, plans, com units. Nate got lost in it all, until everyone was gone, and it was just him, Garrett and Elsie in the cabin.

Elsie was sitting cross-legged on a rickety chair, nose pressed to her screen. None of those light-blocking glasses, and it didn't look like she'd done anything but mainline pop.

"You should take a break. Eat something with substance."

Elsie gave him an eye roll. "I'm working."

Nate grumbled what he thought of that and then slammed around the kitchenette, fixing her some kind of lunch. There wasn't much to work with since Garrett didn't keep it stocked and everything had to be stored in canisters to keep the mice out. But there was some string cheese in the fridge that hadn't expired, and some trail mix in a container in the cabinet.

He put the plate on top of her keyboard. "Eat that."

She looked up from the screen and glared at him. "Do you have to be so bossy about it?"

"Do you have to be so ridiculous about taking care of yourself? You need a keeper."

"Oh, do I? Were you volunteering for the task or was it assigned to you?"

Garrett cleared his throat. Nate had fully forgotten about his brother's presence until that moment.

"I'll, uh, just…take a walk. Check things out," Garrett said and then backed out of the cabin. Quickly.

Nate looked at Elsie. Clearly, they weren't really arguing about food, and *clearly* it was absolutely the wrong time to argue about anything. "I shouldn't let him out there alone."

"No, you shouldn't," she agreed. Sitting there. Staring at him. The temper in her eyes had dulled into something else. "I've got work to do." She pointed to her computer.

Nate nodded. But he didn't move. They didn't have time for this, but it bubbled up inside him. Bigger and more confusing with every passing hour.

So, he kissed her. Because, no matter how little sense *that* made—or yelling at her about taking care of herself— it was the one thing he knew he wanted. The rest was a confusing jumble of noise. But Elsie's mouth on his? Arms wrapping around his neck?

Yeah, that was clear. "I don't know what this is," he murmured against her mouth, because at least that was honest. Even if it didn't help.

Elsie looked up at him from her seat at the table, wide-eyed, her arms still wrapped around his neck. "I don't, either."

"Well, as long as we're on the same page." He thought about kissing her again, even in this awkward position, but she disentangled herself from him. And that was a surprise. She'd been the one who'd wanted to take it a step further earlier, or yesterday, or whenever that had been. Now she was getting out of her chair, putting space between them and looking at him with a wariness he didn't understand.

"Eventually, this will be over," she said, clasping her hands together. "And I'll go back to Nor—my group, and you'll go back to Revival."

She at least seemed disappointed about that, even if he would have preferred her *looking* for a way they could be together. But he was struck by a new thought before he could fully absorb the hurt of hers. "If this is really over, I won't need Revival anymore."

She swallowed and looked down at her feet. He didn't know why. Didn't know what she was feeling. But it didn't matter, did it? It wasn't his job to figure out *her* feelings. It was his job to figure out his own.

In a way, he'd learned an odd lesson when no one had believed him. He just had to do his own thing. Make his own plans. Follow what he thought to be right, no matter what.

Even when people didn't think you were crazy, that was the way you built a life. Sometimes it might be right to lie or to try to deal with someone else's feelings because you cared about them. Doing what was right didn't mean doing whatever you wanted.

Yet sometimes, it had to be…laying out what you wanted. No matter what a person thought or did with that information.

He took her by the chin so she had to look at him. He didn't know what he saw in her expression. Something like fear, which didn't fully make sense to him. Or maybe it did. Wasn't part of what was rolling around in his gut *fear*?

"I don't know what happens next for me, but I hope you can figure out a way to be a part of it."

Her eyes widened and she swallowed, but she didn't

say anything. Not yes or no. And that was fine. She could think about it. They had time. Sort of.

He let go of her chin. "I'm going to go stick with Garrett. We'll keep the cabin in sight. Yell if you need anything or find anything."

She nodded, watching him go, clearly reeling. The kind of reeling a person needed to figure out on their own.

Garrett hadn't gone far. He was picking up the shells from their shooting endeavor this morning and dropping them into an old coffee can.

"Want some help?"

"Sure."

They worked in silence for a while, until Garrett paused and studied at him for a good minute. "Elsie Rogers, huh?"

Nate shrugged uncomfortably. "Guess so."

"Smart."

"Yeah, so?"

Garrett laughed. "That was a compliment. Man, you've got it bad."

"I don't know what I've got," Nate grumbled, hunching his shoulders. "She's got no plans to stick around here and I…" Blue Valley was home. After Revival seemed like a pipe dream, but he didn't want to leave. He didn't need to get out anymore, like he had as a teen.

He needed to stay.

"Dad could always use the help," Garrett said casually enough. But it struck Nate that his brother immediately realized he wouldn't need to stay at Revival any longer, as well.

"Yeah, maybe." But no matter how much closer to his future than he'd been a few days ago, there were still some answers to find before he could make those decisions.

They finished cleaning up then walked the length of shore that allowed them to keep the cabin in sight. Both searching the horizon for a threat. Something.

All was calm and quiet. Almost peaceful. As time stretched out, it was almost possible to believe peace might be an option.

But then Elsie darted out of the cabin, running toward them.

"What is it?" Nate demanded.

She came to a stop in front of them, breathing a little heavily. "It was a decoy. The man who got off the plane." She heaved in and out a breath. "It wasn't Vice Admiral Loren."

"You think he knows we know he's coming?" Garrett asked.

"I really don't know what to think. It might have just been a precaution. I didn't know until he was already in the air, so it's difficult to believe he somehow figured out I'd gotten into his computer system before they sent the decoy."

"He wasn't on that plane, but that doesn't mean he's not coming," Nate said, scanning the horizon again. "What's Shay's next step?"

"They're all heading for Courtney. They'll keep watch there until someone shows up."

Nate nodded. "Good."

Chapter Nineteen

Elsie didn't like the look Nate and Garrett exchanged, but she didn't like any of this. Down to Nate saying things like he hoped she'd be part of his life.

Life.

North Star might have saved her, but it had also been an opportunity to ignore all that *life* around her. Not constantly be there while her sisters built relationships and marriages and *lives*. Had kids and raised them. Elsie preferred to be proud of them…from a distance. See a glimpse of it then go far away and bury herself in a computer screen.

"What if he doesn't go for Courtney?" Garrett asked.

Elsie was reminded she had a *job* to do, not a personal crisis to deal with. "I have to get back and watch the computer movements. It might tell us something, but I want at least one of you guys to keep an eye on Mal's body cam so we see what happens as it happens."

They immediately followed her back to the cabin. She set up her computer for Nate and Garrett. "You'll be able to see what Mal sees, and hear most everything," Elsie explained. "If there's trouble, we'll deal with it." If she had to call Granger off her family…

She shook her head as she settled herself in front of her computer. She couldn't think about that. One step at a time.

Surely Loren, if he was really coming, would head straight for Courtney. Nothing else made sense. Now Courtney had four people on her, so clearly North Star was in good position to deal with that.

"They're just watching Courtney and Don's place," Nate said, studying the screen in front of him and Garrett. "Not moving. Not talking."

"So Loren hasn't arrived yet."

"Presumably. Maybe he's not coming."

Maybe. Elsie dug into the charter plane reservation. It appeared to be for Loren, so it was clearly meant to be a decoy. That meant she had to find some other kind of travel information.

"She mentioned working for a group," Elsie mused, delving deeper into what she was beginning to believe was Loren's computer.

"She didn't care if we knew about the group. That's fishy, isn't it? Even if she was pretending to be black-mailed by them, she was acknowledging and clarifying their existence."

Elsie nodded, hit a few more keys. "Maybe she's going rogue from the group?"

"Yet she was still trying to turn me against Garrett."

Elsie tried to listen and work, but eventually she got caught up enough in what she was doing that she tuned Nate and Garrett out as they discussed Savannah and Courtney. She put all her tech people on Loren. The program he'd run to watch her, his emails, his bank records. The more eyes they had on this, the quicker they could find…something.

Elsie wasn't sure how much time had passed when she finally found something of interest, or if anything had happened on the monitor, but this could be a clue as to Loren's whereabouts. "I don't think Loren was in DC in the first place," Elsie announced.

"Where else would he be?" Nate asked.

"I found a credit card. It's not Loren's, but it's connected to the computer. I could figure it out for sure, but we don't have time. There's a hotel charge in Bozeman for the past week."

"That's before you came," Nate pointed out.

"But not before we got your name," Elsie returned, looking up from her computer. "We had a few days with your name before I got here."

"Your group telling tales out of turn?" Garrett said, his voice cool.

Elsie tried not to be offended, though it was hard. North Star wasn't dirty. It wasn't possible, considering she manned the computers, background checks and the like. "No. No, but… We got your name from another group. A group with their own agenda. It's possible someone on that side either purposefully let it slip or accidentally. I don't know their tech person's credentials."

"You sure it couldn't have come from your group?"

Elsie pulled her gaze away from the computer to look Nate straight in the eye. "Positive."

"Okay," he said with a nod. Believing her. Or at least trying to.

"Why wait? None of this waiting makes sense," Garrett said. "It's giving us time to understand everything. To protect Nate. I'm glad he's not more of a target before he's ready, but why?"

"I don't know if this answers anything, but there's another line one of my guys found when looking at bank records." It didn't all make sense, but she knew there was something there. She jotted notes as she went through what her subordinate had sent her. They'd followed a payment through its circuitous route to… "This all started when you were in Yemen, right?"

Nate nodded.

Elsie frowned at her computer. "Loren is paying someone in Yemen. Sums of money over the past two years. There isn't a great pattern, except it's a lot of money and it starts at Loren's personal bank account, then he hides it, and then the receiver hides it. But I can track it. Why would he be paying someone in Yemen? Repeatedly. For two years."

"Blackmail?" Garrett asked. "Someone there knows what he's doing and is demanding payment?"

"Could be," Nate agreed. "My civilian informant knew about Daria, sort of. I certainly wouldn't have gotten that far on Daria without him leading me to answers."

"This could be him, then."

Nate shook his head sadly. "Died in the explosion."

"Someone who knew him? Knew what he was doing? This kind of money screams blackmail." Elsie clicked on the email another tech agent had sent her and skimmed the information. "Or ransom."

"Ransom?"

"Loren has a recording on his computer. It's a garbled message, but the basic gist is 'we have your son.'"

"Who's Loren's son?"

Elsie switched gears. She'd looked at Loren's family and knew there was a son, but she'd been preoccupied with Courtney and Savannah. "Ewan Loren. Courtney's father." Elsie did a remedial search and it took no time to find… "He was reported missing from a military base in Yemen."

"When?"

Elsie pointed at the date.

"That's the day after I was injured," Nate said flatly.

"What does all that mean?" Garrett asked, clearly irritated with the way nothing seemed to add up.

He'd have to join the club. "I don't know."

NATE WAS STARTING to get a picture of what was happening. It wasn't fully clear. It didn't fully make sense. But there was something to this.

"What was he doing at a military base?" Nate asked carefully, trying to weave the disparate threads in his mind together. "You said Courtney's military connection beyond Justin was her grandfather."

"There aren't any military records for Ewan." Elsie tapped keys and frowned. "Nothing that I can find."

"Why was a civilian at the military base in Yemen?"

"To visit his father?"

"Loren wasn't there." Nate shook his head. "Daria was there."

"So, the son is part of it. Somehow. Working with Daria. Then he's there, doing whatever, and you have a local civilian who knew about it. Maybe he's the reason someone took Ewan and has been extorting money out of Loren."

"It doesn't explain Nate's connection," Garrett insisted.

"I know," Elsie agreed. "But we keep finding as we dig. Maybe we'll find the connection. But we know there is one. There has to be one."

"If Loren is in Bozeman, he hasn't made a move for Courtney yet," Nate said. "At least, as long as we've been watching. Maybe you should send your team to the hotel."

"That's Shay's call, but I'll update her and suggest it."

Elsie picked up the com unit Shay had left her and spoke in low tones. Nate watched the video and Garrett watched out the cabin window.

Nate tried to make sense of what Elsie's tech team had found out. The civilian who'd basically exposed Daria to Nate had been killed in the explosion. Nate had assumed it was something set by the insurgent group they'd been trying to find, but what if…

What if Daria had known about the civilian informant,

or had found out, and had had him killed. Maybe Nate was supposed to have been killed, as well.

But then, why not kill him anytime in the past two years? What was keeping Nate alive? All this time? While they actively worked to discredit him, push him into PSTD or mental illness or something.

"Shay's sending Gabriel and Connor to Bozeman. Mallory and Shay are staying on Courtney."

"We need to be looking out here, too," Nate said. "If Loren wasn't getting off that plane, if he knows more than we think he knows, we could be the target as easily as him connecting with Courtney."

Elsie nodded. "I'll transfer the body cam feeds to my tech people so we can focus on information and making sure no one shows up here."

"Good."

They rearranged. Garrett stationed at the window, watching the docks. Nate watched the side window. On the other side of the island, the rocks would prevent anyone from landing. This was the only access point to the island, and they could see the entire shoreline from the two windows.

There were other possibilities. Someone could parachute in. They could attempt to navigate the rocky shore on the other side. Military men with deep pockets were certainly capable of the equipment needed to do those things, but it would require so much work. And once again, Nate had to go back to the fact that they hadn't tried to kill him or to terrorize him.

Something was protecting him. God knew what.

Yet no matter how long he stood watch at the window, he couldn't work it out. No matter how many connections Elsie made… Maybe that was the takeaway here.

None of it mattered. Not really. The hows. The whys. Maybe it only mattered that they ended things one way or another. Elsie's group was working on it. He and Garrett were helping.

And someone was closing in on them. So maybe the only directive here was to survive.

"We've got company," Garrett said grimly.

"Already?" Elsie said, alarmed enough to look up from her computer.

Nate moved to the front window. "How many?" He looked over Garrett's shoulder and out the window.

"Two boats that I see. Two in each. Nobody I know."

Nate scanned the lake in front of them. He hadn't been able to see this end from his vantage point, but there were, in fact, two small boats. Motorboats, speedy and agile. But not silent.

"They don't care that we might know they're coming."

"If they think you're dead, maybe this is just a 'make sure he is' type thing," Elsie suggested.

"Possibly."

"We need a better vantage point." Garrett looked back at Nate. He didn't need to speak what he had in mind for Nate to understand.

"You think it'll hold the three of us?"

"Maybe. Maybe not. But if we can get one shooter up there, it's better than being sitting ducks in this cabin that can be surrounded."

Elsie grabbed his arm before he could tell her to get ready to hike. "You have to stay out of sight. They think you're dead. They wouldn't have time to prove otherwise yet."

Nate pulled himself out of her grasp then took her by the shoulders. "If they think *I'm* dead, I doubt they sent four men after me. That means they're likely here for *you* and what you can do with your computers. Now, come on."

She shook her head, gesturing helplessly at her computer. "I can't find the connections if I go with you."

"You can't find the connections if you're dead. We're running out of time."

Elsie blew out a breath then marched away from him. In a whirl of movement, she shoved the laptop into a backpack and slid her arms into straps. She took her gun and held it.

"You can't carry—"

"It's Courtney's laptop. I'll toss it in the lake if I have to. But I'm going to keep it with me for right now in case I have a chance to do more digging."

Nate looked at Garrett, who shrugged.

"Fine," he muttered. "Out the back." He pointed to the back door and Elsie and Garrett followed. "Once we're outside, don't say a word. You need attention, tap someone." He looked sternly at both of them. "Not a word. Not a noise."

Garrett nodded and Elsie saluted him. Like this was a joke. But he saw the way she gripped that gun till her knuckles were white—and she hated guns. Preferred her computer. Maybe she needed to lighten the mood.

"Garrett first. Then Elsie. Then me. Go."

They funneled out, a single-file line heading immediately for the cover of the trees. The four men in boats wouldn't be too far behind. Nate figured he'd have about a five-to ten-minute head start.

So, they had to book it.

The terrain was rough, the tree cover dense, but Garrett knew this island like the back of his hand. Nate hadn't spent much time here since he'd been a kid, but he and Garrett had spent days upon days out here back then, pretending to be frontiersman and such.

But this was more important. This could be life and death. They hiked in silence. Nate was impressed. Elsie tripped over a rock at one point and didn't make a peep even as he caught her from falling with a jarring jerk of the arm. She mouthed a thank-you instead and kept walking.

They finally got to the highest point of the island. Twenty some years ago, Nate and Garrett had worked all summer to build the tree house that still sat on the branches of an old, thick tree.

"It's a tree house," Elsie said, in an awed whisper, looking up at the structure in the leaves.

"Yeah. It is. You're up first."

Chapter Twenty

Elsie eyed the planks nailed to the tree that were allegedly supposed to hold her weight as she climbed the giant tree and into the rough-hewn house above. A *tree* house.

She looked over her shoulder at Nate and Garrett, standing there like twin sentries who certainly weren't going to let her chicken out.

She swallowed. It wasn't that she was afraid of heights so much as she was afraid of *falling*. But falling was better than getting captured or shot.

Probably.

She handed Nate her gun and then started climbing, and immediately felt Nate below her. Almost around her. Like he was closing her in. That should have been a claustrophobic feeling...but it very much wasn't.

"The adage is true," he said into her ear. "Don't look down."

"But when you say that to people, they want to look down," Elsie said, taking the next rung and very, very much wanting to look down. To see how far she'd come. Her eyes wandered, she couldn't help it.

She blew out a breath and scowled. They weren't even a few feet off the ground.

"Just climb," Nate ordered, though there was some

amusement in his tone. "And when you make real progress, don't look down."

They climbed, and it wasn't so bad when it felt like if she did fall or stumble, Nate's strong body was right there to catch her.

She managed to reach the top and scramble onto the floor of the structure. She held herself very still, half expecting it to sway or to crumble.

But it didn't. It held her weight, and then Nate's and Garrett's, still feeling sturdy beneath her body. There were walls on three sides, seemingly drilled or nailed or roped to the thick tree branches, but one side was mostly open into the leafy tree branches.

Elsie tried to swallow her anxiety. She glanced up from her sprawled position on the floor, to see Nate and Garrett both standing there looking down at her, twin expressions of concern mixed with amusement.

She wanted to be offended by that, but they didn't have time. Garrett moved to the open side and began to hack away at branches with a pocketknife. Once he'd cut a bunch of them off, the vantage point to the shore was clear, without cutting so much away that they could be seen in return.

"What now?" Elsie asked, pushing herself up into a sitting position. She wasn't quite ready to stand in here yet. No matter how sturdy beneath her body, she knew how high they were and, surely, that was precarious.

"We watch what they do," Nate said. "I guess you were right about bringing your computer. You can sit there and tap away while we watch."

"And if they start coming for us?" Elsie asked.

Nate and Garrett exchanged a look. "Let's take it one step at a time."

She did not trust that response, or that look, but she was sitting in a tree house. With two grown men. Watching for people with guns to come hunt them down.

Elsie looked around the small structure dubiously, but Nate and Garrett moved with sure feet and confidence the wood structure would hold.

Please.

She scooted into the corner of two of the walls, leaned against the wall gingerly, then pulled the computer out of her backpack. She set up her hot spot again and checked her messages from her team. She skimmed the information. There were new layers, but nothing groundbreaking or that fully explained any of this.

She went through the information again, looking for an angle they may have missed or glossed over. She let the work distract her from where she was and what was going on.

The nonmilitary son being taken was something. *Something.* And what exactly were the payments? Ransom? It had been two years. Why would a smart, capable, military commander keep paying someone if they weren't returning the son?

A message from one of her techs popped up.

Some money coming back over to US side. Connects to someone in Montana. Still narrowing down. Sharing screen with you.

Elsie immediately switched over to the screen. She followed the twists and turns, then started her own search. Through all sorts of computer programs meant to hide the money and its eventual endgame. Elsie dug and dug and dug, and then almost dropped the laptop.

Courtney.

But why would she be taking money from the group in Yemen? The group that allegedly had her father?

Elsie had to dig deeper, and fast, but Nate was swearing.

Elsie looked up. Both men were standing there, pointing to the shore in the distance.

"It's not random-looking. They're tracking us," Garrett

said grimly. "Should be hard once they get in the trees, but they can see the direction we went from the cabin."

"Hard to track us, but not impossible for them to be led right here," Nate said, his voice matching Garrett's for grimness. "We'll go down. Elsie will stay here. We can each take two, don't you think?"

"You might be a little rusty," Garrett said.

"Yeah, and you might be a little old."

They grinned at each other and Elsie gaped at them. "What is wrong with you two?"

Nate chuckled and shook his head. "Brothers. Now." He pulled the gun she'd handed off to him so she could climb up, then crouched in front of her and held it out. "Stay put. Don't climb down, no matter what. If someone who isn't us or your group tries to climb up, shoot them."

Elsie looked at the gun. She didn't want to take it. She didn't want them to go down there and start trying to fight off men. "I'll call Shay. She'll send everyone back and—"

"No time. You can certainly call for backup, but this has to be dealt with now. We can handle this, Elsie. Take the gun."

She did, though reluctantly. "I feel like I need to remind you my aim goes to hell when I'm nervous."

He took her by the chin, looked her right in the eye. "Then don't be nervous, Els. You're a hell of a shot, and we're all going to come out of this on the other side just fine."

It was a platitude at best. He couldn't guarantee that, but she nodded anyway. Because she knew he needed to think he'd given her some confidence, some surety.

So she pretended, because as he and Garrett climbed down, she was none of those things.

GARRETT HAD ONE pair of handcuffs. Nate found some rope that had once hung from a branch as a tire swing. It was frayed, but it might do the trick for a quick hold. He used his pocketknife to cut quick lengths of it and then handed a few to Garrett.

Garrett may have never been in the military, but he understood Nate's quick hand signals. From the base of the tree house, they spread out.

If the men coming had any tactical experience, they'd move forward in sets of two. One pair would follow whatever tracks they found and the other would be watching for signs of life.

Nate scanned the area for tracks himself. Or anything that might lead the men to Elsie. A few prints in the mud, a few broken twigs. Nothing too overt, but Nate didn't have any idea what kind of trackers these men were.

He wouldn't let anyone get to Elsie, no matter what it took. That meant he had to calm himself. Focus. Slow his raging heart so he could hear above its thundering beat. He took a moment to breathe, to center.

Then he inched forward, gun in hand. He moved silently, listening, watching. He kept an eye on Garrett. They were yards away from each other, each moving forward carefully.

Nate heard someone talking and stopped, moving behind a tree. When he couldn't make out the murmurings, he moved closer. Avoiding twigs and anything that would make noise with ease.

"Yeah. Okay. So what?" There was a pause. "You handle the computers. We'll handle the confrontation."

Nate could see the man now. He was on the phone. Nate didn't see anyone else around him, but the guy held a powerful sniper rifle with an impressive scope. As he talked on the phone, his grip on the gun loosened and his alertness to the world around him waned.

Nate filed away what he'd heard, but he couldn't think

about or analyze the information right now. He had to take his moment and disarm him.

It was easy enough. The man had been so preoccupied with a phone call, he hadn't been listening for Nate's approach. A quick grapple and Nate used the rope he had to tie the guy's wrists and ankles.

"You won't stop all of us," the man growled, clearly trying to get out of his bonds. Nate wasn't sure how long they'd hold, but he took the gun and the phone. He searched the man's pockets, narrowly avoided a head butt.

He looked right at the man. "Watch me."

Nate didn't frown, but he studied the man's face and knew something was…off. Maybe the guy was a good shot, and he was certainly dressed tactically, but he didn't hold himself like military or anyone skilled in tracking or combat. He was wrestling with the bonds in a way that would only tire him out.

Nate stepped away, dread skittering up his spine. Something was off, but he didn't have time to figure out what. He glanced back at the tree house, half a thought to send Garrett back there to keep watch—though the chances of his brother listening to him were slim. Still…

Nate heard the *snick* of a tree branch being stepped on. A total lack of tactical strategies. The phone call. The noise. Could be accidents, extenuating circumstances, but Nate didn't have the feeling he was dealing with trained assassins here.

So, who the hell *was* he dealing with?

Still, these men were armed. So, trained or not, Nate needed to disarm them. He moved around where the noise had come from. He made someone out through the heavy brush, and then advanced from behind. The man hadn't even turned before Nate had him on the ground, securing his wrists behind his back.

It wasn't even hard, and the quick ease of taking these

men down had a cold ball of dread sitting in Nate's stomach. Still, he tied the man's wrists and then flipped him over so he could do the same to his ankles.

The guy had to be in his seventies. And, while he was in good physical shape, why would anyone send an older man to do a young man's job?

"Where is my son?" the old man demanded, wriggling against the bonds.

Nate blinked, fumbled, but quickly recovered and got the man's ankles tied tightly. It dawned on him, no matter how little sense it made, that this was Loren himself.

"Why do you think I have your son?"

"Why do you think you're alive?" the man said, wriggling like the other captive. Desperate to escape the bonds. He wouldn't escape. He'd be exhausted by the time he managed to get any sort of freedom.

Nate almost felt sorry for him.

Nate heard the approach of someone else and ignored Loren and the other guy for a moment as he readied for another attack. But it was Garrett who appeared.

"Handcuffed one and tied the other to him about ten yards north," Garrett said. He was breathing a little heavily, and his lip was bleeding. He looked at Nate's two conquests.

He frowned at the older one, clearly as confused as Nate had been by his age. "It's… Loren," Nate said, still trying to work out what the man had said. "He asked me where his son is."

Garrett's confusion matched Nate's. "Doing his own dirty work?"

"Thinking I have something to do with his son's disappearance." Nate immediately turned and scanned the woods around them. "Something is very wrong here."

Chapter Twenty-One

Elsie fretted. She couldn't help it, and for once she couldn't concentrate on her computer. How could she just sit here and do nothing?

She'd updated Shay. Shay was reticent to take someone off Courtney and Loren watch, and Elsie had insisted she not let Granger leave Revival. Shay had grumbled about it, but had eventually agreed to send Mallory.

Still, it would take some time, and Elsie didn't know how much time they had. She tried to meditate. Count backward from one hundred. She tried to lose herself in following the information her team was unearthing.

But she couldn't do it. She got to her feet and gingerly moved toward the open edge. She peered through the hole in the trees Garrett had made. She could see the cabin, the length of the shore, and the lake itself stretching out. Sunshine glinted off the water. It would have been downright beautiful if she wasn't scared to death of what was going on down on the ground.

She blew out a breath, ready to force herself to turn away, when she caught a glimpse of something out there on the lake. A tiny dot, but moving closer. A boat.

It couldn't be Mallory yet—Elsie had just gotten off the phone with Shay five minutes ago. Was it reinforcements for the first four men? Nate and Garrett wouldn't know to expect more men and then they'd be captured and killed and...

Elsie took a deep breath and ordered herself to slow down. Nate was always saying one step at a time, and that's what she had to do. First, she had to understand who or what was in that boat.

She needed binoculars or something. She pulled out her phone. Surely she could find some kind of app. She muttered and cursed at how long it was taking, and then silently chided herself for making noise.

Once she got the app up and running, she pointed her phone at the boat. It had gotten closer, and the app allowed her to zoom in. The picture was still blurry, but she could make out two people. They were rowing. So, unlike the four men who'd come before with their noisy motorboats, these two wanted to be undetected.

If she had to guess based on size, shape and hair—a woman and a man. But if they were North Star, Elsie would be able to recognize them. It had to be more of the group Nate and Garrett had gone after.

Elsie forced herself to think. She could rush down and run after Nate and Garrett to warn them, but they were men with experience. A former Navy SEAL, a cop. They knew how to deal with this sort of thing, and Elsie running in with half-formed warnings wasn't going to help them any.

She had to know what they were dealing with. Her job was information, not action. She used the binocular app again. She still couldn't make out the faces, but she took a few pictures and then sent them to Courtney's computer.

It was more time, but she uploaded the picture into her team's systems with the instructions to make an ID. ASAP. Once they did, they'd spread the information to everyone, including Shay and the team in the field.

But she didn't know how she was going to get the information to Nate and Garrett. She'd figure it out. She would.

She resumed her watch. The boat was making slow progress, so she scanned the forest below. Could she find Garrett or Nate? Make out what they were doing? Give them some kind of sign from here?

She scanned and scanned. Sometimes she thought she caught movement, the flash of color, but the leaves were too thick to be sure. The only way she'd be able to see them was if they went past the cabin and onto the shoreline.

Her computer pinged and she went to look at what her techs had found out.

Clear match.

Elsie gasped at the information. All alone in the tree house, she *gasped*. Because she hadn't expected this twist, and she certainly didn't know what it meant.

The woman in the boat was Courtney. *Courtney*, whom North Star was supposed to be watching. The man with her was Justin Sherman, her half brother at Revival.

And they were armed.

Elsie stood abruptly, forgetting all her earlier trepidation about the sturdiness of the tree house. She hadn't told Garrett and Nate about Courtney getting money from the group in Yemen, because people had come and they'd gone off to take care of them and...

Stop. Focus, she commanded herself. She made herself breathe slowly, evenly. She couldn't be of help to anyone if she panicked.

You can be tactical, Elsie Rogers. You are a North Star operative, one way or another. Start acting like it.

She let her mind focus on that, repeat the words over and over. On her last mission, she had been drugged because she hadn't ever considered that someone might come after her. She'd believed in the safe cocoon of her computers and information.

Now, she knew better, and she'd use that knowledge to make the right choices. Nate and Garrett had to know Courtney was out there. It was imperative. Because this was bigger than just the potential for danger. Somehow, Courtney was the central answer to all of this confusion.

Elsie looked at the planks nailed to the tree branch and the long, *long* way to go to get to the ground.

"I will not be a coward," she muttered to herself. She tucked the gun, safety on, into the waistband of her pants and then began the long climb down. She bit her tongue to keep her limbs from shaking with fear—the pain a good distraction.

She kept her eyes on every plank as each foot reached for the one below, and then the next, slowly picking her way along even as her heartbeat echoed in her ears. She didn't look down, no matter how much the impulse plagued her. She would *not* look down until she hit solid ground. She let her feet lead the way.

But then one of the planks gave out, and her grip on the one above wasn't enough to keep her steady. She was air-bound, falling and—

"Oof." She landed on her butt, not a second or two later. Because, thankfully, she had been almost at the bottom. She sat there for a good few seconds catching her breath, the adrenaline buzzing through her.

She had not fallen to her death or injury. She was fine. Fine. And she had work to do.

She got up, dusted herself off and looked around. Nothing. No one. Everything was silent, and though her butt kind of hurt, she was uninjured. So, she moved into the woods, gun in hand, ready to find Nate and Garrett.

And get to the bottom of this once and for all.

NATE HAD HELPED Garrett move the two men he'd taken down to where Loren was. All four tied-up men were now in a small clearing where Nate and Garrett could keep their eyes on them. Just in case they escaped the rope bonds.

But these were not well-trained men. That's what struck Nate as the biggest issue. Who came en masse and untrained?

"You were supposed to be dead," Loren said, sneering at them. "If anything happens to my son, you can bet you will be."

Nate was tempted not to talk. After all, he didn't need to give anything away to this man. But maybe he'd find out more with the truth. "I've got nothing to do with your son. I didn't even know you existed until a few days ago."

"You're a liar," the man next to him said. "We have proof you're working with them. *Proof.*"

"Shut up," Loren muttered.

The way they spoke, in general and to each other, Nate had to assume the second man was related to Loren, as well. Not some band of experts. *Family.*

Garrett leaned in. He nodded toward the south. "More people coming."

"Elsie's group?"

"Doubt it. Too loud."

Nate paused and listened. Yeah, whoever was coming wasn't trying to sneak up on anyone. Both he and Nate aimed their guns at the direction the noise was coming from. But the new person showed absolutely no fear.

"Let's put the guns down, boys," Courtney Prokop—or Loren, or whatever—said. Courtney didn't have a weapon of any kind.

"Why would we do that?" Nate returned. "Two against one."

Courtney held up a hand. A gunshot exploded in the air and Garrett jerked back. Hard. Nate felt his whole body freeze as Garrett fell to the ground.

"Now, drop your gun, Nate, or I signal for a head shot for your brother."

Nate knelt to place his weapon on the ground. He looked at Garrett. Blood stained his shirt.

"Just my shoulder," Garrett gritted out.

Nate didn't say anything. Garrett might survive the gunshot, but not without medical attention. The clock was ticking. He had to get them out of this fast.

"What do you want, Courtney?"

"Justice," she said earnestly, like it was obvious. "My grandfather tried to *use* me for his dirty business deals. Didn't you?" she said, facing Loren now. "You thought you could pull one over on me. You thought Savannah and I were dumb because we were women. Well, we showed you."

"What are you talking about?" Loren rasped.

"*I'm* the one who convinced Dad to go to Yemen. *I'm* the one who told the civilian group what was happening. I orchestrated everything, Grandpa. Because you thought you could cut me out of the profit."

She turned to Nate, pointing at Loren. "My grandfather and father are the bad men here. They were stealing military weapons and selling them to the highest bidder."

Loren paled. "Courtney."

"You didn't think I knew? You thought you could send me on your little errands and I wouldn't *know*? I'm smarter than you. All of you. And I am the good person here. I'm doing what's right. Stopping bad men. Like my father. Like you."

"What about Garrett?" Nate asked. Garrett was pressing his hand to the wound to try to stop the bleeding, but the pressure was not enough. And Nate had no idea where Courtney's shooter was so there was no way to stop him. Yet.

"Garrett shouldn't have gotten involved. He certainly

shouldn't have gotten Savannah pregnant. That was his biggest mistake of all."

Garrett made a noise, but Nate didn't know if it was in pain or out of reaction to what Courtney said.

"We took care of that, though. Didn't we, Grandpa?"

"Where is my son?" Loren demanded. This time of Courtney.

"I made sure that little group in Yemen kept him alive. I mean, what a cash cow, right? You were so funny, giving us all that money and running all those sad attempts to find him. You're sad, Grandpa. And you thought you could use *me*." She laughed.

She was *unhinged*. That was all Nate could think. But he had to...he had to get Garrett out of here. Alive.

Elsie was his only chance. She had to have heard the gunshot. Hopefully she'd sent her group an SOS.

He just needed to keep Courtney's attention on him, so help could arrive. "How do *I* have anything to do with this?"

Courtney turned to him. Wide-eyed innocence. "Fate? Luck? Divine intervention? You name it. I gave the information to the civilians, and they chose you. They chose you. Daria tried to kill you, but he failed. So you became the perfect scapegoat. But to be a scapegoat, I needed you alive, so I made sure my friends in Yemen put that stipulation into the blackmail against Grandpa. Sent Savannah here to keep an eye on you, from afar. I just had to keep you alive. Had to keep an eye on that friend of yours, too. Gosh, he became a problem when you sent him that evidence. Really shouldn't have done that."

Nate couldn't afford to be knocked off his axis by that, but he was. It was just too many different blows. "He's just fine."

Courtney shrugged. "He didn't know anything, though, did he? And all he got was Daria." She waved a hand.

"Who cares about that. I wanted the head honcho. The big guy." She turned to her grandfather. "Since he thought so little of me."

Loren just sat there, looking at Courtney like she was a stranger and ghost rolled into one.

Nate couldn't say he blamed the guy.

Courtney shook her head. "But I'm forgetting myself. At this point, Nate, you've outlived your usefulness. And your little friends got a little too close to the truth. I gave you the chance to take care of things yourself, but you didn't take it. Shame."

"You're going to kill me."

Her expression became outraged. "I am *not* a murderer. I am the innocent victim here!" She held up her hands. "I don't even have a gun. Or any weapon, for that matter, be-cause *I'm* the good guy."

"Then you can't kill me."

"*I'm* not going to kill you, Nate." She smiled. "But that doesn't mean you aren't going to die. Just remember, it's your own fault. Not mine."

Chapter Twenty-Two

Elsie was sweating. Even though it wasn't hot at all. But as she moved through the trees, doing everything she could to control her body's reaction to stress and fear, she felt winded and sweaty.

But she persisted, moving as silently as possible in the woods and toward the open shoreline. If she didn't find Nate and Garrett on her way to shore, she would follow the tracks back into the woods and catch up with them that way. Maybe she'd even help surround someone. Or capture Courtney and Justin herself.

She knew it was crazy, but she thought maybe if she believed herself capable of North Star operative–level things, she'd actually be able to do whatever was needed.

Then, out of nowhere, a gunshot went off and Elsie narrowly swallowed the scream in her throat. She still made a sound, but it was little more than a gasp.

She held herself very still, looking around her without moving her body. She counted, carefully. When no one burst out of the trees, or shot at her, she turned in a slow circle. She held her gun at the ready, and did the nerve-racking thing of turning the safety off.

She had to be strong enough to defend herself if it came to that, and she had to be *herself* enough to think. To use the brain she'd developed to put the pieces together and get to the bottom of this mystery.

The gunshot had not been that far away. Not down on the shore, but near her. Had Nate or Garrett shot someone? Or the other way around?

She tamped down the spurt of panic. She was a North Star operative, and she would do her duty. She began to make her way toward where she thought the shot had come from.

Each step steadied her. She wasn't going to hide in the corner on her computer. She was going to act. Protect. Save.

If she ended up hurt like Sabrina, or worse, she'd have *done* something. Something important. Little Elsie Rogers, who'd been nothing more than a sad story in Blue Valley her whole childhood.

But she was a survivor. She would survive this, too.

She moved. She searched. And when she finally saw someone, it didn't fully make sense.

Justin Sherman was in a tree, spread out over a thick branch. Courtney's half brother held a sniper rifle, pointed at the world below.

He was somewhat obscured by branches and leaves, but Elsie could see him well enough to make out who he was.

She stepped silently behind a tree, then tried to position herself to see whatever Justin was aiming his rifle at. She couldn't see through the trees, not from her angle, but she could see little snippets of color. People.

He was pointing a gun at a group of people. A group of people who likely included Garrett and Nate. Even though the rifle was trained on them, Justin's gaze and hold was relaxed.

But something changed after a few minutes. He tensed. He lowered his eyes to the site of the rifle.

Elsie knew she had to act.

Don't be nervous. Obviously, telling yourself something didn't usually have the desired effect, but she heard the words in Nate's voice. Felt his belief in her. She pretended Justin's leg was a target. A pop can swinging in the breeze.

Nate was depending on her. Garrett was depending on her.

She aimed. She pulled the trigger.

And prayed.

THIS TIME, WHEN A gunshot went off, Nate didn't see anyone around them jerk or fall. Everyone in the clearing looked around at each other trying to determine who had been hit.

After a few seconds, everyone seemed to realize no one had been shot.

Courtney let out a groan of disgust. "That idiot missed!"

She only had one sniper. That was good news. And if a shot had gone off that hadn't hit anywhere near them after hitting Garrett… "Or 'that idiot' got caught," Nate pointed out.

Courtney's face… It reminded him a little bit of a witch melting. Her expression changed into a slow, dawning horror tinged by madness. That was when she reached behind her.

She'd claimed she had no weapon, that she was a good person because of it, but a person in this situation didn't reach behind them if they didn't have something there to reach for.

Nate lunged. He tackled her to the ground, but she'd pulled a gun out and was waving it wildly.

Nate ripped the gun out of her hand, held her in place beneath him by pinning her legs with his, and grabbed her flailing arms and shoved them between his leg and hers, as well. She was rendered mostly immobile, except for her head, which she thrashed back and forth in an attempt to wriggle herself free.

"Still think you're smarter than everyone else?" he asked.

She let out a primal scream, thrashing and wriggling with renewed vigor. But Nate held her as immobile as he could, holding the gun aloft just in case she got an arm free.

Someone tried to take it from his grasp and Nate looked up to see Garrett. Blood seeped from his wound, but he was on his two feet. He took the gun.

"You need to—"

"I'll manage," Garrett rasped, but he was downright gray and certainly unsteady on his feet.

"Sit."

"We've got to find the gunman."

"The gunman was clearly taken care of. As he's not currently shooting at us." Nate looked down at Courtney. "Let me guess. Justin?"

Courtney screamed curses at him, and didn't tire of thrashing.

"I definitely need some backup, though." He could hold her as long as he needed to, but he wouldn't be able to get her anywhere to have her arrested or taken care of or *whatever* without some help.

"We need to check on—"

Before he could say her name, Elsie appeared through the trees. She held a gun. Wide-eyed, she looked a little pale herself.

"Didn't I tell you to stay put?" Nate growled.

"You're very welcome for saving your life." She looked down at Courtney, not seeming the slightest bit surprised to see her. "I shot Justin."

"What?" Nate almost lost grip of Courtney, but reapplied pressure when she wriggled.

"He was in a tree, with a sniper rifle." Elsie looked up, pointed vaguely, then took in the sight around her. "He was shooting down below. I figured at you guys, so I... Before he could… I…" She was clearly in some kind of shock, but then she surged forward. "Garrett, you were shot."

"I'll live."

His teeth were chattering now. He looked awful.

But they were…alive. All of them. And Courtney and Loren had been taken care of, more or less, and… God, he wanted to get out of there. Get Garrett to a hospital. "Where is everyone?"

"I called Shay, but—"

"Right here," Shay interrupted, stepping through the trees, Mallory and Gabriel behind her. "When Elsie called us, we decided to go ahead and close in on Courtney. But it wasn't Courtney. It was some woman who claimed Courtney was paying her to house-sit. I pulled everyone, except Connor."

"We need Betty—ASAP," Elsie said.

"She's on her way. I sent Connor to get a helicopter. He'll rendezvous with Betty and be here soon." Shay surveyed Nate. "Allow us."

Nate transferred Courtney over to the trio. She screamed and raged, but they tied her up and Gabriel dragged her away.

"She told us everything," Nate said, still kneeling and not quite able to move yet. "Loren tried to use her for his little business, without telling her what was going on. But she figured it out. Started working with the Yemen group, got her father kidnapped, then convinced whoever got too close who wouldn't believe I was crazy that *I* was the one with the Yemen connections, and that I needed to stay alive or Loren's son would die."

Shay nodded. "Once we're all in better shape, we'll go over the details, but for now we'll take Loren into custody in partnership with our military group. They'll take care of the legal side of things."

"They might have a leak," Elsie pointed out. "Courtney knew a group was helping Nate."

"They're working on that. But for today? We stopped a multilevel military corruption scheme. For good."

The faint sound of helicopter blades chopping through the air met them, and Shay shaded her eyes at the horizon. "I've got backup along with our doctor. Betty's going to see what she can do about Garrett's injuries herself. We'd like to avoid a hospital if we can, but I promise you, if it's necessary, she'll get him to one."

"I want to be with him."

Shay nodded at Nate. "Of course."

"I'll be fine," Garrett said.

"I'm going with you," Nate insisted.

"Justin is alive," Elsie said. "I shot him in the leg and he fell out of the tree, but he's alive."

"On it," Mallory said. "Why don't you show me where?"

Elsie nodded, gave Nate one enigmatic look, then disappeared into the trees with Mallory.

Nate didn't know what to say or to feel. The only thing that mattered right now was getting Garrett medical attention.

Shay clapped him on the shoulder. "It's over, Nate. Might not feel like it yet. But you did it."

You did it.

He didn't know what to feel about that. His two-year-long nightmare was finally over. But his brother had been shot and Elsie was...

Accomplishing something sure didn't mean life could go back to normal, but now there was the chance at normal.

Time to figure out what he wanted his normal to be.

Epilogue

Elsie helped Mallory find Justin. North Star got the island cleaned up after Garrett and Nate were helicoptered out. Elsie wasn't sure what she was feeling, or what to do next, so when Shay told her to join her in the boat, then get in a Jeep on the other side, she did as she was told.

Shay began to drive, and though Elsie wondered where they were going, she didn't ask. She was too tired.

"Granger talked to your family," Shay said after a while.

Elsie straightened in her seat. "What?"

"There was some concern about Nate's welfare, and yours, so Granger talked to your sister and Nate's therapist at Revival. Assured them everything was fine and explained that Nate had actually been right all along."

Elsie could only stare at Shay's profile. "He told them Nate was right."

Shay nodded. "Proved it enough, everyone believed it. I think your sister believed it because you'd already told her, but everything is set at Revival. I'll take you back there after."

"After what?"

"Where do you really want to go right now?"

"I want to make sure Garrett's okay."

Shay gave her a quick glance and smile. "That's what

I figured. I'm taking you to Garrett's house. That's where Betty's been working on him."

Elsie slumped in her seat again. "Well, good."

"Listen, Els. This was a lot."

Elsie forced a smile. Shay was worried about her. Because she'd basically been in the field, without being a field operative. "I'm okay, really."

"I know you are. But you earned yourself a vacation."

Elsie's brow furrowed. A vacation? A *break*? Shay didn't want her... "You need me," Elsie protested weakly.

"Yeah, we do. Whatever comes next, we're definitely going to need you. But you know the great thing about computers?"

"They aren't people?"

Shay laughed. "Elsie, you have a family here. You love your sisters. Isn't it time you let yourself have that?"

"You want me to quit?"

"I want you to stay here and enjoy that before we move on to the next assignment. And maybe I want you to consider working remotely. Sure, you'd have to come into headquarters sometimes. But you could also do a large portion of your work from Blue Valley, with your family."

Elsie looked forward. She didn't know what to say. She'd never thought about living in Blue Valley before.

"Elsie, I never fully understood... I knew you had sisters here, of course, but I didn't realize you actually *liked* them." Shay shook her head. "You have family you love, who loves you. You should be *with* them. And I don't want to lose you at all, but I want what's right for you. You're part of my family, Els."

Elsie swallowed at the lump that formed in her throat. Shay hated displays of emotion, but she was giving one and...

"This isn't about Nate," Shay continued. "It's about your family. But... You're young. You have your whole life ahead of you. Burying yourself in your computer was fine for a while, but there's a big world out there. You shouldn't limit yourself. You should stay here for your family, if it'd make you happy, but I can't deny the Nate factor. If you like him…why not go for it?"

"Where is this coming from? You were mad when Reece and Holden left for women."

"I'm not asking you to leave. Certainly not for any man. I'm asking you to build a life. Believe it or not, mad as I was, mad as I *am*, Reece had it right. We all deserve to build a life at some point. You're not in the field. You're not putting anyone in danger. You could do everything I depend on you for here. Enjoy your family. Start something with Nate—hell, maybe eventually end something with Nate. Or maybe it works out. I don't know, but you deserve the *chance* at all those things."

"What about you?"

"What about me?"

"Don't you deserve a chance at all those things?"

Shay hunched her shoulders a bit. "Too late for me. Now, look, we're here." She pointed to a house on a pretty stretch of land, the mountains big and imposing in the background. Blue Valley, Montana.

Even when it had been her prison, it had been her home. And now…did she really want to come back?

"Go. Check on Garrett. Talk to Nate. I'm *requiring* you to take a weeklong vacation here. After that? You get to decide."

Elsie looked at Shay. She had no words. Only feelings. So she did something she knew her boss would hate, but she couldn't quite stop herself. She reached over and gave Shay a hug. "You're my family, too."

Shay stiffened, but she didn't let Elsie go. They held on to each other, the years they'd worked together, gotten to know each other, had each other's backs… It didn't need repeating.

They were family. Sometimes a hug was enough.

Shay pulled back, eyes suspiciously bright. "Go check on your friend," she muttered, waving Elsie away.

Elsie got out of the car and walked up the little sidewalk that led to the door. The house looked like it had been cheerful once, but had been ignored for a while, so it was a little sad around the edges.

Elsie knocked, and it was Nate who answered. Tall and broad. She remembered distinctly when she'd seen him on her drive up to Revival. Had that just been a few days ago? He'd made her nervous and now…

He pulled her into a fierce hug and she wrapped her arms around him, pressing her face into his shoulder. Everything that had been coiled too tightly inside her relaxed.

"Hi," she murmured into his shirt. "How's Garrett?"

"Good. Betty said it was a clean shot. Take a while to heal, but she sewed him up. She said she already had a line on getting a paternity test for his kids, though Courtney pretty much verified that in her rant."

He didn't let her go, and she didn't try to move.

It felt right here. Nate felt right. Did the bad memories of Blue Valley really matter when she had good memories with her sisters, building their families? When she'd met a man as good and amazing as Nate?"

"Betty's great. She'll take good care of him, and we'll do everything we can to get Garrett to his kids."

"Why would you guys…?"

Elsie pulled back a little. "Garrett was hurt because he got mixed up with our mess. My group will do *everything* to make it all right. No matter how long it takes." She met Nate's dark gaze. There were so many words in her head, but she couldn't seem to put them in any discernible order.

So she simply got up on her toes and kissed him.

NATE KISSED ELSIE back with all his relief, all this *emotion*.

A throat cleared behind him and Nate belatedly remembered the presence of Betty, a doctor from Elsie's little group.

"Garrett's asleep," Betty said. "I'll keep an eye on him. Why don't you two go for a walk or something?" Betty gave Elsie a wink.

Elsie blushed and Nate realized…he got to do things like this now. Take a walk with a pretty woman because he wanted to and he liked her. No threats. No worries about who believed him.

Just life.

He moved outside and closed the door behind him. The sunrise rioted around them when Nate had figured it was still nighttime. His days and nights were off but… It was all over. Things were going to go back to normal.

Whatever that was.

"I talked to Monica. My therapist," he said, not sure why he needed to tell someone. Out loud. Explain…what had changed inside him.

"Shay said one of our guys explained everything to her."

Nate nodded. "She apologized for not believing me… She also told me in the beginning she tried to verify my story. It was just that nothing matched. I realized…people didn't even automatically not believe me—even Garrett. Courtney and maybe Loren were working to discredit me and I…" She slid her hand into his.

Elsie's hand. And it felt right to walk hand in hand with her. Here.

He wouldn't wish what had happened to him on anybody, but it had turned out…pretty okay.

Revival wasn't the place for him anymore. He wasn't sure what place was, but walking around Garrett's yard with Elsie felt good enough.

"I can't be mad or bitter at anyone. Except Courtney

and Loren and Daria and the rest. But not anyone in my life." His life. His *life*. He got to build his now. "So, what happens now?" he asked.

"My group will work with the government to facilitate all the legal channels to bring Loren, Courtney, Justin and all of those involved to trial in a court of law. We'll keep an eye on it and watch for corruption, and step in if need be, but usually these things go smoothly."

"Yeah, Betty ran me through all *that*. I meant for you."

"Oh. Well." She looked at the mountains, a strange frown on her face. "Shay wants me to take a vacation. Here. Visit my family and all that."

"Good, you could use one."

She looked up at him, studying him. Clearly looking for some answer he wished he had for her. She stopped walking, so he did, too.

"Then she wants me to stay here. Work remotely from Blue Valley. She said I had a family I loved, and I should be with them more."

Nate's heart tripped in its beat, but he didn't let it show. He didn't know *how* to let it show. He wanted Elsie here. He wanted that *after* he hadn't known how to dream about.

But more than all the things he wanted, he needed her to be happy. To make the choice that was best for her. He had to clear his throat to speak. "Oh, yeah? What do you think about that?"

She looked at the world around them again. "I never thought about coming back to Blue Valley permanently."

He followed the path of her eyes. Mountains and the town of his youth. "Me neither."

Her gaze met his again. "Are you going to stay?"

He nodded. "I figured out sometime during all of this that Blue Valley is where I belong. Not sure exactly how that'll work. For now, I think I'll help at my parents' ranch while I think about what I want to do."

Elsie swallowed. "I think I want to stay, too."

His mouth curved, no matter how he tried to pretend he was indifferent. That she could do whatever she wanted and if it was right for her, he would be happy for her and support her.

But he wanted her here. He took her other hand in his. "Good."

She laughed then shook her head. "Yeah, I guess it is. I'll get to spend time with my sisters. See my nieces and nephews grow up. And there's this really cute cowboy I think might ask me out."

Nate laughed. Outright. He couldn't remember the last time he'd done that. And now…*now* he'd get to do it whenever he wanted. He vowed then and there, to do it often.

"You better be talking about me."

Elsie shrugged, but she was grinning and when he pulled her to him. She molded to his body like she belonged.

Like they did.

So, he kissed her. A promise. A bright chance at a future. Here in Blue Valley, where they'd once been victims but now got to be survivors. *Thrivers.*

Together.

* * * * *

DISAVOWED IN WYOMING

JUNO RUSHDAN

This one is for my tribe.
I couldn't do it without you.

Chapter One

The phone rang, jolting Kate Sawyer awake. She didn't remember falling asleep but must've drifted off after the noise from the bar beneath her apartment had finally died down. She peered at the alarm clock. The red lights blinked 2:23 a.m. Nobody called at this hour with good news.

Bolting upright, she reached out and turned on the light on her nightstand. Her work cell was ringing. Not her personal phone. There was an emergency with a sick or injured animal for someone to call in the middle of the night.

"Loving Paws Mobile Veterinary Services," Kate said, rubbing the sleep from her eyes.

Anything urgent she referred to the local animal hospital. Alpine was the closest and offered 24-7 critical care.

"Help me," a woman said. Her voice was low and tight, thick with emotion.

Kate pushed back the covers and put her bare feet on the carpet. "Ma'am, do you have a wounded pet? If so, Alpine Animal Hospital would be better suited to handle the situation."

Not only did they have an on-call vet available, but also a technician to assist and any equipment that she might not have at her disposal. She operated out of a twenty-six-foot La Boit truck that consisted of an exam table, a small surgery suite for minor procedures, digital radiology, a handheld ultrasound and dental equipment. Routine well checks and running basic diagnostics for about fifty patients a month were her bread and butter.

"Please," the woman said in a strained way that unsettled Kate's stomach.

Something horrible must have happened. "What's wrong, ma'am? Can you tell what the problem is?" Was it a poisoning? An intestinal obstruction? Animals ingested things they shouldn't all the time, from chocolate to Legos. If she had more information, she could try to provide some immediate assistance over the phone.

"You have to come now." The woman sucked in a deep, shuddering breath that tugged at Kate's heart.

"Come where?"

"Downstairs," the woman said. "I'm here. Hurry. Please." The call disconnected.

Kate lurched from the bed and rushed to the window overlooking the private parking area for owners of the street-level businesses and residents of the second-floor apartments. She shoved back the blackout curtain. Lights on the exterior of the building and streetlamps across the road ensured the lot was always well lit. So illuminated it made it difficult to sleep at night. She had a clear line of sight to her mobile pet truck, but she didn't see anyone.

Beside her truck was the Jeep Renegade that belonged to the bartender, Davis Johnson, whom everyone called DJ. Farther down were two other sedans she recognized as her neighbors'.

Scurrying around her bedroom, Kate quickly got dressed, slipped on her sneakers and threw on her lab coat. She grabbed her keys and rushed out the door of her corner apartment.

A cold February breeze slapped her in the face, making her reconsider whether to go back and grab her coat. But there was a hurt animal who needed her right this minute.

A poor dog or cat was suffering, could even be bleeding out. No time to waste going back for her jacket.

Wyoming's winters were harsh and bitterly cold, but soon enough she'd take shelter from the elements inside her truck. At least it wasn't snowing.

She raced down the exterior staircase, her feet pounding against the metal steps. As she turned onto the walkway, she stopped short.

In the shadows, a woman was leaning against the brick wall of the bar, bent over...holding her pregnant belly. Wearing a thin dress, a zippered hoodie pulled up over her head, tattered boots and coatless, she must've been freezing. She peered up at Kate. Her face was gaunt, as if she hadn't had a decent meal in a while, and her skin was smudged with grime. She had large blue eyes and pale skin. Kate guessed her to be about nineteen, twenty at the most.

"Dr. Sawyer?" the young woman asked. "You're Kate, right?"

"Yes." Kate had never seen this woman before, but she seemed to know her somehow. If she did, then she should know that Kate was a veterinarian, not an obstetrician. "Are you in labor?"

The woman nodded and sucked in a sharp breath on a contraction as she tightened her frail arms around her midsection. She was so thin that it made her pregnant belly look the size of a watermelon.

Kate hurried to her, wrapping an arm around her shoulder and lifting her from the wall. "Come on. We've got to get you to the hospital."

"No." The young woman recoiled. "No hospitals."

Uneasiness crept between Kate's shoulder blades. "It looks like you're pretty close to having this baby." She got the girl moving and guided her along the walkway toward the truck that she used professionally as well as personally to save on the expense of a second vehicle. "What's your name?"

"Cheryl." Her teeth chattered through bluish lips. She clutched Kate's hand, her bony fingers digging into Kate's. The young woman's skin was ice-cold.

"Listen to me, Cheryl, I have to take you to the emergency room. That's the best place to deliver this baby."

The sudden look of terror on her face punched Kate in the gut. "You can't." Cheryl shook her head. "They'll find me there." She glanced around. "They're looking for me now. We have to get inside."

"Who will find you? Who is looking for you?"

Clenching her teeth, the woman grunted through another contraction. Squeezing Kate's hand, she stopped walking and hunched over in pain. This time her grunt bloomed into a full-blown scream.

The contractions were coming fast, way too fast. Kate estimated less than two minutes apart. Was there even time to get her to the ER?

"I'll call an ambulance." Kate fished her cell phone from her lab coat pocket.

"No hospital," the woman growled, but her eyes, glazed with fear, reminded Kate of an abused puppy. "Help me or my baby is going to die."

Die?

Who was going to find her at the hospital? Why would anyone want to hurt an innocent child?

All Kate knew for certain was that Cheryl was terrified of something or someone. She had to help this young woman and make sure her baby was delivered safely.

The back door of the bar opened. DJ stuck his head outside and spotted them. "I thought I heard a scream. Is everything okay?"

Kate exhaled in relief, pleased to see him. "No, it's not. Can you give me a hand?"

Without uttering another question, DJ rushed outside to assist them. Kate couldn't think of a better person to help her with this situation—other than an obstetrician.

The older man was well into his late seventies, but his calm disposition—no matter what, even if a bar fight broke out—always put her at ease. Despite the permanent worry lines etched across his forehead and dusting of gray at his temples, he never seemed to fret about anything.

DJ slung one of Cheryl's arms over his shoulders and helped her walk.

"She won't go to a hospital," Kate said, getting closer to her truck.

A gush of fluid splashed to the pavement beneath Cheryl as she groaned, doubling over.

"Her water just broke." Kate tried to quicken their step, but the expectant mother was in so much pain it was difficult for her to walk. "This baby is coming right now."

DJ scooped Cheryl up in his arms in a startling display of strength that belied his elderly frame. He was thick around the middle and didn't appear athletic, but he carried Cheryl to the mobile pet clinic at a pace that had Kate running to keep up.

She fumbled with her keys, looking for the right one. A brutal gust of wind whipped her long blond hair around her face, obstructing her vision. She raked her hair back, angled the keys toward the light and found it.

The harsh hum of a heavy car engine making its way down the road snagged her attention. She stole a glance over her shoulder. Headlights crept along the side street, drawing closer. Whoever was in the vehicle would spot them if they didn't hurry.

She shoved the key into the slot and unlocked it. Swinging the door out, she ushered DJ inside.

He carried the pregnant woman up the three steps as though she weighed nothing.

Hurrying in behind them, Kate closed the door and locked it. She peered through the blinds, scanning the area.

A muscle car, one of those super coupes she'd seen around town, rolled down the street, passing the parking lot, and drove out of sight.

That had been close. She didn't think they'd been seen.

Hoping it was safe, Kate switched on the lights. It was going to be hard enough delivering a baby—she didn't need to complicate the situation by trying to do it in the dark.

"What's going on, Kate?" DJ asked. His voice was deep and scratchy, sounding as weathered as he looked.

"I'm not sure." Her gaze dropped to Cheryl, who was panting through another contraction. "She says someone is looking for her."

Kate led the way down the narrow aisle to the exam table at the back.

The flat-top metal surface was only forty-eight inches long and not designed for a human, but it was sterile. They'd have to make it work.

She pulled out some supplies from the cabinets. First, she covered the metal table with a blanket for comfort and put a sterile surgical drape on top. "Set her down here."

DJ gently eased Cheryl from his arms onto the table. She pushed her hood back, revealing dishwater-blond hair that was matted to her forehead from perspiration.

Helping the woman into a seated position, Kate put a folded blanket behind her to prop her up. She had never delivered a baby. Assisting with the birth of a calf out at the Sullivan ranch when the local bovine vet had been unavailable was as close as she'd ever come.

Kate had been in the delivery room in Omaha, Nebraska, the day her niece had been born last year. Although her brother-in-law had been at her sister Claire's side, Kate had read *The Birth Partner* cover to cover to prepare.

That was her, a type-A overachiever in everything. So

she avoided doing anything impromptu. It only increased the chances of failure.

A flutter of doubt set her nerves on edge. The thought of what rested on her shoulders now—the lives of Cheryl and her soon-to-be-born child—gave her a moment of pause.

"Hey." DJ's voice drew her gaze to his. "You're the sharpest doctor I know. If anyone can do this on the fly, it's you," he said, as though he were a mind reader. "I'll be right here with you every step of the way."

One of the many things she appreciated about DJ was that he always knew the right thing to say at just the right moment to make things better. The perfect bartender. Poured her drinks strong. Listened to her troubles without judgment or trying to fix her problems with unsolicited advice. Knew how to give solid encouragement.

DJ took her hands in his, which were covered in latex gloves as always, due to his obsessive-compulsive disorder regarding germs. "You've got this." His brown eyes searched hers, reflecting a familiar warmth that imbued her with confidence. Then he lifted a hand, cupping her cheek in a manner that felt more flirty than fatherly.

Once again, she found herself thinking that if there hadn't been a forty-year age gap between them, and he wasn't such a germophobe, she would've asked him out on a date months ago. Probably shortly after he'd moved to town.

"Okay?" he said.

"I've got this." Kate nodded, trying to convince herself. She leaped into action, tugging on a pair of sterile gloves, and grabbed some green operating towels.

"Tell me how to help," DJ said.

"Talk to her. Keep her calm," Kate said. "Cheryl, can you put your legs up for me? I need to examine you. See how far dilated you are." A single finger inside the cervix would be one centimeter. Once the cervix was about the size of a cantaloupe or a large bagel, it would be time for her to push.

Kate pulled her long dress back to the top of the young woman's knees and covered her with another surgical drape to give her some privacy.

Extensive bruises covered her legs in various shades that ranged from red-purple to yellowish brown. Some marks looked as if they'd been made by a cord. Cheryl had been beaten.

Did she have an abusive husband or boyfriend after her?

But she'd said *they*. Maybe his family was helping him look for her, but why would they want to hurt an infant?

"I've got to get the baby out." Cheryl grimaced. "Now! I've got it get out. It burns! Hurts so much."

DJ took her hand. "You see that sign on the wall?" He pointed to the one that read, Free Belly Rub With Exams. Sorry, Pets Only.

"Focus on the sign," DJ said, "and breathe like this. Hee, hee, hoo." He demonstrated, blowing two short breaths followed by a long one as he made the noises.

"Where did you learn that?" Kate asked.

He shrugged. "Saw it in a movie."

It might have been a tip from a movie, but it worked. Cheryl calmed, her gaze focused on the sign, and her breathing regulated.

DJ had the magic touch.

If only Kate could find an age-appropriate guy like him.

She peered under the surgical drape, prepared to check her cervix, but there was no need. "The baby's head is crowning." That explained Cheryl's urgent feeling to get the baby out. They didn't call crowning the ring of fire for nothing. "We're in the home stretch." In minutes, Cheryl would be holding her newborn. "The next time you feel the need to push, I want you to take a deep breath and slowly release it while you bear down."

Cheryl nodded. Seconds later, she was doing as Kate had instructed. The young woman let loose a guttural cry as the baby's head slipped out.

"A couple more pushes," Kate said, eager to usher this new life into the world. "Wait for the next contraction."

A loud pop sliced through the air as the lock on the truck door gave way. The door was flung open and banged against the side of the vehicle.

Kate flinched at the sound, her heart jumping into her throat.

Two men burst inside the mobile clinic. Both were big and burly, radiating menace. The first guy had a tattoo of a snake on his neck and a crowbar clenched in his fist.

DJ let go of Cheryl's hand. Turning toward them, he stood defensively, blocking the aisle.

"Give us the girl and that baby, and we'll let you two live," the man with the tattoo said.

Fear flooded Kate. The taste of old pennies suddenly filled her mouth. Fragments of panicked thoughts bombarded her. But her mind snagged on one—the only thing standing in the way of those two thugs was a senior citizen.

There was nowhere for them to run. The only door was blocked. Cheryl couldn't move even if there was some way to escape. And that baby was being delivered right now. What were they going to do?

Violence pulsed off those men. They obviously had no qualms about threatening women and a baby. That made them capable of anything. She sensed it in her bones.

But handing over Cheryl or the child was an unthinkable option. Only over her dead body would those men get their hands on either of them.

Kate shoved aside the panic. If she surrendered to it, the feeling would consume her. She had to keep a clear head.

Cheryl groaned at the onset of the next contraction and

bore down again with another gut-wrenching scream, pushing the baby's shoulder's out.

"We gave you fair warning," the guy with the tattoo said, stalking forward, and dread welled in Kate's chest.

The taller man cracked his knuckles, following his buddy deeper into the truck.

Horrible scenarios raced through her mind, making her light-headed, but she had to focus on helping Cheryl. The young woman needed her, and this baby was coming, one way or another.

The guy with tattoo scowled. "Now we're going to make it painful, old man." He swung the crowbar.

A whoosh prickled her ears as the metal slashed through the air.

"DJ!" Kate said, not wanting him to get hurt.

But the elderly man had ducked, avoiding the blow. Then he popped up lightning fast and launched a fist, punching the bigger guy in the windpipe.

The crowbar clattered to the floor. The man gasped. Falling to his knees, he clutched his throat.

DJ jumped over the man who was in a heap in the aisle and kicked the other one backward.

Cheryl pushed again, and Kate caught the baby in a towel. The umbilical cord was wrapped around its little neck. But thankfully it was loose. Moving quickly, she gently eased the cord over the baby's head.

The sounds of a vicious struggle resonated in the small space. Kate only caught glimpses of the scuffle.

DJ blocked an incoming punch and threw a leg up into the man's groin. The brawny guy doubled over with an *oomph*. DJ grabbed him by his jacket and bulldozed him backward, down the steps and out of the truck.

Kate dried the baby off with a towel. The little one started crying. The sweet sound was reassuring. "Those are some nice, healthy lungs." She handed the baby to Cheryl. "It's a boy. A beautiful boy."

Cheryl clutched the baby close to her chest. "He's so small."

The baby did look premature. Probably caused by malnutrition. But he had a strong pulse and good muscle tone and color.

"He's healthy." Kate tied off the umbilical cord, clamping it.

"She was right," Cheryl said, staring down at the baby. "She told me that you'd help me."

"She? Who?" Kate asked. "Who told you to come to me?"

Metal scraped against the floor as the guy grabbed the crowbar and climbed to his feet. "Give me that baby," he said, rubbing his throat and drawing closer.

Cheryl held the newborn tighter. "Please, don't!"

The young woman's scream, the sound of her fear, jumpstarted Kate's adrenaline.

She whirled and scoured the shelves for something she could use as a weapon. Desperate to grab anything, her fingers curled around an orthopedic bone saw. She threw the surgical tool at his head.

But he swatted the saw to the floor with the crowbar.

Blind panic threatened to overwhelm her. Why hadn't she taken her purse? Inside it she always carried bear spray.

"Please, Smitty," Cheryl begged. "Let us go. I won't say anything."

Reaching behind her, Kate grabbed the first thing she touched. A stethoscope. She closed her fist around the chest piece and swung, whipping the binaural device through the air, trying to keep him back.

He snatched hold of the tubing and wrenched the stethoscope from her hand, tossing it behind him.

Her first instinct was to protect Cheryl and the baby. She

threw herself in front of the mother and child, standing with her arms stretched out to shield them from any blows. To stop this monster from taking them by any means necessary. Punch. Kick. Bite. Anything.

Smitty raised the crowbar, and Kate swallowed the wave of terror that almost choked her.

Movement behind Smitty had the big guy shifting around toward it. DJ leaped up, wrapping the tubing of the stethoscope around his neck and hauled him out of striking distance. The old bartender had crept back onto the truck without making a sound. Silent as a ghost.

The two men wrestled, locked in a tense struggle.

She had to do something to help DJ before that thug maneuvered to hit the old man with the crowbar. A hard enough blow would break his bones.

Frantic, she looked around and spotted a stainless-steel instrument tray. She snatched it from the counter. With the metal clenched in both hands, she charged the man.

Desperation and anger made her strong and wild. She slammed the tray down on Smitty's arm. His head. His shoulder. Anything she could strike.

He knocked her off him, throwing her against the counter, but the crowbar slipped from his thick hand. Someone kicked it, sending the metal bar sliding to the rear of the truck.

She scrambled down the aisle and scooped up the crowbar from the floor. By the time she managed to stand, the man had pulled something from his pocket.

A switchblade glinted in the light.

Before she could run to the front of the truck, before she could swing the crowbar, before she could scream in warning, Smitty plunged the knife into DJ's stomach.

"No!" Kate cried out.

DJ flinched. But he didn't stop fighting, didn't even slow down.

Smitty kept stabbing him. Each strike drove a spear through Kate's own heart.

That animal was killing him.

Smitty swung with his other hand to defend himself from the older man's relentless blows. His open hand struck DJ's face, ripping off skin. The big guy stumbled back, pulling out the knife.

There was no blood. Not on the switchblade. Not on DJ's abdomen. No blood anywhere.

For a second, she doubted her eyes.

Smitty stared down at the skin in his hand. At the *face* that he was holding. "What the hell?"

Kate's gaze flew to DJ. Instead of a wrinkled white man with gray hair, she stared at a Latino face with smooth, deep olive skin, framed by inky curls. But that shock wasn't what made her heart seize.

She knew that handsome face all too well.

Senior citizen DJ, the perfect bartender, was Dean Delgado. Someone she'd thought she'd never see again.

Smitty threw the wrinkled face down and ran out of the truck.

DJ—Dean—looked at her. "Crowbar," he said, holding out his hand. His voice crackled, wavering between the old man's and the real one.

Now she could tell that it was digitized.

"Throw me the crowbar, Kate!"

She snapped her mouth closed once she realized she was gaping and tossed the crowbar to him.

He snatched the piece of metal from the air and took off after Smitty.

There was a roaring in her head that sounded like a giant wave was about to break on top of her, smashing her to pieces. In a way, one already had seconds ago.

She stood there, trembling, her hands shaking, her mind whirling from the violence and shock. But it was the gut punch of seeing *him* that truly left her reeling. She felt as though she were floating. Untethered.

Questions piled up in her head, an avalanche of queries. About Cheryl. About who'd told the pregnant woman that Kate would help. About those men.

About Dean Delgado.

Her first love. Her first heartbreak. Her first everything.

A pang sliced through her chest, and she set her teeth against it. He was alive. Back in Laramie. A bittersweet surprise.

Far more bitter than sweet.

Why was he here after all these years? What was with the disguise?

"Don't…" Cheryl said, pulling Kate from her spiraling thoughts.

She turned and staggered to the new mother's side like she'd just been in a car accident.

Cheryl caught hold of Kate's lab coat and tugged on the pocket. "Don't let them…get the baby," she whispered. A tear surfaced, rolling down Cheryl's cheek before her eyes fluttered closed. Her arms went limp, and her legs dropped, dangling from the sides of the table.

Oh, no. Something was wrong with her.

Kate ensured the baby was in a stable position in the crook of his mother's arm and in no danger of rolling off the table. Then she went to examine Cheryl.

Blood poured from her, running over the edge of the metal surface, dripping to the floor.

Cheryl was hemorrhaging. A number of things could've caused it. Placenta problems. A tear in the cervix or a ruptured blood vessel in the uterus.

I can't lose you now. Stay with me.

If Kate couldn't get the bleeding to stop, the young woman was going to die.

Chapter Two

Dean dashed from the mobile van, leaped over the dead body of the first man he'd taken out and raced after the second scumbag who'd had the audacity to threaten a pregnant woman and a helpless baby.

He was going to kill him when he caught him. Not *if*, but *when*.

Not only would that man come after Cheryl and her baby again, but also he had seen Dean's real face. That made him a threat who needed to be put six feet under.

As the would-be kidnapper reached his muscle car, he slowed and patted his pockets. Then he glanced over his shoulder at Dean and kept running.

No keys. They must have been on his buddy. Smitty's bad luck.

Fate was practically gift wrapping this guy for Dean, and he was never one to look a gift horse in the mouth.

The guy rounded the corner of the building and fled out of sight.

A problem that Dean quickly remedied by running at a full sprint.

Tearing around the corner, he spotted the man bolting down the sidewalk. The long side street was deserted. Quiet, aside from the sound of their pounding footfalls against the pavement.

The crisp night air sharpened his focus, helping Dean

strategize how best to kill him. He couldn't beat the guy to death with the crowbar. It had to look like an accident. Self-defense.

Assassination was his specialty, or it had been when he was active with the CIA. A skill he'd hoped to have no use for while hiding out in Laramie. Killing was not something he took pleasure in. The marines had showed him that he was very good at it, and the CIA had cultivated that talent. Taught him to elevate it to an art form.

Not once had he orchestrated *Giselle* or *Swan Lake*. But every job had been calculated perfection.

Except the last one, which had gone awry. A full-blown fiasco that had landed him in a world of trouble. Had him literally and figuratively on the run.

Dean was closing the gap between himself and Smitty, like a heat-seeking missile ready to destroy. His mind was calm. He was driven. Bristling with clear purpose. A few more feet and he'd have him.

Casting a frantic glance over his shoulder, Smitty ran wildly, panicked, straight out into the street.

Tires squealed as a pickup truck plowed into the guy. Metal hit flesh and bone with a sickening thud. Smitty's body bounced into the air, flipped, then landed against the pavement. His neck and left leg were at bad, unnatural angles. Both broken.

There was no escaping fate.

The driver of the pickup truck was a middle-aged guy. Frozen in shock, he had one hand locked on the steering wheel and the other wrapped around a beer bottle. He stared out the windshield, stricken.

The accident couldn't have been more flawless if Dean had planned it.

He peered around, scanning up and down Third Street and Main Avenue. Not another soul in sight. No bystanders to worry about. He spun on his heel before the driver got a good look at him, but when he did, he realized exactly which corner, bathed in light, that he was standing on.

The only one in the small town that had full closed-circuit TV coverage from multiple angles.

A sliver of ice shot down his spine.

Lowering his head, he slipped out of the light, sinking into the shadows as nothing more than a looming specter. But in his gut, he knew it was too late. His real face had been captured on CCTV.

He was a hundred percent certain.

Dean made a beeline back to the parking lot behind the bar. A tingle of awful possibilities crept over his skin.

Local law enforcement wasn't his concern. He wasn't hiding from the cops.

The CIA had put him on a termination list, right along with every other member of Team Topaz. They would be running a facial recognition program that used the most sophisticated algorithms to search for a match from anything an analyst could tap into. ATM security cameras, photos posted online, smart technology video surveillance doorbells and, the most ubiquitous of all, CCTV footage.

Fate was laughing at *him* now. No escaping it. There wasn't a damn thing he could do besides grab his go-bag and run. Again.

The smart thing for him to do was hop in his Jeep, clear out his long-term room at the motel and hit the road ASAP. But...

Kate.

She knew the truth, that he wasn't seventy-seven-year-old Davis Johnson, bartender extraordinaire, who made all the time in the world to lend her his ear and gave her drinks on the house just because. Cheryl was another factor. The girl might have seen his face, too. But perhaps the help he'd provided would buy the new mother's silence.

Kate was a different matter.

The thought of facing her, fielding questions that he couldn't answer, made his stomach churn. What was he going to say? What explanation could he offer that she would understand, much less one that she'd accept?

A dark haze of anxiety swirled inside him. He stared at the Loving Paws truck, and on the next breath, his gaze swung to his Jeep.

Simply disappearing with no explanations given would be easier. But then history would repeat itself.

Easy wasn't always best, he'd learned the hard way.

A lifetime ago he'd been the biggest jerk and had made the worst mistake by leaving without saying goodbye to anyone. At the time, he had no clue the devastation that would follow in the wake of his absence. But now he had some inkling of what those he'd left behind had been through. His mother. His brother, Lucas. Kate.

The first giveaway had been the fact that Lucas refused to speak to him. Treated him as though they were strangers. Never made eye contact if they happened to pass each other in the halls of the CIA. Never uttered a word after their first encounter at Langley when he'd gone up to his little brother, excited, surprised to see him.

"Lucas, what are you doing here?" Dean had asked, noting he wasn't wearing a visitor's badge but had bona fide credentials. "How long have you been working here?"

"I'm sorry, do I know you?"

Dean had rocked back on his heels, thinking time hadn't changed him that much. "It's me. Your brother."

"I don't know you," Lucas had said with a deadpan expression. "You've mistaken me for someone else. I used to have a brother, but he died."

The words had been a knife to Dean's heart. Once they'd been best friends, as close as brothers could be, and Dean had ruined it.

The second clue had been more insightful, but still

vague. One night Kate had had too many drinks, and after the right kind of prompting, she'd spoken his name. Then her eyes had filled with tears. She'd hurried out of the bar, running as though she had been chased by a ghost.

Exactly what the people he loved most in the world had endured escaped him. But it had been painful. Dark.

Only a heartless SOB could take off, disappearing on her twice.

In the moment, Dean made a choice, regardless of the consequences. He ran up the steps of the truck, shutting the door behind him, and scooped up his mask from the floor.

"Call 911!" Kate said, drawing his gaze. She was working feverishly on Cheryl. Blood covered the table and the floor. "She's hemorrhaging and I can't stop it. We need an ambulance. I'm losing her."

He whipped out his cell phone. Made the call. Listened to the operator.

"Laramie 911, police, fire and medical. What's your emergency?"

"Yes, there's been…" His voice fluctuated between the real one and the altered one from the modulator on his throat. He pressed on the tiny piece of equipment. "We need an ambulance," he said, his tone holding steady. "A woman has given birth, but she's bleeding out." The hemorrhage was severe. The young woman had already lost too much blood to save her, but he wasn't going to say anything to Kate. "Come to the Loving Paws mobile pet clinic parked behind Delgado's Bar on Third Street." He thought of the body outside in the parking lot and the other one in the street. "She was attacked by two men. All of us were. But they're dead. Please, hurry." He hung up before the operator could ask any questions or eat up precious time keeping him on the line. "I'll be right back," he said to Kate.

"Where are you going? Help me!"

There was nothing more anyone could do for Cheryl. She wasn't going to make it.

"I'll be back." Turning, Dean jumped down the steps of the truck and bolted for the bar. He started a timer on his wristwatch.

Three minutes. That's how long it would take for the ambulance to arrive. The sheriff's office was right down Main Avenue. Someone from there would show up around the same time. Unless whoever was on duty got caught up handling the car accident first.

He flung open the back door to his family's bar, hustled inside and made his way to the office, where he kept an emergency kit in his sling bag.

Darting into the private bathroom, he fished out the kit. He unzipped it and dropped the bag on the countertop. First, he shed the soiled gloves, tossing them in the trash bin. Germs didn't faze him. The only thing he was fanatical about was leaving his fingerprints behind. Not to mention, applying latex skin on one's hands was tricky. Too many opportunities for tears, particularly while tending bar. Gloves made better sense, far more practical.

He touched up what he could on the foam latex skin on his throat with a topical glue for adhering makeup components to skin. But when Smitty had yanked off his disguise, the fake layer on the throat had been ripped and the voice modulator damaged. They were beyond seamless repair here in the bar with limited time.

A rush patch job was the best he could do under the circumstances. He glanced at his watch for a quick time check. One minute fifty seconds left.

He tugged on the hyperrealistic face mask. The state-of-the-art material had been specially designed and fitted for him courtesy of the CIA and what their deep black budget could afford. On certain missions, it had come in handy to alter his appearance to get close to a target. Looking in the mirror, Dean massaged the lifelike skin, molding the foam to the contours of his face. Special care had to be taken around the eye area. It was delicate and the easiest place to spot that he was wearing a mask. That's why he'd chosen the face of an older man. Wrinkles helped hide the flaws, and people always underestimated the potential physical prowess of a senior citizen.

This face allowed him to blend in, disappear into the background. To be easily dismissed.

It had also almost prevented him from getting the job at the bar.

His dad and stepfather were dead, and his mother was in a nursing home with middle-stage Alzheimer's. A cousin, who had relocated from Fort Collins, managed Delgado's, but she hated the environment, working late nights and had put her private psychotherapy practice on hold. Dean had waltzed in as DJ, claiming to be an old family friend, dishing details only an insider would be privy to, and offered to take the job at half the salary if he were paid under the table. The only stickler was he had to prove he had the stamina for the long hours and the ability to quash a bar fight without too much damage to the property or to himself.

The first few days on the job, his latex gloves had drawn stares and whispers. After he continually mentioned the longtime judge on *America's Got Talent* and an old television show about a detective who both had contamination OCD, the stares had dwindled and the whispers had faded.

Now all his hard work was down the drain.

Sirens wailed in the distance, the approaching sound ticking up his pulse. They would be here any moment. He stared at the obvious jagged tear along his throat and drew in a deep, steady breath. Remained calm. Didn't panic, not ever.

Panicking got people killed.

Digging into his bag, he found a tubular sports bandanna. It was versatile, could be worn as a neck gaiter, face mask, balaclava. Like a loaded gun and a med kit, he found it handy never to leave home without one.

His timer beeped.

He slipped on the stretchy bandanna, concealing the damage to the foam skin around his neck, but the only way to get the voice modulator to function properly was to press down on it while he spoke. Although it wasn't an ideal situation, it was a manageable one.

Sirens blared, drawing closer.

His shirt was slashed through. The midsection was practically in tatters. If not for the silicone false belly he wore to disguise his athletic build, he would have taken a knife to the stomach several times. He hadn't seen Smitty draw the switchblade. The thick, fake paunch had saved his life.

For good measure, Dean changed his shirt, putting on a fresh flannel button-down and tucking it in his jeans.

A loud whoop announced the arrival of the ambulance.

He tugged on two pairs of fresh gloves. Always two. Quickly, he wiped down anything he might've touched with his bare hands. He hurried from the bathroom, switched off lights, threw on his sheepskin leather bomber and locked up the place.

Flashing lights painted the mobile truck an eerie color. He squinted against the harsh glare.

EMTs were loading Cheryl into the back of the ambulance. A sheet covered her face. She was dead.

Such a pity.

Kate must have been devastated to lose her, and now that newborn was motherless.

Holding the baby, who was wrapped in a towel and blanket, Kate stood, talking to Sheriff Jim Ames. Just shy of six feet tall and broad shouldered, the man had a tough yet pleasant disposition. He carried himself like a man in charge, even out of uniform, but he was never arrogant or overbearing the way some of his deputies could be.

With his bag slung over his shoulder, DJ approached slowly, trying to pick up on the conversation and gauge what he could from the sheriff's body language.

"I did what I could for her to stop the bleeding," Kate said, clutching the baby to her chest and rocking him.

"Then you called 911?" the sheriff asked.

"No. DJ did."

The sheriff spotted Dean coming and redirected his attention to him. Kate's gaze followed. "Evening, DJ," Jim Ames called out when he got close enough for him to greet Dean without yelling.

Dean tipped his head at him. "Sheriff."

Their interaction over the past few months had been limited and casual. Only in passing. Jim struck him as a hardworking, reasonable man. The sheriff never came into the bar for a drink, and during their run-ins on the street he'd never harassed Dean by playing twenty questions with the newcomer. Unlike the deputies. But Laramie was a small, tight-knit community, so it was to be somewhat expected.

"Rough night?" Jim's face might have taken on a sympathetic look, but the sheriff maintained that wary appraisal in his eyes.

Dean gave an affirmative shrug.

"You're responsible for that?" the sheriff asked, hiking a thumb over at the dead body.

Pretending to rub his throat, Dean pushed on the voice modulator. "Yeah. Not sure how I did it, though. Guess I got lucky."

"Some kind of luck." The sheriff looked him over from head to toe and back up again. "She says you chased after the second man. There's another fella a block over. Ran out into the street. Deputy Powell is getting details now from the driver who hit him. Would that be the other assailant?"

"Yep." Dean nodded wearily. "Thought for sure he'd get away. He was so fast."

"Got lucky twice, huh?"

"A fluky coincidence."

"That's one explanation. Certainly odd. In my experience when there's a coincidence, it's better to examine it. Not ignore it." The sheriff assessed him for a long, uncomfortable moment. "Where were you just now and why did you leave the mobile clinic?"

Kate shivered as she made sure the baby was protected from the cold and wind, shielded by the heavy wool blanket.

Dean took off his jacket and draped it around Kate's shoulders. "I went to the bar. To grab my keys."

"Why did you need your keys?"

The quicker to get the hell out of Dodge. But Dean couldn't say anything to make him look as though he'd given the situation serious thought. Normal people didn't plot and strategize in emergencies.

Dean shook his head and gave another shrug. "Not really sure," he said, pressing on the modulator. "A lot happened pretty fast. Figured I might need them."

"Did you get injured in the altercation?" the sheriff asked.

Frigid wind cut through Dean's clothes. January and February were the coldest months of the year in Wyoming, but an Arctic blast had frozen Laramie solid. He clenched his jaw, swallowing a groan. "I'm a bit banged up, but I'll live."

"Is your throat all right?" Jim gestured at his neck. "You keep rubbing it, like it hurts."

Bunching his shoulders against the cold, Dean coughed. "I got hit a few times, but with all the exertion, my throat's dry and little irritated."

Kate's gaze bounced between them. "Yeah, I was worried about him. It was awful." Her voice was so fast and fluttery that Dean suspected she was teetering on a tight-rope of emotions. "He took a terrible beating all right, and one of those guys punched him in the throat."

Dean glanced at her for a heartbeat, refusing to let a grimace surface, keeping his face impassive. Why on earth had she said that?

The best lie was a vague one. He shifted his focus back to Jim Ames.

"Is that so?" Crow's-feet deepened as the sheriff's eyes narrowed on Dean. "You took a punch to the throat and still managed to kill one assailant and chase after the other?"

Her eyes flashed wide as the realization of her mistake became clear on Kate's face. Thankfully the sheriff was staring at Dean and not her.

"The blow to my throat sounds a lot worse than it was." Dean coughed again. "I just need some water. Rest. Really, that's all."

"We're ready to go," the EMT called from the ambulance. "We need to take the baby with us."

"I don't want to leave him." Kate shook her head. "His mother was worried about his safety. Can I ride along? To make certain he's okay?"

"Sure," the EMT said with a nod. "I don't see why not. You did help bring him into this world, after all."

Kate looked at Dean like she was reluctant to leave him.

"I'll meet you there," he said, reassuring her that he wouldn't simply take off. "And drive you back when you're ready."

"Okay." She nodded and turned to the sheriff. "Can we finish this later?"

"Sure, Katie," he said, using the nickname for a little girl. "Get that kid and yourself out of the cold." He waved her off.

Dean watched her climb into the back of the ambulance while the sheriff looked around at the crime scene. The ambulance doors closed, and the emergency vehicle pulled out of the lot.

"Something about this isn't adding up for me," Jim said, studying Dean once more. "Why don't you run me through what happened?"

On a deep shiver, Dean let out a long, hard exhale, and his breath crystallized in the frigid air between him and the sheriff. "I'm freezing. I should get to the hospital, too. Can this wait?" All he needed was a couple of hours. Enough time to talk to Kate, give them both the closure that had been fifteen years in the making. Then he'd hit the road and disappear for good.

"No problem," the sheriff said. "I'll follow you to the hospital. We can finish talking there. It's probably a good idea if a doctor gives you a full, thorough exam, to be sure there are no internal injuries. And we'll get pictures of any bruises for the report."

A physical examination was at the top of Dean's immediate *not-to-do* list. There was no way to avoid discovery under the probing hands of a doctor. "Sure, Sheriff." He gave an easy nod. "Whatever you think is best."

One way or another—*no matter what it took*—Dean was leaving Laramie tonight.

Chapter Three

Reluctant to let go of the baby, Kate handed him to Ellen Fossey, a nurse in the maternity ward on the third floor of the hospital. "You don't understand. There were these men who wanted to take him."

Smitty and his buddy were dead, but Kate didn't know why they had been after Cheryl and wanted the baby. Did the danger end with those two, or had they been a part of something bigger? Had they meant to do harm to a newborn?

Without any solid facts, other than Cheryl's undeniable fear before she died, all Kate had to rely on was the unsettling feeling still tying her stomach into knots.

"Don't worry," Ellen said, offering a gentle smile, "he'll be safe. There are several nurses on duty each shift, and we have security guards and cameras." She gestured to a couple.

Surveillance cameras with tiny red lights hung in a multitude of corners in the nursery and hallway. A security guard came around the corner and stopped at the nurses' station, which faced the elevator, and spoke to a woman wearing pink scrubs.

It should have alleviated Kate's concerns, but she sensed there had been more to Cheryl's troubles. Then there was the mysterious woman who had told the expectant mother that Kate would help her.

Every nerve ending burned with the certainty that the infant wasn't safe.

"We're going to take excellent care of him," Ellen said in a reassuring tone. She was about the same age as Kate. They'd been a couple of years apart in high school, with Ellen being older. Although they were friendly, they'd never become more than casual acquaintances. Back in school, Ellen had always been the first to protect a target of bullying or offer encouragement to others. She had a reputation for being the best neonatal nurse in town. "I'll get him cleaned up, and then the doctor will take a look at him."

"Okay." Kate took a step back. What other choice did she have? She wasn't the parent or legal guardian and had absolutely no say regarding the child.

She stood in the hall and watched through the large nursery window as Ellen gave the baby a sponge bath, put a diaper on him and swaddled him in a warm blanket.

The baby was in the best, safest place he could be at the moment. The nurse at the reception desk had already called Child Protective Services, and now the sheriff was aware of the situation.

Maybe Kate was being paranoid. Her basic instinct to protect the innocent was on overdrive. Or perhaps it was something else, another deep-rooted impulse fueled by her desire to be a mother herself one day. A longing she doubted that would ever be fulfilled.

She pressed her face against the soft sheepskin collar of Dean's jacket and inhaled the smell of him. Woodsy and earthy. Natural. Not some artificial scent from aftershave or cologne. The unique male essence that was pure Dean. Her muscles loosened in response, relaxing, all but the one pumping blood in her chest. Her heart clenched. The scent of him hadn't changed. He still smelled strong and safe.

Tears stung her eyes. The snapshot of him standing in the mobile clinic with his real face exposed was burned into her mind. She didn't want to dredge up the past, but with each breath, every lungful, it was the only thing she could think of.

The elevator chimed, and the doors opened. Sheriff Jim Ames stepped off alongside Dean, disguised as DJ.

Her heart squeezed, thinking about the face hidden beneath that disarmingly deceptive mask. A face she hadn't seen for fifteen years before tonight. Had dreamed of more times than she could count until she had forced herself to stop thinking of him. A bad habit that she'd had to break.

He had been right in front of her for the past seven months. No, almost nine. Pretending to be her friend, joking with her, laughing with her, flirting with her. Listening to her ramble on about everything that weighed on her heart. Things no one else in town knew. About the struggling business she'd taken over from Doc Fitzsimmons when he retired and how she was having a hard time making ends meet. About her happiness for her younger sister, and Claire's perfect life, that sometimes skewed toward envy. To her shame.

And all about her darkest secret... Tyler.

Telling her friendly neighborhood bartender had been akin to sharing with her pastor. But what Dean had done felt like a violation. The depths of his deception made her chest burn.

If the sheriff hadn't been with him, she would've slapped the mask right off his face.

Taking deep breaths, she did what she'd learned to do to endure his disappearance. She compartmentalized. She shoved her feelings, the memories of the past and thoughts of Dean's glaring deceit deep down. Put everything in neat little boxes to be dealt with at a more appropriate time.

"How's the baby?" Dean asked in that fake voice.

"Healthy, I think." She looked back into the nursery.

"The doctor's examining him now, and one of the nurses called Child Protective Services."

"That's good," Jim said. "They'll put him in the system, then they'll be able to help me track down the mother's family after we identify her." He touched something attached to his duty belt. A digital recorder. "Katie, did the woman give you her last name?"

Only her parents, her pastor and Jim called her Katie. Though the sheriff wasn't quite as old as they were, she guessed he was in his late forties. He had one kid in college, and the other was a senior in high school. Everything about him was strong yet appealing, from the features on his rugged face to his muscular build, which he'd retained from his days as the star quarterback for the Plainsmen. She appreciated his commanding presence that anchored the town.

"No," Kate said. "Just her first name, Cheryl."

Jim removed his stiff campaign hat, a brown Stetson, exposing his thick, dark hair. Only his lightly silver-flecked sideburns betrayed his age. "Did she mention who those two men were? Why they were after her? Whether one of them might have been the father?"

"I'm afraid not. She didn't tell me anything." But Kate wished that Cheryl had given her some information to go on, the smallest tidbit that might help protect her son. "I have no idea why they were after her or the baby. I suppose one of them could've been the father."

"I'll have the nurse get a cheek swab," Jim said, "and I'll run it against the DNA of the two assailants. If we get half as lucky as DJ has been tonight, one of those fellas will be a match."

Kate squirmed inside in her skin, trying not to let it show. Jim suspected something about Dean. Her days of loving him and watching out for him were long done. He'd packed his things, dropped out of school and walked away from his family and her. No note. No email. No phone call.

The worst part was that she'd been so hopelessly in love with him that if he'd confided in her, she would've gone with him.

Even though she should be over it, he haunted her. She missed him so much that at times her heart still ached, but there was no way she was ever falling back into the bad habit of Dean Delgado. Getting burned once was more than enough for a lifetime.

Still, no matter how furious she was at him, the instinct to protect him was strong as ever. "You should probably speak with Ellen now," Kate said to the sheriff, hoping to redirect his attention. "It'll be easier to get a cheek swab while the doctor is examining the baby. Once he's finished, they'll feed him and he'll probably fall asleep. You won't want to disturb the little guy then, will you?"

"I hadn't considered that." Jim hit the recorder on his belt, stopping it. "It's been so long since my boys were in diapers. I'll go take care of it, and I'll be right back."

They both nodded.

The sheriff walked a few feet away, a discreet distance, poked his head inside the nursery and spoke with the doctor.

Dean clutched her forearm. "Kate." His voice was a whisper, but the intimacy in the way he spoke her name roared through her.

"Not now," she interrupted, struggling to stem the emotion welling in her chest. Any explanation he offered would only upset her, and getting in a dither in front of the sheriff wouldn't help matters.

"He wants me to get a medical exam," Dean said, and her gaze flew to him. "That can't happen, for obvious reasons." He looked around. "Stall the sheriff for me."

"What? Why?" Her skin prickled. "How am I supposed do that?"

"You're clever. You'll think of something." Dean crossed the hall, casual as he pleased, and ducked into a bathroom.

Who in the heck did he think he was? Slipping into the bathroom to do only goodness knew what while leaving her to cover for him. Assuming that she would. *The nerve.*

Jim closed the nursery room door and turned toward her. His gaze darted about, no doubt in search of Dean, as he came back to stand in front of her. "Where's DJ?"

"The bathroom. I'm sure he'll only be a moment." She grasped the edges of the jacket draped around her to keep from fidgeting. "I'm glad you were on duty tonight to handle this." It was true. She didn't care for Chief Deputy Holden Powell anymore. He used to be a nice guy, but somewhere over the years he'd turned into an arrogant, pushy jerk. And he was one of her exes. A rebound after Dean had left town. The first in a long line of mistakes in her effort to forget her first love. Tyler had been the last. "Taking the occasional night shift must be tough."

"It's only tough when people start dying. Thankfully that's rare. Tomorrow was supposed to be my day off, so I could get back on a day schedule. But with everything that's happened, I'll be in the office in the morning for sure."

Kate chewed on her lower lip, thinking of how to change the conversation until Dean reemerged. "How's your son Colton doing?"

"Connecticut agrees with him. He loves Yale and has been getting good grades. Maggie and I are so proud of him. Plainsman to Yalie. But," he said, his eyebrows lowered in a grimace, "it's expensive."

"Tell me about it. I'm still paying off my student loans." She was drowning in debt and hadn't even gone to an Ivy League school. Rather than take on Doc's business, she should've left Laramie and started over with nothing, no remnants, no mementos. Moved to a larger city out of state. Maybe Denver, far from the constant reminders of the past that plagued her. Worked at someone else's practice for a few years, established financial security.

A fresh start would have done her good, if one had been possible. The only problem was she didn't know how to lose the baggage she carried in her soul.

"Depending on where our youngest decides to go," Jim said, "we might have to take out a second mortgage on the house."

"I can think of worse concerns for a parent." Concerns Cheryl would never get the chance to have. She looked back at the precious newborn. What was going to happen to him?

The doctor pushed through the door of the nursery and handed Jim a cotton swab sealed in a plastic bag. "Be sure to let us know if you find anything."

"Will do." Jim stuffed the swab in his inner jacket pocket. "How long will he have to stay here until he's released to CPS?"

"Three days if all his tests check out."

Jim gave a nod, and the doctor left.

"How long to run his DNA to see if it matches either man?" Kate asked.

"About the same amount of time," Jim said. "Maybe two, but if the lab is behind, it can take as long as five."

The bathroom door squeaked open. Dean trudged out into the hall and made his way up to them as though exhausted.

He was one hell of an actor. She'd give him that, but she wondered what he'd been doing in the bathroom all that time.

Jim tapped his recorder, starting it up again. "DJ, let me get your basic information and then I'll take your statement."

"Of course." Dean rattled off a full name, someone's date of birth, a phone number and a motel room as an address.

"Can you go through what happened for me?"

"I was getting ready to lock up the bar when I heard a woman scream outside," Dean said, rubbing his throat. "I went to take a look. Saw Kate and Cheryl. Offered to help. We got into the mobile pet clinic. As the baby came, those two thugs showed up. There was a scuffle, and then I don't really remember. It all happened so fast."

Jim's gaze sharpened. "I understand, but I need you to take your time and try to recall as many details as possible," he said, in a calm, patient voice. "The more details—" The squawk of the sheriff's radio hooked on his tan shirt cut him off.

"Sheriff, it's Holden," the male voice on the other end of the radio said. "We just got a call about a break-in in progress at Nelson's Gun and Outdoor Sports shop. I'm leaving the scene of the car accident with the driver handcuffed in the back of my cruiser to respond, but I could use backup."

"On my way," Jim said and keyed off the radio. "It must be a full moon or something." He raked back his hair and put his campaign hat on. "Why don't you two get some rest and swing by my office tomorrow to finish your statements? Oh, and DJ, you should get checked out by a doctor."

"I'm fine, really, Sheriff. The evening wiped me out and I want to get Kate home, but I'll take care of it tomorrow. Scout's honor."

"Okay." Jim tipped his hat at Kate and hurried down the hall.

Once he hopped in the elevator and the doors closed, she spun on Dean. "You were never a Boy Scout."

He shrugged. "I only said it for effect."

"What have you become? Some kind of a pathological liar?"

"My gift for lying isn't pathological, it's professional."

"Huh? What are you, a lawyer hiding out from the mob?"

Dean took her by the elbow and hauled her into the hallway bathroom.

Inside, she yanked her arm free of his grip.

He locked the door. "Look, I know I owe you an explanation. And an apology."

The apology was so long overdue she couldn't care less about it, but the explanation she wanted. "Start talking, and if you ever cared about me, even a little, please, no more lies."

"Of course I cared about you," he said, and she rolled her eyes. "How could you doubt that?"

How could she not?

"What's with the disguise?" she demanded.

"I am hiding out, but not from the mob."

"Then from who?"

"You asked me not to lie, so let's leave it at that. Telling you would only endanger you."

"Are you kidding me?" she asked, poking him in the chest. "You creep into town after fifteen years of turning your back on everything and everyone here—" she poked him again for good measure "—wearing this getup, and you expect me to swallow half-baked truths with no substance? You really never cared about me at all if you think that's what I deserve. What was I to you? A distraction, something to help you pass the time? A plaything you could toss away without a second thought?" She turned on her heel, unlocked the door and opened it to leave.

Dean slammed the door closed. "Please." The supplication in his voice made her pause.

"Please what?" she snapped. "Listen to your baloney and nod my head in sympathy like a good little *ignorant* accomplice? I don't think so." She grabbed the doorknob and twisted it.

Dean slapped a gloved palm to the door and shoved his foot up against it. "Give me ten minutes."

She sucked in a strained breath. "Only if you promise to give me the whole truth."

Clenching his jaw, he shook his head. "When they come looking for me, I don't want you getting caught in the middle, used as a pawn or hurt because you know too much."

Didn't he understand that no one could hurt her as deeply as he had? Not even if they tortured her slowly for days.

"I don't care what kind of trouble you're in." She wasn't concerned for her safety. At this point, she cared more about her sanity and hearing something that made sense. "But I need to know what *it* is." What would drive him to such lengths. Putting on a costume and pretending to be someone else, every day for nine months. The attention to detail, the self-discipline that required boggled her mind. "I've always kept your secrets. You can trust me."

He cocked his head to the side. "That's not entirely true… Is it?"

She recoiled. "What are you talking about?" Not once had she betrayed his confidence. "I would never."

"You're the only person I told what I wanted to be one day." His eyes were cool and unblinking.

Had she told someone?

Kate racked her brain. After he'd taken off, his parents and the sheriff had interrogated her, and she'd given them nothing. Because she'd known nothing. Dean hadn't shared his plan.

It wasn't until years later, at his stepfather's funeral, that his mother had admitted to Kate that she'd received a letter from the marines, congratulating them on Dean's completion of basic training. His mother had burned it, not wanting to upset her husband, but she had been relieved to know her son was alive and well.

Growing up together and later while they'd dated, not once had Dean mentioned the military to Kate. Only about becoming a CIA operative. To be an American version of James Bond.

She'd never taken him seriously and certainly had told no one except...

"You mean the CIA?" she asked.

"You told Lucas."

She'd been a senior and Lucas a sophomore. The two of them heartbroken and alone, they'd bonded over Dean. Became close friends. Inseparable. Lucas had even encouraged her to date Holden in a futile effort to purge Dean from her system.

"I guess it slipped one day," she said. "We only had each other after you abandoned us. But it was your brother, for goodness' sakes—that doesn't count."

"He found me. Did you know that?"

"What? How?"

"He joined the CIA."

The words hung in the air between them, sucking all the oxygen from the room. Light-headed, she suddenly couldn't breathe. Lucas had found Dean and didn't put her out of her misery by telling her where he was, what he was doing. That he was okay.

She could kill the Delgado brothers.

"For the longest time," Dean said, "I thought it was coincidence, him becoming a spook like me. Then I connected the dots back to you." His voice was full of accusation.

"I didn't do anything wrong." Yet, he stood here, wearing a mask and latex gloves, trying to make her feel as if she had. How dared he. "This isn't about me. This is about you. Remember? Take off that disguise and tell me why you need it. Right now."

Crossing her arms, she waited while he removed the mask. She wasn't going to back down until he spilled his guts. It was the very least that he owed her.

He looked up at her with his real face, and all her careful compartmentalization unraveled. Their days and nights together came back in a dizzying rush. Holding hands. Kissing. Sharing their highs and lows. Making love whenever they could, wherever they could, as often as possible.

Her heart pounded faster, her blood singing in her veins. She longed to press her palm to his cheek and caress his two-day stubble. Touch him. Verify with her hands, not only her eyes and her heart, that he was real. But she resisted the temptation.

The man was an itch she longed to scratch. But like a severe case of the chicken pox, if she indulged and gave in to the urge, it would only lead to scars she'd later regret.

"Why have you been lying to me for months, pretending to be DJ?" When he could have climbed a flight of stairs to her apartment, located right above the bar, and told her the truth. Given them a chance to talk, to heal.

A part of her desperately wanted to believe that he'd come back to town for her.

He lowered his head a moment, as if debating whether to be honest. So help her, she would shake it out of him if need be.

"I owe you the truth." His gaze met hers. "You can't repeat anything I tell you, not even under duress. When I chased after Smitty, my face was caught on CCTV. People will come here looking for me. You've got to play dumb. For your sake. Do you understand?"

Without a doubt, she could play as dumb as she felt. For nine months she'd believed his charade, hook, line and sinker. Like a complete idiot.

"All right." She gestured for him to continue.

"I was with the CIA," he said, and the past tense struck her. "On my team's last mission, something went wrong. We—I—killed someone who was only supposed to die as collateral damage with the intended target. But the high-value target wasn't on-site. Everything went to hell in a handbasket. The CIA thinks that my team was turned, that we're traitors."

"What?" This was serious. Big. As in treason and jail time–type trouble.

She looked at him, really looked at him. This time she noticed the changes. He was older. More ridiculously attractive as a man than he'd been as a boy. But there was an intensity to him, a dangerous aura that hadn't been there when he was younger.

"My entire team was forced to scatter to the four winds and stay off the agency's radar."

"You need a lawyer. A real shark who swims in intelligence agency waters. The best money can buy." Too bad she didn't have two nickels to rub together.

"A lawyer?" he scoffed. "They don't want to arrest us and put us on trial. They want us dead. Permanently silenced. Erased from existence."

He was so steady and sure, the exact opposite of her. It made her doubt reality, but she shook her head. What he alleged was preposterous.

"You're an American citizen entitled to due process," she said. "What you're talking about only happens in movies. Not real life."

He moved into her space and pressed so close that the smell of him engulfed her senses. On reflex, her body tightened, guarding against it.

"Oh, Kate." He tucked a lock of her hair behind her ear, trailed his fingers along her jaw.

Heat jolted through her. His proximity, the warmth radiating from his body played havoc on her ability to think, to breathe.

The bone-deep ache she'd found hard to ignore for the last decade flared up as she stared at him. His luscious curls were long enough at the front to run her fingers through them. Skin she wanted to touch. Brown eyes that went straight through her.

She realized all the anger and sorrow and confusion she'd had festering inside would never end.

His presence, the memory of him, was an albatross around her neck.

"After I ran into you at the bar and realized you lived upstairs, every single day I thought about knocking on your door and telling you." His voice was soft as cotton. "Showing you who I really was. But this," he said, gesturing toward her, and the insult in his tone was clear, "is the reason I didn't."

Her stomach twisted into a knot. *"This?"*

"You're a candy-coated civilian ill equipped to handle the truth. I told you that my life is in danger, and you're in denial. Talking about lawyers and due process. I kill people for the CIA. Or used to. Bad people to make the world a better, safer place. Nonetheless, *assassin* would be the job title on my résumé. You wouldn't believe the things I've seen. The things I've done. That's how I know, for a fact, that a team will have boots on the ground in Laramie in twenty-four hours. Thirty-six, tops. They will have one objective—to eliminate me. So I'm going to be long gone by then."

Every word that left his mouth gathered momentum, building speed, barreling forward, and plowed into her with the force of an eighteen-wheeler.

It was a wonder she was still standing without shattered bones. But it was her heart that was in pieces. "I just found out that you're here and you're leaving tomorrow?"

She'd thought she had died inside when he'd disappeared the first time.

Stripped to nothing.

But now hurt was like a concrete block in her chest, weighing her down, making it impossible to breathe. How could he keep killing her?

"Not tomorrow," he said. "I'm leaving tonight."

Chapter Four

Ten minutes to talk to Kate was taking twenty. Dean needed to go.

The clock ticking in his head was counting down to the arrival of a very real team of trained killers, despite her doubts.

She squeezed her eyes shut as if in pain, her lips pinched. Her long hair fell forward, covering her face. Wavy and thick, it was still the color of sunshine. He remembered the silken feel of it between his fingers the same way he remembered the feel of her pressed against him. How she smelled of wild summer flowers even in winter.

In all his years, he'd never desired a woman the way he had her.

He pulled off his gloves, tucked her hair back and caressed her cheek. She was so beautiful, had the face of an angel. It tore him apart to see her upset.

"Kate?" He curled his hands around her arms, wanting to hold her, to make this better or at least easier, but he seemed to be making it worse.

She trembled in his hands, and it frightened him. All he wanted was to keep her safe and out of harm's way.

"Are you all right?" For the second time she didn't respond. So he did the only thing he could think of. The one thing he'd longed to do the moment he'd set eyes on her again.

He lowered his mouth to hers and kissed her. His lips trembled, or maybe it was hers. For a heartbeat it was perfection. She stopped shaking, her body softening as she deepened the kiss. His bare hand cupped her face, her lips warm and soft under his.

And then that perfection disintegrated.

Wrenching back, she stumbled away from him, her eyes snapping open. She fixed him with a stare and wiped the back of her hand across her mouth as though he'd tasted rancid. "Why are you here in Laramie?"

The question caught him off guard, a complete blindside. "I don't understand."

"You're a superspy 007 knockoff now. You claim you're on the run and need to hide, so why come back home? Why did you pick Laramie?"

He shook his head. The answer was complicated. Convoluted on too many levels to explain in a hospital bathroom. Leaving all those years ago hadn't really been a choice. A terrible, necessary act to prevent something more horrible from happening. Every important thread in his life began and led right back here in a vicious tangle. Knotted up forever.

The one thread that shone the brightest was standing right in front of him—Kate.

But he chose one word to sum it all up. "Closure."

She pulled away from him with an anguished look on her face, as though he'd said the worst possible thing. "You're still the same selfish coward who ran away with his tail tucked between his legs fifteen years ago."

The accusation knocked the breath from his lungs.

His hands dropped from her arms, and he stepped back. "I'm a lot of things, but a selfish coward isn't one of them." He had risked his life countless times in the marines and with the CIA for his country and national security. To preserve a way of life he didn't have the privilege to enjoy.

"Is that what you tell yourself so you can sleep at night?"

He deserved her anger considering the way he'd handled things, but after all this time, he had assumed she would've guessed the reason he left. "Things had gotten bad at home."

"I know. I was there. I saw the bruises on you and Lucas."

But she'd only been aware of a fraction of the darkness he'd lived with. There had been so many things he'd been unable to say at the time. Even now.

Perhaps that's why he'd made a great bartender. He'd spoken little and had listened a lot, especially to her, over the past few months. That was his one other undervalued talent. Listening.

People loved to talk to him. Bartending was an easy cover. After he'd learned that Kate lived in the apartment above the bar, it had sealed his conviction to wheedle his way into the job.

Kate had been his anchor back then, and when his world had turned upside down again, fleeing for his life, he'd been drawn back here. To her.

"You don't know," he said, shaking his head.

"It takes courage to stay and fight for what you love. But that's not what you did, is it?" She took off his jacket and threw it at him. "You ran. Without saying goodbye. If you need to go again, then do what you do best, and leave. But I could really use your help."

Hollow dread opened in his chest—a sinkhole threatening to swallow his future. "My help with what?"

"Figuring out what happened to Cheryl and making sure her baby is safe. I'm going to find out who she was, why she was scared and who sent her to me."

Dean sighed. "Let the sheriff handle it."

"The sheriff didn't see a pregnant, malnourished girl so terrified for her life and her baby's she went to a veterinarian instead of a hospital to give birth. As soon as Jim finds out that you, DJ, disappeared without a trace, he'll be more interested in your whereabouts than that infant."

"You're only going to invite trouble by asking questions." Dean got the sense that the situation with Smitty and his cohort had gone deeper than a lover's quarrel. If he had to guess, he would bet money this involved organized crime. They didn't have the mob out there in Wyoming, but they sure had shadowy figures doing dirty deeds. "Leave it alone."

"If I had looked the other way and left it alone, where would that baby be now?"

He shuddered to think of the possibilities. "Maybe one of them was the father and he was afraid she'd steal his kid. Maybe they only wanted the baby to use him as leverage with Cheryl because she saw or heard something she shouldn't have. Maybe with the three of them dead, there's nothing more to worry about." The list of maybes stacking up in his head seemed infinite.

"And *maybe* not. I'm going to dig until I get answers." Her tone brooked no argument.

"Why?"

"Because I'm not a coward. Because I think about more than myself. Because I ushered that child into the world. In a way, he's my responsibility, since there's no one else to look out for him. And it's the right thing to do."

"But it's not the smart thing. You're only going to put yourself in danger."

"That's why I need you. Dean, if you hadn't been in the mobile clinic, those men would've killed me to get to her and the baby."

His gut roiled with renewed fury. He'd accepted the possibility of an early death a long time ago, but Kate was meant to live a long, happy life.

Her honey-brown eyes softened, drawing him in. "More

thugs could turn up when I start asking questions. You're a slick agent with all sorts of useful skills. Who better to help me get answers while keeping me safe?"

The knot in the threads of his life tightened. But he couldn't get sucked into this.

"I can't stay." No matter how much he wanted to. He'd give anything for more time with her now that she knew who he was. "Pursuing this on your own could be suicide. Let it go, please. I don't want anything to happen to you."

"Then stay. For me."

Asking him to give her the Hope diamond would be simpler. Kate had no idea what was headed to Laramie. *Something deadly this way comes.* "I can't," he said.

She straightened, her eyes growing cold. "I thought about what it might be like to see you again one day. Good. Hard. Painful. But I hadn't imagined you'd be such a sad disappointment." She opened the bathroom door.

Dean caught her wrist and stopped her before she crossed the threshold. "Give me a second to put this thing back on." He held up the mask. "Then I'll take you home."

He could talk some sense into her during the car ride, make her see reason.

"I don't need a ride. Child Protective Services is on the way. I'm going to hang around until they get here, so I have a point of contact. I'll get a car service to take me home when I'm ready to leave. Goodbye, Dean." The neutral finality in her voice stung.

Her wrist jerked free of his hand, and she was gone.

The door closed behind her.

He took a moment to gather himself and process what had transpired before pulling on his gloves and the mask. After making sure everything was in place with the bandanna covering his neck, he slipped into the hall.

Kate stood with her arms crossed over her chest, staring into the nursery.

He walked up beside her, his head down, staring at his boots.

This wasn't how he wanted to end things. The atmosphere between them was saturated with things unsaid. It didn't feel like closure. It felt like regret.

He noticed the outline of her cell phone in her lab coat pocket. He grabbed it and swiped the screen. The phone wasn't even password protected.

Candy-coated civilian.

In her contacts, he thumbed in the number to his burner phone—a prepaid disposable—not the fake number he'd given to the sheriff and saved it under the name Heathcliff. It was from her favorite book in high school, *Wuthering Heights*. He'd never understood why she'd loved it so much. The two lovers had married other people and died in the end without ever truly being together. Then again, if suffering and tragedy were Kate's gold standard of a relationship, it explained why she'd fallen for him.

"If you need me, call." He held out the cell.

"I thought you were leaving with no plans to come back," she said without looking at him or taking the phone.

"I am."

"Then why bother giving me your number?"

"If you get into a jam or something—"

"You'll be halfway across the country. Maybe even in Canada. Mexico. You're a superspy. Not a superman."

She had a valid point. But he couldn't bear to think this would be the last conversation that they'd ever have.

"Take it anyway." He dropped the phone in her pocket, and it clinked against something that didn't sound like keys.

The sound drew both their gazes.

She stuck her hand in her pocket and pulled out a thumb drive. "Did you put this in there?" She finally met his eyes.

"No. I have no idea where that came from."

She flipped it over, examining the thumb drive. Silver

and nondescript, there was nothing written on it. Kate's gaze roamed as though she was thinking. "Cheryl grabbed my pocket right before she died. I was still in shock from the fight and seeing you. She could have slipped this inside without my knowing."

"If that thumb drive came from Cheryl, whatever is on it will only get you killed."

Dean went to snatch the drive from her fingers, but she clenched a fist around it and pulled it out of his reach. She was faster than he expected.

Raising an eyebrow, she asked, "Were you going to take this to help me?"

In a manner of speaking. "I was going to take it to save you." From herself.

"You don't care about me. And you don't care about him." She nodded toward the nursery.

Care about her?

For a while, he'd deluded himself into thinking that a person's first love was supposed to stick. That not being able to forget and move on didn't mean anything. Then he'd spent the past nine months seeing her, smelling her, talking to her and there was no denying that he was still *in love* with her. He'd never stopped caring. Had only suppressed his feelings over the years. Being back in Laramie brought it all to the surface.

But they weren't kids anymore. The stakes were higher. This mess with Cheryl wasn't his problem, and it didn't need to be Kate's, either.

"You only care about yourself," she said, throwing another barb.

Guilt had gnawed at him for a decade and a half. To push his buttons, she was going to have to try a heck of a lot harder.

"Be smart and stay safe," he said. "Give the thumb drive to the sheriff."

"I'll give it to him after I make a copy of the contents."

Gritting his teeth in frustration, Dean shook his head. "Why won't you listen to me? Looking at what's on it will only drag you in deeper."

Kate shoved the thumb drive in the pocket of her jeans. "I heard every word you said, but you're the one not paying attention. Cheryl chose me for a reason. I need to know why, and I need to make sure her son is going to be safe, too." She drew in a deep breath. "If something does happen to me," she said, her voice going cold, colder than outside, "and I mean the worst possible thing, do me a favor."

"What's that?"

"Don't come to my funeral. I wouldn't want you there." She turned away from him and faced the nursery. "This time stay gone for good."

His gut heated with that final blow from her, got so warm it turned something inside him to mush. Getting soft was the last thing he could afford with a team preparing to descend on this town. It was time to go. "My number is saved under Heathcliff," Dean muttered.

He walked to the elevator and hit the call button. In the shiny reflection of the doors, he watched her.

Her gaze stayed fixed on the nursery. Her bearing hard as granite.

The doors opened. He shuffled inside and looked at her one last time. His beautiful, stubborn Kate.

Not once did she glance in his direction.

The doors closed, and he wondered whether he was making a mistake.

Dean hurried out of the hospital, crossed the parking lot, hopped in his car and raced to the fleabag motel where he had a rented room. He had a long-term rate and an additional discount for taking care of his own upkeep. Convincing the manager that he was doing the motel a service by changing his own sheets, vacuuming and cleaning had been simple when in fact Dean would've paid extra to keep housekeeping from snooping through his belongings.

In his room, it took him two minutes flat to gather his things and pack. Traveling light was essential. He wiped down the surfaces as an extra precaution, taking special care in the bathroom.

He shoved a loaded nine-millimeter in his jacket pocket, took another quick look around to be sure he hadn't forgotten anything and left the room. Popping his trunk, he tossed his things inside. He peeled out of the motel parking lot, leaving his room unlocked, and got on the road. Within minutes, he hit I-80. The interstate was clear. It was nearly five in the morning.

Canada was a good idea. He could be in Calgary in less than sixteen hours.

But the farther the destination, the longer it would take him to get back when Kate called telling him she was in trouble. Not if, but when.

Taking the ramp for US Route 287 South, he headed toward Colorado. Denver was a great city, plenty to keep him occupied, but Boulder was a sounder choice with fewer surveillance cameras.

In the morning, he'd call his cousin Lourdes, though everyone called her Lola, and tell her to close up the bar. Take a vacation. Go back to Fort Collins. Her brother, Jake, was an FBI agent there. She would be out of danger with him in case the kill team showed up at Delgado's Bar.

Then there was Kate. When the time came, he could be back in Laramie in two hours from Boulder. And the time would come if she started asking questions about Cheryl. In his gut, he was certain of it.

Although the baby was safe, Child Protective Services was going to get involved and the sheriff's office would investigate, Kate wasn't going to leave well enough alone.

Not that it should surprise him. She'd always been like

that. A backbone of steel, an iron will and the biggest heart. Even as a child, she couldn't resist picking up strays, nursing wounded animals and helping anyone in need.

In the sixth grade, they'd come across a lost dog on their way home from school. A vicious, mangy mutt with no collar. Dean had wanted to steer clear of the animal, suspecting that it might have rabies and one of them could lose a limb or an eye if they got too close.

All Kate had seen was a scared animal in need. Not taking heed of his warnings, ignoring the bared teeth and foaming drool dripping from its mouth, she'd followed her instincts and approached the dog. Dean had made Lucas stay back and climb on the hood of a nearby car just in case. The mutt had attacked and bitten her hand. Dean had grabbed her, pulling her up onto the car hood, but the dog managed to claw her leg in the process. Gave her scars that'd never fade.

Dr. Fitzsimmons, the local veterinarian, had been passing by, and he'd known exactly what to do to calm the animal and to treat Kate's wounds later.

Turned out, they'd both been right. The dog had been dangerous, but it hadn't had rabies. The mutt had been scared and mistreated.

Kate's instincts invariably got her into her trouble, at times badly hurt, but she was never wrong. Whatever she discovered on the thumb drive was only going to spur her on, not make her back off. Her heart had once been his compass, pointing him true north so that he didn't get lost. Digging into Cheryl might not be the smart thing, but Kate believed it was the right one. She also sensed that child was in danger.

Maybe he *was* the one not paying attention.

Kate thought what he did best was leaving, but the reality was, what he did best was protect her. Despite any pain it caused him.

Only a fool wouldn't be afraid of a kill team, but a marine's core tenet was to defend those who could not defend themselves. No matter the personal cost. Maybe Cheryl's child did need protection. Maybe not. There was only one way to know for sure. And if something happened to Kate because he didn't help her, because he was running like a selfish coward, albeit a smart one, what would his life be worth?

Dean crossed the border into Colorado, took the next exit and turned around, heading back to Laramie.

Chapter Five

"Thank you, Mrs. Smith, for coming in so quickly, at the crack of dawn, no less," Kate said to the representative from Child Protective Services.

"Once a call comes into the twenty-four-hour hotline, our office receives an email about the incident." Dressed in a pantsuit, Regina Smith was a middle-aged woman with glasses, a slight paunch and graying hair in a blunt bob that suited her round face. "I suffer from insomnia, and I'm constantly on the computer. A bad habit, I know. But it's fortunate I came when I did so I could get your account on what happened firsthand."

"All the information you provided was helpful. I feel better knowing you'll personally check on him once a day. I will as well, and the nurses promised to keep a special eye on him."

"I can speak with hospital security if you'd like. Have them do extra rounds on the maternity ward."

"That would be wonderful." Kate hadn't considered that possibility. "Are you sure they'll agree to do it?"

"The head of security and I are old friends," Mrs. Smith said with a smug grin.

Not surprising. There were only two degrees of separation from everyone in town.

"Hopefully the sheriff will be able to locate the deceased mother's family," Mrs. Smith said. "That would be the best-case scenario, placing the child with relatives. But either way, we'll ensure he's in a loving, stable home once he's cleared to leave the hospital." The older woman looked Kate over. "You should go home. Take a shower. Put on fresh clothes. Try to get some rest."

Kate glanced down at the bloodstains on her lab coat. She must've looked a hot mess. "Now that I've spoken with you, I'll call a car service."

"I can give you a ride, if you like."

"Are you sure? I don't want to put you to any trouble."

Flashing a warm smile, Mrs. Smith waved a dismissive hand. "It's no bother. After I drop you off, I'll grab a coffee and go in early to the office. Get started on the paperwork for Baby Doe."

"Thank you. I appreciate it."

They made their way down to the lobby and outside. The Arctic wind blowing down from the north cut straight through Kate. She tugged her lab coat closed and wrapped her arms around herself, fighting off a shiver.

Darkness still hung in the air. Wisps of gray clouds snaked around the moon high in the sky. The sun wouldn't be up for another hour or two.

Mrs. Smith pressed her key fob. Lights flashed on a late-model sedan as the doors unlocked. They both climbed in, and Kate gave a sigh of relief for the shelter from the cold.

"Where do you live?"

"In an apartment above Delgado's Bar."

"Oh, over on Third Street. You're right in the heart of town." Mrs. Smith headed out of the parking lot and turned onto Grand Avenue. "I've always wondered what those apartments were like. Are they nice?"

Kate shrugged. "Comfortable enough for the price. I get a hefty discount because mine is over the bar. It wasn't my first choice, but after..." She swallowed the words, not wanting to rehash the past.

"After what happened with Tyler," Mrs. Smith said with a shake of her head, finishing Kate's sentence, "you probably just wanted to get resettled anywhere quickly. You poor thing."

Kate cringed on the inside. Gossip spread through the small town like a communicable disease, but Tyler's death had made the front page of the newspaper. While out on one of his morning jogs, he'd been the victim of a hit-and-run driver. Killed instantly, according to the coroner. No witnesses. No suspects. His funeral had been a county event.

It'd been common knowledge she and Tyler had been involved and living together at the time.

"How did you know him?" Kate remembered Mrs. Smith from the funeral, but most of the town had shown up to pay their respects.

"His mom and I are good friends."

With all the friends and family relations, it felt like there was no separation in town. Not even two degrees.

Mrs. Smith tsked. "It's awful what happened. He was so young. Only thirty-three. His mother was hoping that Tyler would propose to you. She thought you would've made a fine daughter-in-law. A good wife."

Too bad Tyler wouldn't have made a good husband. Sure, he'd had a stable job, had been smart and funny and charming. Checked most of the appropriate boxes on the list for a suitable partner. But the dark secret she'd only shared with DJ—or rather, Dean—was that Tyler had been cheating on her. For months, she had suspected an affair. When she finally found proof that he'd been sleeping with his editor, she hadn't been angry or sad or humiliated.

Truth be told, she'd been relieved.

Tyler had given her a way out of a seemingly perfect relationship that half of Laramie had sworn would culminate in marriage.

Before Tyler's car accident, she had already made plans

to move and had started looking for a new place. Then he'd died, and everyone had expected her to play the part of the bereaved girlfriend.

At the end of every relationship, she'd felt immense relief. A weight lifted from her.

Whether it had been future deputy sheriff Holden, the teller at the bank, the assistant professor at the community college or investigative journalist Tyler.

The only one she wished hadn't ended had been with the one guy who had broken her heart.

What did make her flush with the heat of humiliation was how she'd confided the truth to her bartender, not knowing she'd been pouring her soul out to Dean the whole time.

Mrs. Smith pulled up alongside the mobile pet clinic and stopped. "I'm so sorry for your loss. You and Tyler made such an attractive couple."

It had been ten and a half months, nearly a year, and still she received comments such as this, when to Kate it already felt like forever. "Thank you."

"I'll give my friend at the hospital a ring as soon as I think he's in the office."

Kate nodded. "I appreciate the ride." She hopped out of the car and waved goodbye as Mrs. Smith drove off.

She glanced at the mobile clinic. It would need a thorough cleaning. Not that she was sure if that was allowed. Was the truck considered a crime scene? She'd have to check with the sheriff and cancel her appointments for the day, perhaps for the next several if she didn't get the green light to sanitize it.

The EMTs had taken Cheryl's body and the baby so quickly. Kate tried to remember if she'd locked the truck. There was no cash in the clinic, but she had valuable equipment inside that someone could hock. A junkie had tried to break in once while she'd been living with Tyler.

One thing she loved about living over the bar was being able to keep an eye on the truck from her apartment.

She hurried up to the door. Sure enough, it was unlocked. *Fantastic.* Stepping inside, she hoped that nothing was missing. After the morning she'd had so far, she didn't think she could handle one more thing.

Kate climbed the three steps and stumbled to a halt. *Oh, my God!*

Things had been thrown and knocked around in the fight earlier, but now her truck had been completely ransacked. Her mind raced, choppy thoughts firing through her head as if in time with her pulse.

Someone had torn her clinic apart. Destroyed it.

Everything could be replaced, she told herself. Her insurance would cover the cost. It would be all right.

She stepped deeper inside. Medical instruments were scattered on the floor. The orthopedic saw, forceps, steel suture wire, stethoscope, handheld ultrasound. Equipment worth thousands of dollars hadn't been taken. She checked the locked medicine cabinet. It hadn't been touched.

This was so odd. Why would someone do this and not take anything?

Even as she drew in a deep, calming breath, telling herself this was a coincidence, it was as though a clammy finger ran down her spine.

What if Smitty had friends who wanted to send her a message? Had more than two men been looking for Cheryl? There must've been, if this was connected.

She eased back out of the truck, trying to come to grips with the vandalism. Part of her didn't think she was capable of handling this on top of everything else. What might happen when she started asking questions about Cheryl?

Backing down wasn't her style. She wasn't going to let some thugs intimidate her.

Closing and locking the door, she decided to take this

one step at a time. First, coffee. Caffeine was a top priority. She needed to think clearly. After a piping-hot cup of joe, she'd call the sheriff's office and report the incident.

Kate slogged up the staircase to her place, vowing never to make the mistake of leaving home without her coat again. She pulled her keys from her pocket and unlocked the door. At least with the unexpected break from work, she'd be able to spend as much time as she wanted at the hospital and looking into Cheryl. Kate wasn't going to let this go. Something inside her wouldn't allow her to.

She crossed the threshold into the dim apartment, flinging the door shut. Warmth wrapped around her. She tossed her keys on the side table, switched on a lamp and headed for the kitchen.

A floorboard creaked behind her.

Kate froze as her blood ran cold. Someone was in her apartment. Then she heard it again, a soft groan of wood. She whirled around, facing the intruder.

A man wearing a ski mask stepped out of the shadows in the corner and into the faint light filtering in from the living room window. "Give me the thumb drive Cheryl stole." His voice was a harsh whisper.

For a split second, she couldn't move. Couldn't breathe. Then he took another step toward her, and adrenaline kicked in. Kate darted into the bedroom, slammed the door and twisted the latch on the knob, locking it.

The man banged against the door, making it rattle on its hinges.

She heard cursing from the other side. Frantically, she glanced around. She snatched her purse from the top of her dresser and dug inside.

Another loud bang against the door.

Oh, God, what's happening?

She grabbed the pepper spray for bears and thumbed off the orange safety guard as the bedroom door burst open.

Shrieking, she aimed at the man's head and depressed the handle on the power fogger. A blast of pepper spray hit him in the face.

The guy reared back, roaring in pain.

If the spray could stop a bear with temporary loss of sight, burning the skin and restricting breathing, it'd certainly slow down a man.

She dashed into the bathroom and locked the door. Her mind reeled.

He's after the thumb drive. What's on it? Did he trash my truck looking for it?

She crossed the room and clawed at the latch on the frosted window. It had been painted over and was stuck. She took the metal nail file with a sharp pointed tip from the counter and scraped at the dried paint until the latch moved.

A faint popping sound drew her gaze. Bullet holes in the wood.

He had a gun. With a silencer.

She yanked the window up and climbed outside onto the fire escape. The door flew open, splintering around the frame, and the man stormed in.

Rubbing at his eyes and coughing, he waved the gun around wildly in his other hand and pulled the trigger. Bullets hammered into the walls.

Kate pinched her lips tight and climbed down the metal ladder.

Ping. Ping. Bullets ricocheted off steel near her head. In the quiet open air, the sound was loud and sharp. Almost earsplitting. She let loose a scream.

He was shooting at her.

More gunfire spit around her with sparks flying from the fire escape. She shrieked as she jumped from the last rung and hit the pavement. Pain zipped up her legs, and her heart slammed against her rib cage.

Move!

Run!

She scurried to her feet, ignoring the sharp ache in her ankles, and forced herself to think. Her mobile pet clinic was around the bend. But she remembered with a sinking heart that her keys were up in her apartment.

Footfalls pounded on the fire escape on the second floor. He was coming after her. She had to get out of there. Find help.

She scrambled to the corner and froze, thinking which way to go.

A car screeched to a halt in front of her. Hysteria bubbled up in her chest. *Oh, no.* Was it more of them?

Then she recognized the vehicle. A Jeep Renegade. Dean was behind the wheel. He leaned over and opened the passenger door. "Get in!"

A bullet struck the side mirror.

She lunged into the car and slammed the door shut.

Dean hit the accelerator, speeding away down the block.

Quivering, she slid down in the seat and wrapped her arms around herself.

"Are you okay? Did you get hit?"

He tried to kill me. He tried to kill me. He tried to kill me.

"Kate," Dean said, his voice growing firm, "were you shot? Are you okay?"

She couldn't speak. She just panted and shook her head.

"No, what?" he asked.

"I wasn't shot," she said, forcing the words from her mouth, but her voice was barely audible. She cleared her throat and tried again. "He didn't shoot me." But she was far from all right.

Dean made lots of dizzying turns, checking his rearview mirror every block or two. Before she knew it, he parked in front of a motel on the outskirts of town. "I can't go back to the one I was staying at since the sheriff might go looking for me. I'll get a room here. We'll talk inside." He took her hand in his, and she wished he wasn't wearing gloves. "It's going to be okay."

A moment later his hand slipped from hers and he was out of the car, moving toward the entrance. She thought about everything that happened in the past few hours to toss her world upside down.

All of it had started with a phone call for help. And landed her here. Outside a dump of a motel, running for her life.

Her chest convulsed as she pictured the man in the ski mask stalking toward her in her apartment. In her home. The one place that should've been safe.

A knock on the window startled her, making her jump. With a hand pressed to her chest, she tried to calm her racing heart.

Dean gestured for her to get out of the car, and she did.

"Here, the coffee is fresh." He handed her a to-go cup with a lid, steam escaping from the hole, and put his jacket around her shoulders. "We'll walk to the room. I'll repark away from the motel once I get you settled, just in case the sheriff puts out an all-points bulletin with the make and model."

He grabbed a bag from the trunk, put an arm around her, guided her to room 114 and unlocked the door. Inside it smelled of cigarette smoke and mildew.

She gazed at the faded green bedspread and sighed. In a handful of hours, this was what her life had become.

Dean locked the door and turned the heat up before urging her deeper inside the room, away from the door. He directed her toward the bed. She stiffened and pulled back, still too shaken, too terrified, but he was having none of it.

"It's okay," he reassured her and guided her to take a seat on the bed.

He sat beside her, so close that their legs and arms touched. His body was rigid, as if he were still on high alert, ready to handle any danger. He just sat there for a long moment, not saying anything, lending her his heat and the comfort of his nearness. Those dark eyes sharp on her face.

"You should drink the coffee." His tone was gentle. "Hope you still take it with two sugars and a splash of cream."

"I do. I'm surprised you remember something so inconsequential about me after all this time."

He pulled off the mask and removed the gloves. Caught her gaze and held it. "I remember everything about you."

A ghost of warmth flickered inside her.

"Go on and have some." He nudged the hand holding the cup up toward her mouth. "The sugar and a shot of caffeine will help counteract shock. I promise."

Taking an obedient sip of the coffee, she was glad to have something hot to drink and for Dean's presence. After she took another swallow, she actually felt a slight lessening of tension in his muscles, as though his worry was draining.

She lifted her head, suddenly more alert, her thoughts solidifying. "What are you doing here?" Not that she wasn't grateful to see him. If not for his fortuitous arrival, surely the man who'd broken into her apartment would've caught up with her. Dean had saved her for a second time. "I thought you'd left town."

"I did, but I couldn't stop thinking about you. How when it comes to you, no good deed goes unpunished. I'd never forgive myself if anything happened to you because I refused to help."

"You made it painfully clear that you weren't in a position to stick around."

"I'm not." He glanced at the clock on the nightstand. "It'll take a team time to mobilize. I figure I have a solid twenty to thirty hours before I need to worry." He put on a brave face, even managed a sad smile.

She envied his courage, wished she could fake it until it was real herself. "What happens at the thirty-hour mark?"

"I'll cross that bridge when I get to it."

Although she had asked him to stay, damn near demanded it, she didn't want him in any danger. To know that he was alive brought her soul-deep comfort. But she needed him. Now more than ever. As selfish and greedy as it was, she couldn't let him go. Not yet.

She latched onto the only hope she had. "If you hadn't come back…" Fear had a cold grip on her heart and tightened its grasp.

Shifting toward her, he rubbed her leg in slow, soothing strokes. "Tell me what happened at your apartment."

Kate brushed her hair out of her eyes with a trembling hand and took a deep breath, recalling the details. "I got a lift from the social worker. I remembered that I hadn't locked the clinic." A shudder rippled through her body, making the cup shake in her hand. "I was worried someone, a junkie maybe, might steal something. Inside, the truck had been trashed, but nothing valuable had been stolen. At first, I couldn't understand why anyone would deliberately vandalize the clinic. I went up to my place, and after I closed the door," she said, sucking in a sharp, shaky breath, "I realized that someone was in the apartment. I locked the bedroom door. But he busted in. I got him in the face with bear spray. Then I ran to the bathroom. Climbed out the window. And he started shooting at me."

A small, startling sound cut through the room, and she realized it had come from her. She clamped a hand over her mouth.

Dean brought her into his arms and wrapped her in a tight embrace. The dark tide of events was about to pull her under, drown her in the bleakness of it, but here in Dean's arms, it was as if he'd hauled her from the treacherous water into a life raft and towed her to safety. She doubted there would ever come a time when she didn't have feelings for this man.

She couldn't stop herself from leaning into his strength, his warmth. He held her, solid and steady, and it felt so good not to be alone. To be in his arms, to have him watching out for her, the way it used to be. Even if it was only for a few minutes and not permanent. Even though he was no longer hers.

He stroked her hair until the shivers stopped, cupped her chin and met her gaze. "It's okay." His husky voice soothed her, calming her frayed nerves. "You're safe now."

She swallowed, eye to eye with him as she nodded.

He shifted, taking her face between both hands. "I won't let anyone hurt you." His voice was soft and his breath was warm on her face.

He leaned into her, or she leaned into him. His lips brushed over hers in a gentle caress she welcomed. Testing. Tasting. So soft and sweet she wondered if she'd shatter from the shock of the sensation that light touch brought. Opening her mouth to let his tongue slide over hers, she kissed him back. A deeper, harder, long-awaited kiss that had her falling to pieces. He made a low, tortured noise in his throat like that of a wounded animal.

This is Dean. My Dean.

Relief seeped in every cell of her body. She had wanted this for so long, and it was so much better than she'd ever imagined.

He eased back, breaking the spell. His breathing was as shallow as hers, but there was regret in his eyes.

"I'm sorry," he said, rising to his feet.

I'm not.

"I didn't mean to take advantage again."

Again?

He meant in the hospital, when their wires had gotten crossed and his timing had been horrible. Who wanted to be kissed after he dropped the bombshell that he was packing up and skipping town, leaving her alone to resolve the situation?

"You didn't take advantage. Dean—"

"Did you get a good look at him? The guy who broke in."

She shook her head, not wanting to think about that. Not when she could be kissing Dean. "No, he wore a ski mask."

"Did he say anything? Tell you what he wanted?"

"Yes. He wanted the thumb drive that Cheryl had taken."

A grim expression replaced the one of concern on his face, and she could practically hear his thoughts. *I told you so.*

Her jaw clenched hard, because he was right. She hated that he was right.

But he was too kind to gloat. That was one of the many things she'd loved about him. She was glad that hadn't changed.

"Do you still have the drive?" he asked.

"Of course." She dug in her pocket and pulled it out.

"The guy who broke into your apartment believes you have it. At this point, I think the only way out for you is forward. We have to take a look and see what kind of trouble Cheryl dragged you into."

Chapter Six

The dawn felt shredded as the sun began to rise. It was an eerie yellow, ringed with red. The color of an infected wound.

A bad omen.

Dean missed his team. *Topaz.* With Hunter Wright, Zenobia "Zee" Hanley and Gage Graham at his side, they'd get to the bottom of this in no time, eliminating any threats to Kate and the baby, making the world a safer place. That's what they did. Or rather, used to.

But he was on his own this time. No support. No backup. No computer whiz to work her digital magic.

Drawing the curtains in the room, Dean would've given anything to get Kate back in the car and head straight out of town, but that wasn't an option.

He pulled his laptop from his bag and plopped down beside her. After firing it up, he slipped the thumb drive into the USB port, hoping it was encrypted. No one would expect Kate, a local veterinarian, to crack that level of security. Under those circumstances, once she turned it over to the sheriff and it became public knowledge the drive was no longer in her possession, she wouldn't be in any danger.

Dragging the mouse onto the folder, he tapped the icon. It opened. There was no encryption.

His heart sank. The hope of an easy out for Kate deflated like a balloon. She was stuck in this mess.

The folder contained a series of Excel spreadsheets. Dated by month and year. He tapped on the most recent one.

The first column was a series of coordinates, degrees, minutes and seconds. Ten of them. Beside those were dates and times.

"This must be some kind of a schedule," he said.

"For what?"

"I don't know. Something illegal for sure."

Next to the dates was a list of numbers, ranging from one to two digits. The last column was money.

A lot of money.

"What is all this?" Kate asked.

Dean opened a couple of the other spreadsheets. More of the same, but the numbers in the last two columns varied. The coordinates didn't change. "Maybe it's drug-related," he said, thinking out loud. "If this column—" he pointed to the second to last with one-to two-digit numbers "—is for weight of product, say, in kilos, then the staggering amount of money would make sense."

She shot him a skeptical glance. "A major drug operation here?"

Why not? "You said yourself you had been worried about a junkie breaking into the clinic."

"I know," she said with a slight shake of her head, "but I guess I hadn't considered the bigger implications of it."

"There are drugs and addicts willing to buy everywhere. You just need to know where to look." That gave him an idea he hoped he wouldn't regret pursuing. "I should go to one of these locations and check it out. It's the only way to know what's going on."

"No, don't." Another shake of her head, more forceful, her face tense with worry. "It might be dangerous."

No *might* about it. "We need to know what Cheryl was involved in. What you're now in. That man who was in your apartment might come back."

She reeled back, staring at him. "I'll turn the thumb drive over to the sheriff."

"That'll prove you had it in the first place. You'll be a loose end someone might want to tie up. Or once the sheriff investigates, you could be a target of retribution for turning it over."

With her shoulders slumping, she reached across him to set her coffee on the nightstand next to the laptop. She propped her elbows on her knees and dropped her head into her hands.

He hated highlighting the worst possibilities for her, but she needed to know. It was the only way to make a decision. The more information, the better.

Dean put a palm to her back and felt a shudder run through her. His fingers tingled with the urge to glide through her thick hair and rub the nape of her neck.

Which was the wrong impulse, since he wouldn't be able to stop there. Then he'd want to hold her, kiss her again…

His attraction to her was still visceral, a craving he longed to satisfy.

Why did the wrong impulses have to feel so right?

"Oh, Dean," she said on a sigh.

He did everything he could to ignore the tightening in his body as a result of the way she'd uttered his name mingled with that soft sound. For too many nights the memory of *that*—the two of them as close as a man and a woman could be, physically, emotionally, that sound rolling from her lips—had been torture.

On other nights, it had been the only thing to get him through.

"We'll get to the bottom of whatever this is, find a way for you to be safe. I won't leave until we do."

"But what about the kill team?"

Nothing was ever simple. Was it? "Sitting around waiting for them to arrive is suicide. Pretty much like you handling this on your own." If he had to choose between her and himself, well, there was no choice at all. He would lay down his life for hers, any day, any time. Without hesitation.

Kate cringed as her face wrenched in worry. "It wasn't fair of me to ask you to help." Tears glistened in her eyes. "I'm sorry. It was selfish."

This was an impossible position. "You're concerned about a motherless newborn. That's the opposite of selfish. I'm glad I came back. You needed me." *Still do.*

"It's such a big risk for you to take."

She was worth it.

"I've got some time before that team will get here." If he was lucky. "I can do a lot of digging in twenty-four hours." But he'd stay longer to ensure she was safe.

"There's so much to figure out, and we haven't even had a chance to talk. That's not much time."

No, it wasn't. No time at all when he wanted weeks with her. Months. Years. A lifetime. "I'll make it work."

He put an arm back around her, bringing her close, and held her. He understood her distress and only wanted to alleviate it.

She rested her head in the crook of his neck. With his other hand, he caressed her face, running his thumb across her cheek. Her skin was delicate under his fingertips.

Everything inside him warned he should drop his hand, but he held her tighter instead, tracing her jawline with his thumb.

She clutched his leg, and he tensed. Shifting, she looked up at him, and her mouth was suddenly dangerously close to his.

Touching her, being touched by her—hell, sitting next to her on the bed and staring into those sad, gorgeous eyes—dredged up memories. Passionate, raw, painful. None he'd trade. Not of her.

But the past wasn't what he needed to focus on. Neither

was the present, with the scent of her hair filling his nose or the softness of her skin still pressed to his palm. Or with his lips tingling to taste her again.

Finding answers and keeping her safe was the only thing he should be thinking about.

"I should go," he said, dropping his hands from her and standing. "This is a good time for me do some recon." Not ideal with the sun rising, but it was manageable. This early in the morning, there wouldn't be much security at the locations on the spreadsheets, and any present would be lackadaisical. More concerned about getting a cup of coffee and breakfast than worried about catching an intruder.

"Maybe I should come with you," she said.

Definitely not. "It's better if you stay here. I'll know you're safe and out of harm's way. This will be easier and faster if my focus isn't split. Just promise to sit tight and don't leave. Okay?"

"Sure. I'll wait for you. Where else am I going to go?"

"Try to rest while I'm gone."

She looked up at him with exhaustion and fear in her eyes. "Highly unlikely. I'll be worried sick about whether you're all right the entire time."

"You saw me handle myself against two of those thugs. Have a little faith." He tucked her hair behind her ear and cupped her face. Her skin was velvety perfection, with a milky complexion that would show the imprint of a hard kiss. He recalled marking her with his mouth years ago, kissing his way down her body until he reached the soft, sensitive folds between her legs. *God*, he needed to get out of that room. "You should still try to sleep. You haven't had much rest." He dropped his hand and turned to the computer.

"You haven't had any."

"I'm trained to go without it for a few days. I'll be fine." He looked over the coordinates and homed in on two on the list. One was in Laramie and the other near Rock River. No need to write down either. He had been trained to memorize things on the fly: telephone numbers, addresses, license plates. Coordinates. "I'll call you when I'm headed back. If you haven't heard from me in four hours, then it means something went wrong." He estimated it should take him no longer than two. Padding the time was only a precaution. Hiccups happened, and there was no need to worry her unnecessarily. He grabbed his keys and headed for the door. "In the meantime, get some sleep."

"Dean." She stared at him, and his heart squeezed at the look in her eyes. "Please be careful."

"I always am."

WARM AIR HIT Lucas Delgado as he strolled through the automatic doors into the lobby of CIA headquarters in Langley. He glanced at the giant American flag hanging from the rafters of the atrium. The security officers at the turnstiles were watching, observing everything, as always. There wasn't much to see yet. Give it another hour and there would be a steady stream of folks passing through.

Lucas scanned his badge and entered his code, clearing the security checkpoint. At the bank of elevators, he hit the call button. He sipped his protein smoothie, and his muscles loosened with gratitude after his grueling one-hour workout. Every day he pushed himself hard, switching up the focus of his exercise, but he never took a rest day.

Rest was for the weary.

The elevator chimed, and the doors opened.

He stepped inside and hit the button for his floor. He'd be the first one there in his section. Two hours before everyone else normally arrived, with the exception of the directors, Andrew Clark, Kelly Russell and Wayne Price. Those three practically lived here.

Lucas was making a name for himself. A fast burner

and rising quickly. The first one in, the last to leave, never griped about an assignment and did anything that was necessary to accomplish the mission. *Anything.* Endured broken ribs, had taken a couple of bullets. Accepted the fact that collateral damage was a part of the job.

His old supervisor had taken notice, given him glowing performance reports, told him to keep up the stellar work and promoted him. All his hard work and sacrificing a life for the sake of his career had finally paid off.

Now he was running with the big dogs as a member of Team Cinnabar.

The name sounded innocuous, even sweet. Like candy or a breakfast treat you could buy at the mall by the dozen.

It was actually a mineral that resembled quartz in its symmetry and optical characteristics, but looks could be deceiving. Although cinnabar was mesmerizing and beautiful, it was also the deadliest mineral known to man.

Lucas was right at home with his new team.

With a ding, the elevator doors opened.

His team leader, a formidable man with sharp features and a permanent scowl, was standing in the hall. Fierce, no-nonsense Butch Helms. "Good. You're in early."

"I'm always in early. What are you doing here at this hour?"

"Waiting for you." Butch gestured for him to get out of the elevator. "I tried your cell, but it was turned off."

"I was in the gym and came straight here," Lucas said simply, with no need to explain further.

Headquarters was a sprawling compound, not a single office building, where thousands worked. The parking lot was color-coded like it was at Disneyland. There was a gym on-site, but the protocol was the same for all the buildings—no cell phones allowed.

He hadn't bothered to check for messages while traveling between the gym and the main building.

Lucas strode into the hall, feeling a sudden rush of adrenaline with each step. "Why are you looking for me?" he asked, too quickly, too forcefully.

If the team had a priority mission, then Butch would be waiting for everyone to arrive in their section, the vault—a locked suite of cubicles and offices set behind a heavy vault door. The design was the same for every section.

"An off-the-books assignment from Clark."

The director of the Special Activities Center, responsible for covert and paramilitary operations.

"For the team?" Lucas asked, dumbfounded.

"No, for you." Butch started walking down the hall, and Lucas got in step beside him.

Of course it was for him. Otherwise this conversation would be happening in the vault with the entire team. Still, Lucas didn't understand. "Why me?"

Not that he wasn't grateful to be chosen. Any chance to shine he'd seize with both fists. But only an idiot wouldn't look a gift horse in the mouth in this place.

"I got a call an hour ago to come in. Clark wants you. But he needed to check with me first."

"To see if I was available?" But that could've been discussed over the phone. No need to haul him in two hours early.

"No, to make sure you were up for the challenge."

"When have I ever not been?" Lucas asked, letting his defensive tone mask his nerves. Why were his competence and capabilities being called into question? He might not have worked very long with Butch, but Lucas had a flawless record that spoke for itself.

"This is different."

"Different how?" Lucas didn't appreciate surprises. Not even as a child. He'd always hated them. In his experience, they were rarely good.

Butch turned the corner to the left. Clark's office was

to the right. They were heading toward the offices of the higher-ups. The deputy director for operations and the director of the Central Intelligence Agency were at the end of this hall.

"You'll see," Butch said. "You better not disappoint."

On the right was Kelly Russell's office suite. The executive assistant wasn't in yet. The light was on in Russell's office with the door partially open, but she wasn't at her desk.

Once again they went to the left.

The director's assistant waved them through. "They're waiting for you. No need to knock."

Butch snatched the smoothie from Lucas's hand and set it on the assistant's desk before opening the door.

"Come in," Director Wayne Price said, seated at his large mahogany desk.

Andrew Clark was leaning back in one of the two chairs facing the director.

Kelly Russell, the ice queen, was standing beside Price at his right hand. With her arms crossed, cobalt-blue eyes hard as sapphires, red hair pinned up in a bun, wearing a perfectly tailored suit as though it were a coat of armor, she looked like a mighty archangel ready to smite someone. The woman emanated power.

Butch took the other seat, leaving Lucas to stand.

He assumed a firm stance, feet planted wide, hands behind his back. The military at-ease position was the most comfortable for him after his time with the marines.

"Do you know why you're in here?" Price asked Lucas.

"No, sir."

"Are you aware of what happened with Team Topaz?"

The shocking news had spread like wildfire, burning everyone's ears. "That's classified, sir."

Price exhaled sharply with a disgusted look. "Don't waste our time by making us explain something you might have already heard. Do you know?"

This was one of those gray, sticky areas. Admitting you knew too much could invite suspicion and an investigation. Lucas didn't mind gray, but he steered clear of sticky.

"The teams have heard rumors," Butch said, like a good team leader protecting his own. "Nothing concrete. Nothing official. You know us, too busy with our noses to the grindstone."

And too damn smart to ask questions.

Price gestured to Clark.

"Topaz went rogue," Clark said. "They were paid to murder an Afghan official. A half a million each in offshore accounts. Then they disappeared."

Lucas's gaze slid to the ice queen, looking for a reaction. All he saw was a block of permafrost.

She had been Topaz's handler on that mission. To his knowledge, no one had investigated *her*.

After one of her teams went up flames, she'd been promoted. From handler to director of operations, effectively skipping Clark's position.

There were whispers about that, too. All behind her back. No one was dumb enough to say anything to her face. Everyone feared her.

Before the fiasco with Topaz, every team had vied to have her as their handler. She was the sharpest, the shrewdest strategic thinker and would cut down anyone who dared get in her way or that of her team.

Questions hung in the air. A stench everybody hoped would pass given enough time since it was clear they were grooming Russell to take over as director one day.

"Gage Graham and Zenobia Hanley popped up on our radar," Clark continued. "In Virginia and Alaska, respectively. We sent cleanup teams after them."

Mercenaries who took care of the CIA's dirty work at a far enough distance to provide plausible deniability for the director.

Official teams, such as Cinnabar, and once upon a time Topaz, handled high-level on-the-books black ops missions.

"Both teams failed," Clark said.

"This time we're considering a different approach," Price said. "One Kelly recommended."

Glances shifted to her. Still, she said nothing.

"This time, sir?" Lucas asked.

Clark crossed his legs. "Around three this morning, we got a lead on your brother, Dean."

Surprised whipped through Lucas, making his heart skip a beat. He had guessed this conversation was going to end up on the topic of Dean, but hearing his name out loud and that he'd made a mistake, exposing his whereabouts, caught Lucas off guard. What Dean lacked as a brother he made up for tenfold as an operative.

"We may be blood and share a surname," Lucas explained, "but he's not family to me."

Price and Clark exchanged an inscrutable look. Russell's gaze stayed glued to Lucas.

"I trust this is no surprise to you," Lucas said. "Otherwise I suspect that I wouldn't be in your office." He had no allegiance to that traitor. His loyalty was to his country. To the agency. To his team. Since he started working there, he'd made certain that was common knowledge to everyone.

Price gave a curt nod.

"We want to send you after your brother, Dean," Clark corrected. "Your assignment will be to find him. Then get close. Close enough for him to trust you. Get him to tell you where the others are hiding. We want the entire team. Dead. This problem needs to be buried."

Price propped his elbows on the arm of his chair and steepled his fingers in front of him. "You don't have to be the one to pull the trigger."

Lucas stiffened. There was no wave of relief. No great

sense of disappointment. He felt nothing one way or the other about whether Dean lived or died. Or, for that matter, who killed him. What they were asking him to do wasn't a betrayal. He didn't owe Dean anything. In fact, it was the other way around.

But it unsettled him that they thought him incapable of pulling the trigger. That they wanted to give him an easy out. One he didn't want.

"You won't be alone," Clark said in a soothing tone, as though Lucas needed reassurance.

"Then this is a Team Cinnabar assignment," Lucas said to Clark while looking at Butch.

"No, no," Clark said quickly. "We can't send Cinnabar on this. There's already too much exposure for us by sending you. But if something goes wrong, it's easy enough to explain your involvement, considering your familial ties, on paper."

Lucas straightened. "You mean I'm disposable."

In the event the impossible happened and he didn't do his job and fled with Dean, they'd say it was in the blood, being a traitor. Bound to happen. Then there was the flip side, where he succeeded but things got complicated: too much collateral damage, law enforcement was drawn into the mix or, the worst for a covert operative, he was identified while operating illegally on American soil.

Either way, they could spin the story, claim he went rogue. Like Dean.

"More like viable. *Disposable* is such an ugly word," Clark said.

That didn't make it any less accurate.

"You're not a Lego block, easily replaced. We've invested a great deal of money in your training." Clark uncrossed his legs and shifted uncomfortably in his chair. "You provide—"

"Plausible deniability," Lucas said, finishing his sentence.

"Yes." Exhaling with visible relief, Clark nodded. Even gave a little grin. "That's the brilliance of Kelly's plan."

Lucas's gaze lifted, meeting her intensely blue eyes. Not a peep from her.

"I still have a concern," Price said, drawing Lucas's full attention once again, "despite assurances from Kelly and Butch."

"What's that, sir?"

"We're asking a great deal here. For you to turn on blood. I understand the two of you are estranged, but I'm finding it difficult to believe that when it comes down to it, you'll follow through."

Lucas drew in a long, steady breath while screaming on the inside. The last thing he should have to do was prove he had no *viable* relationship with Dean.

He had two options. One, he could spill his guts about why he already considered Dean dead as far as he was concerned. Open an old wound and bleed all over the floor, showing them his pain, resurrecting the anger.

Or he could take option number two. "My primary objective is to discover the whereabouts of Team Topaz, is that correct?"

"Yes," Price said. "That's right."

"After the primary objective is met, do I have permission to complete the secondary?"

Price leaned forward, brows drawing down, as he rested his forearms on the desk. "Are you seriously asking if you can kill your brother?"

They weren't biological brothers by choice. Not a damn thing Lucas could do about his DNA, and he shouldn't be punished or held back professionally because of it. "I'm asking if I have clearance to pull the trigger and eliminate a target. Dean Delgado is no different than any other. That man means nothing to me."

The day Dean left him behind, he'd made it crystal clear that Lucas had meant nothing to him, either.

"You're sure you're capable of looking Dean in the face and putting a slug in his head?" Price's eyes narrowed as he studied him.

The hard part would be playing nice with Dean and gaining his trust. Not killing him. "Absolutely."

"All right," Price said, appearing resigned. "But due to the precarious nature of this assignment, the kill team will be wired to hear *and* see everything you do."

Yes! The assignment was his.

"The team is being put together now," Clark said. "I'll send you the file with everything we have on Dean. Wheels up in ten hours out of Dulles. Flight time will be four."

"How exactly did he pop up on your radar?" Lucas asked, the question now occurring to him after the stress of securing the mission had passed.

"An analyst caught him on CCTV with facial recognition," Clark said. "In Laramie, Wyoming."

Lucas flinched before he caught himself.

Price narrowed his eyes again. "I understand it's your hometown. Is that going to be a problem?"

Lucas smiled. "On the contrary." That fool went back home. Because of *her*, and he didn't mean their mother. He didn't care about the woman who'd given birth to him. Heartless SOB. No, Dean had gone back for Kate. On the inside, Lucas rolled his eyes. He would bet dollars to doughnuts that he'd find Dean within sniffing distance of Kate Sawyer. "I think it'll be easier than I first anticipated."

Price nodded in approval.

"One last question," Lucas said. "If you pinpointed Gage Graham in Virginia and Zenobia Hanley in Alaska, what makes you think that Dean knows where the others are now?"

Team Topaz was comprised of the best operatives the

CIA had. They were smart enough not to stay in contact with each other. Weren't they?

"We have reason to believe," Price said, giving Russell a flinty side glance, "that if the members are put under enough pressure, they'll reach out to their old team leader, Hunter Wright. A last measure sort of thing."

"We already put Graham and Hanley in a pressure cooker," Clark said. "You can do the same with Dean. Use the mercs we're sending with you. Play good cop, bad cop."

"But Hunter Wright is one of the best. Why would he give them a way to contact him? That would leave him exposed, vulnerable if they were captured."

"We have it on good authority," Clark said, his gaze bouncing between Lucas and Russell, "that Hunter's one weakness is his team. Safeguarding them, even at risk to himself. Get to Dean and we can find the rest of them."

Lucas stared at Kelly Russell. She stood there, as if she were an innocent bystander with clean hands, a dutiful solider ready to smite upon the orders of Price. When in fact the ice queen was pulling the strings behind this entire operation. "You were their handler—"

Butch shushed him, like Lucas was a dog that had to be controlled.

And it worked well enough to give him pause, but if Lucas didn't finish now that he'd started, he'd lose respect, and rightfully so. "As I was saying, ma'am, you were their handler. You haven't said a word against Topaz or for them, to any of the teams." She could sit in that fancy new office of hers and move on with her life. Put this debacle behind her. But she wasn't. She was in Price's office, stirring the pot. "So why are you spearheading this?"

"Because Topaz needs to learn," Kelly Russell finally said, softly and slowly, her eyes narrowing until they were catlike, "that you don't bite the hand that feeds you. No one crosses me, betrays this country and this institution, spitting on every value we hold sacred, under my watch, and lives to brag about it."

All righty.

This was why everyone feared her. Probably Price, too.

"Yes, ma'am," Lucas said.

Clark cleared his throat, but it did little to clear the suffocating tension in the room. "I'll send the file over now. And Lucas, this is vital for us. Succeed and you'll write your own ticket in SAC," Clark said, referring to the Special Activities Center.

This time, Lucas smiled on the inside. Ambition was a ball of fire in his chest. If he had to incinerate Dean down to scorched earth to achieve his goals, so be it. Dean had brought this on himself, in more ways than one.

Butch stood.

That was their cue to leave.

"Thank you for this opportunity," Lucas said to the room before focusing on Russell. "Ma'am." She was the one who'd given it to him.

Lucas turned toward the door with Butch right on his heels.

"See, I was right about him," Russell said to Price and Clark, her tone smug.

"Never should've doubted you, Kelly," Price said as Lucas reached the threshold. "That kid is a real predator."

"I'm counting on it," Russell said.

Butch closed the door.

Lucas tipped his head in thanks to the assistant and grabbed his smoothie. This was precisely the kind of assignment he needed. He might not be on his own, but the team was only backup. This mission was his.

If he pulled it off—*no, not if,* when he pulled it off— the glory would be all his, too. No sharing the credit with anyone.

Once they cleared the office suite and reached the hall,

Butch stopped him. "Hey, you were pretty convincing back there. The only reason you made it into that office in the first place is because the ice queen chose you and I vouched for you. Do you understand what I'm saying?"

If he screwed up, there would be hell to pay. This assignment would make or break his career. "I understand."

"I'm not sure you do. If you don't succeed, they'll question your loyalty to the agency. To the country. They'll wonder if you're a threat to national security like your brother."

One more reason for Lucas to hate Dean.

"Between you and me," Butch said, "I need the real answer. Once you get the information on the others in Topaz, can you kill him?"

In this life, there would be no forgiveness for Dean. They'd never get square, be good with one another. Not after what Lucas had had to endure alone. Maybe after Dean was dead. "Without a doubt, I can kill him."

"Good. I believe you. But remember that killing him isn't your primary objective. Finding Topaz is," Butch said. "You probably think you know Dean, but I caution you not to underestimate him."

Lucas wasn't kidding himself. He didn't know Dean any more than Dean knew Lucas. They were strangers with the same last name and a shared childhood. Nothing more.

Dean was a highly skilled operative, and Lucas wouldn't forget it.

"I won't."

"Good," Butch said. "Let's go talk about a contingency."

"Contingency for what?" Lucas asked.

"To cover you in case things don't go the way you plan. Expect the unexpected." Butch put a hand on his shoulder, his grip firm. "You're Cinnabar now. We don't fail."

Chapter Seven

Time was short. Dean needed to check out at least one location on the spreadsheet and decided to go with the one to the south of town. After plugging the coordinates into the satellite navigation system, it was only a fifteen-minute drive.

When the satnav pinged that he was a quarter mile from his destination, he knew precisely where he was headed. To an old, abandoned cement plant. The place was on the far outskirts of town and large enough to hide any illicit activity and not draw attention from law enforcement.

Almost at the plant, he drove close enough to park his car out of sight and approach on foot. He didn't bother with the synthetic mask. Instead, he pulled the stretchy fabric of the bandanna up to cover his mouth and nose. A knife and a gun with attached sound suppressor were both good choices to avoid drawing unwanted attention, but he also brought along zip ties and duct tape. Getting entangled in a one-on-one fight or taking on multiple guards would be a last resort. He'd prefer not to engage with anyone. An alarm could be sounded, a phone call could be made and the whole enterprise might close shop and relocate before the sheriff had an opportunity to investigate.

He left his Jeep and headed for the target.

No danger of pedestrian traffic out here. No residences for miles. Doing a full perimeter sweep around the building from a safe distance gave him a chance to choose his point of entry and determine whether it was under surveillance. He hadn't spotted any guards yet, but there were three vehicles parked around the side of the plant behind a brick wall, hiding them from view of any passersby from the road.

Old crates were stacked up in a maze between the vehicles and the building. He ducked in the shadows, observing and listening, as long as he dared before changing position. Moving at the right moment was as crucial as recognizing the difference between patience and paranoia. To slip in and out unnoticed, his timing had to be on point.

There was no suspicious activity on the outside of the plant and no sign of anyone coming to investigate as if aware of his presence. A security camera hung by a hinge above the door and was obviously not functional. A remnant of when the plant had been operational. This was as good as it was going to get.

He checked the doorknob, but it didn't turn. Locked. It took precious minutes to pick it quickly and quietly. Not his favorite activity. Gage was much better at this than he was, but the tumbler was a simple one, old and no longer secure.

Proper safety measures weren't high on the priority list of whoever was in charge of this operation. Then again, no one probably thought to come snooping around a defunct cement plant.

He proceeded inside, easing the door closed behind him, and immediately hugged one wall under the cover of a set of stairs. There were noises mixed with the faint murmuring of voices farther away. Not loud enough to pick up on what was being said, but he recognized the rhythm of conversation. It wasn't coming from the upper level, though. The sounds originated somewhere down on the ground floor.

Crouched low, he advanced into the plant and kept behind cover as much as possible. The air was musty and stale, heavy with dust. But that was to be expected in a place that had once manufactured cement.

Every time he changed position, slipping deeper into the facility, he took calculated glimpses of the plant and his surroundings, listening hard along the way. The more he exposed himself to see what was going on, the more likely someone would spot him. A delicate balance that he had to get right.

He swept closer to the center of the facility, toward the faint sounds of movement and chatter. Maybe three guys. No more than five. All probably armed. But he had no intentions of finding that out the hard way.

Ducking behind boxes and skirting in between old equipment, he inched even deeper.

The men were concentrated in an open area just ahead. Dean could tell by the increase in the volume of voices and how the sound carried with a bit of an echo. This was it. Right around the corner was the reason he'd come here.

He inched out from behind his cover and froze, his every muscle tensing.

A guard was standing less than a foot away with his back to Dean. The guy was tall, but lanky. Yawning, he stretched and scratched his shaggy hair that looked greasy and in need of a good washing.

Two hundred feet away were more men. Four, from what Dean could tell with the other guy blocking his view.

Tense and poised, he waited, ready for the opportune moment to strike. The other men were busy moving something, distracted with chitchat. Once all four had their line of sight shifted the other way, Dean leaped into action.

He crept up behind the guy. In one lightning-fast move, he threw an arm around the guy's throat. Neck locked in the crook of Dean's elbow, the man strained to break loose. Before he kicked something, making noise and drawing attention, Dean yanked him back behind a concrete pillar. He increased the pressure on the guy's throat, closing his windpipe, until the lack of oxygen made him lose consciousness.

When the man went limp, Dean laid the guy down on the ground and reached into his back pocket, pulling out a few zip ties to bind him and some duct tape to cover his mouth.

Securing the guard and preventing him from alerting anyone to Dean's presence was better than killing him. After he came to, it would take him plenty of time to wriggle into sight and catch someone's attention. By then, Dean planned to be long gone. Once they eventually found their buddy restrained but alive, they shouldn't feel threatened enough to relocate whatever business they had going on, especially since no product had been stolen.

If anything, they'd increase and tighten security. But that was the sheriff's problem.

With a guard down, he needed to move more quickly. Find out the nature of this operation and get the hell out of there. He glanced around the pillar.

There were two long tables set up. The guys were sorting little bags and boxing them up, but he couldn't make out what it was. He had to get closer for a better look.

Dean darted behind some equipment, a cluster of cone crushers—compression machines used to take in raw materials and reduce them in size. He peeked out in between two of the large machines.

They were weighing the resealable plastic bags on food scales and boxing them up. Inside each small baggie were clear, chunky crystals resembling ice.

Crystal methamphetamine.

In his gut, he'd known it was drugs. But had no idea which one.

Although the price of meth was comparable to that of cocaine, demand for methamphetamine was greater because it produced longer-lasting effects and was more readily available, thanks to the organized crime groups and people trying the cook the stuff in their garages.

His head was filled with all sorts of *not-so-fun* facts that were useless at a party with civilians as a part of his job.

This site was clearly a hub, a delivery and storage point, because they weren't cooking the stuff here.

So, what was going on at the other locations?

KATE FELT GUILTY for being exhausted and wanting to sleep, but her mind was spinning in circles and her paranoid thoughts no longer made any sense. To think straight, she had to rest. She curled up on the bed and pulled the blanket over her.

She replayed the incident in the mobile pet clinic. How Dean must have sensed the threat since he had turned toward the door before it had been wrenched open. The way he had launched into battle mode, putting down a very large and scary Smitty and then taking on a second man. His reflexes had been sharp, fast as a hairpin trigger, and he was strong.

He'll be okay.

If anyone could take this on out there alone, it was Dean.

Bit by bit, she relaxed and gave in to the heaviness tugging at her eyelids. The darkness called to her, and she surrendered.

Her phone rang, and she jerked awake.

Dean!

What if he was in trouble?

She fumbled for her phone in the dark room and blindly answered it. "Dean, is everything okay?"

"Katie," Jim said on the other end of the line. "Are you all right?"

"Oh, uh…" Pulse spiking, she sat up in the bed and organized her thoughts. "Yes, I'm fine. What can I do for you?"

"We received a call from one of your neighbors. He reported gunshots and a woman screaming. You're the only female occupant in the second-floor apartments. Then another neighbor phoned in on their way to work and said your apartment door was wide-open. Holden is there now. He said you're not at home and there are signs of a struggle. Your bedroom and bathroom doors were busted open. There are bullets lodged in your wall."

Crap! How on earth was she going to explain that?

Why was her door open? Had the guy doubled back and left through the front?

"Katie, what's going on? Did you have a break-in?"

"Yep, I did. Some guy wanted…" Should she tell him about the thumb drive now? "Money. A junkie, I think. You remember how one broke into the clinic?"

"Of course, I do. You were scared half to death and reported it yourself, right away. Are you hurt? Are you safe?"

"Yes, yes. I'm not injured, but I'm pretty shaken up with everything that's happened in a short amount of time, and I haven't had any sleep. I'm not thinking clearly. But I'm safe."

"Well, where are you? Why didn't you come into the office?"

Pinching the bridge of her nose, she sighed. "I'm getting a coffee." That sounded completely bonkers. She was attacked in her home and went to get coffee instead of going to the sheriff? *Way to go, Kate.* "Caffeine relaxes me." *It's a stimulant, you idiot.* "You know, uh, I needed something comforting, familiar and a breather to wrap my head around everything."

"Where are you? The café on Third Street? I can have Holden pick you up and bring you into the office. We need to get an official report while everything is fresh in your head."

"No, no need to send Holden." Was she hyperventilating? "I'm actually on my way to your office this very instant. The fresh air will do me good on the walk over."

"Are you at the café?" he asked again.

"Don't worry. See you soon, Jim. You're the best." She disconnected. Quickly, she hit the ride-share app icon to get a lift and plugged in the information for the motel. Her credit card information was already stored in the app.

Dean had told her not to leave, but the sheriff was looking for her, wanting her to come in and file a report after her neighbors had called and Holden went to her place to investigate. Surely, Dean would approve of this change in plans.

She'd barely had a chance to make a copy of everything on the thumb drive, saving it to Dean's computer, when the car pulled up out front and honked. It shouldn't have been surprising that it had taken no time at all, considering there was little traffic and low demand at this hour. But this worked in her favor. The faster she got to Jim's office, the better.

Before heading out into the cold without a coat, she grabbed one of Dean's heavy pullovers, tugging it on over her top and a pair of his leather gloves to keep from freezing.

She had the driver stop down the block from the Albany County Courthouse, where the sheriff's department was located. She thanked him, hopped out into the cold and hurried down Grand Avenue to the large brick building.

Pulling open the front door, she strode inside past the empty information desk. Janeen Phillips, an old friend from high school, worked at the station and would probably be in shortly.

Kate spotted a sign for the restrooms and realized she had no idea how she looked since she'd left the motel in a rush. She stepped into the ladies' room and glanced in the mirror.

At her reflection, she sighed. Her mother would call her a ragamuffin.

Quickly, she splashed some water on her face, used paper towels to dab her skin dry and finger-combed her hair.

Mascara and a brush would do wonders, but she had bigger things to worry about. Such as coming up with answers that wouldn't lead to more questions.

Best to just get it over with.

On the walk down the hall to the sheriff's department, she gathered her wits about her.

The courthouse had a faint lemony smell that spoke of cleaning compounds. Oddly, the familiar scent settled her pinging nerves a bit. She reached the end of the hallway and turned left. Two doors down another corridor, she came to an open set of double doors with Sheriff's Department stenciled on the front.

Inside was a long room with a high counter running the length of it. On the other side of the counter were several desks, the dispatch radio and two offices, including Jim's, which was slightly larger than the other.

As Kate approached the counter, a woman in her midtwenties wearing a brown deputy's uniform looked up at her. The deputy's long dark hair was in a tight ponytail that pulled at her features, making them appear sharp, almost severe, and she wore no makeup like Kate, but the younger woman looked fresh-faced, with dewy skin.

She must've been new, because Kate didn't recognize her.

"What can I do for you?" the deputy asked.

"I'm here to speak with Sheriff Ames."

The deputy peered over the top of her computer at Kate. "What's your name?"

"Don't worry about it," Jim called from the doorway of his office. "That's Katie Sawyer. Holden is at her place now."

Good. Holden wasn't there. She'd prefer not to run into him.

"You heard the boss," the deputy said. "Come on

through." She indicated a half door at the end of the counter and hit a buzzer.

The door clicked open, and Kate went on through.

"Doughnut?" the deputy offered a box.

The pleasant aroma of sweet fried dough had her stomach grumbling. "Thank you." She pulled off the gloves, grabbed a napkin from the counter and took a glazed one. The first bite was heaven in her mouth. Dessert for breakfast. Whoever invented doughnuts was a genius.

"Want a cup of coffee to wash it down?"

"Bless you, yes," she said around the food in her mouth, now starving. "Just a little cream, please." The sugar from the doughnut was plenty.

Jim greeted her in the doorway of his office. "Morning." Ushering her inside, he looked her over. There was no way his keen eyes had missed the bloodstains on the same pair of jeans she was still wearing. "I see you haven't had a chance to clean up." He frowned at her as he sat behind his desk.

She dropped into a hard wooden chair and set the gloves on the edge of his desk. "The intruder was waiting for me in my apartment after I left the hospital. And he ransacked the mobile clinic, too."

The deputy knocked on the open door as she came in and handed Kate a cup of coffee.

"Thanks."

The deputy went back to tending the front desk.

"Start at the beginning," Jim said. "What time did you leave the hospital, and how did you get home?"

Kate recounted the nightmare, yet again, in between nibbles on the doughnut and sips of coffee until she was finished.

"I'm not clear on how you got away if this man was in hot pursuit after you."

Stalling for time, she crammed the last large piece of

doughnut in her mouth and chewed slowly while thinking of a plausible response. "I flagged down a passing car, and it stopped. I got lucky."

"There's so much good luck flowing around I should buy a lottery ticket," Jim said, devoid of humor. "What's the name of the driver who picked you up?"

"I didn't get his name. Good Samaritan."

"You don't know his name, but he gave you his sweater." He gestured to the pullover she was wearing. "Literally, the shirt off his back."

"Like I said, Good Samaritan. I was freezing. I think he was worried about me going into shock."

"Where did he take you?"

"Oh, I had him drive around for a while. Until I calmed down and could think clearly. Then he dropped me off and I got a cup of coffee."

Jim nodded slowly, his jaw twitching from side to side as though processing everything she'd said. "You needed time to let the adrenaline settle and the fear dissipate?"

"Yes, that's it exactly."

"I can understand that, with a guy in a ski mask ambushing you in your home and shooting at you."

"It was terrifying."

"I'm sure it was." He folded his hands in his lap. "So, you were thinking clearly by the time you asked the Good Samaritan to drop you off?"

"Yes." That's what she'd said, wasn't it?

"Then why didn't you come here instead of the coffee shop? This would be the safest place for you to be, wouldn't it?"

Her heart began to slam against her chest.

The sheriff posed an excellent question.

Chapter Eight

Kate took a gulp of her coffee, and the hot liquid went down the wrong way, causing her to choke.

"You okay?" Jim leaned forward.

Clearing her throat, she nodded.

"Do you need anything?"

She shook her head. "No." She patted her chest, ensuring her airways were fully open. "No, I'm fine." What she wouldn't have given in that moment to be a savvy operative. She would've pressed some high-gadget button and disappeared. "You know, recalling it all, I was actually still frazzled when the driver dropped me off. I wanted to collect my thoughts over a cup of coffee. And it's a good thing I did, too, because I found this in my pocket." She took out the thumb drive from the back pocket of her jeans and held it up. "Cheryl must've passed it to me without my realizing."

Jim perked in his chair and opened his desk drawer, plucking something out. "What's on it?" He held open an evidence envelope.

She dropped the thumb drive inside. "I don't know." She squirmed in her seat and caught herself. "I was in the coffee shop when I discovered it. I didn't get a chance to take a look. But I'm pretty sure that whatever is on there is only more trouble if the guy who broke in was after it. I've had my fill for a lifetime." If only she could advertise that to all the criminals in town to keep them from coming after her.

"The decedent didn't say anything to you about this? Explain why she was giving it to you?"

Decedent. The official term for a person who had died sounded so cold and clinical.

"No, nothing. I mean, I didn't even realize that she had slipped it in my pocket."

"I thought you said the intruder was after money. That's what you told me on the phone."

"Did I?"

She gulped and shook her head.

"You also called me Dean." His eyes narrowed as he studied her, hard.

"I was dreaming when my phone rang. Confused."

"Dreaming? In the café?"

Kate chewed the inside of her lip. "Daydreaming. As I was collecting my thoughts."

"About Dean? That Delgado boy who ran away?"

"Crazy, I know. But the shock and the fear had my mind spinning in wild, unexpected directions. I really need to get some rest. I feel delirious at this point."

"Sure." His features softened along with his tone. He held up the bag with the thumb drive. "Obviously yours and the decedent's prints are on here, but we'll check for others."

What?

Kate stiffened, trying keep the alarm flooding her nervous system from showing on her face. She and Dean hadn't had a chance to discuss how to handle this situation, and she hadn't anticipated Jim checking for prints.

Dean's were all over it.

She couldn't catch a break. Every time she thought a predicament had been averted, another popped up.

"The big problem is," Jim said, "we won't get a match unless someone has been fingerprinted before."

Law enforcement officers were fingerprinted—FBI

also. Reason suggested the CIA would do the same with their folks.

She clenched her jaw. *So stupid.* Why didn't she think of that?

"Is everything all right, Katie? You look like you're going to be sick."

Aside from the mini nervous breakdown she was having, everything was fine. "I'm not feeling well. The sugar from the doughnut on an empty stomach. No sleep. The trauma of everything."

"That's no surprise. You've been through quite an ordeal in the past few hours. Holden should be finishing up at your place soon. You should go home. Get some rest. I'll have my deputies drive by your way a couple of times each shift to keep an eye out. Make sure you don't have any more trouble." He gave her a quick grin, full of small-town charm.

"I think I'll get a room at a motel. I'd rather not run into Holden." She lowered her gaze. "It's still awkward when we're in the same room." After more than a decade. The only time he treated her like they had no pertinent history between them was when his fiancée, Renee Olson, was present, and she wasn't around nearly enough. It was like he went out of his way to get under her skin.

"I can call him back to the station, if you like, so he won't be there by the time you get home."

She glanced up at Jim and smiled at his thoughtfulness. "No, let him do his job. I don't think I'd be able to sleep there, anyway." That was one hundred percent the truth.

"It'll take some time to get over that feeling, of having your personal space violated. You're welcome to stay with Maggie and me. Colton's room is empty and it's free."

Her smile widened as she stood. "Thank you, that's so generous, but I don't want to impose."

"Impose? Maggie would have my hide if I didn't offer. It's no imposition, truly. I insist."

"To be honest, I think I need to be alone." *With Dean.* They didn't have much time together before he had to leave, and she wasn't going to waste any of it.

"I understand." Jim rose from his chair. "If you change your mind, you know where to find me. Do you need me to give you a lift?"

"Oh, no. I have a couple of errands to run. But I appreciate the offer."

Although her parents had moved from Wyoming to Nebraska to be closer to their new grandchild and help Claire out, Laramie still felt like home. Surrounded by people who'd known her since she was little, who looked out for one another, offered a safe place to sleep or a ride. That was hard to find.

"Any idea when I'll be able to use the mobile clinic again?"

"In a few days, and then I'd recommend using a professional service to get cleaned."

"Sure. Thanks." She hesitated at the door. "Did you happen to find out anything about the mother? Cheryl?"

"Her name was Cheryl Gowdy. Her prints were in the system. Turns out she was brought in for drug possession eighteen months ago. Since it was only a small amount and it was her first conviction, the judge sentenced her to probation."

Gowdy. The name was familiar, but she couldn't remember where she'd heard it before. "That's it? Nothing else on her? Does she have any family?"

"Her dad's deceased. Nothing else in the file on her. But don't worry, we'll keep looking for other relatives. See if one of them is willing to assume responsibility for the baby."

"Instead of having the deputies swing by my place on

their shifts, can you have them stop by the hospital and look in on the baby to make sure he's safe?"

Jim frowned. "They have security guards there. That wouldn't be an efficient use of manpower."

"I know. Please. It'd put my mind at ease, help me to sleep better."

He gave a long sigh. "I'll spread the word to all my deputies. Okay?"

"You're the best."

"I'll let you know if anything turns up on those prints," Jim said.

Heading out of his office, she cringed. How was she supposed to explain that Dean Delgado's fingerprints were on the thumb drive?

This wasn't something she'd resolve on her own. Duplicity wasn't her forte. She stunk at it. Lying to Jim just now had almost given her a coronary.

Dean would have a slick idea on what she should say. Provided he didn't blow a gasket over how she'd messed up first.

At the front desk, she spotted Janeen getting settled in for the day.

"Kate," Janeen said, wide-eyed with a bright smile. "What are you doing here?"

"Oh, there was a break-in at my apartment."

Janeen gasped as a hand flew to her chest. "Oh, my Lord, are you all right? Were you home when it happened?"

"I'm fine. I just had to come in and give the sheriff some information for a report."

Letting out a long exhale, Janeen shook her head. "Thank goodness for that. I'm glad I ran into you, otherwise I'd have to go over to your place and check on you." She looked around and lowered her voice. "Nothing happens in this place that I don't eventually hear about."

"Really?"

Janeen sat in her chair. "Oh, yeah, everything comes through the information desk, whether it's officially or unofficially. Mostly the latter. I see and hear it all." She tapped her long, bubble gum–pink nails on the desk, making an annoying clicking noise.

"You wouldn't happen to remember a girl by the name of Cheryl Gowdy, would you?"

Janeen scrunched her face in contemplation as though she'd never heard the name. "I don't think so."

It was probably a long shot by asking. "A year and a half ago, she was arrested for drug possession. She would have been about eighteen, nineteen at the time. Blonde, around my height, maybe a couple of inches shorter. She was given probation and sent to a halfway house."

Her eyebrows shot to the ceiling with recognition dawning in her eyes. "Oh, yeah, I remember that case because it was so odd."

"Odd in what way?"

Janeen pursed her lips and rolled her eyes. "Well, not so much odd as sexist. They gave that girl probation when ninety percent of the others who come through on a similar charge get jail time. The judge let her off easy because she was a pretty little thing. There was an article about it in the paper and everything. Caused a real stink in these halls. I'm surprised you didn't read it. The story was written by..." Her voice trailed off, and she lowered her gaze.

"Tyler." That was why the name was familiar.

Janeen looked up at her with remorseful eyes. "I'm so sorry. About what happened to him. And for mentioning it like that. I wasn't thinking. My mouth goes a mile a minute, faster than my brain sometimes."

"It's okay." Kate backed away from her desk. "You didn't do anything wrong." Her cell phone buzzed, saving her. "Excuse me." She took her phone out of her pocket. "I have to take this."

"Let me know if you ever want to get together for a drink sometime."

Nodding with a forced smile, Kate turned toward the door and glanced at the phone.

Heathcliff.

"Perfect timing," she muttered under her breath and answered. "Are you okay?"

"I'm fine. I told you I would be."

James Bond always was in the end. "Did you find anything?"

"It's a drug operation. Methamphetamine."

"Just like you suspected." She contemplated telling him about the thumb drive but thought better of it, especially with Janeen within earshot.

The news should be delivered face-to-face anyhow. Might be easier for him to hear if he was looking at her.

"There's a hub on the outskirts of town," he said. "The other location I checked out appeared to be a distribution center. The other coordinates might be more of the same."

Kate pushed outside into the freezing air and shivered, letting the door shut behind her. She'd forgotten the gloves in Jim's office, but she wasn't going back in there to get them. "That still doesn't explain how Cheryl knew to come to me." She walked down the steps. "Who told her I'd help?"

"Where are you?"

She considered telling him she was in the motel room. Lying to the sheriff was one thing. A bad thing. She wasn't in denial over that, but she didn't want to lie to Dean. "Why do you ask?"

"The background noise on your end changed."

She blew out a heavy breath. "I'm in town. Outside the courthouse."

"What?" he said, his voice growing tight. "I told you to stay in the room."

"I know, and I would've. I had just drifted off to sleep

when the sheriff called. He wanted me to come in. My neighbors reported gunshots and screaming. One found my apartment door open. I had to come in. I didn't feel like I had a choice."

There was a long pause, and Kate held her breath, wishing she could see his face and tell what he was thinking.

"Okay," he said after an excruciating beat. "I understand."

"You do?" He should be livid, and she wouldn't blame him.

"There's nothing I can do about it now besides adapt and overcome."

Hopefully, he'd feel that way after she told him about Jim running fingerprints.

"I'm ten minutes away. The second location was farther out than I'd estimated. Where should I pick you up?"

She had read all of Tyler's news articles, yet, for the life of her she couldn't recall the one about Cheryl Gowdy. He'd told her something ugly was going on in town but hadn't gotten into specifics, and she hadn't pressed the subject. Half the time Tyler had been chasing conspiracy theories. But the story about Cheryl was legitimate if it had been vetted and printed in the paper.

A thought came to her, and she grimaced with dread. There was one person, at least, who could give her answers—unwillingly, but the woman would talk. Kate was loath to go, but if she wanted to know whether Tyler had been onto something and if it was related to Cheryl, she had no other option.

"Behind the vintage clothes shop on Grand Avenue," she said.

"Why there, of all places? The library would be better. They don't open until ten today. No worries about foot traffic. It's a short walk from the courthouse, and there's a bench in the rear of the building."

Wow, he'd processed that fast.

"I'm heading in the opposite direction of the library. The clothes shop will be closer."

"Where are you going?" His tone slid from curious to mildly annoyed.

She glanced down the street at her destination. "To the *Laramie Gazette*. I have to speak to the editor in chief."

Another pause. "With the woman who was having an affair with Tyler?"

She gritted her teeth. "One and the same."

Chapter Nine

A few minutes after having made up her mind, Kate was walking into the *Laramie Gazette*. As she had expected, Andrea Miles, the editor in chief, aka *the other woman*, spotted her the moment she entered the door.

Their eyes met, and Kate's stomach clenched. The other woman must've been equally uncomfortable, since she went slack jawed as she averted her gaze and hurried into her office, shutting the door.

After Kate had learned about the affair, she'd racked her brain out of curiosity, wondering why Tyler had messed around with her. Andrea wasn't *that* attractive. She had glossy black hair and porcelain skin. An average figure, the same as Kate. Only four years separated them in age—Andrea was older. They were both smart, career-oriented and independent. Maybe he had a professional bond with her that he was unable to share with Kate. Maybe he'd cheated simply because he could.

Even though Kate had never blamed Andrea—Tyler had been the cheater, the one in a relationship, after all—the woman had steered clear of her; she'd even stopped using the services of Loving Paws and started taking her cat to a different vet. Forget about decorum, the loss of a client was the bigger issue for Kate. She needed every one of them to stay afloat financially.

She looked around the open space. Only a couple of reporters were in. Someone could usually be found working almost around the clock.

The story doesn't sleep, Tyler used to say.

Thinking back on it, cataloging the lies, all his late nights probably had less to do with a story and more to do with getting Andrea on her backside.

Straightening, Kate marched to the back of the space to the editor's office. Andrea's head was lowered, her gaze on the computer, her pale complexion florid. Kate rapped on the glass of the door with her knuckles.

Andrea stiffened, not looking up immediately, as if hoping this wasn't really happening. Finally, after Kate knocked a second time, a bit more insistent to show she wasn't going to leave, Andrea raised her head, pasting on a strained smile and feigned surprise.

Attractive, without a doubt. But not *that* much more than Kate.

Taking a deep, affirming breath, she told herself that she could do this.

Kate turned the knob and waltzed in, leaving the door wide-open.

"Morning," Andrea said tentatively, an uneasy expression stretching across her face. "What brings you in?"

"I'm here because I'd like some information about an article."

Andrea blinked, genuinely surprised this time by the direction of the conversation. "About an article?" she repeated.

A weird calm came over Kate. "Tyler wrote one about Cheryl Gowdy. A young woman who was convicted of drug possession but was sent to a halfway house instead."

"Why do you want to know about that?"

"Cheryl died last night. She was with me at the time. There were some men after her. Another broke into my apartment."

Andrea blanched and cast an anxious look toward the

office space where the other reporters were. "I don't think I can help you. If you want to read the article that Tyler wrote, I can give you the headline and the date. You can look it up online." Her attention shifted to something over Kate's shoulder.

Kate turned around and gulped. Dean, disguised as DJ, strolled into the *Gazette*. He caught her eye and waved. She gave him a *what are you doing here?* scowl in response.

"Hey, there," he said, approaching her, the issues with his voice modulator seemingly fixed. "Figured you could use a hand." He leaned in and dropped his voice to whisper only she could hear. "You're too nice to do this alone."

Candy-coated. That's what he meant. Not nice.

Kate looked back at Andrea.

The dark-haired woman was staring at them like she was trying to work out a puzzle. "Aren't you the bartender over at Delgado's?"

"He's my friend." Kate narrowed her eyes at her, not caring for the tone of her question or the sneer that had accompanied it. To Dean, she said, "I was just explaining to the editor in chief I need some information."

Andrea folded her hands on top of her desk. "Public information that's accessible to anyone with an internet connection."

"Public information isn't what I'm interested in. I know Tyler was working on something," Kate said, daring to make an assumptive leap. "Was it connected to this article about Cheryl? Was there more to the story than what was printed?"

"I said I can't help you," Andrea snapped. Her lips pinched in a tight line. "Please leave."

Kate stood her ground, crossing her arms, and gave a cool smile. "I'm not going anywhere until I get answers."

DJ cleared his throat. "Ms. Miles, I figure you owe Kate,

seeing as you were sleeping with her boyfriend on the down low for months."

Andrea's eyes flared wide, hopefully with shame, and she glanced around the office as if searching for inspiration. Finding none, she swallowed hard and licked her lips.

"Just a few answers," he said, "and we'll be out of your hair."

Andrea shoved away from her desk, her chair scraping across the wood floor, and hurried to the door, closing it. Then she glared at Kate but said reluctantly, "What exactly do you want to know?"

"What was the big deal with Cheryl going to a halfway house?"

"Do you really want to open this can of worms?" Andrea asked.

Kate had already crossed the point of no return. The only way out was forward. "Yes."

Andrea sighed. "If I share what I know, do you agree to leave my name out of it?"

"Of course," Kate said. "I'll never mention you." No reason to involve her further.

Wringing her hands, Andrea took another quick glance at the two reporters in the bullpen before she went to a file cabinet, pulled out a thick folder and opened it on her desk.

Kate flashed Dean a grin of triumph. He put his hand on her shoulder and gave it a squeeze.

"This is Tyler's research." Andrea flipped through the documents until she found what she was looking for. "Here's the article he wrote. It was supposed to be the first in a series."

Kate took the paper and held it so Dean could read along with her.

The article talked about preferential treatment for young women convicted of drug-related charges. Tyler had used Cheryl Gowdy as his poster girl.

"When it was published, feathers were ruffled," Andrea said. "The *Gazette* received a lot of heat. I received a lot of heat and realized that I might have been hasty in publishing the article because of my personal feelings for Tyler." Her gaze dropped. "I told him I needed better evidence next time if he was going to continue down this road."

Tyler had been stressed out about publishing a story too soon. He had needed support, and rather than giving it, Kate had made an insensitive remark.

Nobody wants anything half-baked. You've got to do your due diligence.

She hadn't even asked him what the story had been about. "Did he find anything else?"

"Yeah, I think he did." Andrea had a forlorn look. "He came to me excited, said that he was working on something major and that he'd been looking at the story about Gowdy from the wrong angle."

Dean shoved his hands in his pockets. "Wrong in what way?"

Andrea riffled through the papers and pulled out a document. "Look at this."

They glanced at the sheet. It was a list of women, eight of them, all under the age of twenty-five, who had been convicted of drug charges. In lieu of jail time, they had been given probation and sent to the New Horizons halfway house.

On the list, there was another name she recognized. "I know her." Kate pointed to one near the bottom. "Lilah Sanchez. She used to come to the clinic with a stray dog that she'd taken in. A cute corgi-Lab mix. I'd treat him for free, and sometimes she'd swing by just to chat. I got the feeling she was lonely, didn't have many friends. But one day she stopped showing up."

"When was the last time you saw her?" Dean asked.

"I'm not sure. Last spring, I think. Maybe late winter.

I figured she was busy having fun over the summer and then it was her senior year of high school."

Andrea dug around in the folder and plucked out another sheet. "According to this, Lilah was convicted in March. She repeated an earlier grade and was eighteen at the time."

"Charged as an adult. She could've finished school from the halfway house," Dean said. "These are just more women like Cheryl. This supports his first article, but did he find anything new?"

"All of those women are currently on probation, but none of them are at New Horizons."

"What do you mean?" Kate asked.

"No one in administration would talk to Tyler. He staked the place out for a few days from the time they unlocked the doors in the morning until curfew, when the residents are supposed to be in for the night," Andrea said.

Kate vaguely recalled Tyler mentioning a stakeout, and she also remembered not believing him.

"Those women were never seen entering or leaving the facility," Andrea said. "Tyler eventually found an orderly who would speak with him, only off the record with the assurance of anonymity. That was so like Tyler—dogged, determined." Pride rang in her voice. "The guy told Tyler the women showed up their first week and then he didn't know what happened to them."

"What about their probation officers?" Dean asked.

"Officer," Andrea said, emphasizing the singular. "They all had the same one."

"So, where are the women?" Kate asked.

Andrea threw her hands up with a shrug. "I don't know. Tyler suspected it had something to do with prostitution, but he couldn't prove anything. Yet. He kept digging and was getting close to putting the pieces together. He was so clever. I knew given enough time he would figure it out. Then there was the car accident." She sniffled and wrapped her arms around herself, getting choked up as though his death had been recent. Tears brimmed in her eyes, and Kate handed her a box of Kleenex from the desk. "I know our relationship was wrong," she said, taking a tissue. "Neither of us intended to hurt you, Kate. But it was more than a fling." A whining note of self-pity entered her tone. "We were in love."

That was the reason Tyler had cheated. With Andrea, he'd found a woman who thought of him as clever and dogged and who was the cheerleader that Kate wasn't. Who had stars in her eyes when she looked at him. Who loved him.

A pang cut through Kate, and she glanced at Dean. The one man she could never forget. The only man she would do anything to be with.

Andrea dabbed at her eyes with the tissue. "After the funeral, I went through his notes, and I was going to follow up on everything, to pay tribute to him, you know." Her voice was raw with emotion. "But one night, I was leaving the office late. I had locked up, and a man wearing a ski mask shoved me up against the wall, put a knife to my throat and told me to forget about the story that Tyler was working on. If I didn't, he would come back and make me regret it before he killed me. That's when I realized that Tyler's accident was no accident at all. I put the folder in the file cabinet and haven't looked at it until now."

Oh, my goodness. Kate actually felt bad for her. Andrea couldn't even mourn publicly as a girlfriend, and after losing Tyler, she had been terrorized and threatened. She must feel so alone.

"I'm sorry for your loss," Kate said.

"Thank you." A surprised note sounded through the tears before Andrea began to cry full-on. It wasn't dramatic sobs, designed to gain sympathy. Her tears were genuine.

Kate was on the verge of cracking and giving the woman a hug.

"Don't you dare," Dean said as if reading her mind. "Tyler was sleeping with both of you at the same time. That wasn't love. It was selfishness and greed packaged in lies."

Andrea's crying dialed down to hiccuping sobs and then petered out. "You shouldn't speak ill of the dead."

"Well, you're alive," he said, shedding his casualness like a second skin. "You knew he had a girlfriend and that they were living together. Why did you do it? Was it low self-esteem, lust, you simply didn't care? All of the above? But don't stand here and tell her you decided to become the other woman because of love."

The realization of how much Kate had confessed to Dean over strong drinks, the intimate details, made her want to shrivel up like a slug in salt. Thank goodness she'd always insisted on using a condom with Tyler. She'd never fully trusted him or loved him, and she hadn't wanted an *oops* baby tying them together for the rest of their lives.

"And," Dean continued, clearly on a roll, "while he was two-timing you, Kate, you were giving this one—" he hiked a thumb at Andrea "—a thirty percent discount because she was his boss."

Her overweight Burmese cat had needed surgery, too. Kate did a quick calculation of how much money she'd lost on those discounts, and it made her blood boil over the bills she could've paid off.

This woman did her owe her, in more ways than one.

Dean's hard gaze swung back to Andrea. "Any idea who was the last person Tyler interviewed?"

"Uh," she stammered, blinking wildly, thrown for another loop. "The day before his accident, he pushed the probation officer for answers." Sniffling, she dabbed at her eyes. "But she stonewalled him."

"She?" Kate asked. "Who is their probation officer?"

"You shouldn't pursue it," Andrea said. "Tyler was killed over this. It's dangerous."

"I appreciate your concern." Kate believed it was sincere. "But we need a name."

Andrea pursed her lips. "You don't mention me to anyone, or Tyler, because it will only lead back here."

Dean gave a quick nod. "Agreed."

"The probation officer is Renee Olson."

Shock jolted through Kate. "Holden's fiancée?"

"Like I said, you didn't hear any of this from me."

Chapter Ten

Sitting behind the wheel of his Jeep, Dean looked at Kate over in the passenger's seat. She had the thick folder in her lap, clenched in her hands. She was still shaken and processing things, but they needed to discuss what they'd learned.

"Do you think Holden is involved with what's happening?"

"I don't know." She dropped her head into her hands. "I hope not."

"It would make sense if he were. Having an insider in the sheriff's office would be smart. Someone to keep their finger on the pulse of things, keep her out of trouble, make evidence disappear. How long have Renee and Holden been together?"

"I'm not sure. A couple of years, I think. He proposed on Valentine's Day." She blew out a heavy breath. "Is it possible Holden killed Tyler? I mean, even if he's not directly involved in whatever Renee has going on, what if he murdered him to protect her? Holden would do anything for somebody he loved."

"There's a big difference between self-defense and cold-blooded murder of an innocent man. Would he go that far?"

She threw her head back on the seat. "I don't know, okay!"

He put his hand on her leg. "Okay. You know him better than I do after all this time."

"Not really. Things are strained between us. Awkward."

"Why? Back in the day he was such a good guy, and you two were friends. So close sometimes it made me jealous."

"I don't want to get into it." She pushed his hand from her thigh. "You don't have the right to pop up after fifteen years and start asking questions about friendships and grudges and the interpersonal dynamics of everyone. Not when I don't know diddly squat about you. Or what your life is like now, or who your friends are."

"Just to clarify, do you have a grudge against him or is it the other way around?"

She growled at him, teeth bared, eyes crazed.

"All righty," he said. The phrase made him think of his mother. She used to say it from time to time.

He would miss his mom once he left again, but the one positive about her Alzheimer's was that she wouldn't remember that he'd been there. She was too far gone. Didn't recognize anyone from her past these days. He'd made friends with her as DJ, and that had been enough for him. More than he deserved.

"Do you want to know about my life?" he asked.

Kate stilled. "Yes."

"The CIA team I've worked with for the last decade, Hunter, Zee, Gage, they're my only friends. The nature of our work was classified, and the missions were hard and required a lot of time away from home. Over the years, we became close. Tight-knit. They're family to me. Being without them is like missing an arm or leg. It's weird. I've worked so hard, made so many sacrifices for this country, I never thought it was possible for me to be in this position. On the run. Branded a traitor. I feel lost."

He had no idea where all of that came from, but now it was out there. The truth.

"What about your real family?" She shifted in her seat, facing him. "Your mother. Your brother."

He ached to yank off the stupid mask he was wearing, but they were still in town, and he didn't want to take unnecessary risks. "By the time I found out my mom had cancer, she'd already gone into remission and then she'd been diagnosed with Alzheimer's. And Lucas…" Dean huffed a breath. "He wants nothing to do with me. Won't talk to me. Barely looks at me."

"What about me? No phone call. No email. No snail mail. You never looked back. Did your new family simply replace all of us? Is Zee your girlfriend? Or is there someone else?"

Clenching the steering wheel, he wasn't sure how to make her understand. "My mom, Lucas, *you*, none of you are replaceable. And no, Zee isn't my girlfriend." She was brilliant and bombshell beautiful, but she was like a sister to him. "There is no one else. Never anyone serious. I haven't been free to have a real relationship."

"Because of the demands of your job. The traveling and secrecy."

"No." He shook his head. That was a part of it, but a small part. "You think I've never looked back. Are you kidding me?" He gave a sharp laugh that ended in a pitiful sigh. "All I do is look back, to the point where I can't move forward. Because when I left you behind, it was like ripping out my heart." He'd been living as the Tin Man for the past fifteen years.

She stared at him, her eyes filled with sadness and uncertainty. She was weighing his words, trying to decide if he was telling the truth.

Not that he blamed her. He'd spent the past nine months lying to her face, pretending to be DJ.

Her cell phone rang. She pulled it from her pocket and looked at the screen. "It's the sheriff. Which reminds me, I have some things to tell you."

Great. "Go on, answer it."

She hit the speaker button. "Hello."

"Hey, Katie. I hate to bother you. Hopefully you weren't sleeping."

"No, I was awake."

"I need to locate DJ. I tried the number he gave me, but it didn't go through. I contacted the motel he was staying at, they knocked on his door and at my insistence they went into his room. It looks like he cleared out of there. Do you happen to have a good phone number for him?"

She slid a furtive glance in Dean's direction. "No, I'm sorry, I don't. We're not close like that. He's just my friendly neighborhood bartender."

"Okay. Well, if you hear from him, please have him contact me as soon as possible."

"Will do." She disconnected.

"What did you need to tell me?" Dean asked her.

"I gave the sheriff the thumb drive."

"Did you save the information first?"

"Yeah, I thought of that. What I didn't account for was that he's going to check the drive for prints. Yours will come up."

Was that all? "Not in his database. He'll never know about me. It'll ping the CIA, but I'm sure they already know I'm here."

"Moot point?"

"Pretty much."

"One less thing to worry about." Her shoulders sagged, and her gaze dropped to the folder Andrea had given them.

"Penny for your thoughts."

"Lilah. She's the only apparent thing that would explain the connection, why Cheryl chose me, who sent her." Kate looked up at him. "It's just that Cheryl had bruises on her legs like she'd been abused. The thought of Lilah, or anyone, for that matter, going through whatever horror Cheryl must've endured is a lot."

Dean resisted the urge to think about wretched memories of his own.

"Do you think it's true, about the prostitution?" Kate asked.

"Probably. I overheard talk from a couple of the guys in the bar. Ugly rumors."

"When are rumors ever the pretty kind? No one whispers about good things. What did you hear?"

"Talk about buying sexual favors."

"You mean at a brothel?"

"I didn't catch the specifics." He started the engine and put the Jeep in Drive. "But I know who to ask."

Ten minutes later he parked at the Ranch and Home Supply store across town on Snowy Range Road.

"What makes you so sure Mr. Sanders will talk?" Kate asked.

"Trust me, Ed will talk. Sit tight." He left the engine running and hopped out. Inside the store, he glossed over the aisles of supplies and headed to registers at the far end of the store.

"Morning," Ed said with a grin on his beefy face, his thinning gray hair slicked back, as he stocked a shelf. "I'm surprised to see you in here, DJ. This is my wife, Betty."

The middle-aged woman operating the register didn't smile, but she did tip her head in acknowledgment.

"Can I speak to you a minute?" Dean asked. "In private."

Ed frowned. "Sure." He wiped his hands on the smock he was wearing and led the way over to a feed area where bags of food were stacked.

No one was within earshot.

"I've been in town awhile," Dean said, "and I'm looking for some female companionship."

Ed's frown deepened. "Not sure why you're coming to me. Betty doesn't have any sisters I can set you up with.

We're both only children. But there's Friday night bingo at the church. Plenty of widows that go every week."

"I was thinking someone younger. Someone I could *pay* for a couple of hours of company."

Ed froze, flushing darkly. "I don't know what you mean." His anxious gaze darted to Betty.

"Really. 'Cause I think you do. I've heard you talking in the bar. Come on, help me out."

The flush faded as abruptly as it had come, leaving him pale and sweating. "I'm not sure what you're implying, but I don't appreciate it." He cast a swift glance over his shoulder back toward his wife again.

"The implication is clear. I'm not judging. I'm just looking to get in on the action."

His wife was eyeing them at this point. No doubt wondering what they were whispering about.

"How much longer do you think you have until the Mrs. comes over?" Dean asked. "I'd hate for Betty to hear anything about this."

Horror filled Ed's eyes. "Okay, okay," he whispered. "I've only been once. The place changes location every week, but it's always somewhere near Rawlins, Casper or Cheyenne."

Ed knew a lot for a onetime customer.

"How do you know where to find them?" Dean asked.

"Craigslist. Under *Missed Connections* and then *Cleaning Pipes*."

Was he serious?

Considering you could find a hit man on Craigslist, if you knew precisely what to look for, it wasn't too surprising prostitution was being advertised there, but the search terms were a bit too on the nose. "How much should I expect to spend?"

"Fifty to two hundred. Depends on what you're looking for."

"Are they open now? Do they provide round-the-clock service?"

"How the hell am I supposed to know? Fellas tend to go at night. Now get out of here." Ed scurried away and resumed stocking the shelf.

Dean left the store and climbed back in his vehicle.

"Well, did you find out anything?" Kate asked.

"Yeah, he talked. But I think it's best to wait for nightfall to check out what he told me."

"What do we do until then?"

Dean pulled out of the lot and hit the road. "We'll swing by your place so you can grab some fresh clothes, and I'm sure you need to eat. I'm starving. After that I need to take a look at Craigslist."

"Craigslist? Whatever for?"

"Missed Connections."

Chapter Eleven

While Kate was in the bathroom taking a shower, Dean unbuttoned his top and removed the padded belly from over his T-shirt. He washed his hands and face and toweled off.

He had rehashed his conversation with Ed as they'd eaten takeout from a café. It only took minutes for him to verify the information. He'd looked up Craigslist and had found the advertisement just as the man had described. There wasn't any mention of sex, of course. Or fees. Not a word about young women. The only indication there was something odd, and that it wasn't an advertisement for a plumber, were the coordinates.

Dean went back to the laptop and searched the spreadsheets she'd copied from the thumb drive to see if there was a match on any of the sites. Sure enough, the coordinates were on the data sheet. Figures varied on a weekly basis between the location and two others.

In addition to the prostitution ring, they were more than likely running drugs through those sites also. Made sense. The guys who showed up there were interested in partying, probably inebriated, and if not already drug users, then at least they'd be more susceptible to try a narcotic in that environment.

Those sites were a two-for-one money maker.

The bathroom door swung open, letting steam and the scent of Kate's body wash escape—warm vanilla and a hint of pear. Fresh-faced with no makeup, she stepped into the main room, dressed, a towel in her hand, drying her hair. She sauntered to the bed and sat beside him.

She smelled good. Looked good.

So beautiful.

"You took off the fake tummy." She slid her hand along his torso, her fingers lingering on his abs, and every muscle in his body tensed. "Did the CIA give you all that stuff?"

"It's CIA issued, but *give* would be an inaccurate representation." Technically, when he went on the run, taking the disguise with him, he'd stolen it.

She was still touching him. Her hand roamed up his chest, fingers splayed wide, over to a shoulder and down his biceps. "You've been hiding a lot under those clothes." She grinned, and her smile shot right to Dean's core, and the tension that had been a part of him for the past decade and a half, the knot that was so tightly coiled every waking minute, eased.

"Want to watch TV?" He got up and crossed the room. "I can put on something to take our minds off things." He looked around on the dresser. "Where's the remote?"

"Right here." She picked it up from the table and strode over to him.

He reached for it.

But she pulled the remote back. "I don't want to watch television. I want to finish our earlier conversation."

They'd talked about a million things. "Which one?"

"The one where you said leaving me behind was like ripping out your heart."

The ground shifted under his feet just enough to let him know diving back into emotional territory, in this motel room, with a bed a few feet away, and her smelling and looking so irresistible, would not be prudent. "I don't know why I told you that."

Her brow knitted. "Was it true?"

"It's true." And there was no denying the feelings for her that were deepening with every breath.

She set the remote down on the dresser and looked up at him with the most intense stare he'd ever seen on her. They weren't touching, and yet, with their proximity, he felt heat radiating from her, felt the curves of her body close to his. He ached to haul her into his arms.

Get a grip.

Aching for women wasn't his style. Yet, here he was, staring into Kate's eyes, longing to brush the hair from her face and reel her closer.

"Why did you leave?" Her voice was a whisper. "No lies. No evasion. Just tell me. I need to know."

"Things had gotten unbearable at home. I knew that if I didn't leave, it was going to be me or *him*. My stepdad. I'd lie awake at night, bruised and hurting, thinking about how to kill him."

"Dean." Horror contorted her features.

He'd dreaded seeing that look from her. That was one of the reasons he'd never told her.

After his dad died, the bar had fallen on hard times. His mother had remarried, to give her boys a father and as a way to survive financially. When his stepdad had been sober, things had been fine. Then he got injured on the job and hurt his back. Taking Vicodin for the pain had led to drinking. And when he drank, he became mean. Violent. A different person. Eventually, it seemed like he was drunk more often than he was sober.

"I couldn't continue in a constant state of fear and pain, with my mother making excuses for him. And I didn't want to end up in prison for killing that bastard. So, I left."

She stepped closer, putting a palm to his chest. Her touch soothed something deep inside him. "Why didn't you take me with you?" she asked, softly.

"How could I take you with me? We were seventeen.

Underage. Your parents would've had the cops on us so fast. And I didn't have any money. No real plan. I ended up living on the streets, getting my GED, picking up odd jobs until I was old enough to join the Marine Corps without parental consent."

"But you never contacted me. Why?"

The truth wasn't pretty.

The truth sucked.

But if that was what she wanted, needed, he'd give it to her. "I was lost, trying to rebuild myself. In here." He covered her hand on his chest with his own. "If I had rushed contacting you, we probably would've gotten married, and I would've messed up your life. I had to make something of myself to give you what you deserved." Tears filled her eyes, and he brushed damp hair from her cheek, tucking the strands behind her ear. "By the time I had gotten my life in order, had my head on straight and settled at the CIA, it felt like too much time had passed. That I had missed my chance. I thought for sure you were in a relationship with someone else. That you would've forgotten me."

She reached up and touched his cheek. "I could never forget you."

His heart swelled. His body was drawn tight with desire and need. His head was a tangled mess of guilt and love.

Love for this one woman that had never died, despite the time and distance.

"The worst part was," she said, "deep down, I don't think I ever stopped waiting for you to come back to me."

He slid an arm around her waist as he buried his other hand in her hair. Staring at her, all he could think about was kissing her senseless.

Actually, kissing wasn't the only thing on his mind.

Rising on her toes, she closed her eyes and leaned in and then his lips were on hers.

Her mouth was soft and hot and eager. She kissed him

deep and hard, like she never wanted to stop, rubbing her soft curves against him, sending a rush of heat to his groin. Her body was so sensual, so addictive. He took another greedy kiss and another, dragging her closer, falling deeper with each breath he stole from her lungs, with each moan of pleasure from her that he swallowed.

Desperate need took over, and in it, he found that heat, that sense of urgency they'd always had together.

His mind spun, intoxicated by her, his thoughts tumbling to how he'd looked her up and gotten her contact information. To all the phone calls he'd resisted making, the emails he'd typed and deleted. To how he had thrown himself completely into work to force himself not to think of her, to ignore the loneliness, even though he knew his heart would always belong to Kate.

But what must it have been like for her?

It wasn't until then he realized he was cupping her breast, stroking her supple flesh with his thumb.

Drawing back, he tore his mouth away, and they both gasped for air.

He wanted more. A lot more. The need to touch her everywhere, to take her until they were both boneless and exhausted, was a pulse throbbing in his entire body. But it wouldn't be right. Not when he had to leave again.

"We shouldn't do this." He stepped back. "We should stop."

Her rich brown eyes grew wide. Her rosy lips parted, the lower one trembling. "Why?"

"It seems like a good idea right now. But in the morning, when I have to leave, and in the days to follow, I don't want you to think back on this and regret it."

"That's assuming the kill team doesn't find us and we live to see another sunrise."

"This isn't a joke." They weren't in any imminent danger, but the threat was real.

"Who said I was joking?"

"I don't want the memory of me to keep causing you pain."

"It's not the memory of you that hurts. It's being without you. Because I'm still in love with you." She squeezed her eyes shut for a heartbeat and then looked up at him again. Determination burned in her eyes. "I have never wanted anyone or anything as much as I want you. Make love to me, Dean. Don't say no. Not when it's what we both want."

Arousal gripped him like a fist. Fortunately his brain was still functioning—barely, but it was working—and it warned this would be a mistake.

HER FACE, HER whole body, flamed. The truth had poured out of her. Like a dam breaking with no way to stop the deluge.

She could see the war going on in his face. The need to do the right thing. The desire to be with her, even if it was only for one night.

For months, he'd been watching her, talking to her with that glint in his eyes. One she had ignored, thinking he was elderly DJ, but with Dean staring at her like that, she understood what that gleam meant.

He ached for her the way she ached for him.

Over the years, she'd tried to forget him. Had taken drastic steps, such as moving in with Tyler, to force herself to get *over* him. Now he was here, in this room with her, and suddenly the world seemed full of possibilities that she actually desired. For starters, stripping off his clothes and getting *under* him.

He sucked in a sharp breath as though her touching him was torture.

She could tell his last bit of control was fraying, so she pushed it further. Ran one hand up his neck, across the stubble of his jaw and tangled her fingers in his hair. The other hand she slid lower, over his tight abs, and lower still, where she palmed the hard bulge that was proof of his desire.

"You're not playing fair," he groaned.

Well, if this was a game, she had every intention of winning.

"Funny, I never had to work so hard for you to take off my clothes when we were teenagers." She crushed her mouth to his and took what she wanted.

He tasted so good. So *familiar*.

This man set her senses on fire. He was the flame and she was the moth. She didn't care if she got burned. Not if it meant she could have him again, even for a little while.

In the moment of his surrender, he kissed her back, and their tongues tangled together. His arms swooped around her, bringing her body tight to his as he pushed her up against the wall. The release of his self-control seemed to ignite an insatiable need he'd been keeping locked down, and she melted against him.

"Tell me," she said, taking a ragged breath. "Tell me you want me." She felt it in the sureness of his lips, the heat of his tongue, in the roughness of his hands on her body, but there was something special about hearing the words.

"Yes, I want you." He went after her mouth again in a deep, all-consuming kiss.

Winning never tasted sweeter, and she couldn't get enough of him.

She loved that he no longer showed any of the reluctance he'd expressed earlier. His mouth on hers was hungry and impatient, and his hands were equally demanding as they roved over her body. She matched him in every single emotion, stroke for stroke.

She tugged the shirt over her head and tossed it as he did likewise with his.

He slid the straps of her bra off her shoulders, along her arms, and pushed the lace cups down.

Trembling under the heat of his gaze, she thought about her body. How it must look compared to when he'd last seen it. No longer seventeen and lissome and effortlessly lean. Her body was thirty-two. She wasn't sure how much it had changed since then, because she didn't pay a lot of attention. All she knew for certain was that she couldn't squeeze into her jeans from high school, she ate more cheeseburgers than salads and her idea of strenuous exercise was walking to the kitchen for a glass of wine.

"Let's turn off the lights." She reached for the lamp.

But he caught her wrist, stopping her. "Why?"

"Time has had an effect on all this." Lowering her gaze to the floor, she gestured slightly from her breasts to her hips. "It's not the same cute, *tight* teen bod you remember," she said with a nervous giggle.

"Time has had a great effect. I'll take gorgeous over cute and girlish any day." He dropped her wrist and took her face in his palms, forcing her to look at him. As he held her gaze, his eyes changed in a way that made her wish she could fall into them, swim in their fathomless depths forever. "You're so beautiful. More beautiful than before."

The sincerity of it had her rocking back, staring up at him, lips parted, enjoying way too much how that made her feel.

One of his hands lowered, curling around the side of her neck, bringing her closer. The feeling of his strength, his heat through that simple touch made her want him even more.

"If we're going to do this," he said, "I want to see you. All of you."

Oh, they were definitely going to do this, and after what he'd just said, the lights no longer mattered.

She took in the sight of him.

Time had had an astounding effect on him as well. Gone was the boyish work in progress. Now, he was solid muscle. Taut and sexy. Ripped in a way that made her want to enjoy every inch of him. He looked like a dream come true.

"Okay. Lights on." She wanted to see him, too. *All* of him.

A dirty grin tugged at his mouth. With his thumb on her pulse and his palm on her nape, he brought her mouth to his. His other hand caressed her exposed breast and thumbed her nipple. He squeezed it in a not-so-gentle pinch and rolled the peak between his fingers.

The contrasting sensations of his hot, tender kiss, his tongue gently caressing hers, along with his rough hands sent her hormones into overdrive.

Stumbling across the room, they copped feels and kissed as he managed to unclasp her bra and tug her pants off along the way. They fell to the bed, their arms locked around each other. He was only in jeans with the button on his fly undone, and she was in nothing but panties.

She'd missed this. The excitement, the passion, the raw intimacy of being with Dean. But he was no longer a boy. He was all man now and had the body to match. She explored him with her fingers and mouth, memorizing the feel of his chest hair against her skin, his nipples tightening on her tongue, the carved ridges of his abdomen contracting at her touch.

Needing more of him, of everything, she lowered his zipper and slipped her hand down his pants, to find him rigid and thick and long. But then he was kissing his way down her body. The next thing she knew he'd stripped off her panties.

Ripples shot over her as his mouth found its target between her thighs.

His tongue, his fingers—it was incredible. *So, so hot.*

She hadn't expected this, but sometimes the best things in life were the ones you didn't see coming.

Driving her fingers into his hair, she encouraged whatever he was willing to give. She'd take it and give back double. She was close, right on the edge when he took his mouth from her and nipped her inner thigh.

"More?" he asked, his tone playful.

No more games, this was serious business. "Yes. Yes," she begged, squirming as though she was trying to get away while her hands in his hair tugged him closer.

He resumed what he'd been doing, knowing how she wanted to be touched. The knowledge, learned with time and care—something she hadn't received in a long while—was an intimacy so much greater than simply coming together.

With his hands and mouth revering her body, she felt safe. Desired.

Her body squeezed at the surge of his tongue, as if to capture and hold it there, and then his magic fingers had a tide of release rolling through her.

She dug her heels into the mattress, her hips lifting as wave after wave of sweet heat engulfed her. He drew out the sensations, feeding on her pleasure.

"You taste even sweeter than I remember," he said, low and husky.

As soon as she recovered, able to breathe again, she happily reciprocated. Pushing his back to the bed, she took him in her mouth. Licking, sucking, kissing, stroking until he was the one begging.

"Kate, please, *Kate*," he muttered. "Stop, honey. I want to be inside you."

Grinning at the feminine power she still had over him, she crawled up his body, planting kisses along the way.

He rolled them, flipping her under him.

Under was so much nicer than trying to get *over*.

"You have protection?" she asked. This wasn't a matter of trust or love. They hadn't been together in fifteen years, and although he might not have fallen for anyone else, a man this hot had not been a monk.

With a nod, he was moving. A second later, he pulled a condom from his wallet.

Just as she thought. He was prepared.

Climbing back on top of her, he made quick work of the wrapper and slipped it on.

He lowered his body, his hips settling, forcing her legs to spread wider, and buried himself deep in a single thrust. They both gasped at the first stroke of their joining.

"You fit me like a glove," he groaned, rocking into her, steady and hard, and her intimate flesh stretched and pulsed around him.

Everything else ceased to exist. There was nothing but the two of them—no worries for tomorrow, no regrets for yesterday—just this splendid moment, together.

She turned her head to the bedspread, and her lips parted as she went soaring. "Dean," she cried out in another long breath.

"I know." He turned her face back to his. "I'm right there with you." His gaze stayed locked on her for a second before their lips met again, their tongues tangling.

She loved how much Dean kissed while he made love to her. The feeling of his mouth, his tongue, the feeling of *him* on top of her, inside her... She screamed her release.

His rhythm increased, growing harder and faster, and he followed her over the edge with one last thrust and a guttural groan of pleasure.

He glided his lips up her neck, along her jaw and up, where he caught her mouth in a sweet kiss. She held him, kissing him back. Strung out following the most intense orgasm of her life.

Rolling off her, he kept her with him, holding her close in a tangle of limbs. They shared the same air as they caught their breath, their hearts pounding together, neither of them willing to relinquish the intimacy for space.

"It's only ever been you," he said, low and husky. "I love you. Still. Always."

This happiness was sublime, almost a miracle. At the same time, it was frightening. Fragile as a soap bubble that might burst any second.

She wanted to freeze this moment. Both quivering and sated. His body next to hers, his fingers curled in her hair, his mouth pressed to her ear, his breath warm on her neck. She'd think back on this, replaying each tiny detail, when he was in Canada or Mexico, miles away, and the terrible loneliness gnawed at her. She shoved the thought from her mind.

For now, she would revel in this, the two of them laid bare, skin to skin. Heart to heart. Where they belonged to each other and *this* one thing in the world was perfect.

Chapter Twelve

As much as Dean hated putting that stupid mask back on, he was loath to leave Kate behind in the motel even more. He'd never forget the feel of her body molded to his, the ecstasy of being inside her. The pleasure of simply being with her.

She was special. Look at what she had accomplished with her life. A veterinarian who owned her own practice. That wouldn't have happened if he had contacted her at eighteen, straight out of basic training.

The CIA had picked him up right before his first enlistment had ended and changed the course of his life. Apparently, his scores on certain aptitude tests made him a good fit.

If he had reconnected with Kate while he had still been in the marines, who knows where either of them would have ended up?

He was certain he would've ruined her future. Limited her opportunities.

Kate was a triple-threat kind of woman: bighearted, beautiful and unafraid to do the right thing.

Making love to her had been more incredible than he'd dreamed.

He had no idea why she'd been self-conscious about her body. She was sexier than before, fuller breasts, rounder hips. An hourglass figure he would've worshipped all night if he didn't have to drive out near Buford to investigate *Missed Connections*.

Fortunately, it was only a twenty-minute ride.

The satnav chimed that he had almost reached his destination. He was approaching slowly. Now off-road, the terrain was a bit bumpy.

There were lights about two hundred yards ahead. In the surrounding darkness, he made out the shape of a small structure.

As he drew closer, the Jeep's headlights cast the building in enough light for him to see what it was. A tiny house. One of those portable homes that could be hooked up to a heavy-duty pickup and moved without much fuss at the drop of a dime.

He parked a few feet away from an SUV and a motorcycle. In front of the tiny house was a Ford F-250. A tough-looking guy sat behind the wheel with the engine running and headlights off, paying attention to his phone. He must've been a bodyguard for the women.

Armed with zip ties and duct tape, Dean alighted from the vehicle.

The tough guy hopped out of the truck and jerked his chin up in greeting, his nose piercing catching the light. He was big. And tall. Maybe six-five.

"Hey," Dean said, keeping his hands in his pockets.

"What are you interested in?"

"Looking to get the pipes cleaned."

"Want any *ice* for your party?" he asked, referring to the meth.

"Nah, I'll pass."

"What about a little booster to help you along, old-timer?" The guy took out a small plastic pouch filled with blue pills. "One will make sure you get your money's worth. Only fifty a pop. You'll last for hours."

For one pill? That was highway robbery. Not to mention

what those poor girls had to endure. "Thanks, but I don't need any help in that department."

"Suit yourself." He hit a button on his phone and put it to his ear, speed-dialing someone. "Got one coming in."

A second guard was inside. A good thing Dean hadn't taken this one out prematurely. It would've alerted the other to trouble.

The guy disconnected. "All right, have fun."

As he turned to hop back in the warm confines of his truck, Dean made his move.

Jumping on him, Dean snaked his legs around the man's waist, his right arm over his throat.

Panic made the guy start bucking. He dropped his chin to block Dean's elbow.

Dean whacked him in the back of a head with a palm strike, which weakened him just enough. Quickly, Dean gripped his forehead and tugged back to let his elbow snake underneath the guy's chin. The choke hold was locked in place. Dean had him now.

It was only a question of time.

The man staggered while Dean held steadfast before dropping to his knees, and then it was lights out. Dean zip-tied his wrists behind him, restrained his ankles and put duct tape over his mouth.

He dusted off his jeans and hurried to the door. Through the glass windowpane, he spotted the other guard sitting in a chair, reading a magazine. He opened the door and stepped inside, closing it behind him.

Putting down the magazine, the guy stood. "DJ?"

Dean flinched. He hadn't counted on being recognized, and now that he had a good look at this one, he knew him as a regular at Delgado's. "Hey."

"This your first time?"

"Yeah, it is."

"Here are the rules. You let the girl know what you want,

she'll give you a price. If you party without paying, she lets me know and then I have to hurt you. If you rough her up, then I really got to hurt you. Break an arm or bust a knee-cap. Other than that, have fun. Got it?"

"Sure, I got it. Is Lilah available? I heard she's sweet and would be good for my first time here."

"You're in luck. She is free. Room number three."

"Thanks."

Not wasting any time, Dean decided to go for the man's throat but with a frontal attack. He bent his right arm and slammed his forearm into the man's Adam's apple. The guy made a wheezing noise, and the struggle was over right there.

Dean restrained and gagged him.

With the guards handled, he took a look around. As far as tiny houses on wheels went, it was huge at about forty feet long and ten feet wide and tall enough for an upper level. They must've needed a special permit to transport it on the road. The house had been specifically designed to be a brothel rather than a home. Beyond the front door, there was only space for a couple of chairs. There wasn't a living room. No kitchen. No dining area. The rest of the structure contained six bedrooms, three on the bottom and three on the top level. In the rear was a full bathroom and kitchen-ette—a sink, counter space for a hot plate and mini fridge.

What these guys were doing out here was abhorrent. But from a design aspect, the setup was ingenious. No rent to pay, no land or deed in someone's name. The portability of the structure was a huge advantage for staying under the radar and avoiding unwanted attention.

Still, his stomach turned.

From the male grunting noises and fake sounds of fe-male pleasure, he knew rooms one and two were occupied with clients.

He went to the room marked number three. After a quick rap on the pocket door, he slid it open.

The room—more of a six-by-eight cell—had a full-size bed with barely enough space to walk around it. No closets. No windows. One little nightstand. A young woman, a girl of eighteen, with mousy brown hair and sad eyes, dropped a book on the floor, pulled out earbuds and turned off an MP3 player. She sat up on the bed and opened a robe, revealing her naked body.

Dean averted his gaze and turned his back. "Please, cover yourself."

"Don't you want to party?"

"I want to talk."

"That's a first."

"Are you covered?"

She sighed. "Sure."

Dean stood on the threshold, where he could keep tabs on the clients and see if anyone else approached the entrance. "Get dressed. I'm getting you out of here," he said in a low voice.

"We're not allowed to leave the premises. Sorry."

"I'm a friend." Dean met her confused gaze. "Do you know Cheryl?"

Lilah jumped to her feet. "Yeah. Is she all right? Did she have the baby?"

"Kate delivered the baby. A boy. You were the one who sent Cheryl to her, weren't you?"

Lilah nodded.

"What's going on here?" Dean asked. "Why are you women here instead of at the New Horizons halfway house like you're supposed to be?"

She swallowed hard and bit her lower lip.

"I can be trusted," he said, keeping his voice low. "Kate trusts me. She wanted me to come and help you. Please tell me what's going on."

She peered around Dean into the hall. "What about the guards?"

"I took care of them."

Lilah looked him up and down. "You did?"

"Yes. Now before someone else shows up, tell me."

"The story is the same for all of us. We got arrested and convicted on drug charges. Sentenced to probation at New Horizons. Our parole officer—"

"Renee Olson?"

Lilah nodded. "She said we had a week to find a job. Nobody in town would hire us. Not that we were given much time. When the week was up, Ms. Olson told us that she found us a job in hospitality. Either we took it or we went to jail. We jumped at the position, not realizing it was going to be here, working on our backs. Once we arrived, they pumped us full of drugs, wouldn't let us leave."

He glanced back at the hall. By the sounds of it, at least one man had finished. "Listen, we can't talk properly here. I'm going to get you and the other girls out."

"They won't let you take us."

"They're in no position to stop me. I can get you and the others someplace safe. Do you think they'll come?"

Her eyes widened as she chewed on her lip. "There's nowhere safe." She shrank back, looking terrified. "They'll find us, and when they bring us back, there'll be hell to pay."

If he took seven women to Laramie or Cheyenne, the news about them would spread faster than fire through dry underbrush. He still didn't know if Holden was involved, who was behind this operation or the lengths they'd go to in order to silence these girls. "What if I took you out of state?"

"Are you crazy? We're all technically on probation. We get caught over the state line and we'll go to jail for violation of our parole."

"This prostitution ring is illegal. What you're being forced to do is wrong. Would you and the others come if I got the FBI involved?"

"The FBI?" She crossed her arms, her gaze falling, like she wasn't sure if that would make the situation better or worse.

"The FBI will protect you while they investigate."

"The feds won't help. They won't believe us. To them, we'll only be a group of lying hookers."

"This particular fed is my cousin." Getting him involved was the right decision, but Dean would have to be careful on how he handled it. "He'll believe you. This racket that Renee Olson has roped you vulnerable women into is horrible. If you don't take a stand, take a chance and trust me, then she'll keep doing this to other women."

Lilah rubbed at her arm, as if it hurt, her features pinched tight with stress. Her sleeve slid up, and he spotted a purple bruise. Finally, she said, "You're right. They'll never let us go. Not with what we know. They'll keep using us until they can't anymore, and then they'll trap others as replacements. The way they trapped us."

One of the other bedroom doors slid open. Dean could hear a man speaking.

"Get dressed," he whispered. "Start rounding up the others while I take care of these guys."

She nodded and darted to her clothes that were hanging on a hook.

As the man stepped into the hall, shutting the door, Dean swept up on him, easily subduing him and throwing on zip ties and a gag.

Lilah was dressed and made her way up a narrow flight of stairs to the upper level.

In the first room, the client was still going at it. Little did he know that he was done.

Dean wrenched the door open.

"Hey!" the man screamed, a startled look falling across his face.

Dean grabbed the guy by the hair and yanked him off the brunette beneath him. The woman scrambled to cover herself.

Without bothering to let the man dress, Dean kicked his legs out from under him. One punch and he was out cold. After binding him as he had the others, he dragged the man to the front and put him beside the other two.

Lilah rounded up the women, giving scant details and promises of safety. On their way out the door, they searched the men's pockets and took any money they could find.

While the women crammed into his Jeep, Dean pulled his knife from the glove box and flattened the tires on the tiny house and every other vehicle.

Provided those men got loose, he didn't want to make fleeing the area easy for them.

Starting his Jeep, he counted six women. "I thought there were seven of you out here."

"There used to be," Lilah said from the passenger's seat. "But one girl tried to run. They chased her down like she was a dog and brought her back. They hurt her." A hand fluttered to her throat. "Made us watch."

In the rearview mirror, he glanced at the women in the back. Some nodded. One looked out of it, like she was high. The rest sniffled, huddling together, gazes lowered.

"Then they killed her. Shot her. Made us dig the grave and buried her in an unmarked hole," Lilah said. "That's how we were all going to end up. Used. Beaten. Murdered."

This had to stop, and he was going to do what he could to put an end to it.

Dean took I-80 going east. They could be in Fort Collins in an hour. He'd take the women to a local women's shelter he knew, run by a church. Call his cousin. Explain everything. There was no way his cousin would resist the bait: justice, a career-making case, saving lives, helping family. Once his cousin showed at the church, Dean would bolt. They couldn't have any face-to-face contact. It could compromise his cousin and himself. Dean had no way of knowing whether he was aware of his fugitive status.

After his cousin heard firsthand confirmation from these women, Jake would be hooked. To ensure his commitment, Dean would overnight the folder of research from Andrea and the information from the thumb drive. With documentation plus witnesses, there was no way Jake wouldn't pursue this.

"What about Cheryl?" Lilah asked. "Aren't we going back to Laramie to get her? We can't leave her behind."

Dean clenched the steering wheel. "Cheryl didn't make it."

"Oh, God." Lilah gasped, gripping the door handle. "They killed her," she said, and the women in back whimpered and started crying. "Did they hurt the baby? Did they kill him, too?"

"Two men showed up at the pet clinic, but I took care of them. They're dead."

"*You* took care of them?" one girl asked.

"Looks can be deceiving," Dean said. "Those men didn't hurt Cheryl. She died in childbirth. Kate did what she could for her, but in the end, there were complications and she hemorrhaged."

Silence descended. The women stilled, exchanging looks.

"What about the baby?" one woman in the back asked. A redhead.

"He's alive," Dean said. "Healthy."

Lilah exhaled in relief and sagged down in the seat.

"Why did those men want the baby?" Dean wondered. "Was it to use him as leverage, to keep Cheryl quiet?"

"You better explain," Lilah said to a woman in the back.

"Okay." The redhead nodded. "Last year, before Lilah joined us, Cheryl and I and a couple of the other girls were taken to a party. In Cheyenne. A lot of bigwigs. Powerful men were there. We were supposed to be the entertainment. The host took me and Cheryl down to this sex dungeon. Did weird things to us. Cheryl was a better actress than I was. He took a liking to her. Started seeing her over and over again. Sometimes two to three times a week. So often, she didn't have to entertain regular clients. Then she got pregnant. She swore it was his because he was the only one who refused to use protection. Once she started showing, things got tense. They moved her into an admin role. Had her keeping track of the books, making drug runs, that sort of thing. One day she came to us, crying. Said they were going to take her baby. And if it turned out to be *his*, she'd never see the child again."

His?

"Cheryl told us she stole information that would protect her and the baby," Lilah said. "Damaging stuff that would make them leave her alone."

"Who was the bigwig?" Dean asked. "Who did Cheryl think was the father?"

More hesitant looks were exchanged in silence.

"You have to tell him," Lilah said. "He needs to know if he's going to help us."

"Lyle Kingsley," the redhead said, and the name rang a chilling bell. "The governor."

Chapter Thirteen

"You're my official hero," Kate said to Dean, sliding her thigh in between his leg as they nestled in bed.

"I don't feel like a hero. I feel like I did the bare minimum to help those women."

That's what made him the perfect hero, and he didn't even realize it. Sought no glory. No thanks. No pat on the back for a job well done.

Well, she'd shown him her thanks for the past hour in bed, and now he just looked completely wiped out.

"When you called your cousin to explain everything, did you tell him about the trouble you were in?" she asked.

"Not exactly, but Jake suspected something was up because I refused to meet with him face-to-face. I didn't want to risk getting him into trouble."

"Will the women be okay?"

"The shelter at the church had room for them, but that'll be temporary. Once Jake puts all the pieces together, he'll be able to get them into the witness protection program. They'll have new lives somewhere else."

"You did a great thing tonight."

"Only because of you." He kissed her forehead. "You were right to want to pursue this."

She was, but at what cost?

"If the governor is involved, maybe even Holden..." Her thoughts whirled down the rabbit hole again, her brain spinning like the little blue circle on her computer screen, struggling to keep up.

"You won't be safe," he said. "Not until there are convictions and those responsible for orchestrating this are put behind bars. Lilah will tie you to Cheryl. I was identified at the brothel. Well, DJ. And there's a known connection between us."

"I was thinking the same thing." She hesitated, trying to summon the nerve. "I want…" *You. I want to be with you.* She swallowed past the tightness in her throat. "I want to come with you."

"What?" He leaned up on an elbow and looked down at her, his dark eyes unreadable.

"Disappear with you. For a while, anyway. Until it's safe. I don't mean you'd be stuck with me forever. I was only suggesting—"

He tugged her onto her side, bringing her into his body, and touched his lips to hers. Tender and firm. "I didn't want to presume that you'd want to leave with me. I'm a fugitive. It'll be dangerous."

"You'll protect me. We'll keep each other safe."

"What about your business, Loving Paws?"

"I'm in the red." She had hinted things weren't good, but she had never divulged how bad her financial situation was. "I'm struggling to survive as is." Giving discounts certainly hadn't helped.

"I don't want to mess up your life by taking you with me."

"I'm not seventeen." She shoved away from him and sat up, drawing the sheet along with her to stay covered. "I'm capable of making my own decisions and living with the consequences of my choices."

"Hey," he said, sitting up beside her. "That's not what I meant. I'd be lucky to have you with me. For however long you wanted. I love you, Kate. I only want you to be safe and happy."

They sat there, staring at each other.

Maybe she shouldn't have suggested it and waited for him to broach the idea.

"Stop it," he said. "It wasn't a mistake to mention it. I wasn't going to. I'm too terrified of wrecking your life, of still being the wrong guy for you. My situation is worse now than it was fifteen years ago. How's that for irony?"

"I would've left with you back then." She turned to him and leaned against his chest. "Even if I had to live with you on the streets."

"I wouldn't have let you. I would've swallowed my pride and groveled at the door of my cousins in Fort Collins. I would've worked five jobs, done anything to spare you from that."

"Don't you see, that's why we'll be okay. Together." They had a rare kind of love where they would sacrifice anything for the other person. "But I'm still worried about the baby. Especially if he might be proof of the governor's illicit actions."

"Jake knows about the baby, that his DNA could be evidence. There's security at the hospital. And the sheriff is aware that men were after Cheryl and the child. I think he'll be safe."

"The sheriff did agree to have his deputies swing by the hospital on their shifts to check on him. But what if Holden is involved? What if he goes to the hospital?"

"The Holden I used to know would never hurt a kid. I get that you two aren't on the best of terms and it's possible he killed Tyler, but do you really think he'd hurt a baby?"

Holden could be a jerk at times, but he wasn't evil, soulless. "No, I don't."

"He's going to be okay. Trying to make a baby disappear with so much attention already drawn to him would bring serious heat no one would want."

She lay back down. He was right beside her, tucking her close, his skin hot, his muscles dense and solid. She burrowed against him. It felt so good to be wanted like this, to be held. They stayed that way for as long as they could.

The sun was already up.

"We need to get going," he said and headed for the bathroom.

"What about your mom? Are you going to say goodbye?"

"I've been debating about that and whether it's worth taking the chance." He started the shower and came to the doorway. "She doesn't remember me. Not as an adult."

"But she knows DJ. It's incredible how you became friends with her." Kate had never given DJ's visits to the nursing home a second thought. He'd mentioned being a family friend of the Delgados, and it seemed only natural for him to stop by and see her twice a week. The fact he had managed to forge a genuine relationship with her, a friendship, was not only beautiful but also impressive.

"I didn't expect her to take to the disguise, the persona." He leaned against the doorjamb and crossed his arms.

"But she did. Don't squander this opportunity to say goodbye. The guise doesn't matter. You don't know if you'll ever get a chance to see her again."

"That's true. It weighs on me, how I left before. Not saying goodbye. I thought one of you would try to talk me out of it, convince me to stay, and I knew how that would end." He sighed. "I'll swing by the nursing home to see her one last time. Any loose ends you want to tie up?"

"I think I need to tell the sheriff about what's going on."

"That brings us back to Holden."

"All the more reason he needs to know. Holden is his top deputy. I have to give the sheriff a fighting chance, so he doesn't get a knife in the back." Or a bullet.

"Do you want to take my backup gun with you?"

She was a good shot. Her dad had made certain of that. But it was broad daylight, and she was going to be in the center of downtown. "No, I don't think I'll need it. I'm going to hit the bank and speak to Jim while you're visiting your mom. I'll wait for you to pick me up at the café."

"Then we hit the road. Together."

"I like the sound of that."

"Want to join me in the shower?"

She smiled. "Just to wash up?"

A devilish grin hitched his mouth. "We can get dirty again before we get clean."

She liked the sound of that, too.

CHEWING A PIECE of gum, Lucas sat alone, low in the back seat of one of the three SUVs that had been waiting for the team when they landed last night. Going to Kate's apartment had turned up nothing. Apparently, she'd run into some trouble. Her mobile pet clinic was a bloody, ransacked mess, and there were bullet holes in the bathroom wall of her apartment.

A search of hotel records for her name had given them zero results.

Lucas was certain she was with Dean. The only question was where?

Since he was in charge and the one calling the shots, he had half the team surveilling Kate's place in case she came back. The odds were good that she would return if she had left in a hurry. The other half of the team he'd sent to Nebraska to see if she and Dean had gone to her parents' place.

Two days ago, he never would have thought an operative such as Dean would risk going somewhere familiar, expected, yet, the target had shown up here. Their hometown, of all places.

Target. Not brother.

Using binoculars, he stared at the entrance of the Silver Springs Senior Living and Memory Care Center through the front windshield. Sitting in the back seat, rather than behind the wheel, made it easier to go undetected. Anyone driving by wouldn't notice him, their eye trained to scan the front seats. The only reason to sit in the driver's seat was if you had to give chase quickly or make a hasty getaway.

Lucas kept his gaze on the entrance.

Dean had proven he wasn't big on sentimentality and saying goodbye. But Kate was. If they were together, as he suspected, her influence would hold a lot of sway over him.

It was a long shot he'd show up here, but one worth gambling on. The only other option was to simply wait and hope for another facial recognition hit on him. Going that route was a recipe for failure.

He was hedging his bets on Silver Springs and Kate Sawyer's influence.

Lucas took out his phone and dialed the front desk.

"Hello, this is Lucas Delgado," he said, well aware that the kill team were watching and listening to everything through a device disguised as a button on the collar of his shirt. "I'm the son of Miriam Delgado as well as her agent, fiduciary, for all matters concerning her."

"Yes, Mr. Delgado. If you'd like to speak with Miriam, she's eating breakfast right now."

"No, I don't want to disturb her. I'd just like to know who her visitors have been over the past six months."

"One moment and I'll take a look for you." There was the clack-clack of typing on a keyboard.

A Jeep came down the street. A Renegade. That was the third time it had passed. The very same one. Lucas was certain of it. But this time, it turned into the Silver Springs parking lot.

"She's only had three different visitors," the attendant said. "Lourdes Delgado."

His cousin, Lola, from Fort Collins, who managed the bar.

"Kate Sawyer."

That was nice of her to check in on his mother. Kate was that kind of person. Thoughtful. Sweet.

The Jeep pulled into a spot and parked. The driver stayed in the vehicle a moment, checking his mirrors.

"And DJ. Davis Johnson."

Bingo. "Could you describe him for me? A Latino guy in his early thirties with dark curly hair?"

"No, not DJ," she said, with a smile in her voice. "He's in his late seventies. White. Gray hair. A full head of it, too."

"Any identifying marks on him, such as tattoos or scars?"

"Um, none that I can recall. But there is one distinctive thing about him. He always wears latex gloves. He has OCD."

I bet he does. OCD about leaving his prints behind.

The driver got out of the Jeep, an elderly gentleman matching the description. He hit the key fob, locking the Jeep, and Lucas caught sight of his hands before he slipped them in his pockets.

Latex gloves.

Well, I'll be damned. "Speak of the devil."

"What's that?" the attendant asked.

"Nothing. Thanks for your time. You've been very helpful."

Lucas stabbed the red icon, disconnecting the call, and took out a case from his canvas duffel bag. The contingency kit was smaller than a fishing tackle box. Inside were a myriad of different GPS trackers—among other things—designed to be hidden on vehicles, in clothing, inside a cell phone case.

Smiling, he grabbed one for a vehicle.

A CRAWLING SENSATION skittered down Dean's spine again. Like spiders on his backbone. That feeling wouldn't leave him—that he was being watched.

He hastened his steps, darting a quick glance over his shoulder.

Nothing.

He'd even taken the precaution of circling the block twice before pulling into the lot to be sure it wasn't being staked out by a team. He'd spotted no one.

The doors to Silver Springs whooshed open and a warm gust of air greeted him. It was convenient that nursing facilities were prohibited from imposing *visitation hours* on the residents. They were free to have visitors at any hour, in theory, provided the resident hadn't withdrawn their consent.

Dean strode inside and went to the front desk. "Good morning," he said.

The attendant hung up the phone and looked up at him. "That's so funny. Speak of the devil is right."

"What do you mean?"

"I was just talking about you."

An icy chill shot through his blood, making the hairs on the back of his neck prickle. "About *me*? To who?"

"Oh, it was just Miriam's son. Lucas. He was asking about her visitors, that's all."

Damn it.

Maybe he should turn around and leave. The CIA must've had Lucas making calls from Langley, trying to get a bead on him.

If a kill team was already here in Laramie—possibly here as in outside those doors—there was nothing he could do to change that fact. Taking sixty seconds to say goodbye to his mother wouldn't alter his odds of living or dying.

Sixty seconds, then he was gone.

"Where is she?" Dean asked. "In her room?"

"In the dining hall. I'm sure she'll be happy to see you."

Dean hurried down the hall and around the corner, with his hand squeezing the butt of his nine-millimeter in his jacket pocket. Weekday mornings had always been the best time for him to visit her. The bar was closed, traffic was light and there were usually only the residents and staff.

Entering the dining hall, he spotted her. Three tables over sitting alone. Her silvery-gray hair was in a single braid down her back, and she sat with a bowl of oatmeal in front of her. As soon as she saw him, her eyes lit up.

"DJ!" His mom smiled and waved.

He hurried over to her table. "Hi, Miriam. You're looking lovely as ever."

"Oh, stop it." She laughed and clutched his arm. "I wasn't expecting you this morning. Did you bring me anything?" she asked, looking to see if had a bag in his hands.

Usually he brought her a breakfast sandwich or a pastry. Anything he knew she'd enjoy. Today, he'd been in such a rush, he'd forgotten to swing by the café after he dropped Kate off.

"Sorry. Not today."

Her smile fell, but the light didn't dim in her eyes. "That's okay. I guess it's oatmeal for breakfast after all. Sit down."

"I can't sit this morning." He put a hand on her shoulder and crouched down beside her, so he kept physically low in case a sniper had a line of sight through the windows, and where he could spot anyone entering the room.

"If you stay down low like that, you might not be able to get back up." Worry washed over her face.

"I'm fine. I've got good knees."

She grinned. "Lucky you."

As much as he hated to admit it, he was going to miss this. Seeing her smile. Their fun little chats. Playing cards together. Being her friend after years of being angry and frustrated, disappointed, in her choice to stay with their stepdad.

Back then, he didn't understand that the decision couldn't have been simple or easy for her. She didn't have any skills or a degree. Delgado's Bar was all she had left of their dad, of his dream to be a business owner. Leaving the marriage while staying in that small town, when their stepdad owned a piece of the bar once he bailed it out of trouble, when his name had been put on the mortgage after they refinanced, it would have been a living nightmare for her.

There was no such thing as a reasonable negotiation with someone drunk, mean and violent.

"Something has come up, Miriam. I have to leave town today. Right now."

"Oh, no." Her shoulders sagged.

"I want you to know that you're an incredible woman," he said, and she beamed. "I know you were a devoted mother. That you love your children, and I'm sure they love you, too. I'm sorry your eldest, Dean, left without saying goodbye. He didn't mean to hurt you."

Confusion swam in her eyes. "Did I tell you about Dean?"

"I love you. More than you know. I'll miss you and I wish I had done things differently."

She put her palm to his cheek, and her expression changed, her brows drawing down. "Your face feels strange. The texture is—"

Rocking on his heels, he drew back, away from her hand. It was the first time she'd ever touched his face, the mask.

"Weird," she said after a beat.

A whistle sliced through the air in the room. The sound mimicked the call of a cedar waxwing. He didn't need to look up to know who it had come from. Years ago, he and his brother had used that whistle to signal to each other that

their stepdad was drunk and the other should run and hide.
Or that the coast was clear, and it was safe to come home.

Lucas was in Laramie. In Silver Springs.

Dean stood, drawing his gaze up.

"Isn't this nice." Lucas strutted over to the table. "We're having a family reunion."

Chapter Fourteen

The line at the bank had been so long, she would've thought it was payday. Kate didn't close her account, not wanting to draw suspicion. What little money she had she withdrew. All of her debts and bills she'd have to sort out when she could. Her landlord already had her last month's rent, and she wouldn't see a dime of her security deposit.

But none of that mattered. She was going to be with Dean. *Finally*.

Kate crossed the street and entered the courthouse. The same lemony scent hit her, relaxing her the tiniest bit. She had no idea how to explain to Jim. Accusing Holden of anything would be a bad start. There was no proof he was involved, and she wasn't going to presume his guilt by association with Renee.

"Hey, there," Janeen said. "Twice in one week. Consecutive days, no less. It's a sign we should get together for drinks. How about tonight at Delgado's? You just have to walk down the stairs from your apartment."

"Wish I could, but I've got a lot going on these days. Maybe some other time." Kate hurried past her and to the sheriff's department.

The station was abuzz with activity. It was a reasonable hour and three other deputies were in, including the brunette with the severe ponytail.

"Is Sheriff Ames in?" Kate asked her.

"No, he's out," she said.

"But I'm here," a male voice called from the other side of the room. Holden stood, leaning on the doorjamb of the smaller office. A smug smile was on his face. His arms were folded across his chest, and his legs were crossed at the ankle.

The entire department fell silent. It was quiet enough to hear a pin drop. Everyone's gaze bounced between them.

She didn't need this today. "That's okay." Kate edged back toward the door. "I can speak to him another time."

"Don't be a scaredy-cat. Come on." Holden gestured to his office with his head. "I won't bite."

All those gazes swung to her.

She *so* did not want to do this.

"I could make you come into the office and talk to me," Holden drawled. "If I had questions about your statement regarding your intruder."

The sounds of a clucking chicken blasted in the room, coming from someone's computer or phone. The male deputies snickered.

"Real mature," she said with her eyes narrowed. *Jerks.* She went to the half-open door and pushed through after the buzzer rang. "Thank you." She tipped her head to the female officer, who hadn't been laughing at her.

"Okay," Holden said to the deputies, "knock it off."

The clucking stopped. Thankfully.

She brushed past him into his office.

He closed the door and strode around behind his desk, taking a seat. "Sit," he said, as if issuing a command.

"I'll stand since I won't be staying long."

"You're always avoiding me."

Because he always acted like a blockhead. "Sorry you feel that way."

"It's the truth. The sheriff told me you didn't want to go home because I was at your place."

"What questions do you have about my statement?"

"None." He leaned back in his chair, a grin tugging at his lips, and put his feet up on the corner of his desk. "What do you want with the sheriff?"

She gritted her teeth. This was exactly what she meant. He loved going out of his way to get under her skin. "I had asked him to have the deputy on shift swing by the hospital and check on the baby. Cheryl Gowdy's son. To make sure he's all right. I wanted to see how the patrols were going. If there was any trouble."

"Patrols?" he scoffed. "They've got security guards at the hospital. What's so special about this kid that he needs protection anyway?"

"The men that were after Cheryl had threatened her and the baby."

"You mean the dead men?" he asked slowly, purely for effect to make her feel like an idiot.

"Yes, but they might've been part of a gang or something."

Holden blew out a heavy breath. "The sheriff isn't going to waste that kind of manpower. Even if the request is coming from you, princess."

She squeezed her hands into fists. "Did the results come back on the paternity test? To see if one of the dead men was the father?"

His face darkened in a scowl.

To think she had once been attracted to him. He was good-looking, in that all-American, blond hair, blue eyes way. Tall. Strapping. But his personality had become so ugly.

"I don't know anything about that," Holden said. "The sheriff probably had it run through the morgue. At the hospital. Is there anything else, your highness?"

"Yeah, what exactly is your problem with me?" she snapped.

"Do you really want to know?"

"Yes." It wasn't a rhetorical question.

He set his booted feet on the floor with a thud and stood. "You don't know how to treat people."

"Excuse me?" She always minded her manners. Said "please" and "thank you" and went out of her way to help others.

He hooked his thumbs in his utility belt. "You heard me."

"If you don't want to tell me, fine." She turned on her heel to leave.

"You never gave me a reason."

She spun back around, bewildered as to what he meant. "Huh?"

"The night before prom. You dumped me. In a text. No explanation. Nothing. I drove out to your place and you were too yellow-bellied to face me. Remember?"

Of course she remembered. It hadn't been one of her finer moments. She'd been depressed over Dean and wallowing in self-pity. But that had been fifteen years ago. "Are you still holding a grudge about that?"

"We were friends before we started dating." He put his fists on his hips. "Good friends. I always had a thing for you, and when Dean disappeared, I was more than happy to be your shoulder to cry on. For months, I listened to you go on and on about him. Deep down, I knew that you might never love me like you did him. He was your first and all. But I figured that it had to count for something that I was the one there for you when he wasn't."

It was as if the wind had been knocked out of her. For a long, interminable moment, she couldn't speak. Only stared at him. "Holden, I…"

"I was a good boyfriend."

"Yeah, you were." The best a girl could ask for back then. Considerate. Affectionate without being handsy or pushy. Holden had been the sweetest.

"But I wasn't him. So you ghosted me."

She lowered her gaze to the floor, unable to look it at him because it was true.

"I didn't deserve to be treated that way. Like I meant nothing," he said, his voice low and soft. "Nobody does. You should know that better than most. Instead, you turned around and did to me what he did to you. For a while, I thought it was me. Something I had done. Then I noticed your pattern." His tone turned cold. "You did the same thing to every guy you dated."

Her head snapped up, and she stared at him. Had he been keeping tabs on her? Did he have a logbook of her dating activity?

"You would've done the same to Tyler, too, if he hadn't died."

Mortification doused the flames of her anger. "Are you finished shaming me?"

"Yes."

"You're right. I never thought about it that way." Not until she saw it through his eyes. "I'm sorry I waited until the last minute to bail on prom." If she had given him enough notice, there would've been plenty of other girls who would've gone with him in her place. "I'm sorry I hurt you and never gave you an explanation. You did not deserve that."

None of the guys she'd dated had.

Holden drew in a deep breath and stepped closer. "Was that so hard?"

Yes! "No. Are we good now?"

He extended his hand. "Water under the bridge."

She accepted the truce and shook his hand.

"You don't have to avoid me from now on," he said. "I won't give you any more grief."

"Thanks." She rolled her shoulders. "Being with Renee must've driven you to hash this out with me."

"I guess so." Holden shrugged. "Maybe it was just time for us to clear the air."

"How long have you two been together? I mean, how well do you really know her?"

Holden narrowed his eyes, and she immediately regretted the question. "Well enough to ask her to marry me. Are you about to give me a new reason to hold a grudge?"

"Nope. I've got to run." She edged to the door. "It was good to chat with you." The resolution was one weight off her shoulders, though the situation with his fiancée was the size of a boulder and still bearing down.

She skedaddled from the office without appearing to flee. On the way out of the building, she threw one last wave to Janeen.

The plan was for her to meet Dean at the café. She headed down Grand Avenue, her hands stuffed in her coat pockets, her head down against the wind. Two blocks away from the coffee shop, someone called her name from the street.

"Katie, there you are."

She halted to see the sheriff in his vehicle stopping alongside the curb. Relief poured through her. "I could say the same. I was just in your office."

He held up the gloves she'd forgotten in his office. "Hop in out of the cold."

She opened the door and climbed inside.

"I'll drop you at your hotel. Which one are you staying at?" He pulled off, cutting into traffic, and headed down the street.

"Oh, that's not necessary. Really."

"I've been looking for you. Actually, I'm still trying to find DJ. I need to get his statement about what happened the other night." He took a left, going in the opposite direction of the café. "The hospital said he was never examined.

At this point, I'm worried he may have suffered a head injury. Could have lost consciousness."

"I'm sure he's fine. You shouldn't worry."

"Have you seen him?"

"Uh." She lowered her gaze to her hands in her lap and realized how guilty that must appear. She forced herself to look up. He turned onto South Corthell Road.

Where was he going? This was the scenic route, whatever the destination.

"I haven't seen him," she said.

"Do you have a good phone number for him? A way to contact him?"

Her gaze dropped again. *Darn it.* "I don't," she said, meeting his gaze. "Sorry. I, um, I think he left town."

Jim pulled over and stopped the vehicle. "When did he leave?"

"I don't know." She glanced around. They were parked near the barren field on Corthell. No other traffic. No sidewalks with pedestrians.

"Where did he go?"

"I, um, I don't know." She looked out through the window. There wasn't a soul around.

"Then why do you think he left?"

Unease slithered over her. "He mentioned something in passing." She clutched the door handle.

Jim hit a button. The locks engaged. "Katie, I know you're lying to me."

She pulled on the handle, but the door wouldn't open. Panic bubbled up inside her. She yanked harder.

"Child safety locks on," Jim said.

"Let me out." Her racing heart dropped into the pit of her stomach. "I'm supposed to meet someone."

"Who? DJ?"

"No."

"Maybe Dean Delgado."

She froze. "No."

"There you go, lying to me again," he said in the disappointed tone a father would use with a child, but something in his voice made her skin crawl. "You've been lying a lot lately."

He pulled a resealable bag from the door pocket. A piece of cloth was inside.

"Open the door, Jim." She yanked on the handle again, knowing it wouldn't open. "Let me out!"

He pried open the bag, and a sweet smell, similar to ether, wafted out. "Afraid I can't do that. My property was stolen last night. And I want those girls back." Jim pounced, shoving the cloth into her face, and pressed hard against her mouth and nose.

With each panicked gasp, she sucked in that sweet smell. She swung at him, hitting his arms, landing a fist to his face, but he was stronger, so much stronger than her.

The strength leached out of her limbs, and then searing darkness swallowed her.

Chapter Fifteen

Dean stared at his brother and tightened his grip on the gun concealed in his pocket.

Likewise, Lucas had his right hand shoved in a coat pocket with a distinct bulge. "The only one missing from this get-together is Kate."

Miriam looked between them, confusion clouding her eyes. "What's going on?"

"Hi, Mom. It's me, Lucas." He stepped up to the table.

Dean tensed. He didn't want to shoot his brother, hurt him, but if he was part of the team sent to put him down, execute him, then Dean would do what he had to. Wound his brother to get past him.

"You're not Lucas," Miriam said. "Lucas is a boy. My sweet, cute boy. I don't know you."

"That's what you said to me, at Langley." Dean put his finger on the trigger but kept the gun in his pocket.

"What?" Lucas asked. "Did I call you cute and sweet? I don't think I did."

"You said you didn't know me. That your brother was dead."

"Brother?" Miriam asked, glancing between them. "You two can't be brothers."

"I have to go now," Dean said to her while staring at Lucas. "I love you, Miriam."

Lucas scrunched his face in a sad-puppy-dog look. "How touching."

"Will I see you again?" Miriam reached for his free hand.

"I don't know."

"Don't count on it, Mom," Lucas said. "Dangerous men are after him. He's going to have to take a trip. No return visits allowed."

"Do I know you?" Miriam asked again. "You seem familiar, but…"

Dean kissed her temple and stepped toward Lucas, angling the muzzle of the gun toward him.

"I come in peace." Lucas pulled his hands out of his pockets and raised his palms. "I mean you no harm."

"Yeah, and I'm Santa Claus."

"Where are you hiding your sleigh and reindeer?"

"Walk." Dean put a hand on his shoulder, turned Lucas around and shoved him toward the door. He checked his brother's pockets. No gun. Only a candy bar. "What's this?" Dean asked holding up the candy instead of the gun with attached sound suppressor he'd expected.

"Breakfast of champions. Don't judge."

Dean kept them walking toward the exit with Lucas in front of him. "What are you doing here?"

"Saving you. Even though you don't deserve it."

"How many men are waiting outside?"

"None."

Dean pressed the muzzle of the gun into Lucas's kidney. He had no intention of shooting him, if he could avoid it, but he wouldn't fatally wound him. "Try again. How many?"

"On my life, on Mom's life, there are no men waiting outside to my knowledge."

"Funny, I don't believe you."

"I heard what was happening. That you'd been found. Here in Laramie. I had to come."

"Why?"

"To help you."

"Why?" He pressed the muzzle deep into his back. "I'm nothing to you. Your brother is dead. Remember?"

"After what you did, leaving me behind to deal with everything on my own, if anyone is going to kill you, then it should be me."

That Dean believed. "This is how we're going to play it. I'm going to use you as a human shield. If a single shot is fired in my direction before I'm safely in my vehicle, I put a bullet in you."

"All righty. Sounds fair."

Dean's heart clenched as his thoughts flashed to his mother.

It was hard not to think about the teenage boy he'd left behind. His sweet, funny brother, who had to deal with the chaos and the fear and the violence all by himself.

In the lobby, Dean stopped before the motion sensors triggered the entrance doors to open. "Is the kill team waiting outside?"

"All I know is that one was dispatched. Destination Laramie. I would be shocked if they didn't have boots on the ground before me."

Dean shoved Lucas against the wall, throwing one forearm under his chin and putting the muzzle to his belly.

The front desk attendant was staring at them, but he didn't cast a glance in her direction.

"I didn't lead anyone here to Silver Springs," Lucas said. "Mom is in both our files, so they know about her. But I didn't spot any surveillance. Only you." Lucas held his gaze, and it didn't waver. "You circled the block twice before pulling into the lot on your third time around."

Fear whispered over Dean. His kid brother had found him, surveilled him, and he'd been none the wiser. "Why are you here?"

"Do you think I want you getting shot down in front of Mom? We've never even talked about it. What you did. What happened while you were gone. What I went through. You don't get an easy out with a slug to the head by some kill team."

Dean believed that, too. "Move." He shoved Lucas forward. "Let's see how many friends you have waiting outside."

Lucas didn't fight it. With his hands raised high on either side of his head, his brother did as he was instructed.

The doors whooshed open. Freezing air washed over them, but Dean's blood was so heated with adrenaline he barely noticed the breeze.

Peering over his brother's shoulder and using him for cover, Dean remained in a position where a sniper—if there was one—couldn't take a shot. He was waiting for any men who might be close by to make a move.

There was nothing but the wind.

"Let's go. To my vehicle. Quickly. If you run, I shoot you."

Lucas hustled to the Jeep Renegade while Dean ducked behind him, moving in time with his step. Dean kept his eyes peeled for movement, for any sign of danger.

Still, nothing. But the quiet, the stillness only amplified that niggle in the back of his brain that this was wrong. Off.

If Lucas was here, surely a kill team wasn't far behind him.

At the vehicle, he had to let go of Lucas's collar to grab his keys. He hit the fob. The doors unlocked. "Where's your vehicle?" Dean asked.

"Across the street. Black SUV."

Dean took a peek. "Looks like standard government issue."

"More like standard rental issue. It was that or a beast of a truck, because there was no way I was getting a sedan."

Dean shoved Lucas away, hopped in his Jeep and cranked the engine.

"You're going to need my help!" Lucas called to him.

Pulling out of the spot, Dean rolled down the window. "The day I do it means hell must've frozen over." He tore out of the parking lot and bulldozed across the street. Taking aim at his brother's SUV, he shot out two tires.

Lucas was yelling something at him with his arms thrown up in the air, clearly peeved, but Dean was not taking the chance of having his brother follow him.

Pressing down hard on the accelerator, he raced down the street toward downtown. He whipped out his cell phone and dialed Kate. It rang and rang and rang. Voice mail picked up.

His pulse pounded, his heart banging against his ribs. He waited a couple of minutes before trying her again. Each second drove his blood pressure higher.

He ripped off the mask, tossing it into the passenger's seat, and scrubbed a hand over his face.

Her line rang twice and was answered.

"Thank God, Kate." Relief flooded him. "I was worried sick when you didn't pick up the first time. Did you get your money? Are you ready to leave town?"

"Sorry, Katie can't come to the phone right now," a man said. A voice Dean recognized.

Jim Ames.

Dean's stomach twisted and roiled as he pulled off onto the shoulder and stopped.

"No need to clam up now. You were so chatty a second ago, Dean Delgado. Or should I call you DJ? Or is it *Heathcliff*?"

Dean was shocked into stillness.

"Yeah, I know who you are," the sheriff said.

"How?"

"That doesn't matter right now. What does matter is that

I have Katie. You stole something from me last night. Six girls, to be specific. I want them back. Return them to me and you can have Katie."

Emotion welled in the back of Dean's throat. "If you hurt her, I'll kill you." The words came like broken glass.

"In two hours, I'll call again to give you a location. You'll have twenty minutes to get there and make the exchange."

His mind whirled. The women were an hour away in Fort Collins and already on the FBI's radar. His cousin had interviewed them last night. Taken statements. Not that he would ever hand them back over to suffer again. But he needed time to think. To strategize.

"I can't do it in two hours. That's not enough time," Dean said.

"It had better be, for Katie's sake."

The line went dead.

Dean beat his fist on the steering wheel. He fought through the rage and the fear surging inside him and pushed through the red haze clouding his mind. That bastard had taken Kate, and Dean couldn't just sit there, spinning his wheels. Not when she might be hurt.

Even if he showed up with the women, there was no way that dirty sheriff was ever going to let Kate and him simply walk away. Not with everything they knew. The meeting would be someplace where Ames would have the tactical advantage. Where he could have armed men hidden and waiting to strike. No telling how many thugs he had at his disposal.

Dean would be walking into a trap, outmanned and outgunned.

Hauling in a deep breath, he forced himself to focus, and that's when it occurred to him that all the coordinates from the thumb drive were only in Albany County. The sheriff's jurisdiction. He should've dug deeper into a possible link between the sheriff's department and the drugs and the prostitution.

Too late now.

All he could do was find a way to get Kate back and keep them both alive.

As if a kill team and his brother weren't enough to worry about.

An idea came to him. A bad idea. One that might end up being a colossal mistake.

But what other choice did he have?

LUCAS KICKED AT the flat tire and swore. Then he remembered the others were listening and watching him lose his cool. At least the communication was only one-way. "Monitor the GPS tracker and get your tails over here ASAP. We'll trade vehicles."

They could also swap the license plates. No doubt Dean had taken note of the tags.

There was only one compact spare in the trunk. A doughnut. Dean had flattened two tires. They'd need the spares from both vehicles.

He popped the trunk and pulled out the jack and spare. Might as well get started. He didn't want those mercs thinking he was above menial labor and intended to rest on his laurels waiting for them to do it. Messing up with Dean in the nursing home was his first mistake. He wouldn't be allowed a second.

His phone buzzed. He took it out and looked at the screen. *Ava.*

It was the team calling him. Butch had suggested he save whatever contact number the team gave him under a woman's name. In the event Dean considered trusting him, he would check Lucas's phone and search his call history. Easy to explain a girlfriend checking in. Multiple calls could be dismissed as relationship issues, yada, yada.

He answered. "What's up? Is there a problem?"

"The target is headed back in your direction."

"What?" Lucas glanced at the road.

"ETA to your location two minutes."

That was unexpected. What could've possibly possessed Dean to turn around?

"Got it. Keep your distance. One to two miles back. If he gets a whiff of you, senses you near, this won't work."

"Roger."

Lucas put his phone away.

Quickly, he plotted his next move and the one thereafter and determined what he needed to do. He opened the back door and grabbed the contingency kit. Inside he looked over the various items and decided to take only one.

It was small, and if Dean searched him, he wouldn't find it.

He slipped it deep in his pocket and stowed the kit under the front seat.

Then he grabbed the tire iron, removed the hubcap and started loosening the lug nuts.

Lucas sensed Dean drawing closer before he saw his Jeep Renegade. Glancing over his shoulder, he met Dean's wary gaze. No mask this time. The vehicle inched up slowly. Dean's head was on a swivel as if still waiting for others to appear.

"Are you really here on your own?" Dean asked.

"I am, Santa. If I was with a team, I'd have a little help with this." Lucas gestured to one of the flats and stood. "What brings you back here?"

Dean clenched his jaw. "Hell has frozen over. I need your help."

Chapter Sixteen

Cold water splashed onto Kate's face ripped her from unconsciousness. Snorting some up her nose, she coughed. She went to push the wet hair from her face to discover that she couldn't move. She was tied to a chair in the middle of a large, open dusty space.

In front of her, Jim sat in a folding chair, watching her.

Little by little memories came back to her. Being in the car with Jim. The questions. The sweet smell.

A guy came over to Jim, and that's when she saw the other men. Five more. Armed with guns. They all had the same rough, edgy look to them.

"The truck is loaded," the man said.

"Get the product moving. I want the distro done today." Jim glanced at his watch. "Let the others know that once I make the call and give Dean the location, they need to stay vigilant. That one is crafty."

"Yes, sir." He flounced off back to the others.

"Dean?" she asked, her brain still a bit foggy.

Jim got up, grabbed a handful of paper towels from a table and wiped her face gently, as if he actually cared about her welfare.

She shrank back from his touch, knowing nothing could be farther from the truth.

"Yes. I pieced together that DJ is Dean Delgado."

"How? When?"

Jim sat back in the chair facing her and crossed his legs. "Well, the other night when he took down my two guys who went after Cheryl, the first red flag popped up. DJ is supposed to be going on eighty, and he bested young, virile men with little to no injury to himself. Then you said his name, Dean, when I phoned you. Another red flag. You came to my office yesterday wearing a man's sweater, spouting off some cockamamie story about a Good Samaritan. In your haste to leave, you forgot the gloves. A pair of men's gloves. I went after you to give them back and overheard your conversation with Janeen. I watched you walk down to the *Gazette*. Saw *DJ* waltz in shortly thereafter. The two of you left with a folder, looking thick as thieves. Then I called you. Asked you if you'd seen him or had a working phone number for him."

A sinking feeling washed through her, from her head to her toes. If she'd been standing, she would've swayed on her feet from the sickening rush of it.

"You were with him. Lying to me. So naturally, I had to wonder why a good girl like Katie Sawyer, who had never lied to me before, was suddenly pathological in her attempts to safeguard her friendly neighborhood bartender."

Kate dry heaved, wanting to retch, but nothing came up.

"Then I recalled how eighty-year-old DJ gave chase after Smitty. Witnessed the car accident. So, I checked the CCTV footage from that night. Lo and behold, who did I see? Everything *almost* made sense. It took me a little bit to figure out why he's been traipsing around town, for months, in disguise." Jim tapped his temple. "Because Dean is in some kind of trouble. He's running from something or someone. And that's why you and lover boy were planning to leave town together."

"We'll disappear. We won't say anything to anybody. You'll never see us again. We won't be a problem."

"You're absolutely right. After you're both dead and buried, that'll be two less problems to worry about."

Oh, God! Oh, God! He was going to kill them.

"I didn't want it to come to this, Katie. After Cheryl died, I checked her belongings for the thumb drive before I left the hospital. When I sent one of my guys to your place to see if you had it, I gave strict instructions not to kill you. I was so pleased when you ended up bringing it to me. But then you lied to me over and over again. You brought this on yourself."

"You murdered Tyler, didn't you?"

He cocked his head to the side. "I gave the order. One of my boys carried it out."

Her chest tightened as if caught in a vise, her mind racing over everything Jim had said. "Andrea. Please don't hurt her. She won't talk."

"She was warned. She didn't heed it."

"You don't have to kill her."

"Andrea Miles is dead. She died this morning. Slipped in the shower. Broke her neck. Unfortunate freak accident. They haven't found her body yet. But they will soon."

Kate shook her head, fighting the rising panic. "What about the baby? Are you going to kill him, too?" Where did the trail of bloodshed and horror end?

"Do you think I'm a monster?" He reeled back in his chair with a look of disgust. "I wouldn't hurt an innocent baby."

"You never even got the paternity test done, did you?"

"I definitely did." He nodded. "My guys aren't the father, but I already knew that. I was just looking for confirmation that the kid is the governor's son. That boy is going to give me all the leverage I'll ever need against him. The governor has aspirations to run for president one day." Jim whistled. "It's going to be nice having the power of the White House at my beck and call. An ace up my sleeve that he won't see coming. That chump doesn't even know the baby has been born. Cheryl wasn't due until next month."

"Why are you doing this? Drugs? Forced prostitution?" To think she had once admired this man.

"Money and power. I can't afford an Ivy League tuition on a public servant's salary. I'm up for reelection this year. Campaigning and billboards cost money. This operation funded the governor's campaign as well. He picked a circuit judge who owed him a favor, so we could get the right girls for this enterprise. We have a lucrative side hustle, a good thing going."

"It's not good for the women you force into this. Is Holden a part of this, too?"

"Holden?" Jim snickered. "That Boy Scout. Heck, no."

"But Renee…"

"I encouraged Renee to sidle up to him. So I could keep an eye on him. Make sure he doesn't go sticking his nose where it doesn't belong. I like him. A good deputy. I'd hate to have to kill him." His watch beeped. "Almost time to call lover boy."

"Tell me again," Dean said to Lucas, wishing he could torture him to get honest answers. It was his operational instincts talking. Torture would only alienate his brother, and he didn't want to hurt Lucas. But the method was effective at getting the truth.

"How many times are we going to go over this?"

"As many as necessary." Asking the same questions over and over, making a person repeat their story, exposed cracks in the lies. But Dean was aware that Lucas was just as highly trained as he was, which would make it difficult to distinguish between lies and the truth.

This was a drill Lucas was familiar with. A game he played well.

Hands clenched on the steering wheel as he drove them

to Nelson's Gun and Outdoor Sports shop, Dean said, "I'm waiting."

Lucas sighed. "Butch was waiting for me when I stepped off the elevator."

"He didn't call you in early?"

"No. He ambushed me. Hauled me into Price's office. Clark was seated. Your old handler Russell was standing. They said you had been caught on CCTV in our hometown. They were putting a team together and wanted me to give them any information to help track you down."

"What did you tell them?"

"Everything," Lucas said bluntly. Quite convincingly. "About mom, her Alzheimer's. I explained that you wouldn't go creeping back to Laramie for *her*, though."

Dean tensed, hating the grain of truth in that. If Kate hadn't still been living here, he probably would've chosen a different location.

"I told them to look for Kate."

"Every time you say that, it makes me want to wring your neck."

"It shouldn't. I came here to intervene. To find you. To make sure those mercs never laid a finger on Kate. And I'm here, right? In this car with you, ready to risk my life to rescue her from the sheriff. Why? Because I care about her, too. She means a lot to me. I wouldn't have made it out of this town alive without her."

A flicker of something darted across his face, so fast if Dean had blinked, he would've missed it. *Pain.*

The pain his brother felt was deep and genuine.

But was it deep enough to poison Lucas, turn him into a backstabbing liar out for revenge?

That was the question he still hadn't answered.

Dean pulled up in front of Nelson's. "Only purchase the items we discussed, and pay in cash."

Lucas rolled his eyes. "I'm not an amateur. This isn't my first rodeo." He pulled the handle, opening the door.

"Hang on," Dean said. "Give me your phone."

"What for? You still don't trust me?"

"Trust has to be earned. One baby step at a time." Dean held out his palm. "Phone."

Lucas took out his cell, entered the pass code and dropped it into his hand.

For good measure, Dean felt his jacket pockets and pulled up his pant legs, taking a gander at his ankles, to be sure he didn't have a second phone hidden on him.

"Satisfied?" Lucas asked.

"Not even close. Hurry up. The call will be coming soon."

Lucas jumped out and went into the shop.

As much as he wanted to believe that his little brother was willing to set aside his grievances and had come here to help him, something in his gut simply wouldn't let him.

He only trusted him enough to partner up to save Kate.

Dean swiped across the screen of the phone and searched his recent call history.

Missed calls from a Langley number. Even more missed calls from Butch, his team leader. Which would make sense if Lucas had left work and hopped on a plane as he had claimed.

The only call he'd taken in the last twenty-four hours was from Ava. Probably a girlfriend.

Dean glanced in the back seat at Lucas's duffel bag. Unzipping it, he riffled through his things, searching for anything suspect. No gun. No ammo. He wouldn't have been able to fly commercial with one. That made sense, too.

If it looks like a duck and quacks like a duck, it's a duck, right?

Then why did he feel as if he was playing a game of

Duck, Duck, Goose instead? One where Lucas was going to turn out to be a spiteful goose.

The CIA was the best at this, painting any picture they wanted you to see while hiding the truth.

It didn't help matters that even as a kid, if someone wronged Lucas, he never let it go.

Dean swiped the screen again. This time he checked his text messages. Not a single one from *Ava*. No calls from her last week, either.

He blew out a heavy breath. That didn't prove anything. Ava could be someone new. A girl he just met.

Dean's cell phone rang. His heart pounded as he answered. "Yes."

"Do you have what you stole from me?"

"Yes."

"Come to the old cement plant on the south side of town. Do you know the one?"

Did he ever. The perfect spot to meet. Isolated. No one would hear gunfire. Plenty of places for armed men to hide. "Yes."

"Be here in twenty minutes, or she dies." Jim hung up.

Dean's gut burned. He ached to put Sheriff Jim Ames down. Six feet under with one bullet to the head.

Lucas pushed through the door of the shop and came back to the car, holding a bag of guns, ammo and a big black case with the words *Electric Fire Remote Ignition System* printed across the front.

"The call came," Dean said as his brother got settled in his seat.

"Where do we meet?"

He handed Lucas his cell phone. "The old cement plant."

"Good choice on the sheriff's part. You definitely need me."

That was true.

Lucas passed him the shopping bag. "You load while I set these puppies up." He patted the case.

Inside the bag were two tactical nine-millimeters. Both used, probably to keep the costs down. Threaded barrels. Nelson's didn't sell silencers. Dean would loan Lucas his sound suppressor, but his brother wasn't touching his personal weapon.

Not that Dean would be able to bring it with him inside the cement plant. He fully expected to be searched and for any weapons found to be confiscated.

While Dean loaded the guns for Lucas, his brother took out the sport smoke canisters and programmed them to go off with the remote control. Lucas would search for the men who were lying in wait and eliminate them. Along the way, he'd leave behind a smoke canister.

When Dean gave him the signal, Lucas would ignite them with a press of a button.

"Once you're inside the plant, you'll need to be fast and quiet. We have to get Kate out of there and to safety."

Lucas took the gun with attached sound suppressor. Checked that it was loaded and chambered a round. "I know how to do a job."

His brother had a reputation for being one of the best in-house assassins.

But once you were trained and had enough ops under your belt, the hard part wasn't killing. It was not losing your humanity in the process.

Dean didn't doubt that Lucas would be able to take out a bunch of thugs.

He worried that the man beside him might not be his brother anymore.

Chapter Seventeen

Dean had looped around to the back of the plant and stopped the Jeep.

Lucas hopped out with the gear he needed. Standing between the car and the open door, he stared at Dean. "Do me a favor?"

"What's that?"

Lucas pointed the gun at Dean's head. His finger was on the trigger. If Lucas had still been in the car, in close proximity, he could've taken him. But with his brother out of the car with a clear, clean shot, Dean didn't stand a chance.

"Once the dust settles," Lucas said, "I want you to look back on this moment and remember that I had a choice." He lowered the gun, shut the door and gave him a two-finger salute.

Dean let out the breath that he'd been holding. For the longest heartbeat, he hadn't been sure if Lucas would've pulled the trigger.

After watching his brother sneak into the plant, using the entrance he'd indicated, Dean took out his cell phone and tapped the iHere app, activating it. He'd downloaded the app ages ago, and it was paired with a triangular device, smaller than a key fob, that was attached to his key chain. He put the cell phone to sleep. When he was ready, with a push of the button on the device, he could secretly begin recording a conversation. The phone would appear as if still in sleep mode, but every word would be captured.

If he was lucky, the sheriff would be feeling cocky, emboldened to say more than he should.

Dean drove around to the front and parked. He leaned over and took out a flip phone, a burner, from the glove box. Getting out of the car, he scanned his surroundings.

One guy was waiting for him by a door. "Where are the girls?" he asked as Dean approached.

"That's a conversation for me to have with your boss." He extended his arms in preparation to be searched, the keys with the iHere device in his right hand and the flip phone in his left.

The guard did a quick pat down of his arms, torso and legs, pausing to take a look at the cell phone in his pocket. It never occurred to the obtuse man to ask why Dean had two phones. Noticing that the smartphone was asleep, the guy stuffed it back in Dean's pocket.

The guy turned a gun on Dean, and they walked through the cement plant to the large, open area where he'd witnessed them loading drugs the last time he'd been there.

Kate was standing beside a chair with her wrists bound. The sheriff was beside her, gun in his hand pointed at her.

Seeing panic race across her face almost did Dean in. A killing rage spiked through him, and that red haze clouding everything thickened.

"Dean Delgado, as I live and breathe."

Not for much longer, if Dean had anything to say about it. He pressed the button, activating the recording app. "Kate, are you okay?"

She teared up and pressed her lips tight like she'd been instructed not to speak.

The sheriff grabbed her by the arm. "Don't talk to her. Talk to me. Where are the girls?"

"Do you think I was stupid enough to bring them here? They're somewhere safe."

"Now that was a mistake." The sheriff pressed the muzzle of his gun into Kate's ribs, and she winced.

The look of pure fear in her eyes hit Dean straight in the gut. Jim Ames was going to die today.

"The mistake would be killing Kate, Sheriff. I may not have those poor women you forced into prostitution, innocent girls—"

"They weren't innocent." An ugly grin spread across his face. "According to the law, they were all found guilty as charged. If they had been good girls, keeping their noses clean, doing the right thing, then they would be innocent."

This hubris would be the sheriff's downfall. He was used to controlling everything and everyone. Thought himself above the law. Had grown to think he was invincible.

"You had the parole officer Renee Olson intimidate and coerce them," Dean said, stalling to give Lucas time to work and hopefully to get something that would strengthen the FBI's case. "I assume the judge must be getting paid off, too, sentencing them to that halfway house."

"Sure, the governor's second circuit man gets a kickback."

"It's disgusting. Pumping those women full of drugs, using them like pieces of meat."

"We've all got to make a living. Those girls don't bring in nearly as much money as the drugs, but it's a nice slice of the pie that I'm not willing to give up. You have until the count of three to tell me where my cash cows are, or I put a bullet in her. One."

"Don't tell him," Kate said. "He's going to kill us anyway."

The sheriff raised his hand and hit Kate with the gun he held—a quick, startling smack to her cheek. She cried out as blood dribbled from her mouth, and then she held her face.

Dean took a step forward, but the other man, a punk with a gun, pressed the muzzle to the right side of his head. The proximity was excellent. Just right for Dean to maneuver when the time came.

"I warned you, Katie." The sheriff hit her again. This time in her stomach, and she doubled over, crumpling to her knees. "Shut your mouth."

The breath stalled in Dean's lungs, and his knees went weak. The sheriff was a sick, evil man, but Dean hadn't been prepared for him to strike her. To hit her with such brutal force. "Don't you dare touch her again."

Jim stared him in the eyes as he grabbed a handful of Kate's hair and yanked her up to her feet. "Two."

"I'll give you two reasons you're not killing anyone today," Dean said. "First, this phone in my hand is a remote detonator. I hit the send button, the number is called and one of your distro sites along with a whole lot of crystal meth goes *boom*."

Jim's eyes narrowed. "You're lying."

He was. This was a total bluff.

Dean rattled off the coordinates of the other location he visited. "The one near Rock River. I planted quite a bit of BLASTEX," he said, referring to the brand of packaged explosives used by construction workers. And that was true. He had planted explosives somewhere. Months ago. But it wasn't at one of the drug sites. "My fake demolitions credentials came in handy."

"I could just have him shoot you." Jim gestured to the guy holding the gun on Dean.

"My finger will hit the button before he pulls the trigger, but if he kills me, you'll never find those women. Which brings me to my second reason. I'm not here alone. Now!"

The Electric Fire canisters detonated, emitting huge

bursts of white smoke in various spots where Lucas had placed them. A perfect distraction that drew the sheriff's and the other man's attention, their heads swiveling, their gazes flying around wildly.

Dean moved lightning fast. He dropped his keys as he cocked his arm, swinging his elbow back and rotating his body. The pointy bone collided with the man's head and sent him reeling. Seizing the momentum, Dean struck the guy's arm. Then he twisted the weapon loose from his grip and fired two shots at his chest.

With the gun in hand, Dean whirled and took aim on the sheriff, but Jim had his arm wrapped around Kate's throat, holding her in front of him as a human shield.

No matter what, this was ending here, with Jim Ames in a pool of his own blood. "You're the one dying today," Dean vowed. "Let her go."

Jim laughed, so arrogant, so sure of himself. He had no idea whom he was dealing with.

In his peripheral vision, Dean saw Lucas emerge from the smoke, holding the sound-suppressed nine-millimeter at the ready.

He gave a little nod of thanks to his brother, and both men trained their weapons on the sheriff.

Jim had missed this one important fact. His skills were nothing up against theirs, those of trained killers, molded by the CIA. The sheriff's greed paled in comparison to Dean's fear for Kate and his determination to keep her safe, even at the cost of his life.

"You won't shoot me." Jim tightened his hold on Kate. "Not while I have her."

"Dean," Kate muttered.

His gaze fell to her terrified face. *Please, don't talk, honey.* He needed to focus. Couldn't afford the distraction of looking at her, hearing her.

Lucas glanced between them. He must have had some

idea of how this was messing with Dean's head, because he spoke up. "Kate, let us do what we do best. Just be quiet."

But Kate kept her gaze focused on Dean's. The intensity of it burned through him. "It's okay." Her bloody lip trembled. "Do it."

He shook his head. "What?" She couldn't possibly mean...

"You have to stop him." A tear ran down her cheek.

Jim tightened his arm around her throat, choking her, and it was as if someone had knifed Dean and ripped him open. He couldn't lose her, and he couldn't risk her life by taking a dodgy shot that wasn't clean.

"I'm walking out of here." Jim shook her as he dragged her along with him, creeping toward an exit. "And you're going to let me leave if you want her to live."

Kate struggled against him, trying to pry his arm from her throat. "I love you." Her voice was raspy, the words crashing together. "Kill him. Take the shot."

Dean's vision blurred. *No, not like this.* He couldn't take the shot with the gun pointed to her head.

"Rotten bastard! I never liked you," Lucas said. "I called 911 and you didn't arrest him. I was bloody and beaten. My mom was bloody. And you didn't arrest him!" Lucas charged the sheriff.

Jim swung his gun away from Kate toward Lucas, giving Dean the opportunity. The opening. He took the shot.

The force of the bullet knocked Jim Ames backward, but the arm locked around Kate hauled her down to the floor with him.

Dean and Lucas rushed to her. His brother pried the arm loose from her throat. Dean hauled her up into his arms. He ran a hand over her hair and face. Fear released the icy grip it had on his heart.

She was shaking. Her cheek was bruised. Her abdomen must've hurt as well. There was blood in her hair and dust all over her clothes.

The dazed expression didn't clear from her eyes and probably wouldn't for a while.

But she was alive.

Unlike the sheriff, who was dead with blood pooling around his head.

"We should get out of here," Lucas said, scooping up Dean's car keys.

Dean gave a nod. "Let's go."

With Dean on one side of Kate and Lucas on the other, they got her to the car. Lucas tossed him the keys. Dean put her in the back where she could lie down with Lucas's bag under her head.

"Give them to me." Dean held out his hand to his brother and waited for him to pass over the guns.

"After that, you still don't trust me?"

"Lunging at Ames wasn't about me or Kate, that was about you." Getting revenge and not letting go of anything from the past.

Lucas put the two guns in Dean's hands.

Dean dropped them in the foot well beneath him, did a quick pat down on Lucas to be sure he didn't have others from the men he'd killed and took off. He sped toward the motel and didn't slow until they had arrived. "Help me get her into the room."

Lucas gave a slight nod.

They got Kate out of the car into the motel room.

"Smells like sex and stale coffee in here," Lucas said.

Dean grimaced at him. "Shut up."

They sat Kate down on the bed.

"Hon, are you all right?" Dean asked. She nodded but didn't say anything, and that's what worried him. "I'm going to get some ice for her face." Dean jumped up, grabbing the plastic bag from the ice bucket and darted out of the room.

He ran to the ice machine. Put the bag under the opening of the chute and slapped the button. Once the bag was full of ice, he dashed back to the room, swiped the key card and rushed inside.

Kate was saying something low to Lucas. His arm was around her, and her head was resting on his shoulder. An inkling of jealousy twisted through him, but his relief at seeing her come out of that trance and responding was worth so much more.

Lucas looked up at him. "Dean loves you so much he actually let me help."

"Thank you," she said to Lucas. "For coming. For helping us."

"That's what family is for." Lucas rubbed her arm, holding her close.

Dean stepped up to Kate and handed her the bag of ice. "Put this on your face. The sheriff hit you pretty hard."

"Thanks." She took the bag with one hand and clutched his wrist with the other. "I know how much you risked by coming for me."

"I'm nothing without you." That was the extent of what he could say, confess, in front of his brother. "Put the ice on your face."

She did and winced.

Tomorrow, she'd thank him for it.

Dean went to the laptop on the nightstand and got to work. First, he connected his phone and began the download of the recorded conversation. He dug in his bag and found a spare thumb drive. After he erased anything on it, he copied all the pertinent files for the FBI, including the recording from earlier today of the sheriff at the cement plant.

Taking the drive from the computer, he turned to his brother. "Why are you here?"

Lucas's gaze lifted from Kate to his. "Isn't that obvious by now?"

No, it wasn't. "What was the first thing you felt when

you saw Butch in the vault and he told you he'd been waiting for you?"

"I was in the elevator when I saw Butch that morning. And the first thing I felt was surprised."

Dean believed that when Butch had approached him it had been in the elevator.

"Who was in Price's office?" he asked, stepping closer, wanting to hear the story again.

"Clark was seated in a chair. Kelly Russell was standing beside Price. At his right hand."

Details were important, especially if you were lying. But this hadn't changed. The positioning of the players.

But this time around Dean homed in on something he'd missed before. "I get why they might call her in for this meeting, but why was the ice queen standing next to Price? Why wasn't she sitting when you came in?"

Lucas got up and walked over to Dean. "I forgot to tell you the best part. Russell was promoted after your disastrous operation that made you all traitors."

"What?" Dean stared at Lucas, horrified, disgusted. "She didn't get fired or quit in outrage over the injustice of what happened?"

"No, they didn't fire her, and she most certainly didn't quit." Lucas said the words plainly, matter-of-factly. "She was promoted to deputy director of operations, and she's gunning for Topaz."

If that was true, then either Kelly Russell had set them up on that ruinous mission and she wanted to tie up loose ends, or... "She believes we're traitors. She doesn't question our guilt?"

"Everyone believes you're guilty."

"Why?"

"Because of the money."

"What money?"

Something shifted in his brother's eyes. "The offshore accounts with your names on it. Half a million dollars each."

This was bad. Worse than he'd imagined.

"The ice queen spearheaded this operation to hunt you down, Dean. She was the one who wanted me to give them information about you."

And that's where his dear little brother had given him too much truth.

Lucas had almost convinced him that he was there out of brotherly concern.

No one was better than Kelly Russell at reading people, sizing them up, measuring their strengths, assessing their weaknesses.

Maybe Russell had let Lucas waltz out of Langley in the middle of the day after questioning him, let him come here and had him followed, had a tracker put on him.

But then a kill team would have taken Dean out by now.

Maybe Russell had sent Lucas for some other reason.

Either way, Lucas wasn't a duck. His brother was a big, fat, golden goose.

"I have to run an errand," Dean said. "Mail some information, overnight express it to someone. I'll be back in a little while."

"I can go to the post office for you," Lucas offered. "It's best you don't flash your face around town with a kill team hunting you."

Dean put a ball cap on his head. "Your concern warms my heart, but I'll take care of it myself. You stay here." He grabbed the thumb drive with all the data, the hard-copy folder from Andrea and his personal duffel bag with all his stuff. No way he was leaving any of his gear within his brother's reach. He kissed Kate's forehead. "Keep the ice on your face," he said to her, "and an eye on him." He gestured to his brother. "Don't let him out of your sight."

Chapter Eighteen

Kate watched Dean waltz out of the motel room with all his belongings, and for a startling heartbeat, she wondered if he was coming back.

He loves you. He won't leave you again.

"Kate." Lucas held one of her hands in his. "I'm so glad you're okay. Safe."

She pressed the ice to her cheek, where the sheriff had hit her. "I'm just glad you were there to help us. When I saw Dean walk in, I was so scared for him. I knew Jim had four other men hiding, waiting to kill him." She squeezed her fingers around his. "What are you doing here?"

"The CIA tried to recruit me to help track down Dean. But when I heard he was in Laramie, I knew he was here because of you."

"You did?"

"There's no other reason he would've come back here."

Pride and her ego swelled for moment, then Kate thought of his mother. "Did the CIA ask you to come?"

"No." Lucas shook his head, holding her gaze. "In fact, I'm going to get into a lot of trouble for coming here. If they don't fire me, they'll probably send a kill team after me, too."

"Oh, no."

"But I had to help him and to protect you. I inadvertently told them about your relationship as teenagers. When I did,

I saw it in their eyes, that they considered you to be a viable target he'd make contact with. I couldn't let anything happen to you because I'd slipped up."

"Lucas, you've risked so much."

"I never thought I would. Not in a million years. Not for him. Not after he abandoned us." The crestfallen look on his face broke her heart.

She recalled far too vividly the grief-stricken, angry boy he'd been. His grades at school had nosedived; he constantly got into fights and was a regular in detention. Until she helped him. Studied with him. Invited him to her house for dinners to give him a break. Did her best to fill the hole Dean had left behind.

"He regrets it," she said. "He's sorry for leaving the way he did. It wasn't to hurt us."

"But it did hurt us. Both of us. Do you know he's never apologized to me?"

"He said you won't talk to him. That he's tried."

"He's a liar." Lucas got up, took off his jacket and tossed it on the dresser. "He hasn't tried. Dean saw me once in the hall, and when I blew him off, the way he deserved, do you know what he did?"

She set the ice down. "What?"

"Nothing. Not a thing. I'm his brother, not only in blood, but in the Corps, too, a bond that's supposed to be unbreakable. That transcends blood. A lot of good it's done me."

"You joined the marines, too? How did you know he joined the Corps?"

"Mom received a letter congratulating her on his completion of basic training," he said.

Kate knew his mother had burned the letter, but she didn't know she'd shown it to Lucas.

"She cried. She was so happy to know that he was alive and okay. Not dead on the street." He clenched his jaw. "If Dean was really sorry, if he cared about me at all, he would've tried every day. He never would've stopped trying until I forgave him. But here I am, like a fool. I'm the one trying to help him. He doesn't even appreciate it. Treating me like I'm the enemy instead of giving me a chance when I'm the one who's done nothing wrong."

He was still so angry, so hurt.

"Lucas." She got up and embraced him.

"I've risked everything, and he's just going to leave me behind. Again."

"No." Kate pulled back and looked at him. "He won't. I won't let him."

"He doesn't care about me." The pain in his eyes, in his voice, tore her apart.

"That's not true. He loves you. I'll talk to him. You'll see." Dean needed to mend this fence with his brother. It was his responsibility. He was the one who left; he was the oldest. Dean had to make this right.

"What would I do without you, Kate?"

She smiled, but the searing pain was too much.

Lucas put a gentle hand on her shoulder. "I'm so sorry the sheriff hurt you."

"At least he's dead now." Thank goodness for that.

Lucas looked her over. "You're a mess. There's blood in your hair and you're covered in dust. Do you want to clean up?"

"Yeah, actually, I do." Her muscles loosened at the thought of a warm shower. She headed for the bathroom. "I'll only be five minutes."

"Take your time. I'll watch something on TV."

DEAN DISCONNECTED THE call after talking with his cousin Lourdes, who was there in Laramie. Lola wasn't going to open the bar today and would head straight to Fort Collins. It would have been faster to simply hand her all the evidence he had for the FBI so that she could give it to her brother, but a kill team would most certainly have her under surveillance.

Hopping out of the Jeep, he walked into the post office and sent everything overnight express. Back at his vehicle, he grabbed his bag of gear and took out a device that looked like a black wand. He toggled the switch, turning it on. Then he swept his vehicle for a tracking device.

It didn't take long for the wand to beep.

Bingo.

Well, that answered his question about whether or not Russell had had Lucas followed or had sent him.

Dean had to hand it to the ice queen. Her plan was pretty brilliant. But what was she after? Why wasn't he already dead?

Leaving the tracking device undisturbed, he stowed the wand back in the bag and dug around until he found what he was searching for. It looked like an EpiPen, but it was loaded with ketamine instead of epinephrine. He slipped it in his pocket, closed the door and crossed the street.

Keeping his head lowered, he walked one more block. Driving would have been faster, but he didn't want whoever was monitoring the tracker on his vehicle to know where he was going.

He strolled into Nelson's, the same gun shop he'd stopped at earlier, and went up to the counter. "I'd like to get a box of blank nine-millimeter cartridges."

WITH A TOWEL wrapped around her body, Kate finished blow-drying her hair. She ran a brush through it, feeling more like herself. The last couple of days had been the toughest in her life, and the best.

Because she had Dean.

And now it was up to her make sure the Delgado brothers made amends. They'd been estranged far too long.

Looking around, she realized she'd forgotten to bring in a fresh change of clothes with her. She opened the bathroom door, and Lucas was standing there, fist raised like he was about to knock.

"Here you go." He handed her some clothes, neatly folded.

"You must be a mind reader."

He smiled, bright and warm. Both he and his brother were tall and handsome, Dean in a sexier, rugged way, but Lucas was so darned cute with those dimples.

"Just observant," he said. "You didn't take any in with you."

"Thanks."

She shut the door. He'd chosen jeans and a sweater. Not that she had a lot of options in the bag. Putting on her underwear, she flushed at the thought of Lucas touching her unmentionables, but it was sweet of him to get her clothes.

Kate left the bathroom, dressed, and packed up her things. When Dean got back, they'd probably head straight out.

Lucas was in a chair watching a show on the home and garden channel about a house renovation.

She heard a vehicle pull up and glanced out the window. Dean was back. She put on her coat, zipped it and grabbed her bag. "I'm going to talk to him."

"He won't listen to reason, because I mean nothing to him."

"You're his brother, and he loves you. I'll make him listen."

Kate stepped outside and shut the door just as Dean reached it. She dropped her bag.

"What are you doing out here?" he asked.

"We need to talk."

"You should be in there watching him," he snapped, pointing a finger at the room.

"He doesn't need to be watched. He's not a criminal."

Dean rolled his eyes and tipped his head back. "You've got to be kidding me."

She grabbed his arm and tugged him two doors down. "I can't believe you."

"Me? What did I do wrong?"

Oh, let her count the ways. "You ran into your brother after not seeing him for a decade and a half and only spoke to him once."

"He wouldn't talk to me."

"He's angry. He's hurt. And it's all justified. You were in the wrong." She stabbed his chest with a finger. "You should have gone to his apartment. Stopped by his desk at work. You should have tried to make things right with him every single day. But you didn't. How do you think that made him feel? Huh?"

"Damn it, he got to you."

She recoiled. "Got to me? Do you have a heart in there?" She stabbed his chest again.

Dean lowered his head. "You're right. I should have done better. I could have done more."

"You should have gotten down on your knees and begged for his forgiveness. You have no idea how hard it was for him without you."

"I'm not the bad guy here."

"Neither is he."

"Oh, yes, he is."

"Stop." She raised her palm. "I won't listen to you say one bad thing about him. Do you understand me? After he left Laramie, did he forget about you? Forge his own path? No. He joined the Marine Corps and the CIA. Why do you think that is, Dean? He's been following you, hoping that you'd care enough to notice. He is your little brother. And he's going to come with us."

"No." Dean stepped back. "No, he's not. You don't understand—"

"If he doesn't go, I don't go. I love you and want nothing more than to be with you, but this is where I draw the line." She turned on her heel.

He ran around in front of her, stopping her.

"I mean it, Dean Delgado. There's *nothing* you can say that will make me change my mind."

"I believe you."

She rocked back, not expecting that response.

"We will leave this motel together, but you have to promise to do two things for me."

It had better not have anything to do with leaving Lucas. She would not agree to it. "What?"

"If I ever use the word *Heathcliff*, you are to move away from me and him and take cover."

Her heart seized. "Why?"

"Do you agree?"

She hesitated. "Yes," she said uneasily. "What's the second thing?"

He handed her an EpiPen.

"What's this for? You don't have allergies."

"You hold on to it. Put it in your coat pocket," he said, and she did. "When I ask you for it, you give it to me."

Her nerves stretched taut. Something was going on, something important was happening in this moment, but she didn't understand what. "Is that it?"

"That's it."

"He goes with us?"

"We're all getting in the car together."

She reached up and threaded her arms around his neck, her heart so full she was sure her chest couldn't contain it. "Thank you." She kissed him, lightly, tenderly since her face still ached. "I love you."

"I love you, too. I'm doing this for you."

Pulling back, she stared at him. "You should be doing this for yourself and for him. Not for me."

"Still. This is all for you."

Chapter Nineteen

"Here you go." Dean reached toward the back seat and handed Lucas the two guns he'd purchased.

"So, does this mean you finally trust me?" Lucas asked.

Not a snowball's chance in hell. "I have to at some point, right?"

Lucas smiled, putting one gun in his coat pocket and the other in his bag.

Kate put her hand on Dean's leg and rubbed his thigh, her eyes gleaming with approval.

Dean pulled out of the motel parking lot and drove to Route 287, taking it south. Everything that Kate had said weighed on him. Lucas wasn't a bad person. He was a good guy, twisted by pain and rage, misled by the CIA. Dean realized Lucas had never asked for his side of the story, his version of events that had gotten him branded a traitor.

Everyone believes you're guilty.

That included Lucas, and that was Dean's fault.

If he had done all the things that Kate had suggested, proven to Lucas that he was sorry, made a halfway-decent effort to reconnect, then his little brother wouldn't be in the back seat of the Jeep, feeling justified about betraying him.

This was a powder keg of Dean's own making.

"Where are we heading?" Lucas asked.

Dean checked his rearview mirror. The kill team was out there, following them, but at such a distance, he couldn't spot them. No need for them to keep a visual. Not when there was a tracker on the vehicle. "Someplace safe. It's a short drive."

"Short?" Lucas leaned forward. "We need to get out of the state."

"We are."

But not with him.

First, he had to show Kate that the divide between him and his brother was too great to bridge in a day. It was the freaking Grand Canyon.

Even if he had told her about the tracker on the car, she would've wanted to discuss it with Lucas, give him a chance to explain.

There was only one way to resolve this so that she left with him. Didn't hate him for not taking Lucas along.

Dean drove to The Buttes. A small unincorporated community that had a population of about fifty. Once there, he took an unmarked dirt road to an old airfield he'd scoped out after he'd returned.

"We're flying out?" Lucas asked.

No, they weren't. "Yep." Dean pointed to the dilapidated aircraft hangar that was about four times the size of a garage. Attached to it was a small office building with a few busted-out windows.

He stopped the car a good 150 feet back and to the side of the hangar.

They all got out, grabbing their bags. Dean unlocked the padlock he'd put on the hangar door, and the hinges creaked with a loud groan when he opened it.

Kate and Lucas followed him inside.

There was a broken-down twin prop plane in the hangar. He'd salvaged parts for the exterior and painted them to make the aircraft appear functional. Nothing more than a shell with a hollow interior that he had packed with some

BLASTEX. The preprogrammed number in the flip phone in his pocket would trigger the detonator.

This was his contingency plan. Every good operative had one.

"See, I told you this would work out," Kate said to Lucas.

"Yeah, you were right. I never doubted you."

Dean set his bag on an old, dusty desk, keeping his back to them.

"What's our destination?" Lucas asked.

"Someplace warm," Dean said.

"Wouldn't you like to know, Kate?" Lucas prodded.

"Actually, I would." Her voice was light and so carefree. That was about to change.

"Come on, Dean. If you really trusted me, you'd tell me. Are we going to meet up with the rest of your team?"

There it is. The reason Kelly Russell had sent Lucas. The reason Dean was still breathing. They thought he would lead them to the rest of his team.

He didn't know where any of them were. But he did have a way to contact Hunter, his team leader. Hunter had given them each a satellite phone. One programmed number. Their last-resort measure if they had nowhere else to go.

Only Hunter would answer the line. Then there would be a challenge and response. Hunter would say *parachute.* Dean would have to respond with *rip cord*, and he'd be given instructions and coordinates to Hunter's location.

And that's what the ice queen was counting on. She knew Hunter well. That their team was a family. That Hunter would never leave any of them hanging, blowing in the wind. That he'd given them a way to contact him.

"As a matter of fact, we are," Dean said, facing his brother. "I hope you have a passport that the agency can't track. I've got ones for Kate and me. From here on out, she's going to be Emily and I'm going to be Heathcliff."

Kate's smile fell, and she stiffened.

Dean shot her a hard look. Things were going to get physical with his brother, and he didn't want her accidentally getting hurt because she was standing too close. "I know *Heathcliff* is a mouthful. You can call me Cliff for short if you like."

She glanced between them and slowly backed away toward the plane.

"No worries on the passport for me," Lucas said, focused on Dean and pumping him for information. "So, where are we going?"

Without answering, Dean turned back around to his bag and unzipped it. He stared down at his spare gun, the backup, that was resting on top of his clothes beside the black wand.

"I think I've proven I can be trusted," Lucas said.

"Panama," Dean said, picking someplace he'd been to once on vacation. "Down in El Valle. That's where we're supposed to meet Hunter if we run into trouble. There's a little outdoor bar, a hut, really. He'll be there at noon every day in case we show." He met Kate's gaze, and worry hung on her face. "This will come in handy there."

Dean grabbed the black wand in his bag, toggling it on, and turned as he tossed it to his brother.

Instinctively, Lucas caught it. The wand emitted a series of high-pitched beeps.

Lucas gave a tight smile before he drew his gun on Dean. "You got me there. That was slick." He threw the wand across the room, where it clattered against the wall.

"What's going on?" Kate asked near the tail of the plane.

"Lucas has a transmitter on him. I'm betting there's audio and visual. Am I right?"

"You are correct."

"What?" Kate asked, striding back toward them. "I don't understand."

"Stay there, honey," Dean said. "Lucas isn't here to help

me get away from the kill team. He's working with them. They've been listening and watching everything."

"No." Kate blanched. "That can't be."

"I'm afraid it is." Lucas tapped a button on his collar with his free hand. "They'll be here soon."

Dean was counting on it. "Why would you do this? Are you really that mad at me?"

"Mad?" Lucas scoffed. "I'm not five, having a temper tantrum. I'm furious. You left me there, knowing that I would be the sole focus of that man's violence. Left me when you could've taken me with you. Mom was already sick. She just hadn't said anything. When she started chemo, I was the one to take care of her, watched her waste away, unable to hold anything down, wondering if the treatments would kill her before the cancer. I had to go through that alone. Because you only cared about yourself. So I'm looking out for myself now."

Dean raised his palms and walked up to his brother. "Does that include killing me?"

"You don't think I can do it?" Lucas asked with the muzzle pointed at Dean's chest.

Honestly, Dean didn't know.

"You're a traitor to your country, a disgrace to the Delgado name and nothing more than a target to me."

"If that's true, then pull the trigger."

"Lucas, what are you doing?" Kate asked. "Lower the gun."

"I'm sorry, Kate. But they're almost here now."

"We're leaving," Dean said. "The only way to stop me is to shoot me."

"I can't let you leave. I have to show them I'm nothing like you. That I'm loyal to my country and to the CIA." Lucas began tightening his finger on the trigger. At the last second, he aimed for Dean's leg and pulled the trigger.

A gunshot cracked.

"No!" Kate shrieked.

Lucas's gaze dropped to the gun.

"I loaded it with blanks." Dean launched a fist to his face, propelling him back, and threw a foot to his gut.

The breath left Lucas in an explosive bark, his mouth clutching for air. Before his brother recovered, Dean got off a roundhouse kick that was a strike of force to his head and sent him spinning.

He swept up behind his brother and whipped an arm around his neck, clamping tight over his windpipe and blocking the blood flow to the brain to knock him out.

But Lucas fought back, stomping on Dean's foot and thrashing side to side to get him off balance.

"I'm sorry," Dean said to him. "I never should've left you behind."

Lucas twisted and kicked and bucked. Threw an elbow repeatedly into Dean's side.

Much more of that and Lucas would free himself or break Dean's ribs before it was lights out.

"EpiPen!" he called to Kate, and she started moving, slowly, like she was in shock. Keeping the hold locked in place, Dean wrestled him to the ground and wrapped his legs around his brother's. "You were my best friend," he said to Lucas. "It was selfish of me to go. I should have apologized. I should've begged for your forgiveness." Guilt flared up in Dean, scouring his insides, threatening to consume him. "I should've been there for you. For Mom. I love you, Lucas. You're my brother. One day, I'll earn your forgiveness. I swear it."

Kate dropped beside him. Her face was flushed and streaked with tears.

"Stick him with it," Dean said.

She popped the top and stuck the injector in Lucas's arm.

The fight was petering out of his brother; his body was growing slack. "Track...tracker," he muttered, raising his hand, but then his eyelids fluttered closed, and he went limp.

"I found the tracker on the car." Dean maintained the pressure until he was sure Lucas was out.

Kate hunched over, her shoulders shuddering. "I can't believe he was going to betray you. Shoot you."

"I can, and I knew you had to see it for yourself. But there's no time to discuss it now." Dean popped the button that Lucas had indicated as the transmitter and tossed it. Then he picked up his brother in a fireman's carry and hustled outside.

Too late.

A dark SUV was racing down the only road in or out, kicking up dust, headed straight for the hangar. The kill team would breach in less than sixty seconds.

They hurried back into the hangar.

"Grab our bags," he said to her. His sat phone was inside, and he'd need it to rendezvous with Hunter.

Kate got both their bags.

"Take my backup gun." Dean led the way through the hangar, carrying his brother into the adjacent office building.

She dug in his bag and grabbed the other nine-millimeter.

Dean moved to a far wall, putting as much distance as possible between them and the plane rigged with explosives. He dropped his brother on the floor and rushed over to the reception desk. It was beaten-up and dented, but it was sturdy.

Shoving the desk, he pushed it to the corner where Kate was huddled beside Lucas. That should provide sufficient cover from the blast.

Opening the flip phone, he heard the creak of the rusty hinges that carried with the hangar's acoustics. The team was inside.

It was time.

As he dialed the number, a shadow moved along the exterior of the building. A lone gunman crept around the office building.

Dean pointed him out to Kate and gestured for her to remain quiet.

She gave a quick nod.

Dean withdrew his gun from his pocket. Once that guy walked through the door, he'd spot them. But Dean would have to deal with him after the explosion.

He hit the call button and braced with Kate for the blast to come.

But there was no big boom, and the merc was already at the door.

What the hell?

Had the wires on the bomb loosened? He hadn't checked it in over a week.

The doorknob turned.

Dean leaped out from behind the desk, his adrenaline demanding he play offense, and charged. Just as he reached the man, the explosives detonated. The shock wave from the blast launched both men into the air and sent them tumbling outside.

The breath was knocked from Dean. Debris rained down around him. He tasted dirt and Sheetrock dust. A steady ringing filled his ears, and his body ached. His head throbbed. With his vision clearing, he pressed his palms to the ground, trying to shake the fog clouding his brain.

His hands were empty.

His weapon.

Where was his gun?

Several feet away, the other man stood and staggered, recovering faster.

Dean scanned the ground quickly. Spotted his weapon.

But it wasn't within reach, and the other guy was too far away to tackle.

The merc swung his gun toward Dean, taking aim at his head.

Dean stiffened in expectation of the pain to follow.

A gun went off, and for a split second no one moved.

There was no pain as Dean sucked in a breath. Then blood spurted from a wound just above the merc's bullet-proof vest below his throat. A gurgling sound came from him, and he dropped and keeled over dead.

Dean spun around on his knees to see Kate. She stood in the doorway, holding his backup weapon.

She'd saved his life. In more ways than one.

The air rushed out of his lungs in relief, his heart hammering at his chest. He crawled to his weapon, scooped it up and hauled himself to Kate. She yanked him into her arms, pressing her face to his chest. He held her tight in return, but only for a moment.

"I need to make sure the others are dead. Stay low behind the desk."

"Okay."

They both moved, separating.

He hustled back toward the hangar, taking care not to make a sound along the way. There was nothing left of the plane besides scraps of flaming metal. The wall that had been closest to the aircraft had been reduced to rubble.

Two bodies lay in close proximity to the debris. Killed by the blast.

A third man had taken a large piece of metal to a leg. It must have severed the femoral artery, from the amount of blood that had poured from his thigh. If he were unconscious and not dead, he soon would be.

Dean swept the perimeter outside to be sure he hadn't missed any others. Finally determining that the coast was clear, he made his way back to the office building.

Kate was waiting with the gun at the ready, prepared to shoot if he had been the enemy.

This time he was the one to rope her into his arms. Her body felt so good, so right against his. He let his eyes close in gratitude as he held her.

"I'm sorry for forcing you to take Lucas with us."

"It's okay. It needed to play out. You needed to see it." And Dean had needed to apologize. To tell his brother he loved him. Still.

Too bad he hadn't done it sooner. Maybe this whole thing could have been avoided.

"What are we going to do about him?" she asked, looking at Lucas.

"Nothing. He'll be out for hours. By the time he wakes, we'll be long gone." One day, Dean would clear his name, and once he did, he'd find a way to make things right with Lucas.

"I came so close to losing you," she whispered, tightening her hold on him.

"But you didn't." He looked down at her, and she met his gaze. He could see the pure love shining bright in her eyes. His world, once so dark and cold, was filled with light that warmed his heart, because he'd finally gotten the one thing he needed.

He had Kate. With her he'd found more than he ever thought possible, and he was willing to fight through anything to make sure they never lost it again.

"What do we do now?" she asked.

"Now, I make a phone call and find out where we're really going. Hopefully it's not the North Pole."

"It doesn't matter where we end up. Could be the North Pole for all I care, as long as I'll have you to keep me warm."

He dragged a hand through her hair and cupped her face. "Well, that I can guarantee. We'll be together, I'll keep you warm and we'll be safe."

Epilogue

Three weeks later

As the small motorboat pulled up to the dock for the island off the coast of Venezuela, Kate's nerves pinged to life. It was silly for her to be anxious. This was friendly territory. Nonetheless, she was, despite the vacation-like atmosphere of calm water and a balmy breeze.

In the waning light of dusk, there wasn't much she could make out on the beach besides a white house with a wrap-around porch. Light shone through every window, almost as if in welcome of their arrival. Palm trees stood as a dense backdrop. Three huts were farther down the coast, but each was dark, and she couldn't see much else.

The boat stopped with the engine idling.

"Thank you," Dean said to the driver, an older woman wearing a plain blue bucket hat with a chin strap.

Every one of their contacts along their journey had worn some variation of a blue hat.

Kate thanked her as well, and the woman tipped her head in response.

Grabbing their one consolidated bag, Dean climbed out on to the dock. He took Kate's hand and helped her from the boat.

Her stomach bubbled with nerves. Their final destination had been shrouded in mystery the entire journey. Every step of the way it had been cloak and dagger. But not dangerous. If anything, it had felt *normal*, doing things other couples took for granted. Talking for hours. Sharing meals. Playing cards. Making love.

They hadn't had much access to television, but they had caught the breaking news in Wyoming. The FBI had shut down a major drug operation and prostitution ring in Albany County. Renee Olson and the second circuit judge had been arrested along with several of their associates, and the governor was under investigation. Cheryl's baby had been placed with relatives in another state. The district attorney was looking at further possible corruption among law enforcement throughout the county and had appointed a new acting sheriff.

By the time it was safe for her to go home, they had finally arrived here. On this island. She had no desire to go back, only forward, with Dean. The love of her life.

Dean had told her countless stories about Team Topaz and the members during the trip. She knew Hunter Wright would be waiting for them. That his team leader was as intrepid as he was intelligent and had come up with this last-resort measure. Each story about him had been grander and more impressive than the last. Other than that, she didn't really know what to expect from Hunter. A legend in the flesh? Or a man?

Interlacing their fingers, Kate and Dean walked hand in hand up the beach. Flowers planted around the white house saturated the air with a sultry fragrance.

"There's no reason to be nervous," Dean said in a gentle tone.

"Is it that obvious?"

He tipped his head to one side, and his mouth hitched in a playful smile. A mouth that was sexy as sin. A mouth she longed to kiss, to taste.

"Only to me. So you can relax," he said, making her smile.

"Are you sure Hunter won't have a problem with me being here, a candy-coated civilian?"

They chuckled in unison, but the sound coming from him was heavy and warm, like a hot summer night.

When he had called her *candy-coated*, she'd been livid. Hurt. Far from amused. But looking back on it, through the lens of everything they'd endured, she could laugh with ease.

"I take that back," he said. "Never should've said such a thing. Even when we were little, you were tough as nails, and you've proven you're closer to Kevlar-coated these days. But still delectably sweet on the inside." He squeezed his fingers tight around hers.

It was incredible how when they were teenagers he'd once been the center of her world. Then he'd left, taking a piece of her heart with him. She never thought she'd see him again. And now he was a pillar of support and love she couldn't imagine living without.

"Thank you," she said.

"For what?"

"For coming back to Laramie."

"I guess, technically, I came back twice. Since I crossed the state line before turning around the second time." He stopped walking and tugged her closer, bringing them chest to chest, and held her against him in a warm embrace. "I came back for you. I'm sorry it took you being in danger and nearly dying for me to see it. Not sure how I missed the obvious before. I've never gotten over you."

Staring up at him, she basked in the look in his eyes, in the sincerity of his words that resonated deep in her bones, in how he made her feel strong and delicate and beautiful at the same time.

She ran her hand through his cool, dark hair. The longer curls at the front had that enticing windblown look you'd only see in a commercial or magazine ad.

"I'm not sorry," she said. Not one bit. "Everything that happened brought us back together. Brought us here, where we'll be safe. And it made you realize you love me."

Lowering his head, he trailed a path of kisses from her temple to her jaw. His beard brushed her cheek, his stubble a titillating scrape against her skin, sending a shiver of delight down her spine. "I've loved you since I was fifteen. Always have and always will. Not a day has gone by when that one thing wasn't true."

Her heart hung suspended a moment and then beat again hard. She believed him, without a doubt in her mind. "I love you, too," she said, not a canned response but the unvarnished truth.

She pressed her palms to his cheeks, drawing his full lips to hers, and gave him a greedy, needful kiss. He slid his hand beneath her hair, his thumb stroking the back of her neck, his fingers tightening on her nape. She breathed him in, savoring the taste of him.

Her knees weakened, and when he drew back, they came apart breathless.

He flashed her one of those grins that was loaded with sensual promise. "If you keep that up, we'll never make it inside."

If she weren't concerned about being a rude guest as well as an uninvited one, she would've dragged Dean down the beach and had her way with him.

"All right, let's go, but I have plans for you later," she said, thinking of how she'd worship his hot, muscled body with her mouth.

"I'm going to hold you to that."

"I would hope for nothing less." She gave him a devilish wink.

Another hearty chuckle rolled from his lips. He dropped his arms from around her and took her hand. As they strolled up to the house, she felt lighter, less worried.

The front door opened before they hit the stairs. A guy dressed in khaki shorts and a T-shirt stepped out onto the porch. "I see you made it."

"Hunter," Dean said with a smile.

A couple of inches taller than Dean, tanned and sculpted, Hunter was a rather perfect specimen of a man, like Brad Pitt at any age. But she guessed Hunter was in his mid-to-late forties.

They walked up the steps.

Dean shook Hunter's hand, and the greeting quickly turned into a one-armed hug.

"This is Kate Sawyer."

"Ah," Hunter said with a raise of his eyebrows and a knowing grin, as though he'd heard her name before. "It's a pleasure to meet you, notwithstanding the circumstances."

Up close under a porch light, he was almost impossibly handsome. Smiling blue eyes that drew you in and golden-blond hair that didn't come from a bottle. But Dean was far more alluring in a dark, magnetic way. Or perhaps it was her hormones talking.

Hunter took her hand in a warm, firm grip. "I hope the trip wasn't too difficult. I'm sorry it was so long, but a necessary precaution."

"The trip was fine." Her smile was shaky as fresh nerves fluttered in her stomach. "No complaints." As long as she was with Dean, nothing else mattered.

Laughter came from the back of the house. Several voices.

Dean looked toward the screen door. "Who's here?"

"I've got a full house."

A bright smile stretched across Dean's face, but surprise lit up his brown eyes. "Zee and Gage are here?"

Kate didn't think she'd get the chance to meet Zenobia Hanley, hacker extraordinaire, and Gage Graham, *cleanup* specialist. If she understood correctly, Gage made dead bodies disappear or could make a government assassination look like an accident.

Over the years, they had become more than his friends. They were Dean's family.

"Gage came in first," Hunter said, slipping his hands in his pockets. "He brought Hope Fischer with him. She's a photojournalist. He saved her life and helped her track down her sister's murderer. Somewhere along the way they fell in love. Next was Zee. She's here with Olivia and her fiancé, John Lowry."

"Who's Olivia?" Kate asked.

"Her daughter," both men said at the same time.

"She's eleven," Hunter added.

"Did Zee get engaged while on the run?" Dean asked.

"No. John proposed here on the beach a few weeks ago. With everyone showing up with a significant other, I'm thinking about dubbing this place Love Island."

"Oh, man," Dean said with a shake of his head and a chuckle. "I missed a lot."

"You have no idea. Hope is pregnant."

Dean rocked back on his heels. "Wow."

"Gage still doesn't know. Zee does. I think John might, too. But don't say anything. It's Hope's place to tell him."

"Why hasn't she?" Kate asked, and Hunter gave her a strange look she couldn't decipher. Maybe the team of superspies was used to keeping secrets, but if they'd been a bunch of civilians, someone would've let the news slip by now. "Not that I'm judging. Or trying to stick my nose in where it doesn't belong."

"Every time Hope mentions babies," Hunter said, "Gage talks about how he doesn't want to be a father. I think she's scared and still processing everything. When the time is right, she'll tell him. Or she'll start showing and he'll figure it out."

Dean snickered. "I can't wait to catch up with everyone."

"Follow me." Hunter opened the door and led the way into the house.

As the door closed behind them, a series of low beeps chimed. Hunter and Dean turned toward the sound.

Mounted on the wall beside the door was a rectangular black device with two antennae at the top. An LED display across the front panel had an illuminated bar of green and orange lights.

Dean and Hunter exchanged a look, their faces impassive, but there was a sudden DEFCON 1 high-alert tension swelling in the room.

"What is that?" Kate asked.

Hunter's gaze slid to her. "In laymen's terms, a bug detector."

"It'll ping from any analog, digital, GSM cellular or Wi-Fi-based listening and tracking devices within forty feet," Dean said.

"Did you bring cell phones with you?" Hunter asked Dean.

"Come on, I'm not stupid."

"All right. The two of you stand at least ten feet apart." Hunter grabbed the device from the wall.

Dean extended his arms and spread his legs. Kate did likewise.

First Hunter waved the black device around Dean's head, over his arms, down his torso, in between his legs and across his boots. Then repeated the procedure along his backside, taking particular care with their bag.

Nothing.

Kate gulped. "Maybe the equipment is faulty."

"It's not," Hunter said with sharp finality and turned to her. His jaw was hard, his eyes narrowed in suspicion as he raised the device in front of her.

Beeps pinged, and the LED lights flashed from orange to red.

Kate shook her head. There had to be a mistake. "I don't understand."

Hunter's gaze swung to Dean. "Who would know to plant a tracker on her instead of you?"

Dean clenched his hand in a fist and lowered his head. "Lucas. The agency sent him after me. I made the mistake of letting him get too close. It almost cost me my life." He looked up at Hunter. "I'm sorry. I've put everyone in jeopardy by coming here."

"No, I did. This is my fault," Kate said. "You asked me to keep an eye on Lucas when you left the two of us alone. He got me to lower my defenses, to remember how close we once were, how he used to be." A lost little boy who had missed his brother as much as she did. The two of them struggling and lonely, clinging to each other to get through it. "Then he brought up the kidnapping and encouraged me to take a shower. That getting cleaned up would make me feel better. And like a fool, I did." She could kick herself. If only she'd had the common sense to mention it to Dean, they could've avoided this doomsday scenario. "Lucas had access to my things, and when I came out of the bathroom, he had fresh clothes for me in his hands. I never thought anything of it. It didn't occur to me that he'd plant a tracker on me."

Although it should've. Lucas had turned into a 007 operative, as slick and deadly as Dean. If one of them was capable of wearing a realistic disguise, passing himself off as another person for months, why wouldn't the other be capable of embedding a tracker in her clothes?

"You are *not* going to take this on your shoulders." Dean clutched her arms. "I should've checked our things. This is on me."

"Yes. It is." Hunter's tone was matter-of-fact. "If I had to venture a guess, I'd say the tracker was in your bra. Dean, check for it." Hunter turned around, facing the door.

That's where it had to be. Once they'd reached a warmer climate, she'd picked up shorts, tank tops, a couple of sundresses. The only thing she had no need to replace were her undergarments.

Kate unclasped her bra, slipped her arms through the straps, pulled it from her tank top and handed to Dean. Not bothering with the straps or clasp, he inspected the seam of her underwire. A hole had been made. One she hadn't noticed. Manipulating the material with his fingers, he pulled out a filament-thin device and gave her bra back.

"GPS tracking only," Dean said.

While he showed Hunter, she stepped into a corner and quickly put her bra on.

"Very clever of Lucas." It almost sounded like admiration in Hunter's tone.

"He's on Cinnabar now. I found out Butch is his team leader."

"I bet this was Butch's idea. In case you gave him the slip, he could still locate you."

"Us. They want the whole team."

Kate rejoined them.

"Please tell me you at least got something useful out of Lucas," Hunter said.

"You won't want to hear it."

"When did *want* ever factor into this? If you've learned something, I *need* to know."

"The reason everyone believes we're traitors is because there's a money trail. A half million dollars in offshore accounts for all of us. Deposited two days before the mission."

"I'm aware of that already. Zee told me when she arrived. She found out through tracking Bertrand's research. Is there anything else?"

Dean took a deep breath. "I don't know for certain who set us up, but… Kelly Russell was promoted."

Hunter staggered back a couple of steps, as though he'd been physically hit. "Promoted?"

"To deputy director of operations."

Hunter's jaw dropped.

Kate recalled a similar look of shock on Dean's face and what he'd said to Lucas.

She didn't get fired or quit in outrage over the injustice of what happened?

Kate supposed the same thing must have been going through Hunter's mind. She didn't fully grasp what it meant to be a team's handler, but she understood that complete trust was required for a successful mission. Every time a team went out, their lives were in the hands of their handler.

If this Kelly Russell had been the one to set up Team Topaz, then it was the greatest betrayal imaginable. Though what Lucas had pulled was a close second.

Hunter was standing stock-still, looking at the floor or perhaps nothing at all, almost in a daze.

Dean drew closer to him, slowly, as if approaching a deadly predator. "Hunter?" he asked in a tentative tone. "Are you all right?"

"Surprised." Hunter gave a tiny shake of his head and schooled his features into a blank canvas. "That's all."

From everything Dean had shared, that was a lot. It took something colossal to surprise the great Hunter Wright.

"Kelly could be coldhearted for sure, a royal pain at times," Hunter said. "But always a consummate professional. I didn't take her for a backstabbing opportunist." A spark of emotion flashed across his face.

Kate would've sworn it was pain. That the news of their handler had wounded him.

"Do you think she was the one who set us up?" Dean asked.

"I don't know. But I intend to find out. The one thing that's now certain is she benefited."

Jubilant voices and more laughter came from the back patio, drawing their gazes.

"They're playing Dungeons and Dragons Adventure Begins," Hunter said in a low, despondent voice. "We're all hooked."

The rest of his team had found a sanctuary here. They were couples in love, engaged, pregnant, with an eleven-year-old to boot, outside laughing, playing normal games. And her arrival with Dean put everything and everyone in jeopardy. The entire house of cards was about to come tumbling down around them.

Kate fought to tamp down the nausea rising in her stomach.

"What are we going to do about the GPS tracker?" Dean asked.

"Absolutely nothing. If we destroy it, they'll know we found it. I'll put it on one of my garments to keep it moving."

"So we just leave it?" Kate asked, stunned. "And wait for a kill team to come?"

"Precisely." Hunter's tone was cool and nonchalant.

Way too cool and far too nonchalant to give Kate the slightest chance at having peace of mind. How could he consider that to be a plan, much less a good one?

Dean had raved about Hunter being a master strategist. Well, this was hardly convincing evidence.

"I've been expecting this," Hunter said. "Not the GPS tracker per se, but with the entire team needing to punch out of wherever they'd been lying low and coming here, it was only a matter of time before the CIA found us. This can work out in our favor. Now we have a better timeline of when they'll get here. Once they do, they'll do recon before they strike. Since they don't know that we know they're coming, we'll have the tactical advantage."

"Dean." Kate turned to him with her heart in her throat.

"You said sticking around with a kill team on the way was suicide."

"I did say that. But we got out of Laramie, didn't we?"

"Barely." They'd almost died. More than once.

Dean curled his hands around her shoulders and rubbed up and down her arms. "We need to trust Hunter. He knows what he's doing."

"I've given every scenario considerable thought," Hunter said. "And discussed it with the others. John had some good ideas."

"Is John in our line of business?" Dean asked.

"In a manner of speaking, he used to be. Navy SEAL."

"Aha." Dean nodded like that explained everything.

What was wrong with these two? Why weren't they panicking? How could they act so cavalier?

"Isn't this island the end of the road?" Kate asked. "As in there's nowhere else to run. Nowhere else to hide."

"That's right." Hunter's tone was all easy-breezy. "Our time on Love Island has come to an end."

"But we just got here," she said, realizing the words had been uttered out loud and not in her head. In a voice that bordered on whiny, no less.

"Team Topaz is done running." Hunter caught her gaze as he spoke. "We're done hiding. We need to figure out who put us in this predicament and fight back."

"Fight?" Kate was suddenly dizzy. She thought she'd left the fighting behind in Wyoming. "I'm not a warrior. Or a superagent. I'm a veterinarian, for crying out loud." She breathed through the panic attempting to burrow its way into her mind.

"Oh, good." Hunter nodded in approval. "We could use a doctor."

She treated animals. *Not people!* It wasn't the same thing.

Kate wrapped her arms around her midsection. "I think

I'm going to be sick." Once again, she'd meant to keep that to herself, but it just kept slipping out.

"The bathroom is right down the hall." Hunter pointed. "I hope you'll still be up to eating. It was my turn to cook family night dinner. I made *hallacas*. Corn dough wrapped in plantain, filled with beef, olives, pork, capers and a few veggies. Not to toot my own horn, but they're pretty delicious. Even Olivia raved about them. There's some grilled meat and fish as well in case you don't do carbs."

The glorious days when not eating carbs actually occurred to her.

Their nights of playing games and enjoying family dinners—another ordinary thing under extraordinary circumstances—were numbered thanks to her.

The situation was dire, and she was at fault, regardless of what Dean had told her, but she didn't want to give Hunter the wrong impression. To have him thinking she wasn't up for this, couldn't cut it. That she was candy-coated. Worse, she didn't want him to assume she regretted her decision to come here.

Given the chance to do it all over again, she would still choose Dean every single time. No matter the consequences.

"We'll be okay." Dean slipped a comforting arm around her shoulders, tucking her against his side. "We'll get through this. We've got the whole team and a SEAL."

Swallowing against the fear pooling in her gut, she leaned into his strong frame, absorbed his body heat and hopefully a fraction of his confidence. "I know. It's just…" Hauling in a deep breath, she calmed her mind to get the words right. "I wasn't prepared for this."

Therein lay the problem, the difference between her and the two formidable, unfazed men in the room. They were highly skilled, hardened professionals who had been trained for this. Who lived and breathed it. Danger was nothing new to them. Fighting was second nature.

"Look on the bright side," Hunter said. "At least you're not unprepared *and* pregnant."

Poor Hope. Here Kate was feeling sorry for herself, wallowing in fear when she didn't have nearly as much to contend with as Hope. Or the eleven-year-old, for that matter. Both civilians, unaccustomed to this crazy 007 lifestyle.

Although she hadn't met Hope yet, she was important to Gage, who was like a brother to Dean. That made her important to Kate. The same went for Olivia and John.

She needed to be strong, put on a brave face, not only to alleviate Dean's concerns, but because others were going to need her. They were all in this together.

Buck up. You've got this.

"You're right," Kate said to Hunter. He had a remarkable way of putting things into focus, showing her where she needed to concentrate her energy. "It was selfish to only think of myself and how this affects me."

"Not selfish. Only human. Don't beat yourself up over it. I was only trying to lighten the mood."

More like trying to lighten *her* mood. She was the only one acting as if the apocalypse was imminent while Dean was composed and Hunter was talking about *hallacas* and Dungeons and Dragons.

She needed a mental course correction. To do a complete one-eighty.

Hunter looked at Dean. "You've got a good one. A keeper. But I'm sure you already know that."

"Yeah, I do." Dean's arm tightened around her. "Would you give us a minute before we head out back to see the others?"

"Sure. Take all the time you need. I'll get them up to speed on the latest developments." He gave Dean a pat on the back and left them alone in the foyer. "Hey." He turned her to face him and met her eyes. "It's a lot to take in, especially after I promised you that we'd be safe here. Are you all right?"

She took his hands in hers and stepped in between his spread feet, getting closer. "I had no idea what I was capable of, how strong I could be, until you came back home."

"Until I put you in harm's way, you mean."

"You didn't send Cheryl to me. You didn't put that thumb drive in my pocket. You didn't encourage me to get to the bottom of what was going on. In fact, you did the opposite, trying to protect me. You didn't put me in danger, Dean. I did that, all by myself." She sucked in a shaky breath. But because of Dean, everything had worked out. "I'm not going to lie, I'm scared. But I can face this. With you."

He stroked her hair and cupped her face, caressing her cheek with his thumb. His touch soothed something deep inside her, quelling her nerves, her fears.

"You're not angry," he said in a low, soft voice, "that I broke my promise, albeit inadvertently, about coming here and being safe?"

"We'd be in danger no matter where we ended up thanks to Lucas's tracker." *Sneaky devil.* Instead of kicking herself, she wanted to kick him. "This is the best place for us. It'll be easier to survive here than on our own. One team, one fight. And we've got a SEAL." She summoned a smile, for him.

He took her face between both his hands and stared into her eyes. "You're incredible."

When he looked at her like that, she felt incredible. Like together anything was possible. And she believed they'd not only get through this, but on the other side of it, they'd be even closer. More grateful for this precious love.

"You're not too shabby, either," she said.

He grinned, and she found herself laughing. Even though they weren't safe and soon they'd be thrust into the fray again, this amazing man made the ugliness and violence fade to the background. Just with a smile and brush of his hand.

Dean pressed his lips to hers in a tender kiss. "If you're not ready to meet everyone, they'll understand. It can wait until morning."

"Are you kidding me? After all the stories you told me about them for weeks, I'm champing at the bit." He must've been ten times as eager, and she wouldn't delay the reunion. Besides, tucking her tail and scurrying off would send the wrong message. Not only to Hunter, but to all of them. "I want to meet your family. The people who are going to be my family, too."

"I'm so lucky to have you." He took her hand, and they strolled through the house toward the open door that led to the patio, but they couldn't see anyone from the hall.

"I hope they like me." As silly as it seemed, their approval meant something to her.

"Don't worry," he whispered. "They're going to love you."

"How do you know?"

"Because I love you. They'll bend over backward and sideways, contorting themselves into pretzels to make you feel accepted."

Laughing softly, she followed him across the threshold and into the sweet night air.

They were greeted with bright smiles, arms extended in welcome and an overwhelming atmosphere of joy.

Dean started the flurry of introductions in between hugs.

From the way he had talked about Zee, Kate had discerned that the hotshot computer whiz easily garnered male attention. So, naturally, Kate had expected her to be beautiful, but the woman was downright stunning. Flawless light brown skin, long spiral curls and every inch of her body was lean and toned, yet feminine. Zee's daughter, Olivia, was a mini version of her. There was a rugged handsomeness to John. Everything about him was strong—his features, his build, his presence. It was plain to see that Zee and John were madly in love and couldn't keep their hands off each other.

Gage was quiet yet friendly. Kept a low profile, hovering in the background. Despite the fact he was no less good-looking than the others, something about him gave Kate the impression that he was the type who could blend in most places or could slip away without anyone noticing.

Except for Hope. She'd notice.

Pretty in a girl-next-door way, she had intelligent eyes and radiated a warmth that drew you in. Made it easy to be in her orbit.

Every member of Team Topaz, including John—a de facto member—had a different physique, yet they all carried themselves the same. With a lethal readiness.

She had no doubt their skills were as deadly as Dean's.

Once the greetings were finished, she thought they'd launch into strategy mode, start planning their next move in light of the GPS tracker Hunter had found on her.

Instead, the conversation stayed casual and buoyant, as one would expect at a family reunion.

Dean dropped into a lounge chair and pulled her down onto his lap, slipping an arm around her shoulders and the other across her thighs.

Letting herself relax, she nestled against him.

He tipped his head back and glanced up at her. When their gazes met, he smiled and mouthed, "You're so beautiful."

She grinned from ear to ear, her cheeks heating, her heart filled to bursting with love for him. In the days ahead, no matter what they had to face, they'd do it together. Because what they shared, what they'd found, was worth any fight.

* * * * *

COMING SOON!

MILLS & BOON

THE HEART OF ROMANCE

A ROMANCE FOR EVERY READER

MODERN

Prepare to be swept off your feet by sophisticated, sexy and seductive heroes, in some of the world's most glamourous and romantic locations, where power and passion collide.

HISTORICAL

Escape with historical heroes from time gone by. Whether your passion is for wicked Regency Rakes, muscled Vikings or rugged Highlanders, awaken the romance of the past.

MEDICAL

Set your pulse racing with dedicated, delectable doctors in the high-pressure world of medicine, where emotions run high and passion, comfort and love are the best medicine.

True Love

Celebrate true love with tender stories of heartfelt romance, from the rush of falling in love to the joy a new baby can bring, and a focus on the emotional heart of a relationship.

Desire

Indulge in secrets and scandal, intense drama and plenty of sizzling hot action with powerful and passionate heroes who have it all: wealth, status, good looks…everything but the right woman.

HEROES

Experience all the excitement of a gripping thriller, with an intense romance at its heart. Resourceful, true-to-life women and strong, fearless men face danger and desire - a killer combination!

To see which titles are coming soon, please visit

millsandboon.co.uk/nextmonth

LET'S TALK
Romance

For exclusive extracts, competitions
and special offers, find us online:

 facebook.com/millsandboon

@MillsandBoon

@MillsandBoonUK

Get in touch on 01413 063232

For all the latest titles coming soon, visit
millsandboon.co.uk/nextmonth

MILLS & BOON

Desire

Indulge in secrets and scandal, intense drama and plenty of sizzling hot action with powerful and passionate heroes who have it all: wealth, status, good looks…everything but the right woman.